THE REJECTED WIFE

L. STEELE

For the good girls who know their worth and aren't afraid to claim their own love story!

SPOTIFY SOUNDTRACK

Come Away with Me - Norah Jones
    Come Here - Kath Bloom
    You Are the Best Thing - Ray LaMontagne
    I Like Me Better - Lauv
    Can't Help Falling in Love - Kina Grannis
    Thinking Out Loud - Ed Sheeran
    Fly Me to the Moon - Frank Sinatra
    Lucky - Jason Mraz and Colbie Caillat
    Beyond - Leon Bridges

1

Priscilla

The universe rises to meet your bravery.
-Cilla's Post-it note

"Hold it!" I shout, sprinting down the platform of the train station like my life depends on it. The warning beeps blare—too close. The doors begin to slide shut. My ballet flats slam against concrete. I leap.

Almost make it.

Almost.

Something jerks me back mid-stride.

"What the—?" My voice catches as I twist around. No. No, no, no. My handbag is stuck. Wedged between the train's closing doors, clamped in place like a bear trap.

I tug once. Twice. The strap slips from my shoulders. I grab at it; hold onto it. "Come on!" I whisper-shout, yanking at it with both hands.

The train is going to move. I can feel it, the low hum under my feet, the tightening tension in the air.

The sensors are *meant* to stop this sort of thing, right? I mean you're supposed to trust the system, trust the process, like the online productivity gurus would have you believe.

Yeah. No.

There's no emergency release. No hidden button. No divine intervention.

There's no way to pry the doors open unless my affirmations have magically turned into biceps. Spoiler alert: *They haven't.*

If this train moves, my purse—along with my phone, my wallet, my ID, my entire existence—is gone. Vaporized into the dark, grimy void of the London Underground.

I give the strap another desperate pull.

Nothing.

Around me, no one seems to notice.

A man scrolls mindlessly on his phone. A woman's nose is buried in a Kindle. A teenager bops her head to music, eyes shut, lost in a world far kinder than mine right now.

I'm invisible. A heartbeat passes. Panic bubbles up, hot and bitter. *Come on. Come on.*

"You are not stuck. You are being rerouted to something better." A line from the last self-help book I read flashes through my brain. Cute. Not helpful.

I plant my feet. Grit my teeth. Try again.

Still nothing.

Then—

"Allow me."

The voice comes from above and behind me. Husky. Commanding. Velvet wrapped around gravel. I freeze. The hair on the back of my neck lifts.

Then I turn. *And Sweet. Holy Sweet Law of Attraction.*

The man towering behind me is the kind I've never seen before in real life. He seems to have stepped off a movie screen. Like something out of a fever dream. Tall. Broad. Built like he bench presses

Aston Martins for fun. His face? Sharp cheekbones, strong jaw, lips made for bad decisions.

But it's the eyes that stop me cold—one an icy blue, the other a deep forest green. The look in them piercing. Confident. Like he was born with assurance coded into his DNA.

Without a word, he steps closer. He inserts himself sideways between me and the closed doors—and grabs their edges with his fingertips. His sleeves are rolled up, revealing muscular forearms dusted with dark hair and lined with veins. The kind of arms that promise safety… *Or sin.*

The fabric of his shirt stretches across his back, tight over muscles that should come with a warning label. He braces one leg forward and pushes. Grunts. His thigh flexes beneath tailored pants so well-cut they must be custom. *Probably Italian. Probably cost more than my rent.*

With a groan of protest, the doors inch apart.

I yank my bag free just as the train lurches forward. The momentum causes me to stumble backwards—

He catches me.

His hand wraps around my arm, steadying me like I weigh nothing. His touch? Electric. Hot. Alarmingly comforting.

"You okay?" he asks, voice like midnight whiskey and bad intentions.

I look up. *Mistake.* Because now, I can't breathe. Literally.

This man could end empires with that bone structure. And the way he's looking at me—direct, unreadable, like I'm a puzzle he's already halfway solved—sends heat crawling up my neck.

I try to pull away, but he doesn't let go.

"Just making sure you don't fall." He guides me to an empty seat.

I drop into it like my knees might betray me. He folds himself onto the seat beside me. Casual. Calm. Powerful. The jacket he left on the seat earlier is now draped over one solid thigh. His presence fills the space between us, thick and magnetic.

My gaze once more travels to his spectacular forearms, those veins which stand out against his skin, the sculpted muscles which seem like they're carved out of marble. The skin at the back of my neck prickles. I raise my eyes, to meet his. Flush, when I realize he caught me staring. This man has MMC energy. He rivals the fictional book boyfriends I swoon over. This man can't be friend zoned. My ovaries send up a clamor. I tell them to shut up.

I clutch my bag to my chest like a shield. My heart's still racing. My mouth is dry. My brain is a loop of *What just happened?* and *Who is this man?*

His presence is big and strong and solid and seems to suck out all of the oxygen in the carriage. He renders everyone else in the space diminutive by comparison. I take a look around and find no one has moved. Everyone's lost in their personal worlds. No one noticed how this stranger saved my purse from being lost to the black of the tube tunnel. I prop my handbag in my lap. Noticing the paperback that's slipped out, I slide it in, then lock my fingers over my bag. Then I remember my manners. "Thank you."

"You're welcome," he rumbles.

I sneak another peek at those corded forearms currently at rest on those powerful thighs. Noticing him watching me, I flush and look away quickly.

And then, because the silence is too heavy, and I'm absolutely not thinking about how that forearm would look pinning me to a wall, I say the dumbest thing ever. "I didn't know train doors could do that. I thought they, uh, bounced back if something was in the way."

Smooth.

His lips twitch. Not quite a smile, but close. "Apparently, not."

I nod, gripping my bag tighter. "Well, that's one new thing I've learned today. And I try to learn one new thing every day. It helps… You know… With self-confidence. Growth. That sort of thing."

Why. Am. I. Still. Talking?

His head tilts, eyes gleaming now. "You read a lot of self-help books?"

"Too many," I mutter. "And also…romance novels."

His brows arch. The amusement is still there—soft, curious, curling at the corners of his mouth. "That so?" His stunning mismatched gaze scans my face like he's trying to read between the lines.

Another shiver rolls down my spine. He shouldn't affect me in this way. So, what if his eyelashes could rival a woman's. And his pants are clearly tailor-made; his shoes scream that they were hand-made in Italy.

I recognize class when I see it, considering I, too, was born into one of the richest families in the country. Only, I turned my back on them. My fingers slip on the rough material of my bag. I bought it at the charity shop and take pride in the fact that my entire outfit came off the discount store rack.

My job as a nanny means I don't have the money to afford to cut my hair in a salon, so I've learned to trim off the edges myself. Hopefully, it doesn't look too uneven. At least I have a steady income. No more donating blood, or my eggs—which I'd had to resort to—to pay my bills. I tuck a strand behind my ear.

He continues to watch me. Not in a creepy way. In a...thorough way. Like he's trying to decide something.

And then, just as the train begins to slow for the next stop, he dips his chin. "Have coffee with me."

I blink. "Excuse me?"

"Coffee." That almost-smile is back. Dangerous and heart-stopping. "Just one. You owe me."

2

Tyler

"Thanks for joining me." I send a second message on my phone, then lean back in my seat.

We're in the coffee shop I brought her to, which is a short walk from the tube station where we disembarked.

She smiles wryly. "Not like I could refuse, after how you saved me."

"It's five p.m. It's almost the end of the workday." I drum my fingers on the table. "If you had somewhere to be, you would've told me."

I wait, hoping she'll elaborate. Every little piece of information she shares with me about herself feels like I'm unwrapping something precious.

"I —" She looks away, then back at me. "I didn't."

"I'm a nanny. I have a degree in early childhood education. I currently work at a daycare center. So, you assumed right. I don't have any other plans today." Her gaze narrows, her expression turns considering. "Would it have stopped you from trying to persuade me if I had?"

"Honestly? No."

She looks taken aback, then bursts out laughing. "At least you're upfront." She runs her eyes down my jacket, which I've worn over a button-down shirt. "You're dressed like a business executive, so I assume you were on your way from a meeting? Though, you're not the kind of person I'd expect to see on the tube."

"What's that supposed to mean?" I quirk an eyebrow.

"I get the feeling you don't often take public transport."

"Oh?"

She nods. "That's a tailored suit you're wearing. Between that and your handmade Italian loafers..." She looks me up and down. "You can afford to be ferried around by a driver."

"I prefer to drive myself." I raise a shoulder. "But my car is being repaired. And there was no alternate chauffeur or car available from any of the services my office uses. And no cars on the various ride-hailing apps." I raise my shoulders. "I was enroute to meeting someone. And running late."

Her gaze widens. "Was it a date?"

There's a strange note in her voice. Jealousy, perhaps? *I can only hope.* I lower my chin. "I cancelled it."

"For me?" Her forehead furrows.

"This was more important." I hold her gaze. "I had a sense that if I let you walk away without getting to know you better, I was going to regret it."

"Oh." A pleased light comes into her eyes before she banks it. "You are awfully forthright. And very confident of yourself."

I wink. "I'm also not sorry for using my good deed to my advantage." I should feel terrible for playing on her guilt and insisting she have a coffee with me. I should... But I don't.

When I saw her struggling with her handbag, my protective instincts surged. And when I looked into those warm brown eyes, saw the worry etched into her face and those soft, rosebud lips, something inside me melted. My heart seemed to stop. I felt like I'd been struck by lightning. But that must, surely, be my imagination?

She seems taken aback by my comment, then pops a shoulder. "Is it your military training which makes you this...forward?"

"I was in the Royal Marines," I clarify. "Is it the military-style cut that gave me away?" I run my palm over the very short hair on my head.

"That and—" She nods toward my chest. I look down at where my dog tags peek out from between the lapels of my shirt. "Anyway, when you invited me out to coffee, I didn't realize you'd bring me to the most exclusive coffee shop in London." She waves at our surroundings.

I take in the dark oak flooring, the statement counter, which is the focal point of the space, the mirrored brass countertops, the vibrant barstools, and the elegant, yet comfortable surroundings that provide a home-away-from-home ambiance, then turn to her, not seeing anything wrong with it. But what do I know?

"Do you not like the place?" I begin to push away from the table. "Should we go elsewhere?"

"On the contrary." She reaches over to touch the hand I've flattened on the table. Instantly, a zip of awareness shoots up my arm. She pulls her hand back, but not before I hear her draw in a sharp breath.

A flush smears her cheeks. Her pupils dilate. She, too, feels this...awareness between us. A thrill of anticipation squeezes my chest.

"The place is perfect." She takes a sip from her cup. "As is the coffee."

"As is the company," I respond.

She blushes, then laughs. "Have we now moved onto the flattery portion of the date?"

"No, not yet," I tease. "I'm still compiling my list."

One of my companies is the supplier of the coffee served here. And I ordered a gourmet blend made from one of the most expensive beans in the world. It's why I had to bring her here. I stiffen. *Why do I feel like a schoolboy? Why is it so important that I impress her?*

Unaware of my thoughts, she looks away, then laughs nervously. "I feel like I'm doing this all wrong." She pushes the hair back from her face. "It's not that I'm not appreciative of your having rescued my handbag, but—"

"But?"

She swallows. "But being in your presence makes me unravel."

Some of the weight on my chest dissolves. She's as nervous as I am. It must not have been easy for her to admit that. Indeed, in my experience, women seldom speak their minds. They prefer to play games and make me guess what they're trying to imply. But the clearness in her eyes tells me, she's not one of them. So, I content myself with asking in a mild voice, "It is?"

She laughs again.

The sound, like a babbling stream of water, shoots bubbles through my veins. *Jesus, am I rhapsodizing about her laughter? Really?* I frown, and when I look into her bright eyes and see her curved lips, I feel my heart give another lurch. *Jesus, what's happening here?*

"Are you okay?" she asks softly.

"Why shouldn't I be?"

She shakes her head. "You seemed disoriented for a few seconds there."

I'd have gone with discombobulated; it feels like the rug has been pulled out from under me. I feel like I've lost my moorings, desperately trying to get my bearings and failing. Damn. I run my fingers through my hair. "The truth is, I'm not completely okay," I murmur.

"Oh?" She looks at me with curiosity.

"I haven't been myself since I saw you struggling to free your bag from those doors to the subway train." I reach over, take a sip of my coffee, then place the cup back on the table.

I search for words to express what I'm feeling without coming across as creepy, or even more forward, or indeed, without making her uncomfortable, but also sticking as close as possible to the truth. I raise my gaze to hers again. "I feel like I should get to know you better. It's why I asked you to have coffee with me." I raise both of my hands again, hoping my sincerity communicates itself to her. "Is that all right?"

She bites down on her lower lip, and goddamn, I feel that tug in my chest. And lower down. The blood throbs at my temples. My pulse rate grows insistent. She seems to consider my words, and when she finally nods, some of the tension bleeds from my shoulders. I didn't realize how much I was worried she might want to leave after that confession.

I hold out my hand. "I'm Tyler Davenport."

Something flickers in her eyes. Her gaze grows troubled, but she places her much smaller palm in mine. "Priscilla Whittington."

"Whittington?" I release her hand. "You're Toren Whittington's sister?"

3

Priscilla

"And you're one of the Davenport brothers." I place my hands in my lap.

"You've heard of us, I take it?" His tone is wary.

I scoff, "You mean, have I heard of the one-time feud between our two families which has lasted for over fifty years?"

"The relationship has improved since Toren helped my brother Nathan stave off a takeover of the Davenport Group," he points out.

When I heard about that, I was taken aback. Then my brother explained how it helped him negotiate a deal with the Davenports which, in turn, grew the Whittingtons' market share. Still, it sends a thrill through me that I'm sitting here speaking to someone who, at one point, my family considered a rival.

"Our families are still not the best of friends," I point out.

"They are no longer at each other's throats." He tilts his head. "And even if that weren't the case, it has nothing to do with you and me."

"There is no you and me —"

"Not yet," he agrees smoothly.

The sheer confidence in his voice should piss me off, but it also turns me on. I shake my head. "You have a big ego."

"It's warranted." He smirks.

I can't stop the laugh that bubbles up. "Oh, my God, that should sound cringe, but —"

"But?"

"It's kinda hot that you're so self-assured," I say honestly.

The skin around his eyes creases. Something in his expression softens further. "The relationship between our families has no bearing on my wanting to get to know you better. That is, if you agree?"

The honesty in his eyes is disarming. The sincerity in his voice is unmistakable. I feel myself fall a little further under his spell.

Damn. It feels like I've entered an alternate reality where the man of my dreams has suddenly appeared and wants to spend time with me. I'm so attracted to him. His perfect blend of charm, laced with a healthy dose of delicious sexuality, has my insides twisted with anticipation, and every cell in my body tight with expectation.

The chemistry between us deepens. The very air between us thrums. Little frissons of delight spiral up my spine. It almost feels too much.

So, I reach for the cup of coffee and take a sip. When I place it down, he reaches over and touches the back of my hand, just a whisper of his fingers grazing over my knuckles. It's enough to deepen the connection between us, but it's also reassuring.

"It's okay. We have time," he croons.

I clear my throat. "We do?"

"I didn't mean to make you uncomfortable," he says in a husky voice.

I refuse to look at him, sure he'll see through the contradictory emotions gripping me. "That's not the word I'd use. It's more a sense of expectation," I admit.

There's silence. When he doesn't speak for a few seconds, I raise my gaze to his. I find him looking at me with a knowing gaze.

"What?" I scowl.

He walks around to stand next to my chair. He holds out his hand, and I slip mine into his without hesitation. I should be alarmed at how much I already trust this guy, despite him being a stranger, but my instincts tell me it's okay. That he's okay. And I choose to trust them.

He tugs, and I straighten. As if it's a sign, I hear "Come Away With Me" by Norah Jones come on over the speakers.

He leads me to the front of the shop, and I realize, the servers who brought us coffee are nowhere to be seen. I glance around the now empty place. The other guests, too, seem to have left. It's just us in this gorgeous space.

"Where did everyone go?" I ask, surprised.

"I happen to know the owner of the place. I messaged her on the way over from the train station and asked her to clear the space for us."

I whip my head in his direction. "You did?"

"I wanted you all to myself."

Something shifts inside me—sharp and electric. Like the air before a storm. My breath snags, not in fear, but anticipation. His words settle low, somewhere behind my navel, heat coiling where there should be caution.

It's an early spring afternoon, and the sun's rays slant in through the windows, lighting his face with a golden glow.

"Will you dance with me?" he murmurs.

It feels momentous, like my entire life is about to change. How can I deny him? I'm halfway to falling headlong in love with a man I only just met, while my soul insists I know him in a way I can't rationally explain. Unable to speak, I nod. He takes my hand and places it on his shoulder, then flattens his big palm on the curve of my hip. Heat from his fingers sears through the material of my skirt and into my skin. He begins to move, and I follow.

I meet his gaze and feel drawn into those stunning, contrasting eyes of his. My feet don't seem to touch the floor. I'm flying. This must be the most romantic gesture anyone has ever done for me. My heart melts even more. And when he steers me close enough that my thighs graze his powerful ones, my insides quiver. My core melts. My toes curl in my ballet flats. I can't stop the shudder that runs through my body.

He senses my reaction, and his hold on me firms. "Are you cold?"

I shake my head.

"Do you want to keep dancing?"

I shake my head again.

His steps slow until we come to a halt. Norah Jones' soulful voice sinks into my bones, twines through my blood, and shifts something deep inside of me. As if he senses it, he places my hand on his other shoulder and slides both of his big palms to the small of my back. He spans my waist, and I feel tiny and delicate in comparison to his much bigger frame. I feel protected, and oh, so turned on.

Our difference in height and weight marks him out as the alpha. The male. That primitive part of me recognizes his mastery over me. That animal part of my brain identifies him as the one who has control over my body. It's so wrong that I feel this way. That in one stroke, he's pushed aside the feminist part of me. The one which pushed me to be independent from my family. To refuse their help and try to create my own life, away from their influence.

Yet, here I am, standing inside the embrace of a man who comes from the same kind of background I swore to leave behind. *Is that why a part of me recognized him right away? Because, while we're different in so many ways, he's also similar to me in some?*

"What are you thinking?" he asks in a low, dark voice that has my insides fluttering with need.

"I'm not sure I'm capable of thinking much," I confess.

He lowers his face until his lips are a hairsbreadth from mine. "Good," he breathes. His mouth is so very close, and if I go up on my tiptoes, I'll be connected to him. But his hold on my waist is firm. Without saying a word, he commands me to stay in place. And my body obeys. I can't stop myself from tipping up my chin, though. His gaze lowers to my mouth. His nostrils flare. His chest rises and falls, and it's my turn to feel a tremor grip him. He dips his chin, bridging that gap between us and, finally, brushes his mouth over mine.

4

Tyler

Soft. Sweet. I draw in her breath, relishing the sweet scent of apple blossoms that makes my mouth water. The taste of her lips is like honey; it arrows down to my groin. I'm instantly hard. Sparks flare in my belly. My fingers tremble on her waist with this yearning that grips me. My heart races in my chest, and when I swipe my tongue at the seam of her mouth, she parts it. Instantly, I slide my tongue over hers. The sparks turn into an inferno. My muscles bunch. My chest hurts. The emotions consume me. I can't stop myself from hauling her closer, so we're joined from thigh to stomach to chest. She must feel the evidence of my desire throb against her lower belly, for a moan leaves her lips.

I swallow it down, slide my palm down to cup her bottom and lift her.

She wraps her legs around me, hooks her ankles behind me, and goddamn, feeling the heat of her soft center through the clothes we're wearing turns my blood into gasoline. The fire zips through my veins until I feel my body turn into a nuclear reactor of longing. I need to get closer to her. I need to feel her skin against mine, her hands on me, hear her soft sighs and whimpers, smell her, taste the dew of her arousal on my tongue.

My feet seem to move of their own accord until I reach a table adjacent to the one we'd occupied. This one is empty of any settings.

I place her on it and drag my fingers up the undersides of her thigh. She groans into my mouth, and the sound goes straight to my head.

I tilt my head, drag my tongue over her teeth, and she melts into me. Her surrender spurs my desire further. My thigh muscles bunch; my biceps turn into blocks of concrete. I need...to taste her.

I tear my mouth from hers and sink down to my knees between her legs. "Nobody will disturb us."

She glances down, her eyes glazed, her breath coming in pants.

Did she hear what I said? When I plant my palm on her stomach and urge her back, she doesn't protest. She folds back onto the table. Balancing herself on her elbows, she watches as I push her skirt up her thighs.

"Stop me," I urge her.

She bites her lower lip, then shakes her head.

"I want to eat you out," I say slowly, wanting to make sure I have her consent. "May I?"

When she nods, I groan. "Say yes, baby."

"Yes," she croaks. Then, "Yes," she says in a louder voice.

I drag my nose up the exposed skin of her thigh, and she cries out. She tips her head back until it touches the table. I push her skirt up over her hips and take in the white cotton of her panties. They're plain, almost virginal, and a surge of possessiveness fills me. I bury my nose in the space between her legs and draw in deeply of her essence.

"Oh, my God." She digs her fingers into my hair and tugs. The pinpricks of sensation travel down my spine, and I almost come. I have to stop and command myself to get control. I'm going to pleasure this woman. I'm going to take care of this goddess. I'm going to make sure this gorgeous creature has the kind of experience where she sees heaven.

"Tyler," she moans, and my name from her lips is a different kind of torture. Every part of me insists she belongs to me. That primal part of me surges to the fore. I ease her panties down her thighs, then lick up the seam of her pussy. She shudders. I swipe my tongue up her pussy lips, and she quivers. I stab my tongue inside her slit, and her entire body jolts.

"Tyler," she groans my name again, and it's like a clarion call.

I begin to eat her out in earnest—licking, sucking, circling the nub of her clit with my tongue, then using my fingers to play with her pussy. She whimpers and whines, and tries to pull away, but I don't let her. With one hand on her hip, I hold her in place and continue to urge her up the peak toward her climax.

Sweat breaks out on my brow and more trickles down my spine, but I don't let up. I glance up to find her eyes shut. Her chest rises and falls. A flush colors her cheekbones. She's let go of my hair and now her fingers grip the edge of the table. The skin across her knuckles stretches tight. I lick into her weeping slit, and when I finally close my teeth around that swollen bud between her lower lips and tug, she explodes.

A long, low cry is drawn from her. Her back curves. She squeezes her thighs around my face and comes. Her climax goes on and on. Watching the most beautiful woman in the world come is the most incredible sight I have ever seen. I continue to lick the moisture that trickles from her. And when she finally slumps, I rise up, plant my hands on either side of her, and close my mouth over hers.

I kiss her deeply, sliding my tongue over hers, and it's sweet and life-affirming and turns my heart into an instrument that could shatter any moment. When I finally pull away, I survey her flushed features with satisfaction.

She raises her eyelids and looks into my eyes with a dazed expression. "Wow!" She swallows. "That was—" She shakes her head. "Don't know if I have the words to describe it."

I kiss her tenderly, then straighten and put her clothes to rights. I help her to her feet, twine my fingers with hers and bring her hand to my mouth. I kiss the back of her knuckles.

Her lips are swollen. Her skirt is creased. She looks like a woman who's just had an orgasm. One I was responsible for. *I did this. I made her come.* She stares at me breathless, dazed. Like I shattered something in her and rebuilt it sweeter. Like she can't quite believe what just happened. That look? I'll be chasing it for the rest of my life.

I can't walk away from her. Not now. There's something between us—undeniable, electric. I've never felt this with anyone. Not like this. I can't risk losing it before I even understand what it is. I don't want distance. I want her—close, constant, mine.

I need more—of her voice, her mind, the way she looks at me like she sees past everything I pretend to be. I know how she tastes, but now I want to know the rest. Every breath, every silence, every secret. The things she's never told anyone—I want to be the one she lets in. And to do that, I must keep her close. With me.

She opens her mouth to speak, but I place my finger over her lips. "Will you spend the night with me?"

5

Priscilla

"You want me to spend *the night* with you?" I cough.

Instantly, he reaches over and pats my back. "You okay?"

A shiver squeezes my spine at his touch, but I manage to nod.

He helps me off the table and back to ours. He pulls out my seat, makes sure I'm comfortable. A true gentleman. Completely unlike the hungry man who'd feasted between my legs.

He drops into his chair and slides the glass with water in my direction. I take a sip, more for something to do than thirst, then set it down gently. My fingers drift to the table setting. I adjust the cutlery, nudge the sugar bowl a few millimeters to the right. Small movements. A quiet attempt at control in a moment that feels anything but.

It's a delaying tactic, but that's okay. I need to figure out how I'm going to answer him. Because… *Yes, I want to spend more time with him. Yes, I want to get to know him better.* But also, no way, am I going to spend the night with a man I just met. Wouldn't that send out a signal that I'm easy? *You let him go down on you. That ship has sailed.*

As if he can read my thoughts, he holds up his hands. "I should qualify that I want to spend the night with you… Getting to really know one another. I want to know all about you."

I raise my gaze to his and find humor twinkling in his.

"You want to spend the time… Talking?" I scrunch up my eyebrows.

He must notice my confusion, for he chuckles. "You'd rather we not get to know each other before we sleep together?"

"That's not what I meant." I toss my head. "Only—" I form my words carefully. "Only, I thought someone like *you* wouldn't be interested in…you know—" I hesitate.

"Go on," he says slowly.

"—Oh, in getting to know someone before you sleep with them." Even as I hear my words, I know I'm making a sweeping judgment of this man's character, but now it's too late to take it back.

"Hmm." He drags his thumb under that pouty lower lip, the one I want to dig my teeth into and suck on. *Focus, Priscilla!*

"Firstly, you're not 'anyone,'" he murmurs in that deep and rough-edged voice like velvet over grit.

"I'm not?" A melting sensation coils in my chest.

He shakes his head. "Secondly…" He gives me a considering look. "By someone like 'me,' you mean—"

Oh shoot, he wants me to spell it out. I could try to backtrack, but that would only make me seem indecisive. *Okay then.* I've opened this particular door, and I'm going to have to walk through it. "Surely, you're aware of your appeal?"

"My. Appeal?" There's surprise in his voice.

"You come from a moneyed background, and you look like you walked off the pages of a fashion magazine. Not to mention, you're magnetic and so darned chiseled, you could have any woman you want." I wave my hand in the air. "I assumed you were a rake."

"You assumed I'm morally ambiguous and a womanizer who doesn't care for commitment, based on how I look?"

I flush further. "I don't mean—" *Argh!* I deflate a little. "You're right; that *is* what I meant. Sorry."

"Don't apologize," he says softly. "You're right that I've never lacked for female company. And yes, I have dated women."

A hot sensation squeezes my stomach. Of course, he's been with other women. And he's honest about it, which is a good sign, right? Still, jealousy flares—sharp and unexpected. I have no claim on him. But God, I want one.

"But I'm not with them," he says quietly. "I'm here. With you."

His gaze burns into mine. "You're breathtaking. There's a kind of light in your face that doesn't belong to this world—and your body…" He exhales, as if steadying himself. "It calls to me in ways I can't explain. I won't pretend I don't want you. I do. Every inch of you."

His expression is filled with need. But there's restraint in the way he holds himself, reverence. "But what I feel for you isn't just desire. It's deeper. It's real. And I don't want to tarnish that by rushing into something physical when what's growing between us could be… everything."

"Oh." The jealousy recedes. That melting sensation in my chest spreads to my extremities.

I search his face and realize he is serious. It makes me realize, I misjudged him. I had him pegged for the stereotypical alpha male who'd simply take what he wants and be done with me, but he's actually a decent human being who finds me intriguing enough to want to get to know me better.

Somewhere deep inside, I didn't think I was worthy of his spending the time to get to know me before he tried to sleep with me. I thought I was over the biases that a lifetime of being singled out for my curvy figure has thrust on me. And normally, I'm a confident person. I've learned to love myself. I've learned to be comfortable in my own skin. All those who bullied me for my curves were projecting their insecurities onto me. I know that now. But meeting this man and feeling this fierce attraction to him, seems to have brought a fresh layer of insecurity to the surface. Seems like this time, it's me who's projecting my story onto him. He's made it clear he loves my body. His words make me feel like I'm the most beautiful woman in the world. And the way he made me come was... Unexpected, to say the least.

Tingles of pleasure still course through my body from how I orgasmed. I'm a tad disappointed that he doesn't want to spend the night having wild sex. Which is crazy, because I just told myself I'm not going to jump into bed with him. So why am I finding fault with him for mirroring that same sentiment to me.

"Umm... I'm...not sure how to respond to that," I finally offer.

The skin around his eyes creases. I must have said something right, for his lips quirk. "I really do want to get to know you better." He reaches for my hand again and laces his fingers through mine.

Once more, little pinpricks of awareness stream out from the point of contact. His unmatched eyes flash, and I know he feels this weird chemistry between us, too. And when he licks his lips, I'm sure he can taste my cum. Heat blooms in my chest. My scalp tingles. That was even more erotic than feeling his lips on mine. Almost.

The notes of the acoustic version of "Come Here" by Kath Bloom begin to play overhead. It's heartfelt and evocative. The emotions in her voice. The yearning. The feeling. A flicker of something electric dances beneath my skin. I can't say if it's the plea in the words or the fact that she says that you don't have to run away... Or perhaps, it's the promise in his eyes. That burn of lust mixed with the sweet longing that I sense in him, which mirrors this hankering in mine. My instinct tells me this is a once-in-a-lifetime connection. My logical mind tells me that's crazy.

Yet, something deeper in me, that primitive part of me, overrides everything else. "I do want to get to know you better"—I hesitate —"but..."

"But?"

"Also, I feel weird about this. We just met today, you took me out for coffee, and then..." I trail off.

"The orgasm," he completes my statement.

I flush. "There's that," I agree in a steady voice. It was an incredible orgasm, too. And yes, I let a man who I met only a few hours earlier go down on me. I could claim I got carried away, but it's more than that. I feel a real connection here. But what if I'm reading too much into it? What if—?

"I'd love to make you come again and again. I'd love to take you to bed and complete what we started but…I do want to get to know you better first." His gaze holds mine.

That awareness thrumming between us shoots up a notch. It makes me want to throw caution to the wind and tell him yes. *Yes!* And yet…I hesitate. It's not that I don't feel safe with him. If I didn't, I wouldn't be here. The way he helped me on the train earlier ensured we're past that first barrier of not trusting… Which is why I agreed to have coffee with him. *But to spend more time with him?* My heart leaps within my chest. *Damn, I really want this.* But also, it feels momentous to agree. Like if I did, my life would change forever, which is crazy… *Right?*

When I stay quiet, he leans in and fixes those stunning mismatched eyes on me. "Think about it this way. Twenty years down the line, when you're unhappy with someone else, you'll always wonder how it could've been if you'd said yes to spending the night with me."

The confidence in his voice makes me huff out a laugh. "What if I'm very happy with this hypothetical significant other?"

"You're not," he growls.

"How can you be so sure?"

"Because"—he takes my other hand in his and presses both my palms between his much bigger ones—"that person is not me. Not unless you give me a chance tonight. Take a chance on us, Priscilla. I promise, you won't regret it."

Did the cosmos finally read my vision board? That's intense. His words have a ring of authenticity to them which resonates somewhere deep inside me. I swallow… He sounds so sure of himself. His tone goes beyond arrogance; he sounds certain that we have a connection. He's telling me that he's thinking of me as more than just a passing liaison and what we have is something special. Right?

Also, he *did* rescue my bag, and was the complete gentleman until…he wasn't. And I loved that, too. After all, I *did* orgasm. I could do with more of those.

And is he right? If I don't agree to spend the night with him, will I regret it? Will I always wonder how it could have been to act on such an intense connection?

I shake my head. "You're very persuasive, you know that?"

"Does that mean you're saying yes?" he asks in a low voice. Like silk dragged across stone. Oh. My. God. How can I resist that?

I nod.

A breath whooshes out of him. Some of the tension leaves his shoulders.

Apparently, he wasn't sure I'd agree. This glimpse of vulnerability makes my heart stutter. I pegged him for an alpha male who was used to getting his way. So, the fact he didn't assume anything when it comes to me is refreshing.

It also confirms to me that I made the right choice. Which in turn, makes me want to sleep with him even more. How confusing is that?

"Say it aloud," he urges me.

It doesn't even occur to me to refuse him. "Yes, I'll spend the night with you. Only"—I tip up my chin—"I want to do more than just talk."

Something flashes in his eyes, the intensity lighting a fire that zips through my veins. He lowers his chin until his gaze is level with mine. "You want to do more than talk?"

His dark, gravelly voice sends another flurry of excitement down my spine. I squeeze my thighs together. His nostrils flare, and I'm certain he must be aware of how turned on I am. The knowledge makes me flush. I draw in a breath to calm myself.

"I do," I admit.

He studies my eyes, and whatever he sees there makes him nod. "Good, give me your phone."

"Eh?"

"Your phone." He holds out his palm.

"You realize that asking someone to hand over their phone is more personal than sex?"

He chuckles. "Clearly, you haven't had good sex."

How about *no sex?* Not counting all the masturbation with my favorite toys and spicy romance novels, of course.

When I still hesitate, he murmurs, "You agreed to come home with me. You allowed me to make you come. Your instinct tells you, that you can trust me."

I nod slowly.

"Take it a step further and give me your phone."

Once again, his voice is spiked with that edge of genuineness, which has more of an effect on me than him ordering me to do so.

I pull my phone from my purse. I begin to hand it over when he reminds me, "Unlock it first."

"Oh, right." I do so and place my device on his palm.

He holds it up and takes a selfie.

"What are you doing?'

In response, he keys in a number and presses call. A second later, I hear a buzzing sound. He pulls his phone from his pocket, sliding mine across the table toward me. "Now you have my picture, my name *and* my number. Make sure you tell a trusted friend that you're spending the rest of the evening with me."

6
_____

Tyler

"And I thought you were going to drag me off to your lair right away." She takes in the wall-to-wall books and sighs. "I've come to this borough so many times but had no idea this bookstore was hidden in the alleyway."

"You like it?" I take in her sparkling eyes, the way she almost bounces on the balls of her feet with excitement, and I feel like I'm rediscovering the joy of living all over again.

"I love it!" She clasps her hands together. "How did you find this place?"

We're at The Sp!cy Booktok, a bookshop run by a friend's wife. I had my car delivered to the coffee shop so that I could drive her over here. We're past rush hour, and even if we were stuck in traffic, I couldn't think of anyone else I'd rather spend that time with.

"I know the owner. She was more than happy to arrange for us to browse." I messaged Gio on the way over, and she was excited to have us.

Priscilla takes in the cozy atmosphere, illuminated by soft

lighting that spills from vintage-style lamps, the whimsical decorations, like strings of fairy lights that twinkle softly, and elegant paper lanterns that add a fanciful touch. Large, leafy plants are placed strategically in corners or by windows, their greenery adding life to the space. A velvet armchair with a faded yet comfortable look is pushed up against a wall between the shelves.

Colorful rugs line the floor, offering spots to sit and read. Cozy nooks with comfortable chairs and pillows beckon readers to lose themselves in a good book.

"It's a beautiful space. Thank you for bringing me here." She looks at me from under her eyelashes. "So, is this like…a date?"

I quirk my lips. "It's been a date since I sat next to you on the tube."

A pleased smile curves her lips, then she tips up her chin. "You mean, I'm a replacement for whoever you blew off this evening?"

I chuckle inwardly. She's testing me. She's not accepting me at face value—which only makes me want her even more. I love that she challenges me, keeps me on my feet. She's demanding, but once she gives in to *my* demands… She'll know the kind of ecstasy only I can bring her.

"I already told you—" I bend my knees and peer into her eyes. "You are one of a kind. And I want to spend this evening and tonight getting to know everything about you. If you'll let me…"

That spark in her gaze turns radiant—like she's holding the entire star-filled night sky in her eyes.

"Aww," she sighs. "You know exactly how to sweeten me up. Though you don't have to, you know that, right?" She bats her eyelids. "I did already agree to sleep with you."

"And I already told you that I want to do more than sleep with you." I tuck a strand of hair behind her ear.

Her cheeks turn pink. Her lips curve. She's pleased with my answer. And I'm pleased that she's pleased. Damn. I'm a goner. It's a slippery slope since I met her. I'm falling head over heels for her and it's a bit like being on a roller coaster. I'm afraid I'm not in control of my emotions any longer.

She clears her throat and glances over the bookshelves. Her forehead creases. "Wait, how did you guess I loved books?" She shoots me a sideways glance. "And where is everyone else?"

"On the first, I saw the paperback in your handbag," I confess.

Her eyebrows shoot up. "Observant, aren't you?"

"When it comes to you, there's little I haven't noticed," I murmur.

She blinks slowly. "Should I be impressed by that, or worried?"

Definitely worried. Aloud, I say, "Neither."

She chews on her lips, and I itch to reach out and replace her teeth with mine, but I resist. Instead, I lean in closer, until I'm able to brush my nose up her cheek. "As for the second, I specifically asked the owner of the shop to shut down the place so you could browse until your heart's content without being disturbed."

"First the coffee shop. And now you asked them to shut down the bookstore, for me?" She takes a step back so she's able to look into my eyes.

"Only for you," I confirm. It was a stroke of luck that I spotted the paperback when it slipped out of her purse. She likes to read. And I'd love to watch her read. It's why I brought her here. Without breaking the connection between us, I bend and grab one of the baskets by a shelf. "I'm sure you can't wait to shop."

"You're going to hold my basket while I buy books?" Her voice emerges squeaky.

"Would you rather I not?"

She shoots me a look. "Of course, I'd rather you did, but—" She shakes her head. "Forget it."

She begins to move away, but I step in front of her. "No, tell me."

She blows out a breath. "Umm, no, it's just that"—she hesitates —"it's not something I imagined any man would ever do for me."

Something in her voice gives me pause. *Does she not realize she deserves this, and so much more?* I bend my knees and peer into her face. "It was worth bringing you here just to see that look of wonder on your face when you walked in."

She flushes. For a few seconds, our gazes stay connected. The air is spiked with longing. The attraction between us roars to the

surface. She must sense it, for her throat moves as she swallows. Her
pupils dilate. She begins to sway toward me.

Then, as if realizing how her body is betraying her, she wrenches
her eyes away. Her gaze falls on a shelf, and she does a double take.
"Is that—" She hurries over to it and reads out the category heading,
"Mothers, Madonnas, and Mamma Mia?" She laughs. "Whoever
comes up with these titles?"

"That would be Giorgina, the owner of the store." I walk over
and stand behind Priscilla.

Then, because I can't help it, I lean in and sniff the air above her.
The sweet scent of apple blossoms goes straight to my head. My
groin tightens. I've been painfully aroused since I made her come.
And being this close to her turns my blood to lava. I want to scoop
her up in my arms and carry her off to my place where I can have my
wicked way with her.

Only, I want more than a quick one-night stand. I stiffen. Is that
why I was unable to let go of her after rescuing her from the mercy
of the train door? Is that why I asked her to have a coffee with me?
Is that why I was unable to stop myself from going down on my
knees and worshipping her? Is that why I had to find a way to spend
the rest of the day and night with her?

I feel drawn to her in a way I haven't with anyone else—enough
to realize she's unique. To wonder if these emotions she elicits within
me are something I'll ever find with anyone else. To wonder if there's
a future for us together. *A future?* I lean back, putting distance
between us.

Me, who's never wanted to settle down—is so enamored with this
woman I just met, that I can't fathom a life without her in it. Damn. It's
why I want to spend the night getting to know her better, and not only
in the carnal sense. *No...I need more.* I need to find out everything about
her. I need to...get to the bottom of this strange attraction to her.

She pulls out a book. I look at it over her shoulder. It has a beautiful flower cover, and the title says, *The Proposal* by L. Steele. Then,
she flips it open to a page, and I read, *he slides his fingers up the creamy
flesh and parts her —*

"Whoops, didn't mean for you to read that." She snaps the book shut and is about to slide it back on the shelf, but I hold out the carry basket I grabbed on my way in. "Drop it in here. I know you want it."

She gives me a funny look. "How do you know that?"

"You ran your palm over the cover, and you picked it up unerringly from the line-up, so"—I raise the basket—"go on. I know you want to."

She looks torn by my urging, then slips the book into the basket.

"Good, now what other books do you want to get?"

"Uh"—she hesitates—"not sure I'm going to be able to afford them." Then her forehead furrows. "How do you know I want to get more of them?" she asks me in a suspicious voice.

"The way you ate up the shelves when you walked in? And how you forgot about me when you saw the paperbacks?" I assume a woebegone expression. "Never thought I'd be envious of books for the attention of a beautiful woman. But I know when I'm outnumbered."

She blushes, then laughs. "Glad you know when you can't be competition."

"Oh, trust me, I know." I survey her smiling expression. It was worth bringing her to this hidden bookstore just to see the glow on her face.

Our gazes hold, that chemistry simmering under the surface flaring again. The flush on her face deepens. She glances back at the titles on the shelves. Without hesitation, she grabs two more and drops them into the basket. She scans the shelves, picks out a few more, then a few others. By the time we finish one wall, the basket I'm holding is overflowing.

I grab an empty one, and she keeps adding to the pile. We move to the opposite wall, where she pulls a few more selections from the self-help section until this basket is overflowing, too.

My biceps flex. My shoulders bulge with the strain of carrying her haul. I bench press four hundred pounds every day; carrying two loaded baskets of books is nothing. But I gotta admit, it's heavier than I thought it would be.

She turns around and takes in her stash, then gasps. "Oh my gosh, that's more than I realized. Let me go through and pick out which ones to keep. I can't afford to buy *all* of them."

"Don't worry about it; if you want more—"

"No, no, I wasn't going to buy all of them." She reaches toward the basket.

I hold it out of reach. "Nonsense, you want these books, and you will have them." I nod toward the shelves we haven't come to yet. "Sure you don't want to look at them."

She looks at them longingly, then back at the baskets I'm carrying. "Nope." She shakes her head.

"You sure?"

She hesitates for only a second, then nods. "I'm sure. Don't want to get too greedy, do I?"

"You can get as greedy as you want," I murmur.

She looks at me with that half-bashful, half-stubborn look on her features, then shakes her head again. "Greed is a sin I prefer to avoid." She looks me up and down with lust in her eyes.

"Is that from another of your self-help books?'

"It's actually a form of self-preservation." She swallows. "But I might have to break that particular rule tonight."

"Hmm." I move in closer, until the toes of my shoes bump her ballet flats. "Any other sins I could tempt you to indulge in?"

She flutters her eyelashes. "You're a smart man. I'm sure you'll think of something."

I take in her lips and, like iron pins drawn to a magnet, I lower my head. I move closer, until my mouth is directly over hers. When she doesn't look away, I take it as permission to brush my mouth over hers. Softly. Gently. Slowly. Drawing her sweet breath into my lungs, sipping from her lips until she parts them. That's when I sweep my tongue over hers.

7

Priscilla

He touches his tongue to mine, and goosebumps pepper my skin. The hair on the back of my neck rises. Every cell in my body has turned into a tiny inferno. Liquid heat courses through my bloodstream. A groan rumbles up his chest, and the vibrations squeeze my nipples, turning them into tight buds waiting to unfurl at his touch. *Damn.* He slants his lips over mine, and I feel his kiss all the way down to my toes. My scalp tingles. My thighs tremble.

I hear a thump as if from a distance and realize he must have dropped the baskets of books. The next moment, he slides his big palms under my butt and boosts me up.

As if we're engaged in a well-synchronized dance, I lock my ankles behind his back. And when that thick column tenting his crotch stabs into my core, I whimper. It seems to inflame him, for he deepens the kiss. He thrusts his tongue into my mouth, and his hips follow suit when he plunges forward and grinds the evidence of his arousal into my core. Little fires break out over my skin. My nerve endings hum. I dig my heels in and try to pull him closer.

He obliges by pushing me up and into the row of books behind me. A few of the books unbalance and fall to the floor.

Not that it distracts him, for he continues to plunder my mouth, and my head spins. A weakness shudders over my body. He grasps my hips and fits me even closer, and I can feel every ridge of that thickness between his legs. He's so big and thick, and so long, it's as if I'm being branded by his cock. A yawning gap unfurls in my belly. A neediness grips me; that yearning that awoke when I first saw him, roars to the fore. I hold onto his shoulders and begin to grind up against that steel column.

Every time I hit it, a trembling radiates from the point of contact. He wraps his thick fingers under my thighs and begins to rub up against me. The combination of our opposite and complementary movements sends a rush of sensations up my spine. A lightning strike of sensations roars up from my thighs, surrounds my pussy, and volcanoes up my back, carrying me with it. Before I can stop myself, I orgasm.

The climax slaps me with a force that has my vision grow black at the edges. I shudder and convulse as he continues to brush his arousal up against my core. When the climax finally fades, I slump. I'm aware of him holding me close, of a whisper against my damp forehead. He tightens his hold about me until I finally stir. When I look up, it's to find him watching me with a tenderness that has me blushing all over again.

"I...came," I say unnecessarily, then flush even harder.

"And it was the most beautiful sight in the world." He lowers me to my feet, holding me until he's sure I have my balance.

"That's twice you made me climax."

"Are you keeping count?" He half-smiles.

"Maybe." I press my palm into the tent at his crotch. "Let me —"

He places his broad palm over mine. "You don't owe me anything."

"But" — I pout — "I want to."

And I do. Really. Not that I've given any blow jobs before this, but he satisfied me, and he's turned on. It feels only right that I help him.

"Not yet." He tugs on my hand, and when I let go, he brings my hand to his mouth and kisses it. "Watching you come and taking care of you, pleasuring you and treating you like the goddess you are, feels like the most important thing in the world."

I can't recall anyone ever calling me a goddess before this. I gape at him. Gorgeous, sexy, alpha, and he's so attentive. So caring. "You're not real, are you?"

He laughs. "I am. Very much." He brings my hand back to the evidence of his arousal and slides my palm up and down the length. "Don't mistake my turning down the use of your mouth with not wanting you. I haven't stopped thinking of how it's going to be when I finally bury myself in your pussy, and make you come around my cock, only—"

"Only?" I breathe.

"Only…when I do so, it will be because you're completely sure that it's what you want. Because once I have you, I won't be able to let you go."

A torrent of sensations coasts through me. My belly quivers. My toes curl. My God, this man can talk dirty to me all day, and I'll happily listen and bring myself to orgasm with the cadence of his deep, dark, gravelly voice.

He straightens my cardigan, tucks strands of hair behind my ear, then steps back and surveys me.

"Do I look okay?" I suddenly become conscious of how disheveled I look.

"You look like a woman who's been thoroughly kissed," he says with a hint of satisfaction.

"I can cross being kissed in a bookstore off my bucket list then," I murmur.

His eyes spark. "Want to tell me what else is on it?"

I pop a shoulder. "Perhaps." I can't resist the teasing tone in my voice.

I hear the tap-tap of heels behind him. Moments later, a woman appears. I hadn't noticed her before this, but her confident gait, combined with her presence here when the rest of the shop is empty, indicates she's likely the manager.

My suspicion is confirmed when she tells us, "It's almost closing time. Of course, I'd be happy to stay later, if you want..."

"Gio." Tyler walks over and kisses her cheek. "Thank you for letting us browse."

"It was absolutely my pleasure." She looks at me, a warm expression in her eyes.

"This is Giorgina Mitchell, the owner of this incredible bookstore." He introduces her. "And this is my..." He stops himself from saying— *Girlfriend? Nah. I can't be his girlfriend if we only met earlier today. Right?* He settles for, "This is Priscilla Whittington."

I wonder if she'll recognize my surname, but all I see is a wide smile. I hold out my hand, but she eschews it and hugs me. "Lovely to meet you."

I am surprised at the demonstration of affection, but it feels so genuine, I hug her back. Because anyone who owns the bookstore of my dreams surely deserves it. She steps back and beams at me. "Did you have a good time perusing the books?"

"Did I have a good time?" I roll my eyes. "That would be putting it mildly. I adore this space. What you have here is my every wet dream come true," I say enthusiastically.

Tyler coughs, and when I glance at him, he's smirking.

Heat flushes my face again. Apparently, I can't stop blushing around this guy. "Well... Maybe not all, but this place"—I turn back to Giorgina—"is my every book fantasy come true."

"Right?" She grins. "I am forever grateful that I saw the opportunity and went for it. I wanted a place where readers would be happy to come in and spend time reading and, of course, buying the books, too. The best thing is I get to hold book club events, as well as bookish cosplay gatherings, and author signings."

"Wow! You have the best job in the world."

"I do!" She looks between us. "So, would you like me to keep the shop open for you, or—"

"Oh, no, that's not necessary; I'm done. Also, I'm sorry I put out your customers this evening."

"It's for a good cause. I'm sure they'll understand." A hopeful gleam comes into her eyes as she glances in Tyler's direction. But she doesn't say anything else, for which I'm grateful. "Would you mind posing for a photograph?" she asks.

"A photograph?"

"It's not often I find a man holding the basket of books while a woman shops here."

"Right?" I nod vigorously. "I was telling Tyler the same thing."

"Which is why I'd love to take a picture of the two of you and post it on our socials, if you don't mind?"

"I don't." Tyler turns to me with a question in his eyes. When I don't protest, he puts his arm about me and pulls me in. In his other hand, he holds a basket of books. I look up into his face, and the light shining in his eyes is a mixture of tenderness and heat, need and lust. I swallow. Liquid heat infuses my bloodstream. Is every encounter with him going to be this intense?

"Oh, that's perfect." Giorgina pulls out her phone and takes a few quick pictures. "You guys are so cute together."

Neither Tyler nor I react. I can't look away from those piercing dichromatic eyes of his. The green iris has golden sparks in it. The other one is a piercing blue with splashes of silver. He's Apollo and the God of Thunder and Lightning, rolled into one.

She clears her throat, and I jerk out of the haze which has overtaken my mind. He releases me, and I pull back at the same time.

She looks at us with an even bigger smile; this one has a knowing tinge to it. But she doesn't comment on the moment we had. She nods at the basket that Tyler is holding, and the other one at his feet. "I'm so pleased you found our self-help section. I added it recently. Shall I ring up your purchases? And if you give me your address, I'll have the books delivered to you."

8

Tyler

"You shouldn't have paid for the books." She slides onto the passenger seat of my car. I make sure she has her seat belt on before I shut the door, then walk around and get into the driver's seat.

"I absolutely should have." I turn to her. "It was my pleasure, Cilla."

"Cilla?" She blinks slowly. "Are we on nickname basis already?"

"Aren't we?" I allow myself a small smirk. I pleasured her, tasted her, and watched her come. I saw the delight in her features when she picked out the books she wanted. And the happiness in her eyes as she perused the selection in the bookstore. So yeah, I think I'm allowed to have a nickname for her. I don't say all this aloud. But surely, she must read my mind, for she blushes.

"A gentleman wouldn't be so crass as to allude to what happened earlier between us." She waves an admonishing finger under my nose.

"Ah, but I'm not a gentleman, am I?"

"You took me to the most exclusive coffee shop in the country, then to a hidden London bookshop, which I had no idea existed. And shut both of them down in advance so we could have privacy. I'd say there is a gentlemanly streak in you."

"I did it so I could have my wicked way with you," I say bluntly.

"Oh, my God." She throws up her hands. "Do you have no filter?"

I laugh. "Was that too much?"

She rubs at her temple. "I want to say yes, but strangely, I find your brand of being this open"—she waves her hand between us —"strangely endearing and definitely arousing."

"I find *you* arousing."

The blush deepens on her face and extends down her neckline. "Stop." She fans herself, then looks away before clearing her throat. "Where are we going next?"

It's a clear attempt to change the topic, but I let her have it.

"I want to take you to my place."

The pulse at the base of her neck speeds up. "You did say you wanted me to spend the night with you. So, I shouldn't be surprised that you want to bring me to your place. It's just—" she laughs lightly, "it feels so intimate."

"It *is* intimate that I want to take you home." I shoot her a side-ways glance. "What I feel for you is *very* intimate."

I don't bother to hold back the emotions I already feel for her. The one thing my life in the Marines has taught me is that life is short and when you find something or someone who makes you feel the way I feel for her, you don't want to waste any time.

Her eyes flash. Her lips part. Guess she heard what I'm trying to convey to her. I have a feeling she reciprocates what I'm sensing. That this chemistry, this connection I sense between us goes both ways. I have an idea that she wants more; I want it, too. But I want to make sure I take each step forward with her with great intent. Make each move carefully, so I don't spook her.

No matter that being surrounded by her scent in the enclosed space of my car is playing havoc with my libido. No matter that she made it clear that she wants me. For the first time in my life, I want to go slow, even as the primal part of me wants to take her to my bed and bury myself inside her.

I turn the wheel of my car and take the turnoff leading to my place.

"A penthouse on the top floor of the tallest residential building in the city?" She looks out at the view of the city spreading out before us. "Dare I say how predictable this is?"

I hear the laughter in her voice and acknowledge it. "Couldn't resist being on top of the world." My ego is my weakness. And I have no problem admitting that.

I pop the cork on a champagne bottle. The sound catches her attention, and she glances at me over her shoulder. I pour the bubbly liquid into two flutes and walk around the bar toward her.

When I proffer her a glass, she smiles. "What are we celebrating?"

"You." I clink my glass with hers. "To the sliding doors of the tube train which brought the most beautiful woman in the world to me."

She laughs a little, but her eyes gleam suspiciously.

"You going to cry, baby?" The endearment slips out, and it sounds so natural. It *feels* so natural. So perfect.

Like I've been spending my entire life up to now waiting to call her that. Like every challenge in my life was so I could overcome it and get to her. All the times my life was spared when I went on a mission for my country were so I could bring her here to my place, under my roof, and do everything in my power to make her feel special. For she's mine. *Mine. Only MINE.*

She shakes her head, then brings the glass to her lips and takes a sip. Her eyes widen. She licks her pink lips, and it sends a flurry of heat racing down my spine to my already stiffening dick. I ignore it and focus on the pleasure that ripples across her features. "Wow, that is…incredible."

"It is, huh?" Seeing her relish the taste of the champagne I've poured for her is the most amazing feeling in the world. "I've been saving this for a special occasion."

"Oh?" She tilts her head. "Is that what this is?"

"Isn't it?" I take another sip. Her gaze is drawn to my mouth. When I lick my lips, the pulse at the base of her throat speeds up.

"You're starting to sound like such a player." She gives me the side-eye. "Makes me wonder what game you're up to."

"No game." Then, because I know exactly how it's going to impact her, I lick the drops on my lips.

She draws in a sharp breath.

"Now, *that* was me playing." I scan her face, memorizing every line. "But I have a feeling you're enjoying it, too..."

Her face flames. Damn, she's so cute when she's embarrassed.

"You, Tyler Davenport, are trying to seduce me."

"Am I succeeding?"

She tips up her chin. "Thought you said you didn't want to sleep with me?"

I shake my head. "I said, I want to get to know you better first."

"Hmm..." She pouts. "You think you know me enough now?"

Not nearly, but captivated by the curve of her lips, my cock signals it can't be avoided any longer.

I toss back my champagne, then urge her flute up to her lips. "Drink up, baby."

She takes another sip, and another. "Can I save the rest for later?"

Without removing my gaze from hers, I take her flute, then pivot and walk to the bar. I place both of our glasses on it. When I turn, it's to find she's still standing by the window.

I quirk my finger at her. "Come 'ere."

9

Priscilla

That thick, gooey feel of his voice pours over me like liquid chocolate over sticky caramel. My throat closes. My thighs tremble. My nipples turn into pebbles of longing. And all because he asked me to come to him in a tone that makes it clear what he has in mind is getting to know me better—in the carnal sense. I put one foot in front of the other, and when I'm arm's length from him, I stop.

He drags his gaze from the top of my head down to my chest, my navel, the triangle between my legs, my thighs, my toes. He may as well as be touching me; that's how potent it is. A shiver runs up my spine. Goosebumps pepper my skin. He brings his gaze back to my face, then tilts his head. "You're beautiful."

The compliment slides like honey through my bloodstream. It warms me and arouses me at the same time. "Thank you," I murmur.

He holds out his hand, and when I place mine in his, he tugs.

"Oh!" I wasn't expecting that at all. I tip toward him, and he catches me around the waist. He hauls me so close, I'm plastered to him, chest to thigh. Then, he looks deeply into my eyes with those contrasting irises of his, and instantly, it's as if I've been sucked into a vortex. I place my palms on his chest, and even through the fabric of his shirt, the heat of his skin feels like being exposed to the blazing sun. And the strength coiled in those pecs... *Mercury must be in alignment today,* for it feels like I'm touching a wall forged from granite.

A shudder grips him. I blink. Was that my touch that affected him? I slide my hands down his ridged abs until my fingers brush the waistband of his pants. I flick open the top button and reach for his zipper, but he locks his fingers around my wrist and stops me. Still unable to look away from his piercing gaze, I try to tug on my hand, but he doesn't release his hold.

"I want to," I whisper.

"Not yet." He releases me, and before I can react, he bends his knees and scoops me up in his arms.

I squeak.

He strides toward the inner rooms of his penthouse. We pass the sleek furniture I noticed earlier, highlighted by statement lighting from the ceiling. There's a massive television on the wall and a comfortable sectional with cushions opposite it. Thick rugs are strewn around, and a couple of massive armchairs invite me to sink into them. There are paintings on the walls—all of which depict modern art and I'm sure are originals. It's clearly a bachelor pad, but it also feels lived in.

I notice a kitchen with gleaming built-in appliances. On the countertop is a heavy-duty food blender, as well as a knife block, and a holder with spatulas and other cooking utensils. A large island in the center carries a bowl of fruit. A part of the countertop has been converted to a butcher's block, which looks well used. *Does this man cook?*

The carpet cushions the sound of his footsteps as he stalks up the corridor. We pass the closed doors to three other rooms, and when he reaches the double doors at the end of the hallway, he shoulders them open.

The doors snick shut behind us, and I take in the large room with a massive, super king-sized bed that dominates the space. Floor-to-ceiling windows make up one wall, through which the lights of the city twinkle. A lamp on the nightstand casts a warm glow over crisp white bedclothes.

He marches across the thick carpeting and drops me on the bed. I bounce once, but before I can sit up, he planks over my body. I'm bracketed in with his elbows on either side of me.

For a few seconds, he simply stares at me.

"What?" I try not to give in to the tremors wracking my body.

"I can't believe I have you under my roof, in my bed," he says slowly.

There's awe in his voice, and underlying it is the thickness of lust and something else... *Something awfully close to... Love? Nah. You can't feel love for someone you met a few hours ago, right?*

He lowers his big body onto mine, slowly, slowly. He's only leaning some of his upper body weight on me, but it's enough to pin me to the bed. I sigh. It feels so good. It feels amazing. I didn't realize how much I needed this until now. My pussy clenches in on itself, and my breasts are so swollen, they feel too heavy for my body. I feel the need to be held, to feel his weight on top of me. I throw my arms about his neck and hold on tightly. A moan spills from my lips, and it sounds so yearning, so very needy. I should be embarrassed, but I'm not.

The one thing I've learned through my self-help books is to seek my own gratification and not apologize for it. So far, it's resulted in an intimate knowledge of the various toys I've used to pleasure myself. This is the first time a real-life man is responsible for making me feel like I'm about to self-combust. A shiver grips me. My heart flutters like a butterfly in my rib cage. My scalp feels like it's on fire. I feel like I'm burning up. It's a feeling more intense than the time I realized that I'm the one responsible for my life and my future. No one else. It's what made me leave home at eighteen.

He leans back, putting a little distance between us, and observes me closely. "You okay?"

I nod.

"You sure?"

I nod again.

His gaze softens. He draws his finger down the line of my nose, to the dip in my upper lip. I open my mouth, enough to draw his digit between my lips. I suck on it and am rewarded by his sharp inhalation. He leans more of his lower body weight on me. Instantly, I feel something very thick, long, and insistent stabbing into my upper thigh.

My eyes round. None of my toys, or my romance novels, or the porn I watched prepared me for how weighty, how hefty, how massive, that part of him is. And when he pries my legs further apart so that heavy part of him nestles in the triangle between my thighs, it feels hot and sweet and erotic, all at the same time.

In this position, I feel pinned down. I feel owned. Possessed. Branded by the throbbing arousal which I can feel through the barriers of my clothes and his. Speaking of—I slide my palms down his back, reveling in the peaks and valleys of the muscles until, once more, my fingertips brush up against his belt.

"Greedy, hmm?"

"I just want to feel your skin against mine," I whine.

"All in good time." He reaches one arm behind his back, locks those thick fingers around my wrist and pulls my arm up, then does the same with the other. Suddenly, my wrists are shackled, and my lower body is immobilized. I tug my hands but can't move them at all. I twist and turn against him, not because I want to get free…but because I feel trapped. And that's exciting. He simply watches me with those curiously hypnotic eyes of his. Watches as I feel him grow thicker between my thighs. Watches as his weight grows heavier. Watches as I stop struggling, my breath coming in pants.

"You like being held down."

It's not a question as much as a statement. He sounds confident. And there's a knowledge in his eyes that resonates with a primal part of me I haven't dared acknowledge. *Primal part? What am I even thinking?* I brush aside that spark of carnal awareness yawning in the pit of my belly and frown at him.

"And if I do?" I frown. "Is that okay?"

In reply, he whispers his fingertips down the column of my throat and my chest to where the neckline of my blouse dips. The hair on my forearms stands to attention.

He notices it, and a pleased expression comes into his eyes. "You're so damn responsive, Cilla."

Hearing the nickname from his mouth makes my blood pressure shoot up.

And when he leans in and brushes his lips over mine, every part of me trembles. His mouth is firm, yet the kiss is tender. There's so much feeling in it, so much yearning, so much worship that tears knock at the backs of my eyes. It feels like a promise. A plea. A hankering which zips down to the core of me and ignites my hunger. And as if he feels it, too, he tilts his head and deepens the kiss. He licks into the seam of my lips, and that hunger turns into a roaring fire.

I gasp. He thrusts his tongue into my mouth, sweeps it over my teeth, and my stomach bottoms out. My thighs tremble. My pussy clenches. I writhe, trying to get closer to him.

A growl rumbles up his chest. He leans more of his weight, so I have to stop moving. I stay held in position by his weight, and once again, the fact that I can't move and that he's in complete control of my body is such a turn on.

He holds my gaze and grinds his big, solid arousal into my aching core. I groan and shudder. Sweat breaks out on my forehead. His gaze grows more intense, and he begins to dry fuck me. Through our clothes, he thrusts up and against me.

That massive column in his pants gives me the friction I need. Quivers of pleasure begin to build inside me. My entire body begins to vibrate. He keeps going, gathers speed, making sure to hit my swollen clit with that ridge. That weakness in my knees spreads up my thighs, and centers in my core.

"Oh, my God," I huff.

He thrusts up against me again, and the jolt of pleasure that shoots through my veins makes my brain cells spark. "Tyler," I cry out.

"I fucking love it when you call out for me."

10

Tyler

"Mine," I growl. "You're mine, baby. Mine to own. Mine to please. Mine to hold and cherish. Mine to possess. Mine to make love to all night long."

"Tyler," she says between gasps.

And hearing my name from her lips again causes goosebumps to crawl over my skin. My breath catches. My cock threatens to claw its way out through the crotch of my pants, and I grind it into that honeyed place between her legs so she can understand exactly how much it affects me.

"Sweet girl, you have a way of surprising me that makes me your slave."

I take in the flash of intelligence in her gaze, the blown pupils which tell me how aroused she is, the rosy tint which colors her cheeks, the rise and fall of those gorgeous tits, which invite me to suck on her nipples. Her body has been calling to mine in a way I can't resist.

"You're mine, baby, you hear me. Mine. Now come for me, Cilla. Right now."

Her body arches. She cries out as she climaxes. I continue to grind up against her as the aftershocks ripple through her. When she slumps, I gather her up in my arms and turn on my side with her. I keep my thigh between her legs to keep the slight pressure there, knowing that's going to heighten her pleasure. For a few seconds, I stay with my woman in my arms. Holding her. Luxuriating in the soft give of her curves against my body. I run my fingers up her arm to her biceps, then back down to her wrist.

She shivers. "Tyler." The husky tone of her voice brings a satisfied curve to my lips.

"Yes, baby?"

She looks up again. "You still haven't come." To illustrate her point, she brings up her thigh until it rubs against the swollen tent at my crotch. Vibrations of shock race out from the point of contact. My cock lengthens further. *Fuck, at this rate, I'm going to come in my pants.* My balls are so swollen, I swear, they feel as heavy as mortar rounds. She begins to saw her thigh against the heavy column in my pants. My brain cells seem to ignite.

"Jesus, woman, you're killing me."

Her lips curve in a sassy smile. She slides in and rocks her thigh against my bulging penis. I groan. I tighten my hold about her, throw my head back, and grit my teeth. *I can't come; not yet. Not until I've made her climax again. Her pleasure. Her satisfaction. Her gratification. That's what matters most.*

I draw on my reserves of strength and patience from deep inside. From the same place I turned to when I was on a mission and needed to find my focus. Only, what I felt serving my country seems secondary to this incredibly huge need inside me to serve my woman.

I block out my own craving and, with what feels like my final ounce of self-control, I sit up with her in my arms. All those years of training finally paid off—judging by the way she tenses in surprise when I pull it off without even loosening my hold on her.

"Wow, you're so strong." The words leave her mouth, and she makes a face. "Why does that sound so...cringe?"

I chuckle. "You're not wrong. A hundred push-ups per day will do that to you."

"A hundred?" She shakes her head. "I can barely manage five."

"We can train together. I'll show you how to grow your endurance."

"Not sure I'd look forward to that." She scowls.

When I chuckle, she rolls her eyes. "You were kidding, weren't you?"

"I was trying to distract you. Raise your arms."

She frowns, but unable to stop herself from obeying, she does as I ask at once. *Damn, this need in her to indulge my desires as much as I ache to satisfy her feels like the last nail on the coffin of my bachelorhood.* I can't believe I'm thinking this way, but how can I stop when it feels so natural to envisage a future with her?

I grab at the hem of her blouse and pull it up and off. I toss it aside, and glance down at the swell of her tits in her lacy bra. The dark shadows of her nipples are outlined against the fabric. My cock throbs as blood drains to my groin. Unable to stop myself, I bend and bury my face between her breasts.

She shivers, and when I lick into her cleavage, she groans. I wrap my thumb and forefinger around one nipple and pluck on it. She gasps, digs her fingers into my hair, and holds on.

I bring up my other hand, weigh her other breast, before squeezing down on her other nipple. "Oh, Tyler," she moans.

I raise my head, look into her lust-filled eyes, and tug on both nipples.

Instantly, she arches her back, pushing her breasts closer for my ministrations. I reach behind her, unhook her bra, pull it off, then cupping both her tits, I bury my face between them again.

She tugs on my hair, and the little shockwaves of pain zing down to my balls. Once more, I ignore the need to bury myself in her sweet pussy. *Focus on her pleasure. Her rapture. Her fulfillment.* I move my head and suck on her nipple. She quivers. I squeeze her tits together and move my head to suckle on her other one. I bite down gently on her nipple, and she cries out. I straighten, close my mouth over hers and kiss her deeply.

She responds avidly, opening for me. The candied taste of her sends a rush of dopamine through my bloodstream. It's still not as sweet as the hallowed flesh between her legs. I need to see her naked.

I reach down, unfasten the button of her skirt, and lower the zip. When she raises her hips, I tug the skirt down her legs and pull it off along with her flats. Then I push her down on her back.

Giving myself only a second to admire her creamy thighs, I tug off her panties. Then, because I can't resist, I bring them to my face and sniff.

"You're filthy," she cries. The embarrassment in her voice is tinged with lust.

I look into her eyes and respond, "Only for you, baby." I toss them over my shoulder, and when she tries to rise, I place my palm in the center of her body and push down. "Stay."

She instantly subsides. And her ability to obey me without question tells me she trusts me. And that jolts my need to a fever pitch. Something snaps inside of me. I use the weight of my hand to hold her down while I slide down her body. I settle between her legs and stare at her pink swollen flesh.

"What are you doing?" she asks on a gasp, but doesn't try to close her thighs. Fuck if that doesn't arouse me further. Give me a woman who revels in her sexuality. Who lives life to the fullest like me, and who grabs pleasure and enjoys it because she knows she's worth it. The thought turns my cock to stone.

I drag my nose up the seam of her pussy lips. Her entire body shivers. I lick up and around her clit, and goosebumps pop across her belly.

"Tyler. Please." She squirms under me.

I close my lips around the swollen bud and suck. She cries out. I throw her legs over my shoulders and, gripping her hips to keep her in place, I stuff my tongue inside her slit.

11

Priscilla

He curls his tongue inside me, and little balls of fire erupt under my skin. My blood feels like it's boiling. Sweat beads my temples. I grab at the bedclothes on either side of my body, push my head into the mattress, and try to stop myself from coming again so embarrassingly soon. But when he grazes his stubbled chin up my pussy, I wail.

The sound is so vulnerable, so heavy with lust, it turns me on even more. I'm aware of my inner walls pulsing. Of moisture sliding out from between my legs.

He licks up my cum, then proceeds to suck on my pussy, using just enough of his teeth to cause a combination of pain and pleasure to squeeze my lower body. "Tyler, please. Ty," I whine.

In response, he drags his tongue down my slit to my forbidden back hole, then back up again to my cunt. Then, he pries my pussy lips apart and focuses solely on my slit. He sips and slurps and draws on the swollen bud until I'm out of my head with wanting. My toes curl, my hips quake. Full body shudders oscillate up and down my length. "Tyler, please, please, please."

"What do you want, baby?" he whispers into my cunt.

"You." Half out of my head with need, unable to bear the emptiness clawing deep inside of me, I yank on his hair, desperate to have him, to kiss him. To have him replace his tongue with the part of him that I haven't yet seen. "I need you, please."

The longing in my voice must finally get through to him, for he pushes off of me. In a fluid move which has his biceps bulging and the planes of his back stretching his shirt, he rolls off the bed and straightens. With more than a little swagger, he rolls down the sleeves of his shirt. He undoes a couple of his buttons, then reaches behind his back and, in a very quintessentially male gesture, he pulls off his shirt and throws it aside.

I greedily drink in the expanse of his chest planes, the dog tags which nestle between his pecs, the corrugated eight-pack abs which turn it into a work of art, and then that Adonis belt. *Oh, my God.*

Then there's the tattoo over his heart. I peer at the Japanese-style cherry blossom branch that appears to break through dog tags inked into his skin. The blossoms aren't the traditional pink—they're rendered in the watercolor style using the colors of military service medals. They look like drops of color catching the light. Before I can ask him what the tattoo signifies, a jangle of metal draws my attention to his waistband.

He undoes his belt, lowers his zipper, and then shucks off his pants and his briefs in one sweep. When he straightens, I take in the powerful thighs corded with muscle and the heavy organ jutting up from the nest of hair at his crotch. *Jesus.* He's bigger than I imagined. I felt the length of him pressed up against my core, but seeing his cock in its full naked glory ignites specks of fire in my blood and turns them into flaming cannonballs.

My mouth waters. My jaws ache in expectation. My pussy trembles... And it's not just from anticipation. It's a wariness, which has everything to do with self-preservation. From the primal rush of knowing this is a man at the apex of his masculinity standing before me. So virile. He could probably impregnate me just looking at me.

"Holy shit." I take in his thickness, the proud jut of his penis, the throbbing vein which runs up the length, the swollen bulbous head, and shake my head. "You're so big."

He smirks. "I'm aware."

"You're huge."

"Thank you." He dips his head.

"I did mean that as a compliment, *sort of*." I swallow.

He must sense my hesitation, for a furrow appears between his eyebrows. "But —"

"But I have to point out again that that's a monster dick you have there." As if to emphasize my words, I knock my knees together. It's a purely instinctive response. One born out of self-preservation. One done because, though I appreciate his size, I also am not sure if he's going to fit.

He surveys me closely. "I know I'm well-endowed, but I promise, I'll do my best to ensure I don't hurt you."

I swallow — knowing I won't be able to wrap my fingers around that column, let alone my mouth. As for my cunt... *Holy hell.* Moisture trickles from my slit. But my thighs...quiver, only it's not just from desire. There's a certain amount of doubt, of trepidation of letting that anaconda-like part of him near me. Despite him making sure he made me come first and showing he isn't selfish... Still... It feels like a breach too far — pun intended — to allow him to penetrate me with that thang.

"It's not that I don't believe you..." Which is true. I do think he won't consciously hurt me. I twist my fingers together. "But I have a feeling, despite your best intentions, when you put that... That monster cock inside of me, I'm likely to feel you all the way in my throat, and... I'm afraid it's going to hurt too much."

I'm sure he's going to laugh at my reluctance. Or perhaps, try to convince me to let him fuck me anyway, that I'm going to love it, ultimately. And he's probably right, but to my surprise, he does none of that.

Instead, a tender look comes into his eyes. "I understand your trepidation."

"You... You do?" I blink.

"We only met today. And while we both sense the chemistry

between us, there's no reason for you to trust that I'll take care of you."

The very fact that he says that relaxes something inside me. Some of the tension goes out of my shoulders.

"It's not that I don't want it. And I know I'm the one who insisted that we spend the night 'not-only-talking.'"

"But at that time, you didn't realize what I was packing?" he offers.

I search his features to make sure he isn't inwardly smirking at me. And he isn't. He actually understands my quandary. Ugh. It makes me wonder if I'm overreacting.

Once more I glance at his very impressive XXXL-sized muscle between his legs. "Umm, to be fair, I'm not surprised. You have a certain confidence about you, a certain dominance which told me you had to be well-sized, but yeah, the fact that it resembles the Loch Ness monster is a surprise."

"Dominance, hmm?" One side of his lips kicks up.

"No need to appear so pleased," I mutter. "Though I suppose you're entitled." I'm relaxed enough for my legs to fall apart.

His gaze instantly darts to the triangle between my thighs. His breathing roughens. He curls his fingers into fists at his sides. And damn, if his shaft doesn't thicken further. I gulp, then glance up at him—but his face doesn't betray how turned on he is. The air between us shifts, softening. "We don't have to do anything until you're ready." His voice is tender.

He straightens his fingers and rolls his shoulders. Then he looks around, grabs his pants and steps into them.

To my eternal regret, he covers the baseball bat-shaped thang jutting up from his center... And a part of me mourns it. My pussy is both regretful and relieved. Okay, only one percent relieved, because secretly, I trusted what he said. He'd have made sure I came a few more times and that I was soaking wet. And while I'd have had to stretch to take him inside me, considering women have pushed out babies, I'd have probably accommodated him, ultimately. No doubt, I'd have had the biggest orgasm of them all when we fucked.

On the other hand, I don't have to take his shaft into my body yet. I bet I'd have felt sore for weeks after. And it feels too intimate that I'll feel him inside me in that manner... And it's only been a few hours since I met him. He's right, after all.

I would prefer to get to know him better before taking this final step. *And yes, it is because he'll be my first.* And then, I'll have to explain why I haven't been with anyone else yet, and that'll be awkward.

Guess this isn't just about the size of his dick. It's...some instinct which wants me to spend a little more time with him, out of bed, before giving him my virginity. Which is understandable, right?

He shrugs on his shirt, but thankfully, he doesn't button it, so flashes of those very impressive, drool-worthy pecs of his remain visible.

He walks around and holds out his hand. I glance at it, then up at his face. There's resignation and understanding, and lust and... More than a tinge of tenderness. Which is as sexy as that dominant, bossy, take-charge attitude I've found so hot from the very first time he opened his mouth and ordered me around.

There's no question of refusing him. I slide my hand into his.

His throat moves as he swallows. I realize then, he was worried I'd refuse him. As if I could? I still want him. But he's right; this thing between us is serious enough that I also want to get to know him better.

"Come on, let's get something to drink."

12

Priscilla

"Fall in love with showing up for yourself —
especially on the days it feels the hardest."
-Cilla's Post-it note

"You've got to stop feeding me like this." I chew another forkful of the pasta, savoring the creamy, complex textures of the dish. Turns out, he was hungry. So he wanted, not only to have a drink, but also to eat.

He whipped up what turned out be an Aglio Olio e Peperoncino —pasta with olive oil, garlic, hot pepper and parmesan cheese—in very little time.

After pulling on my blouse and skirt, I was content to sit at the counter and watch his graceful movements around the kitchen. I was right. The man can cook.

I'm surprised that after I called it off after we were on the verge of fucking, he wasn't upset. Instead, he made me dinner—*a very delicious dinner*—and seems happy to sit here talking to me. Which is what he professed he wanted to do all along. So, I shouldn't be surprised. Especially after he'd accused me of holding him to a stereotype. In fact, he's not given me any reason to doubt him so far. So why is it that, after wanting to jump into bed with him, I changed my mind at the last minute?

His size was an excuse. I acknowledge that. On some level, I suspect I'm not ready to take that last step physically. I've always thought being a virgin wasn't a big deal so it wouldn't matter when I decided to sleep with someone. Especially not when I've pleasured myself with toys. But there's a difference between a silicon appendage being inside me and the real thing. And it's not only because the dimensions of my vibrator pale in comparison to how big he is.

Perhaps, on some level, I sense that giving myself to him physically would mean giving him my heart. And I'm not ready yet. Not when there's so much about him I don't know.

I've been waiting for the right person and the right circumstances to give up my virginity. I'm still convinced he's the right person, but giving up something I've held onto that's important to me is scary. Maybe I just need more reassurance that he's *the one,* even if my heart already insists that he is?

He pours us each a glass of white wine; it's clean and dry on the palate. I may have left home at eighteen, but thanks to my parents' moneyed background, my tastes were already refined by then. Enough to appreciate the kind of quality ingredients only money can buy.

"I love taking care of you." He takes a sip of his wine and places the glass down.

A melting sensation swirls in my chest. This man seems hell-bent on breaking the stereotype I have of alphas as being selfish and not nurturing. I'm also not used to a man who is so open with his feelings. I certainly wouldn't have expected that from someone like Tyler —who's a billionaire, who looks like Adonis, and lives and breathes confidence.

I'm stereotyping him again. Something he gently reprimanded me for. Not sure how to respond to his comment, I content myself with pointing to his almost empty plate. "You eat quickly."

He pops a shoulder. "A leftover from my military days, when I had to eat on the go and in shared dining rooms."

Now *that*, I want to know more about. "When did you join the Marines?"

"I was eighteen when I joined the Royal Marines; twenty when I went on my first call of duty. Led five more before I retired at thirty-two. That was two years ago. I joined the family business and have run one of the Davenport Group of companies ever since."

He's nine years older than me. "Why did you enlist?"

He takes a sip of his wine, his expression contemplative. "My uncle served. As did my older brothers. My grandfather thought it would be character-building. And that it was great PR to further the value of the shares of our group company. That's not the reason I joined, though. I did it because…I wanted to." He fixes me with a serious look. "It was a calling. A compulsion, even. I was born into a family with plenty. It felt like I should give back something to the country and the community which gave me so much."

His tone tells me his sentiments are genuine. The expression on his face adds gravitas to his words.

"It's unusual to come across someone who feels called to do something for the greater good," I finally say.

"You mean, it's rare for someone from my background of privilege to do something other than join the family business—" His lips kick up. "Which I did, ultimately."

"But only after you served your country," I point out.

"Don't put me on a pedestal." His lips twist. "There were many moments—especially in the midst of a tough mission—when I questioned the sanity of why I had signed up to do this, but—"

"But you persisted."

He breathes in slowly, cracks his neck as if composing his thoughts. "There was a time, when I first joined the Marines and was back from my first mission… When I saw friends upfront being killed and innocents among the enemy being slaughtered… When the clarity of what I'd signed up for... When the futility of what I was embarking on became clear to me... It was my lowest phase."

There's anguish in his voice and a pain that shines through which dissipates the last of the walls I've tried to throw up around my heart. Whatever he's feeling, whatever he went through, it tested him. It changed him. It made him grow up and become the man he is today... The result of which, I'm attracted to, hugely.

And I love the fact that he's confiding in me. His openness to talk about himself is as intoxicating as his sex-on-a-stick attractiveness.

"How did you get over it?"

"You never really get over it." He looks into the distance, his gaze contemplative. "You realize that, while you might have started out with altruistic intentions, ultimately, you're playing a small part in much bigger program you can't really see. But that you can still make a difference by doing your part well. By being there for your fellow Marines. By doing the right thing by them and most people you come in contact with."

There's a wistfulness to his tone which makes me muse, "You miss the Marines."

That half-smile is back. "I miss the camaraderie. The shared purpose. The going after the bad guys. It's more black-and-white in the Marines. You have a goal. A purpose. You put your life on the line because of your beliefs. You learn to trust your instincts. To savor the adrenaline of the shared mission. Your focus is on bringing yourself and your teammates back home in one piece. You live and breathe your mission. Your every waking minute is spoken for." He shakes his head.

"It sounds stressful."

"It is. That's what makes it addictive." He lowers his chin. "And yes, I do miss it."

"How did you acclimatize back to daily life?"

When he stays silent, I explain, "I've heard it's difficult for soldiers to adjust back to civilian life."

"I didn't do a great job of it, I'm afraid." He shifts in his seat. A sheepish look crosses his features. "In those early days of trying to lead a life outside the forces, I used alcohol as a crutch. I'd often be blind-drunk enough to wake up in a different bed each morning, with a different woman I didn't recognize. A nameless, faceless person I used to try and get the frustration out of my system. Not that it helped much." He shrugs.

He's already been upfront that he's dated other women. This time, I'm somewhat unsurprised by the familiar stinging sensation in my chest. I may have known him for very little time, but this connection between us, which has grown stronger with every passing hour, makes me feel like I have a right to feel possessive about him. After all, by his own admission, he hasn't felt this way about any other woman before me, either.

"By the time I realized how destructive I was being, a few months had passed. It was Brody, my younger brother, who gave me a talking to and told me to pull myself together." He half-smiles. "We got into a fight, which I was too drunk to win. But his thrashing me was the best thing he could have done. I — "

The doorbell rings.

We look at each other.

"Were you expecting company?"

He shakes his head. "No one was announced, so it must be someone security recognizes." He looks around and swears. "I left my phone by the bed, so I don't know if any of them called me, either."

The doorbell rings again, then again. The sound is harsh, jarring, almost insistent. A shiver runs up my spine. A frisson of discomfort stabs into my breastbone. Not sure why I feel like it's an alarm bell, a warning.

I shake my head and attempt a smile. "Whoever that is, is impatient."

"Sorry about this." He rises to his feet and walks out of the kitchen. Unable to sit still, I jump up and follow him through the living room to the front door. He looks through the peephole then steps back.

"There's no one there." His tone is impatient.

He throws the door open and looks around. "I'm going to

complain to security." Then he looks down, and his entire body freezes.

Something about how motionless he is—the bunched muscles of his torso, the way his shoulder blades stand out with surgical precision against his shirt—fires another ripple of alarm through my bloodstream. I hurry and close the distance to him. "Who is it?"

I draw abreast, stand next to him, and look down at a carrier with what seems like an oversized diaper bag left next to it. *Huh?* A carrier? A *baby* carrier? What the—? I peer closely at it. Is that the curve of a tiny head with downy hair peeking out? My heart leaps into my throat. My mind recognizes what I'm seeing, but the connection between my brain and my mouth seems to be lost.

It's Tyler who recovers first. "It's a baby."

13

Priscilla

Someone left a baby on his doorstep? What the — ? Can this really be happening? Doesn't this happen only in the movies? This is real life. Things like this don't happen in the real world. But the evidence to the contrary is in front of my eyes. Maybe they do...

Tension radiates from Tyler's big body. He looks around the short hallway, his jaw set. His eyebrows drawn down. I look from him to the baby in the portable carrier then back at him. There's also a diaper bag next to the carrier. A *very expensive* designer diaper bag too.

I feel discombobulated, like I'm watching the events unfold from far away.

There's a baby. On. His. Doorstep. The hair on the back of my neck rises. A sense of foreboding grips me.

The noise of the elevator's engine running reaches us. It cuts through the sensation of suspended animation that has gripped us.

Tyler springs into action, walking around the baby carrier and toward the elevator. The numbers count down as the elevator descends.

He spins around, rushes into the apartment, then stabs the button on the intercom near the doorway.

"Someone came to visit me just now. You need to stop them from leaving."

I assume he's calling down to security. He listens to whatever the voice on the other end says, then barks, "Yes, they are on their way down in the elevator. Intercept them and keep them there. I need to talk to them."

I glance down to find there's an envelope tucked between the clothes. A stone forms in the pit of my stomach. I can't let myself give shape to the possibilities which are crowding my mind. *Take a breath. Don't let your imagination run away.* I calm myself enough to bend and pick up the envelope.

I'm half-aware of Tyler saying something else to whoever he's talking to. Then he hangs up and walks back to me. I silently hand over the envelope with his name written on it.

He glares at it like he could set it on fire with his eyes. Emotions ripple across his face—anger, curiosity, surprise, dread…and, finally, resignation. He cracks his neck, draws in a slow breath, and turns to me. My heart pounds harder. Unease twists in my stomach, but somehow, I manage to nod.

I'm apprehensive about what's in the note. But also, I'm curious. Whatever it is, it's not going away. The baby is proof of that.

Tyler seems to come to the same realization because he glances at the still sleeping child. Another cascade of expressions follows—but this time it's tinged with softness—the kind I saw on his face when he told me how much he loved to take care of me. The man's a teddy bear at heart.

He takes the envelope from me and rips open the flap. He pulls out a single piece of paper. Whatever he reads in it makes the blood drain from his face.

My heart leaps in my throat, tight and unrelenting. A strange, weightless feeling comes over me. Whatever comes next won't just change us. *It already has.* And there's no undoing it. No going back.

As if in a dream, I reach over and take it from him and read it.

Tyler,

She's yours. Her name is Serene. She turned one last week, on the fifth.

I can't do this anymore. She's better off with you. I relinquish all rights to her.

Take care of her, please.

It's unsigned. My breath hitches. A weightless sensation squeezes my chest. I feel like the ground has disappeared from underneath my feet. I feel unable to process what I'm feeling.

There must be a simple explanation for it... Except... There's a baby in a carrier on his doorstep, and I can't help but wonder what this means for my relationship with Tyler. That weightless sensation intensifies—like the world has tilted beneath my feet. I look up to find him staring at me.

"Did you know about her?" I nod toward the baby.

He shakes his head. "Of course not." His features are granite hard. His jaw is set. And the look in his eyes—there's shock, panic, and a touch of horror. It tells me this is a surprise for him. It eases the knot in my belly somewhat.

I try to hand the letter back to him. He stares at it then shakes his head again. "It... can't be."

"You did say you slept with a lot of women," I say dryly.

"I always wore a condom." He drags his fingers though his hair. "Always."

"It's not always a hundred percent effective."

"Clearly not." He glances at the baby carrier, and something like panic flickers through him. He swallows hard. He looks so lost, it's almost comical. As if aware that she's the focus of attention, the little one lets out a shrill cry.

He instantly jumps back. "Fuck."

"Don't swear in front of the baby," I admonish him.

"She...she's crying." A panicked tone enters his voice.

This time, I do chuckle. "She must be hungry. Or maybe, she wet her diaper."

"Wet her diaper?" His voice stumbles over the words as if it's the first time he's spoken them aloud—which admittedly, it must be.

I resist the urge to roll my eyes and, closing the distance to him, I thrust the note at him. He has no choice but to accept it. I head for the carrier and pick up the child. "There, there, sweetie. You're okay now."

I rock her, and her cries slow down. I brush past him inside the apartment. When he doesn't follow, I glance at him over my shoulder.

The irony is not lost on me. I thought I met the man of my dreams. I thought he was the one. I thought he was going to rock my world. That my future as I knew it would change. And it has. Just not how I expected.

"Better bring her carrier and the diaper bag inside, big guy."

14

Tyler

"There; all done." Cilla leans back from the bathroom counter where she just finished changing the kid's diaper. She wraps up the used diaper in a disposable bag and holds it out.

When I make no move to take it from her, she frowns. "Can you bin this please?"

Pushing aside this feeling of being discombobulated, like I've been transferred into an alternate reality, I push away from the entrance to the bathroom where I've been lurking and inch in her direction. When I reach her, she waves the package at me. I catch a whiff of something unpleasant and wrinkle my nose.

"Go on," Cilla says in an impatient voice.

I pinch the pungent package between my thumb and forefinger, head to the trash can, and drop it in. I'm not proud to say that my hands won't stop shaking. My stomach twists, flips, churns. I can taste the panic on my tongue, bitter and metallic. *There's a baby in my house. And apparently... It's mine?*

Nope; not possible. I've always wrapped it up. But has there ever been a time I didn't? I try to think back and come up with... Nothing. Nope. I've never been tempted to do it bareback. Not until I met... her. The woman who's turned brisk and focused on the child since it...landed on my doorstep.

"You'll have to get a diaper disposal bin to lock in the odors," she throws in my direction.

What the—? I pause, then pivot to face her. "What do you mean?"

"The garbage bin you have won't suffice to stop the smell from spreading in the bathroom," she says slowly, as if I don't understand what she's saying. Which I don't. Because I've never had to think about the consequences of throwing a baby's soiled diaper in the rubbish bin.

On the other hand, my mind is reeling with trying to come to terms with the events of the past half-hour. One moment, I was sure I'd met the woman I was going to spend my life with. I was looking forward to making love to her and convincing her to never leave. The next, there's a baby at my doorstep—and it's, apparently, *mine?*

The security guard called to explain what had happened. A woman showed up carrying a baby carrier and told him she was there to see me. She sounded so confident that I was expecting her that he didn't think to check with me. He let her in, figuring it was legitimate. Later, he realized she must have left through an emergency exit, because he never saw her leave through the main doors.

She gave a name, which I'm sure is going to turn out to be fake. He didn't bother to check her ID—a serious lapse—nor did he check in with me first. And he allowed her to come up unaccompanied. It's going to cost him his job. *I don't feel sorry about it, either.* He should not have let that woman in.

I have no idea who she could be. I've never brought a woman to this place before. If I wanted to spend the night with a woman, I've always preferred it to be in a hotel. And could one of those nights have resulted in this kid?

Priscilla brought it into the living room and tried to soothe it. When it continued to cry, she held up the baby and smelled her diaper. *She smelled her diaper!* Jesus Christ. Then she rummaged around in the diaper bag and found additional diapers. She headed to the bathroom, and I followed her. Because really, what else was I supposed to do?

Her actions were competent, her tone soothing as she spoke to the baby while changing her nappy. I watched from the safety of the bathroom entrance for as long as I could.

I'm only putting off the inevitable. My rational mind knows that. But emotionally... Fuck. I'm unraveling. This whole thing is a minefield, and I'm walking it blindfolded. Every instinct I have is screaming — sharp and loud like sirens in my blood. My skin prickles, too tight for my body. Nothing makes sense except the one thought which keeps repeating in my head: *Surely, this kid can't be mine?*

"Look at the shape of her eyes." Priscilla stares down at the infant looking up at her. "They're similar to yours."

"What? No." Once more, I sidle over to her — because I feel like any sudden movement might alarm the child. I confess, a part of me might be holding onto the hope that if I don't get too involved with her, perhaps, I can find a way to foist the responsibility off on someone else. *Because she's not mine.* Nope. But I'm curious enough to want to see what Cilla is talking about.

I reach her and peer over her shoulder. The baby trains her big brown eyes in my direction. At least they aren't mismatched like mine. And the shape of them? Honestly, I can't tell if they look like mine or not.

"Also, her jawline," Cilla says softly. "Do you see the resemblance?" She traces her finger in the air over the kid's face. "So like yours."

"I don't see anything," I say irritably.

"Well, she does seem like she's yours." Cilla nods in a way that makes me realize she's made up her mind.

"Hold on. Until I have a DNA test, nothing is proven." My voice comes out harsh, and it must frighten the kid, for she scrunches up her face and begins to cry.

"Look what you did now." My dream woman scoops up the little one and rocks her against her chest. "There, there. Did your papa scare you? Don't worry about that. He's not as grouchy as he comes across, I promise."

Papa? What the fuck? I'm not ready to be a father. *This is some B-grade soap opera bullshit happening here.* Outwardly, I glare at Cilla. "How do you know that?"

"Because I do?" She turns to face me with the kid nestled in her arms.

"You barely know me," I point out.

"I know enough." Her lips turn up at the side. "You booked out a coffee shop, then a bookstore, for me. You cooked for me. You wanted to get to know me better. You brought me home because you wanted to spend the night getting to know me... And then you accepted my 'no' at the very last minute without a single complaint. You, Tyler Davenport, are a decent human."

My heart constricts. Warmth pools in my chest. I stare into her melting brown eyes and see tenderness. And something close to *love?* Nah. It can't be love. Not when we just met. And now, she's found out that I might possibly have a child. *A baby.* Shit.

She continues to sway the baby in a calming rhythm. And when her gaze roams my face, she must see the conflicting emotions. "It's a lot to take in. You must be feeling confused."

"That's putting it mildly." I shift my weight from foot to foot.

"Would you like to hold her?" She holds the now silent infant out to me.

I glance at the kid, and my gut churns. I can taste panic on my tongue, bitter and metallic. If I hold her...I might not be able to let her go.

There's an innocence about the child, a helplessness that calls out to the protector in me. If I take her in my arms, it means...I won't be able to part with her. And I'm not sure I'm ready to make that decision yet.

When I make no move to take the kid, disappointment flickers across Cilla's features. She begins to pace the floor of my bedroom, holding the kid against her shoulder. The child yawns. Cilla croons a tune under her breath. Something that sounds like a nursery rhyme, though I can't quite hear the words. Watching her with the kid, causes funny sensations in my chest. Maybe it's heartburn? Yeah, that's what it is. It's definitely not my heart stuttering with something suspiciously like tenderness at seeing this woman taking care of this child so competently.

"She's almost asleep." Cilla looks down at the child, her expression gentle. Then she steps past me and heads out of the room.

In the living room, she places the child carefully in the carrier. She sits down in the armchair next to it, keeping a hand on the carrier in a protective gesture.

I'm grateful she knows how to change a diaper. Of course, she does. She's a nanny. A natural caregiver. If she were in my life... And if—and that's a *big* if—the child turns out to be mine, would Cilla want to play a role in the kid's life? *Hold on. That's a big leap to make.* Especially since I only just met her. Besides, the child can't possibly be mine... *Can she?*

"Tyler, are you okay?" Her forehead furrows. "You look troubled."

That's the understatement of the century. I'm completely wrecked —spinning, drowning, with no idea how to make sense of any of this. *What the hell is going on?* Is this some cruel joke one of my brothers cooked up, or have I lost my mind? Nah, springing a kid on me isn't their style. I shake my head to clear it.

Calm down. You successfully led tours of duty and walked away alive. You can do this.

I stalk over and drop into the couch opposite her. "I need to make some calls and figure out what to do about her." I nod in the direction of the child.

She glances at the now sleeping baby, and her features turn gentle. "She's so beautiful." Cilla reaches inside the carrier and touches a finger to the kid's cheek. "So soft."

I stare at the child's face, a knot of troubled emotions forming in my chest. I can't remember feeling this conflicted ever before. But then, I haven't been dealt with two emotional blows in one night, and so close to each other either. I shift my gaze to Cilla's gorgeous features. Not even seeing my brothers-in-arms killed has affected me this deeply. They didn't necessitate the kind of upheavals to my life that this woman and this child may precipitate.

She must sense my perusal for she raises her gaze to mine. Whatever she sees there makes her knit her eyebrows.

"What are you going to do?"

"Call my lawyer and have him call social services to understand what the next steps are with the child. Then, I'll get a private investigator to track down the person who left her here. I'll bet they've been captured on at least one of the security cameras in the building. And then, I need to arrange for a DNA test—" The weight of the decisions I must make pushes down on my shoulders. I feel exhausted. When I pinch the bridge of my nose, Cilla makes a noise of sympathy.

She crosses over to sink down on the couch next to me. "It's a lot of change. A lot of responsibility. There's much to process."

She slips her arm about my shoulders and leans her head against mine. For a few seconds, I allow myself to absorb her comfort, her softness. To revel in her curves against mine.

Whatever I decide to do with this child, my life is going to change irrevocably. I'm going to need time to process it. To understand what led to a woman dropping off a baby at my doorstep—to figure out what to do with the kid, whatever the results of the DNA test turn out to be. That's my responsibility. And I won't shirk from it… Even if it turns out the kid isn't mine. And there's a strong chance she isn't. *I hope…*

And Cilla—? Would I want to saddle her with the responsibility of taking care of a tiny tot? It's different when you have a job and can go home or take time off and forget about it. This wouldn't be that way. And she's still young. She has her entire life ahead of her.

Sure, I've always assumed that one day, I'd want to have children with a woman… And earlier tonight, I thought it would be this woman. But not right away.

And I care for Cilla too much already to want to burden her. I've already formed an attachment to Cilla. I care for her, and I want what's best for her. As for the baby?

I'm not sure how to feel about her.

I've spent all my adult life on my own. And now, to suddenly find I have both the woman of my dreams and an unexpected kid who might not even be mine? My head spins.

Between the two... Right now, Serene has to be my priority. And it doesn't seem fair to ask Priscilla to tie herself to me when... My immediate future feels like it's going to be a shit show while I figure out the story behind this child and what to do with her.

It's not fair to weigh down Cilla with all the complications headed my way—whether the child is mine or not.

Maybe once I've figured things out with the kid, once I've tracked down her mother and returned the kid, or arranged for social services to take her...I'll have the time and space to give Cilla my full attention. She deserves nothing less.

I pull away from Priscilla gently and put some distance between us.

She tips up her chin, a quizzical expression on her face. "What's wrong?"

15

Priscilla

"I need to figure things out." His jaw is rigid, his features closed. And those heterochromatic eyes are cold. Colder than I've ever seen them. He looks so remote. So unlike the man I met earlier today. I glance at the clock on the oven and realize it's almost midnight.

Exhaustion drags at the edges of my mind. I yawn.

His gaze narrows, and he scans my face. "You're tired."

"It's been an eventful few hours." I try a small smile, but he doesn't respond. Another shiver runs up my spine. That frisson of discomfort that settled behind my breastbone when the doorbell rang intensifies.

"Tyler?" I search his eyes. "Talk to me."

"You should leave. I'll call my chauffeur and have him take you home." He looks away. My heart sinks into my stomach.

"What do you mean, you'll call your chauffeur?" I cry.

He rises to his feet, staring straight ahead. He's not meeting my eyes. *Oh, my God.* My heart drops to my feet with a thump. "Tyler?" I feel the hysteria bubble up in my throat and manage to rein it back. "What is it? What are you *really* thinking?"

His expression grows even more remote. "It's late. And as you said, it's been a lot to deal with. You should head home." He rises to his feet and heads off in the direction of his bedroom. *Because that's where he left his phone?* On the bedside table, while he was making me come on his fingers and his tongue, and where he almost fucked me with that massive cock of his. Despite being pissed off with him, my pussy reacts to the image of his monster dick by squeezing in on itself.

I shove the images aside and scramble up to my feet. With a last look at the cutie-pie asleep in her carrier, I follow the big man in.

"Tyler," I begin to call after him. Then, in deference to the sleeping child, I flatten my lips and march into the bedroom in time to see him snatching up his phone from the side table.

His fingers swipe over the device, then he holds it to his ear. "Yes, I need you to take my guest home." He listens. "Ten minutes." He pockets the phone and turns to me.

His expression is remote. His face could be carved into the side of a mountain.

Icicles form in my bloodstream. My heart seizes up. My instincts jangle with foreboding. I know this is not going to end well for me. But I have to be strong. I *need* to be strong. I push aside the premonition and focus all my attention on this gorgeous, larger-than-life man in front of me.

"Tyler, I am not leaving." I set my jaw. "Not until you tell me what's bothering you, and why you're so insistent on sending me away, when a few hours ago you were—" I swallow. "You claimed that you loved taking care of me. You hinted that you wanted something more long-term with me."

"That was before—" He nods in the direction of the living room.

"It's a baby. Her name is Serene. Can you, at least, bring yourself to say that?"

A muscle pops above his jaw. The skin around his eyes stretches.

"I know this is all a shock. I can only imagine how difficult it must be to find a child abandoned on your doorstep, but if you talk it out—"

"I don't want to... Not yet. And not with you."

The vehemence in his voice takes me by surprise. Where is the tender lover? The man who was so conscientious about my tastes, enough to take me to the kind of bookstore he knew I'd love?

I scan his features again, take in that gaze fixed on something other than me, and shake my head in frustration. "Just tell me what you're feeling. I can help."

"You can. By leaving." He folds his arms across his chest.

I stiffen, feeling like he just slapped me. But I'm also aware that he's hurting inside. Which is why he's lashing out at me. I take a step forward, and another, until I reach him. Standing in front of him, I realize, again, how big this man is. How massive, how immovable. The heat leaping off his body could power the electric supply of a city; that's how intense it seems.

Pushing aside my nervousness, I place my hand on his forearm. It feels like I'm touching a wall. "Tyler, you can't push me off like that. I need to know what's brought about this... Sudden change in attitude."

For a few seconds, we stand there, him looking off into the distance, and me taking in his gorgeous face.

"You told me you wanted me. You said... I'd regret it if I didn't come home with you. You told me to take a chance on us—"

"And that was before. Things change."

He sounds so firm. So confident. And his features are so emotionless, I almost believe him.

"You wanted us to get to know each other better. You were so sweet to me. So caring—"

"None of that was faked," he admits. "I wanted you. I felt something for you. It felt monumental when we met—"

Oh God, he's talking about us in the past tense. Like what we have is over before it's even begun. My heart beats with such force, I can barely hear my own thoughts. I draw in a sharp breath, calm myself, then tip up my chin.

Something shifts in him—subtle but unmistakable. He seems to wrestle with whatever's going through his head, jaw tight, shoulders tense. When he finally speaks, his voice is lower, heavier.

"But as you can imagine, I've got a lot to deal with—" He gestures toward the child. "I need to figure out what comes next. It's not unreasonable for me to ask for a little space...is it?"

"Of course not. Your entire life has been turned upside down. Until yesterday, you were a single man, living life on your terms. Today, you need to figure out what your relationship to this child is. It's not easy."

His beautiful throat moves as he swallows. A nerve tics at his temple. He looks both remote and confused. Both standoffish and in need of reassurance. But the look in his eyes—it's one of determination.

"Look Priscilla, I meant what I said then. But that was before"— he waves a hand in the air—"before all this. I need to figure things out. Need to track down the person who left that...kid here. Need to find out if there's any truth to the claim in the letter. Which means, I won't have time to think about anything else. Not even you."

Of course, I know that. "The child takes priority. That's the right thing." I nod. "It's what I'd have done in your position." Still, I can't stop my stomach from sinking. To have met the man who I thought was my future, only to have him ask me to leave less than twenty-four hours later is...unexpected.

Some of my misery must show on my face, for the skin around his eyes softens. "I need to figure out what to do. There's a lot I need to resolve. I need space to think about what to do next, Priscilla."

He called me Priscilla. Not Cilla, but *Priscilla*. That convinces me how much things have changed between us. And the fact that he needs space? It's completely different from what he told me when he asked me to come home with him. When he implied that he wanted me in his life.

"This is not how I'd have wanted to part, but perhaps, it's for the best. Perhaps, our timing is off just now. Perhaps"—he shifts his weight between his feet—"perhaps, when things settle down..." He trails off. A muscle moves at his jaw. His lips firm. Those gorgeous, mismatched eyes grow remote in a way that sends chills down my spine.

He's asking me to leave. Oh, he's implying that he might call me when things settle down, but will he? Does this mean he still wants me? He's implying he just needs time, and there's no reason not to believe him, right?

A message pings on his phone. He glances down at it, then back at me. "The car's here."

"So that's it, huh?" I attempt a smile and fail.

He holds my gaze with a depth that makes my breath catch. The ice in his eyes, melts. For a few seconds, I see something flash in them. Something poignant. Something which has hope bubbling up in my chest. Then it's gone. That mask is back on his face. The one that makes him seem so completely different from the vital, caring man I was sure I'd met. The man I'm sure he still is.

"Perhaps, the emotional punch of having a baby delivered at your doorstep is making you act like this. But it would be a lot easier for me to understand if you'd try to explain your thinking to me." I square my shoulders, jutting out my chin. "I want to give you the benefit of the doubt... But honestly, I'm not sure what to think anymore."

For a few more seconds, our gazes hold. He curls his fingers into fists at his sides. Once again, he seems on the verge of saying something. Only he doesn't. He flattens his lips and ensures there's no expression on his face. Then he pivots and walks out of the room.

What the hell just happened? My head spins, trying to make sense of everything. A headache drums against my temples. I pull myself together, stepping into my flats, which he dropped by the side of the bed, scan the room to make sure I'm not forgetting anything. Consider leaving something... Then, turn and hurry after him.

I reach the living room to find he's holding up my purse. *That's how quickly he wants me gone?*

As if in a dream, I approach him and take my handbag from him. It all began with this bag... And it looks like it's going to end with it, too.

He stalks to the door of the apartment and holds it open. I take a step in his direction when a mewl sounds from the bassinet. I glance at the baby to find she has her eyes open and is watching me. She yawns, and my heart melts. I want to lean toward her, but I force myself to keep going.

The baby must sense the tension in the air for she lets out another wail. My pulse rate spikes. My heartbeat ramps up.

The child is not my problem. She's not. He's made that clear. And I'm not going to stay where I'm not wanted. It doesn't stop my stomach from bottoming out while stupid tears clog my throat.

I keep my gaze straight, and head past the door he's holding open. As I reach the threshold, the baby sends up another cry. Damn it. The pressure builds behind my eyes. I would have to be made of stone not to throw a final glance at the child over my shoulder. Every fragment of my soul wants me to stay...but he wants me gone. The man I was sure was *the one* wants me gone.

And I'm not such a self-sacrificing idiot that I'm going to beg him to allow me to stay and soothe the child until she stops crying.

I reach the elevator and punch the button. I stare woodenly at the doors. The silence stretches. I curl my trembling fingers around the straps of my handbag. *Come on. Come on.* If I stand here any longer, I'm going to lose it. And if I let him see me crying, I'm going to hate myself.

The doors slide open. Thank God. I step inside and turn to face him. I try not to look at him, but he's standing right in my line of view. Big, and solid, *and delicious*. And goddamn him—I sneak a look at his face. I see the burning gaze in his eyes. The regret. The need. The frustration.

Tell me to come back inside. Please?

He opens his mouth, but all that comes out is "Goodbye, Priscilla."

16

Tyler

Fucking hell! She's gone.

I told her to leave. I told her I need space, when nothing could be farther from the truth.

I stare at the closed doors of the elevator, wondering why it feels like my heart just left with her. My life, my soul... Everything is tied to her. And I cut it off and allowed her to walk away with the best parts of me.

It felt like my life was incomplete without her by my side. In the few hours I've known her, she's already come to mean more to me than anyone else I've ever met. It's why I had to ask her to leave. I had to piss her off enough that she wouldn't feel compelled to plead with me.

Enough that she wouldn't return to insist that she help me take care of the baby. For if she did, I wouldn't be able to say no. And I will not thrust the burden of being responsible of such a young life on her. I need to do this myself.

I need to set her free so she can live her life and not be weighed down by my problems. I made the right decision. I did. So why does it feel like my heart is breaking? Like my soul has been crushed? Like I've made the biggest mistake of my life.

Another thin cry splices the air. I startle. *The kid. Shit.* I spin around and head to the carrier. She looks at me, scrunches up her features, then opens her mouth and cries even louder. Fuck. I squat down and rock the carrier from side to side. Will this calm her? I sure hope so.

It doesn't make any difference. She continues to cry. Her face turns red. Her eyes are squeezed tight. Her entire body seems to shudder with the intensity of her wailing. I look around the living room helplessly, wishing Priscilla were still here.

It's up to me to solve the problem of how to stop a baby from crying. How difficult could it be, huh?

I scoop the child up in my arms and cuddle her close. She's so tiny. So fragile. Rising to my feet, I begin to pace. I place the kid against my shoulder and rub her back. "There, there, little one. You're going to be fine." I hum to her. Croon under my breath. Say nonsensical words of comfort to her. The vibration of my voice seems to help. She's still crying, though. I continue to walk back and forth across the living room.

Her crying only seems to grow louder. *Shit.* "Are you hungry?" I rub my hand in circles over her back. "Do you want something to eat?"

Her wail grows to a crescendo. I take that as a yes. My pulse is racing. Adrenaline fills my bloodstream. And it's all because she's crying, and I feel helpless. I need to do something. But what? I head into my kitchen, open the refrigerator, hoping to get her something... But what?

I pivot and make a beeline for the diaper bag. The baby's tucked tightly against my chest, wailing louder by the second. I dig through the chaos inside the bag—diapers, more diapers, some mystery cream, a squishy toy, wipes. Come on, come on. There. A couple of jars of baby food. I grab one and squint at the label, trying to focus. But the cries keep rising, slicing through my nerves. Damn it. My chest tightens. My pulse kicks into overdrive. I've defused IEDs with steadier hands than this.

Thankfully, the baby food is ready to eat, some mashed blend of vegetables with pasta, tuna and cheese. Still holding the kid and the baby food, I race into the kitchen and grab a spoon. Then, heading for the breakfast counter I sit onto a stool. I place the spoon, the jar of baby food and the kid on the counter. Holding the kid close, I manage to open the jar. Then, I scoop out some of the food and offer it to her.

She instantly closes her lips around the spoon. The cries cut off. *Thank fuck.* I feed her another spoonful. And another. The baby eats, all the while watching me with her big eyes. An image of Priscilla's big, brown eyes flickers across my memory, but I push it away. *Just like I pushed her away.* I can't think about her now. I focus on Serene and the fine, chestnut-colored curls forming a halo around her head.

For the next few seconds, the only sounds in the room are those of the kid slurping up the gooey stuff. She doesn't look away, as if my face is fascinating to her. Strangely, I can't drag my eyes away from her, either.

I scoop out the final mouthful from the jar and offer it to her, she bats it away. Some of the goop drips from the spoon and onto the floor.

"You're done, huh?" I place the spoon in the empty jar.

"Feeling better?" I glance at her.

She yawns.

"Are you sleepy?" I watch her features carefully. From somewhere in the hidden recesses of my mind, I recall that you're supposed to burp a baby after they've been fed. I scoop her up in my arms and rise to my feet.

I hold her against my shoulder with great care. Now what? Guess I should pat her back? I can feel her little heart racing against mine. She places her cheek against my shoulder. Then she burps and spits up over my shirt. *O-k-a-y?* So that's what happens when they burp? She snuggles against my chest, and that strange melting sensation against my rib cage intensifies.

She begins to get restless. Huh. I begin to pace. Then, copying what Priscilla did, I start to hum the first Green Day song that pops into my head. *That it's called Basket Case is probably my Freudian comment about myself.* Thankfully, it seems to work, for her cries lessen. The tension in her small body begins to ease.

I keep humming, slow and steady, rocking her gently against my chest. Her breathing evens out, soft and rhythmic, and when I glance down, her eyes are closed. Her cheeks are warm with color, a faint crease still etched between her brows. But she's resting now—finally, asleep.

That catch in my chest turns into a wave of something soft. There's a cracking sensation around my heart. That would be another of the barriers I built to protect myself, breaking down. Meeting Priscilla and this little one within the space of twenty-four hours has rocked the foundations of my world.

I head into the living room and place the baby in the portable carrier. Then carry it into the bedroom.

I place the carrier on the floor next to the bed and sink down onto the mattress, then reach for my phone and dial Connor.

"What?" He answers on the third ring.

When I stay silent, I sense him scowl. "Fine, if you don't want to speak—"

I sense him about to disconnect the call and burst out, "A baby."

There's silence, then he yawns loud enough for me to hear his jaw crack. "No idea what you're blathering on about, ol' chap, but it seems like you said—"

"A kid. An infant."

"You drunk ol' chap?" He chuckles. "Or high on something else?"

"If only." I bark out a laugh that is far from humorous. "I'm sitting here looking at a carrier holding a tiny tot. And she's fast asleep. In my bedroom." I rise to my feet and head into the living room, so as not to disturb her.

"You kidding?" His words tell me he's struggling to believe me. But the clarity in his tone indicates he's finally caught up with the program.

"Do I sound like I'm kidding?" I glance out the window. "Someone dropped her off with a note."

"And it says the child is yours?" he asks in a disbelieving tone.

"Exactly," I admit slowly.

He chortles.

"It's not funny," I growl at the phone.

It only makes him laugh louder. There's a sound of a woman's voice, which fades in the distance. I assume he's moving away from whomever he spent the night with. It strikes me, suddenly, that it's going to be a very long time before I'm going to do that. A child and a dating life don't go well together. I wouldn't dream of bringing a woman home, as long as this baby is in my home. The only woman I'd trust with her is… Gone. And I'll never reach out to her. Unless it turns out that the kid isn't mine. Which I'm going to have to put a rush job on to find out.

Connor continues to chuckle, and I wait until he seems to find some level of composure. "You made my day, arsewipe. Should have wrapped it up tight."

I squeeze the bridge of my nose, deciding not to defend myself. It's not like it's going to make a difference. So, I fume silently. A good move, as it turns out, for my lack of words seems to get through his thick skull.

"Damn, you weren't joking about the kid, were you?" he finally offers.

"Glad we're on the same page," I say dryly.

"What are you going to do now?"

"Get a private investigator to track down whoever might have left her, and order a DNA test — something I hope you'll help me with?"

I stalk back to the bedroom and peer in the direction of the infant, making sure she's still asleep.

"Me?" he asks cautiously.

"Yes, you. Is there anyone else on this line?"

"Hang onto your panties. I just want to make sure you know there's a hard limit to my involvement."

"A hard limit?" Not content with watching the child from a distance, I decide to head closer. *Only to make sure she's comfortable, and so I can see her face properly, to ensure she doesn't need anything.*

"Not going to babysit the kid. Don't have anything against them, but no way, am I going to take on the responsibility of someone else dependent on me so completely," Connor warns.

I sit down on the bed next to the carrier, taking in her relaxed features. Her forehead is smooth. She's sleeping deeply. Some of the tension slides off of my shoulders. I release the breath I wasn't aware I was holding. Who'd have thought getting a kid to fall asleep would be this stressful?

I rise to my feet and head into the living room again. "I'm going to have to hire a babysitter," I confess. *Just not yet.* The thought of having anyone else watch over her makes my stomach shrink. *Watching Priscilla with her made me realize how good she was with kids.* I push that thought away. I'm going to have to find someone who's half as good.

"Never thought I'd hear that word come out of your mouth," Connor marvels.

I rub at my temple. "You're giving me a headache with your constant prattling."

He scoffs. "Likely, it's the thought of dealing with the load of crap that got thrown your way that's causing it."

"Don't call the kid a load of crap." I scowl.

There's silence, then Connor murmurs, "I meant, the paperwork you'll have to deal with, no matter which way this goes."

"Right." I hunch my shoulders. It's not like me to jump to conclusions. I must be more stressed than I realize. "The entire situation sucks balls," I confess.

"It does," he agrees. "Any idea who'd do this to you?"

I roll my shoulders. "Don't have a clue. The kid's a year old. So, she would have been conceived twenty-one months, ago."

"Any flashes of memory? Any woman who stands out who you'd have been with then? Any encounters where you weren't sure about the condom?"

I squeeze the bridge of my nose. "I always carry my own. And I always, always wrapped it up."

"I'm not saying you didn't." Connor's voice softens.

I blow out a breath. My brother's only trying to help. "I wasn't discerning in who I decided to date or have a one-night stand with at that time, but I remember every woman I slept with. And I was always careful to carry my own condoms. I never had sex without protection.

"You were in your fuck 'em and leave 'em phase," he adds.

I open my mouth to argue, then shut it again. He's not wrong. I did go too far then. But it was the only way I knew how to survive — adrift between the structure of the Marines and the corporate strait-jacket of being CEO in the Davenport Group. I see it clearly now: I should've channeled all that restless energy into something else. Hitting the gym more often would've been better than what I chose.

"Is there any reason you'd be targeted this way, you think?" I hear Connor moving around. "Why would someone drop a child off on *your* doorstep specifically? Any demands from the mother?"

"None, just a note." I recite out the contents from memory, the words burned into my brain.

Connor whistles. "She seems to be confident it's yours."

"Yeah." I need something to drink. Hard liquor, preferably, so I can forget about this mess for a while. I head over to the wet bar.

Balancing the phone in the crook between my neck and shoulder, I reach over the bar counter for the bottle of whiskey, then pause. A baby. There's a baby in the house. A tiny life I'm responsible for. Guess I shouldn't be drinking. I set the bottle down.

"You sure you can't think of anyone who could possibly be behind this," he asks again.

"It's a little hard to narrow it down when I was sleeping with so many women around the time the kid would have been conceived."

He blows out a breath. "The perils of being a man-ho, huh?"

"Pot meet kettle," I snap.

"Big difference. I haven't been saddled with a fruit of my loins yet," he points out.

Suddenly, my shoulders feel heavy again. I rotate them to ease the load, not that it helps. "You going to spend all your time gloating, or are you going to help me out?"

"Let me think." I can hear the smirk in his voice. "I'll take the gloating, I believe."

"Connor," I warn.

He huffs out a laugh. "Where's your sense of humor? Or did becoming a guardian already rid you of that?"

"A guardian?" I eye the sleeping kid carefully. *A guardian?*

"Either the DNA test is positive and she's yours. Or she isn't. But considering she landed on your doorstep, and you're the kind of guy who takes responsibility seriously... You're going to want to play some kind of role in her life." He pauses. "Am I right?"

17

Priscilla

Doing nothing is self-care.
Especially when the 'nothing' is done
in a robe with snacks and zero guilt.
-Cilla's Post-it note

The buzzing of the phone reaches me. I don't pick it up. It buzzes again and again. Then stops. Then buzzes again.

With a sigh, I reach for my purse on the bed next to me, pull out my phone, and realize it's my alarm. I switch it off, and drop it on the pillow next to me. Then wish I could go back to sleep.

The headache knocking against the backs of my eyes tells me I should not have had another glass of wine last night. But I couldn't resist. Since leaving Tyler's penthouse, I've thrown myself into my job, and accepting invitations to go out from all of my friends.

And yes, I've also started using dating apps. Not that it's helped. Because every man I've met has spectacularly failed to live up to Tyler. Argh! He's spoiled me for everyone else. And I hate that I compare everyone I've been on a date with to him.

I've ended up cancelling on dates or running out, then coming back home and spending evenings with take-out and a bottle of wine, watching my favorite series on streaming platforms. All in a bid to not think of Tyler and Serene.

The worst times are when there's a baby on a show I'm watching, or a dad who reminds me of Tyler. Then, I find myself tearing up, before scolding myself for my weakness.

It's hard to believe it's already been three months since I walked out of his apartment.

Later in the day after I got home, the books Tyler had bought for me had arrived. It was proof that I hadn't dreamed up that encounter with him. Proof that I actually met the man of my dreams and lost him on the same day. It took me a week before I could unpack the books. Then I pushed them to the back of my bookshelf where they weren't in plain sight. I hoped it would stop me thinking of him.

I've tried to keep myself busy, in a bid to rid my mind of thoughts of him. Not that it's worked. Unfortunately, my dreams seem to feature him. And when I'm awake, despite my best efforts, everything seems to remind me of him. I've also managed not to peek at the selfie he took of himself on my phone... Okay, maybe I have peeked... Twice... Fine, a few times. But I'm not keeping count.

I also couldn't stop myself from looking up the socials of The Sp!cy Booktok. I checked out the picture of the two of us Giorgina had posted online. We looked so happy. We looked like we were a couple. *But we're not.* He'd made that clear.

Only good thing? I'm proud to say that I've stopped myself from reaching for my phone and calling him. If I did that, I'd never forgive myself. He has my number.

I hope he's doing okay with Serene. I'm sure he is. He's resourceful, after all. Of course, I wonder how he's coping with her. Taking care of a child is a big responsibility.

I've been through the denial phase. And the angry phase. Then the bargaining, and the sad phase. I think I'm easing into the acceptance phase now. At least, I hope I am.

Then again, the mere fact that I still find myself fantasizing about a life with him belies my hope that I'm ready to move on. They say the stages of grief are never sequential. But I don't want to spend any more time feeling upset about what happened.

Clearly, Tyler didn't want me in his life. He felt a connection to me; that much, I know. But Serene arriving when she did took up a lot of his emotional resilience. He wasn't able to think past the necessity of having to figure out what to do about her. He seemed convinced he wouldn't have time for a relationship while he had to sort out the situation with Serene.

A part of me doesn't blame him. That's one heck of an emotional sucker punch he was dealt. Of course, he could have shared some of his feelings with me. But... It's not like we were in a relationship. Not really.

Hell, we weren't even dating. In fact, it's not like we even had a one-night stand because we didn't sleep together. We...fooled around a little. No, it was more than that. We had an intense connection. And I loved talking to him. I loved spending time with him. He was gorgeous, stunning even, and he swept me off my feet. And if Serene hadn't come along—I shake my head. I won't think about that.

I gave myself a few days to nurse my broken heart—then tried my best to move forward. I told myself that if he wanted to call me, he would. If he *really* wanted to reach me, nothing was stopping him. But he hadn't. And I wasn't going to sit around waiting for him. I decided to focus on myself. My life. I'm going to look out for me from now on. I am not going to let a six-foot-four-inch, sex-on-a-stick man occupy my thoughts and overrun my life.

Today isn't just a fresh start. It's a full-blown rebrand.

Sure, it sounds like something you'd find on a mug at a wellness retreat, which it is, but today, I'm claiming it. Because the alternative? Curling up like a sad cliché in last night's mascara, watching my heartbreak on a loop is not acceptable.

Yes, I met someone who cracked me open. Yes, I lost him. And yes, I'm still standing.

I have my health. And clean hair—I sniff the strands and make a face—mostly. And the roof over my head—barely. That's practically enlightenment.

So no, I'm not falling apart.

Today, I'm the CEO of my own damn energy.

As for manifestation? *I'm making her my bitch.* So what, if I did attract the man of my dreams and lost him within twenty-four hours? I'll simply have to try harder next time.

And if I have been self-sedating with wine? Well, I owed it to myself. But I'm done with that now. I stumble into the bathroom, grab the aspirin, and swallow down two of them with tap water. Then I brush my teeth and head toward my tiny kitchenette to make myself a cup of coffee.

By the time I've downed it, I feel better. The intercom buzzes. I frown. Who could it be? I'm not expecting anyone. It can't be him, could he? *My heart somersaults into my throat.* Ugh, I hate that I'm so excited at the thought. It's definitely not *him. Calm Down.* I purposely slow my steps before I head over to answer it. "Hello?"

"It's Toren." My brother's voice comes over the receiver.

I slump, half in relief, half in disappointment. "Come on up." I buzz him in, then head into the bedroom to pull on a sweatshirt before returning to open the door.

I survey the tall, broad-shouldered man who brushes past me and into the apartment. He looks around, and when he turns to me, there's a look of distaste on his face. One I choose to ignore. Nothing but the best for Toren Whittington.

My little, one-bedroom apartment doesn't measure up to his standards, but it's more than enough for my needs.

"What are you doing here?" I frown.

My brother doesn't bother replying to my question. Typical Toren. He's the quintessential rich billionaire, who acts like a prick and is not even aware of it. He's always been so self-assured; he oozes confidence from his pores.

He looks at me closely, and his brows draw down. "You look terrible," he drawls.

"Gee, thanks?" I toss my head, then grab my now cold cup of coffee, walk over to the kitchen sink, and dump it in. "Want some coffee?"

Without waiting for his answer, I top up the cafetière fresh coffee grounds and switch on the kettle.

"You've lost weight since I last saw you." I can hear the accusing tone in his voice and resist the urge to roll my eyes.

Given the fifteen-year age difference between us, Tor's often felt more like a father than a sibling. To his credit, he also supported me when I wanted to leave home at eighteen and fend for myself. My father was upset, but my brother stood up for me.

He hasn't interfered in my life or offered to bail me out the many times I came close to losing the roof over my head, which only made me respect him more. Which is why, seeing him today is a surprise. We've kept in touch on the phone and the Christmas dinners I've gone home for. He checks in on me by text message and insists on taking me out to dinner every month. But this is the first time Tor has come to visit me.

I pour the now, almost-boiled water into the cafetière, stir it, then slide the plunger down without depressing it fully, and turn to him. "What brings you here?"

"You missed our dinner last night."

"Huh?" I'm normally good at keeping track of my appointments, both work and social.

I walk into my bedroom and pick up my phone from the nightstand. I check my calendar and, sure enough, dinner with Tor shows up as an entry under yesterday's date.

"Sorry, I'm not sure why that happened." I turn to find him leaning a shoulder against the doorway. "Guess I was—uh—preoccupied."

"Hmm." He slides a hand into his pocket.

"What's the hmm for?"

"I know we had this dinner planned for a while. But you've never agreed to meet and not shown up."

"So, you felt you had to check on me?" I turn back to the cafetière, pour out a cup of coffee for him, and refill my own, then walk over and hand him his cup. "I'm a big girl. I can take care of myself."

His expression gentles. "You're a strong, independent woman who I'm very proud of, you know that."

My anger fades. "Thanks, big brother." I take a sip of my coffee. "I'm sorry I missed our dinner. Time just got away from me, that's all… I promise, I'll make the next one."

"Hmm." He studies me again, eyes sharp with something unspoken.

"There's that hmm again. I'm getting the feeling this visit isn't just about checking in on me." I walk over to the tiny breakfast nook and slide onto a stool. "Want to tell me what's really going on?"

He walks over to place his coffee on the counter opposite me. "You mean, I can't drop in on my sister and say hi?"

I roll my eyes. "You're the hotshot CEO of the Whittington Group of companies. Your time is money."

"And I was worried about you." His tone is serious. His expression is grave.

Warmth coils in my chest. I can't help but feel moved that he's here and concerned about me.

Only, I'm not five. And he's not the twenty-year-old who came to my aid when bullies teased me on the playground. Tor would show up in his black suit like an avenging angel and glare down at the boys who made fun of my wiry hair and my being overweight. It took one glower for him to send them scrambling. They left me alone. And my brother became my hero.

He'd already started working at our father's company by then, so he wasn't around as much as my middle brothers. But he was the one we all went to for help, especially since my father was too busy running an empire.

When I told my father I wanted to leave home and strike out on my own, he threatened to disown me. I left anyway. My father carried out his threat. Tor tried to dissuade him, but to no avail.

Since then, my brother has made sure to continuously check in on me. He knows I won't accept money from him, so he's settled on ensuring that I'm doing fine.

My mother passed when I was five. I don't need a shrink to tell me it's one reason I turned out to be such a rebel. Then at nineteen my father passed away, which made Tor more protective about us. My brothers and I are adults, but Tor took it upon himself to become our de facto parent. He makes sure to support us emotionally while expanding the company our father built.

"I really am sorry I missed our dinner." I rub at my forehead, wishing my headache would lessen. "It won't happen again, okay?"

My brother gives me another grim look, then spins around and begins to open and close my cabinet doors.

"What are you doing?" I ask, bemused.

In reply, he opens a couple of the drawers, then holds up a bottle of Advil. He shakes one out, fills a glass with water, and places them in front of me.

"Thank you." I swallow the pill with some of the water and shoot him a small smile. "You haven't said why you came here."

"I told you; I was worried about you."

"You could have called." I arch one brow. "What's the real reason?"

He gives me another of his looks, then props a foot on the footrail of the stool opposite me. "I have...a proposition for you."

I level a quizzical expression in his direction. "A proposition?"

He slides a hand into the pocket of his slacks. "It's something to consider. And I'll never push you to do it."

I tilt my head. "Sounds ominous."

"It's not. It's straightforward." My brother hesitates, which is unusual for him A prickle of unease runs up my spine. The fine hair on my forearms stands on end. I push aside the foreboding that crowds in on my senses.

"It doesn't seem straightforward, considering you're trying to figure out the best way to spring it on me." I nod in his direction.

He raises the cup of coffee to his mouth, takes a sip, then makes a face.

"Sorry, it's not the expensive-as-gold coffee, made from beans that nocturnal mammals shit out, that you've grown accustomed to," I drawl.

"If you're talking about Kopi luwak that are made from partially digested coffee cherries that have been eaten and defecated by the Asian palm civets, then I'm not apologizing. I like my creature comforts. I've earned them," he says with a straight face, though his eyes gleam.

"Creature comforts?" I chortle. That was an intended pun. My brother has a dry sense of humor.

He glances around, voice suddenly serious. "You, too, could live in style and not in this—" He looks back at me.

I pop my shoulder. "I like my hovel. I earned it on my own merit, too."

The skin around his eyes softens. "And I'm proud of you, Pri. I knew it would do you good to earn your living and be away from the family money. But there comes a time when one must also deliver on one's responsibilities to the family."

"You mean, like you are?" I tip up my chin. "Besides, our father disowned me, remember?"

"But I haven't." He tilts his head. "And neither have your other brothers."

In addition to Tor, I have four other older brothers. All of whom are protective. My mother was the only other feminine presence in the house. And when she died, it felt like I'd lost someone who'd have been my greatest ally in that male dominated household. Perhaps, that's why I felt compelled to go out into the world to find my place?

Not that I've succeeded, yet. Is that why I empathized so much with Serene? At least, I knew my mother didn't have a choice in leaving me. For Serene—she'll have to grow up with the knowledge that her mother gave her up. Poor mite.

"I took over the family business so I could take care of all of you. It certainly wasn't out of love for our sperm donor." His eyes grow hard, his lips firm.

Nope, there was certainly no love lost between him and our

father. He expected a lot from his sons. Enough for him to be at loggerheads with my brothers.

"I assume business is going well?"

Tor's features turn into granite. "Getting the board to embrace new technology has been challenging. Left to them, they'd run the company into the ground."

"But that's where you come in, right?"

"And you," he points out.

My brother is ruthless, highly successful and used to getting his way. Another reason I'm intrigued by the fact he's not simply commanding me to do whatever it is he came here to ask of me.

"You're deflecting." I take a sip of my coffee.

He seems taken aback, then nods. "I am." He squares his shoulders. "I want you to consider an arranged marriage."

Surprise twists my guts. Arranged marriages aren't unusual in wealthy families like mine—but I never thought my brother would suggest one.

He must see how taken aback I am, for he raises his hand. "I know. You didn't expect me to say that, and I'd never coax you into it. It's only a possibility I want to raise with you."

I blink, trying to get my head around what he's suggesting.

"I'll be honest. You marrying this person will help me expand the Whittington Group's market share. And again, I want to stress—" He raises his hand. "You're under no compulsion to accept it."

I shake my head. "Why suggest it to me then?"

"Because—" He shifts his weight from foot to foot. "Because I'm not one to pry in your personal life, as you know, but as your brother, I'm concerned that you are, uh—suffering from affairs of the heart and, perhaps, this might be one way for you to move on?"

I search his features, looking for any clue that he knows what's occurred in my life over the last few months, but Tor being Tor, he gives nothing away. "Is this you making an educated guess, or—"

"It's my summation, since you haven't answered my calls, and you missed our dinner. And now that I've seen you in person, given how bedraggled you look—" He raises his hands in a gesture that's meant to convey that he was right.

"Thanks, big brother; you always were good for my ego." I begin to pace. This out-of-the-blue suggestion from Tor has taken me totally by surprise. I don't know what to make of it. On the other hand, it's the first time in months I haven't thought of Tyler, so there's that. I blow out a breath. But an arranged marriage? Nah, that's so not me. The thought is ridiculous. Then, just for shits and giggles, and because I'm just a little curious, I turn to my brother and ask, "Who's the lucky guy?"

Tor seems to have been expecting the question because without preamble he says, "It's one of the Davenport brothers."

18

Tyler

"Come on, honey, just one more mouthful." I offer the spoon with the boiled vegetables and the half cube of cheese to Serene.

She raises her hand and knocks my hand aside. The vegetables bounce off my shirt. The half cube of cheese joins its twin on the floor. I wince. Did I really think I could get her to eat her lunch and tuck her in for a nap while I jumped on my conference call? When am I going to realize I'm now on someone else's time schedule?

"I'm not a quitter; you know that, right? My boys in the Marines called me Major Rock, not because I had a hard head, though that, too. But I'm one hell of an obstinate mofo—" I wince. "Sorry, ignore the swearing."

She blinks. "No."

Yep, that's the first word she learned. Right after Papa. It was like, one day she woke up and decided to start speaking.

"I'll take that as a yes." I scoop up more of the food and offer it to her.

Serene firms her lips, shakes her head, and stares at me with her melting brown eyes. Her chestnut curls form a halo around her angelic face. There's an adamant look in her eyes which I'm coming to recognize. Yeah, she's a chip off the ol' block, all right. She's as headstrong as me.

It's been six months since she came to me, and my life has changed beyond belief. Now, it revolves, not around me, but around the whims and fancies of another person. A tiny little child who has a mind of her own. First lesson of taking care of a kid? Don't expect them to follow the routine you want to set for them. Second lesson? Forget that you ever had a life. Because now, they rule yours. And the third? Well, there's no third because, by the time you learn the first two, you're so starved for sleep, you can barely keep your eyes open during the day. I open my mouth and yawn widely.

My jaw cracks. My eyes water. Man, what I wouldn't do for just an hour of uninterrupted sleep. Then I blink, for the little rascal in front of me opens her mouth. Wide. For a second, I don't compute; then I realize, she's imitating my yawn. Whatever works.

Before she can lock her lips together again, I spoon the food inside. She wipes the spoon clean, then holds the food in her mouth. I blow out a breath. "You're supposed to chew it, sweetheart."

She merely watches me with that unblinking gaze. The one I'm still not used to. The one which so often reminds me of Priscilla. I shake my head. I must be more sleep-deprived than I realized. Thoughts of her have been lurking at the back of my mind far too often, and for far too long. It's an effort to keep them at bay. But truth be told, taking care of Serene while trying to maintain my role as CEO has been the most difficult thing I've ever done. More challenging than any mission. While not being life and death, it feels like I still live life on tenterhooks. Wondering what surprise Serene is going to spring next on me. Life with a child...is definitely not boring, I'll give you that.

"Chew, Poppet." I mime the action, moving my jaws. But there's no reaction from her. She's clever, this one. She knows when I'm trying to get her to do something against her will.

"You're done, huh?"

She chews. Once. I count that as a victory.

"Okay, then." I eat the lone piece of cucumber clinging to the spoon. My stomach grumbles, reminding me I haven't eaten lunch or breakfast. Missed meals are a part of my new reality. Most meals consist of eating whatever Serene refuses. I've learned it's best to eat when I get a chance. So, I scoop up the rest of the cheese from the plate and shove it into my mouth, then the vegetables. And the shredded chicken. She's eaten some of each. That's going to have to be enough for now. I place the spoon down and wipe her face with the wet wipe.

Then I scoop her up from the highchair. My phone buzzes, and I shift the munchkin to one arm to answer it. "Hello."

"You sound breathless, Bro. Serene been giving you a hard time again?" Connor's cheerful visage fills the screen.

"No need to sound so pleased... *Bro*," I say through gritted teeth.

"Just calling it as I see it, and I'm entitled to make fun of your plight. Remember all the times you kicked my arse when we got into fights as boys? This is my revenge."

"I could still kick your arse," I promise him.

"Sounds to me like it's my niece who's kicking *your* arse — Hey Serene, how are you doing?" He flashes her a big grin.

And my daughter smiles a big toothy grin at him. "Conn-o-r. Uncle Connnnooor," she warbles.

"Hi honey. Hope you're not behaving, and giving your ol' man a lot of trouble."

She giggles and nods.

Would you look at that? In front of Connor, she's so well-behaved. All the tantrums and non-cooperative antics are, apparently, saved for me.

"That's my girl," Connor croons.

"Thanks for nothing," I mutter, half amused, half pissed off. Children know how to present a different front to different people, huh?

"I've got to put her down for a nap before I jump on my conference call."

"Yeah, I know, the busy life of a single dad. Also"—he pauses halfway through his sentence and looks at me closely—"you have something on your"—he gestures to his forehead.

I touch the place on my forehead, bring my fingers down, and stare at the brownish smudge. Then I smell my fingers—"Crap"—and rub it off on a wet wipe.

"Don't swear in front of the little ears," he admonishes me.

"No, I mean that was shit. From Serene's nappy. I changed her earlier, and—"

"Argh. Enough already. TMI." He screws up his face like he's the one who caught a whiff of the bad smell.

"Yeah, this is what is in store for you, too, Bro." I chuckle. "Wait until your spawn comes along."

"Not a chance," he says with confidence.

That's what I thought, too. I was so sure that life would continue as it had been, with me at the center. Then, a curvy woman swept in, this little sprite on her heels, and suddenly, I went from wondering which woman I was going to take to a hotel that weekend to wondering if I could get through the rest of the day. My brother has a rude awakening coming. I want to tell him all that, but I stay quiet. Of course, there's a chance he'll never settle down—but given Arthur's machinations, I sincerely doubt that.

I wasn't sure how my grandfather would react to Serene, but the old coot welcomed her with open arms. Apparently, confirmation that she shared my genes, *and his*, was enough.

Gramps was over the moon to welcome Serene into the family as his great-granddaughter. Every time he sees her, there's a new gift, whether it be a toy or a new dress. It's so out of character for him, I suspect he's allowing Imelda, his Harley-riding, shit-kickers-wearing girlfriend to make these purchases on his behalf. On the other hand, maybe he's just thrilled to have a girl in the family. He even set aside a bedroom just for her—which is really more of a playroom—filled with everything a little girl could want.

Bonus: I suddenly went up in his esteem for having fathered a child. An archaic attitude, for sure, but one I didn't question.

I'm glad the family has accepted her. Becoming a father made me feel vulnerable. I'm conscious of all the ways my daughter could come to harm. The world is suddenly a place filled with people who could hurt her. I've vowed to keep her safe, no matter what. Which, in turn, made me all too conscious of my own mortality. Nothing like having a child to make you conscious of your age and everything you've lived through.

And just watching her grow and blossom in the last few months has made me realize, I, too, am growing older. I worried that, one day in the future, I might not be around. *Then, what would happen to my child?* It made me appreciate the old man and my family, knowing they'd step in if anything happened to me. I've never valued the presence of my brothers or my friends. I took them for granted. But now, I'm cognizant of the fact that my brothers will watch out for my daughter. It makes me feel more secure.

"I called to make sure you're coming to the family lunch at Arthur's." Connor says.

I'm about to make an excuse and refuse, then remember: *Family's important.* I owe the old man that much. And yes, I'm being more amenable to him because he accepted Serene so whole-heartedly. I nod. "I'll be there. So will you, I assume. Or are you off on one of your trips again?"

Connor has his own biotech firm and is often away on research trips. "I would be, but the old man insisted I attend. He's got his panties in a twist about something, I tell you."

Serene wriggles around, then tugs on my shirt. "Papa, play. Now."

"The princess has spoken." Connor flashes her another big smile. "You have your Dad wrapped around your little finger, don't you?"

He has no idea.

Serene grabs hold of another handful of my shirt and pulls.

"I really do have to go."

"Bye, Poppet" Connor blows her a kiss.

"Bah. Bye." Serene blows him back a kiss.

I disconnect the call, place the phone on the table, then I place her against my chest and begin to pace. "You gotta sleep, baby."

"Play. Sheep. Dog. Play." She means her toys. My heart sinks. I really do need to get on that conference call. I'm a dad, and she comes first. But I also want to ensure I don't neglect my company. I'm going to pull my weight as the CEO. I can do this.

"Plaaaay, Papa," she screeches.

I can do this. I can do this. On my own. *No, you can't. You need childcare help.* Though the experience I've had with hiring nannies has put me off them. The first one claimed a family emergency and quit in two days. The next one kept coming onto me, and that was very uncomfortable. So, I had to let her go. The third and fourth, Serene hated on sight and refused to let them near her.

The last nanny I hired, Serene seemed to tolerate, but she spent too much time on her phone instead of paying attention to my kid. I came home from a meeting one day to find Serene bawling her head off with a dirty nappy. I fired her right then.

I can do this. I have to do this. I'm a good father. I am.

I walk Serene to her room. I moved to this townhouse in Primrose, not far from my brothers and my friends. Serene now has an entire back garden with her own swing set and sandbox. I also have more space in the house, so I can work from home. I walk into her room and place her on the bed.

She sits up at once. "Papa, no. Play now."

"Honey, you need to nap. Otherwise, you'll be tired and cranky, *Serene*—"

She slides down from the bed and crawls toward her toy bin. She picks up her stuffed dog in one hand, her toy sheep in the other. Then proceeds to bang them together, head-to-head.

"Way to go kid." I sink back, defeated, then yawn again. I check my watch. Perhaps, *I* could take a little nap? But no, I can't. I need to keep an eye on her. I yawn again. Then freeze as Serene pushes up to standing. On her own. Without any support.

She turns and beams at me. I watch, open-mouthed, as my daughter takes her first step toward me. Then another. My heart blooms in my chest. I have a big-ass grin on my face. And not lying, there might be a tear rolling down my cheek, too. Nothing like having a kid to put you in touch with your emotions.

I go down on my haunches and hold out my arms. She stumbles forward, then throws herself at me.

19

Tyler

"Serene's walking," I announce.

Brody nods and smiles. I have a sneaking suspicion he's humoring me, but I push it aside. "In fact, she's running. Won't be long before she's playing football."

"That's awesome. Have you signed her up for football lessons already?" Connor's voice rings with enthusiasm.

"Not yet, but I will. Also cricket. Don't forget ballet. Really, whatever she wants to learn." I know, I'm beaming like crazy and all puffed up. But hey, I'm allowed, right?

"Where is she today?" Connor looks around. "Can't see her."

"Dropped her off with Victoria." She's my friend Saint's wife, and one of the few people I trust to take good care of my kid.

I pull out my phone, swipe the screen, and show Connor. "Look at her. She's so cute, all dressed up." Yes, I'm now one of those parents who can't stop pulling out pictures of their kid and shoving it under the noses of unsuspecting fools, but whatever.

To Connor's credit, he seems genuinely interested in seeing pictures of his niece. Both of my brothers flip the screen, seeing the pictures I've taken of Serene.

"She's growing like a weed." Connor hands me back my phone.

I pocket it and try to wipe the proud smile off my face. *Focus. Focus. You don't want to keep talking about your daughter's accomplishments and bore everyone to tears.* Then, and only because I want this lunch over with, so I can collect my daughter and spend the evening with her, I nod in the direction of Arthur's house. "Anyone know what Gramps is up to?"

We're in the backyard of our grandfather's townhouse in Primrose Hill, for the weekly family meal. According to Arthur, the family that lunches together stays together. Given each of my brothers has a strong personality, these family meals make for lively discussions.

Tiny, Arthur's Great Dane, ambles into the backyard, making a beeline for the long table packed with foodstuffs. He surveys it, and his ears droop. The mutt looks crestfallen, then walks back to Arthur.

Guess he's unhappy he didn't find any champagne. The dog has a weakness for the bubbly drink. But since Arthur's diagnosis, Imelda has banned Arthur from drinking alcohol, and there's no smoking of cigars at the house. To my surprise, the old man didn't protest. *Is it true love?* Probably.

You wouldn't have caught Arthur listening to anyone else before Imelda came into his life. Now, he seems less hard on himself. When Arthur walks out to take his seat, it's a signal for the rest of us to take our places.

A petite blonde woman whom I identify as Knox's assistant turns to leave, but Knox indicates she should take the chair on his right. She hesitates, then complies. The chair to his left stays vacant. The rest of us take our seats. There's a general buzz around the table. Otis, Arthur's butler, tops up our wineglasses with a non-alcoholic beverage then stands to the side. Knox is the only one guzzling liquid of the alcoholic variety like it's going out of style. He must've brought his own. He seems on edge. *Huh.*

Arthur clinks his knife against his glass, and the chatter dies down.

"No doubt, you're all curious about why you've been summoned."

"Why should we be? We only had to drop what we were doing and turn up here," Brody growls under his breath.

"Something you want to share with the table?" Arthur arches an eyebrow in his grandson's direction.

"It's Sunday, but it's still a working day for some of us." Brody points out.

"And I am the patriarch of this family... Still. So, you boys will come when I call." Arthur looks around the table, his expression leaving no room for argument.

Brody groans. Connor—who's returned from another research trip to a far-off corner of the world—chugs down water from a bottle like it's going out of style.

And Knox? His gaze is focused on the house. I frown. *What is he waiting for?*

"Felix"—Arthur nods in the direction of my young cousin—"you have something to tell us?"

"I'm joining the Marines." Felix clears his throat. "I hope to be half as good at it as my father was." Felix meets his father's gaze.

Quentin's throat moves as he swallows. He's visibly moved by his son's words. Then he raises his glass. "To Felix."

"To Felix." The rest of us toast him.

Then, Knox places his glass on the table and rises to his feet. He heads toward the house, where a woman steps out onto the porch. She's tall, willowy, and wearing a green dress that reaches below her knees. It's sleeveless, baring her gorgeous shoulders. Her auburn hair is a waterfall of health that flows down her back. Her eyes are almond shaped, her skin creamy, and so pale the sun seems to be reflecting off of it to bathe her in an ethereal light.

My heart slams into my chest with such force, I'm sure I've broken a few ribs. *What. The. Fuck?* What is Priscilla doing here? And why is Knox leading her over to the table?

He seats her on his left.

I drink in her features, unable to believe it's her.

That creamy expanse of her neckline, those pink rosebud lips, the pert upturned nose, the thick auburn hair which is longer than it was when I last saw her—I can't take my gaze off her. It feels like I've been rewarded with a ray of sunlight after scrambling in the dark for six months.

Taking care of a child subsumes your own life, as I've discovered. So, it was easy enough to tell myself that I didn't miss Cilla. That I was too busy with my new reality. That she was better off without me. But seeing her now, in all her glory, is a gut punch. One that turns my heart into a live volcano and my blood to molten lava. I draw in a breath, and the oxygen seems to inflame my desire, my need, my yearning for her. I've missed her. Missed her smile, her spirit, her curves. I've missed having her in my life.

In a matter of hours, she wormed her way into my heart, dissolved into my soul, her scent embedded in my skin in a way that I haven't been able to shake off. And the time and distance bring home just how much I've wanted to see her.

I will her to look at me, but she avoids my gaze.

Her eyelids are lowered, and she folds her hands in her lap, her expression almost serene. It's only the pulse beating at the base of her neck which gives her away. She's nervous. And the way she holds herself stiffly, with her spine erect and shoulders squared, I have an inkling that she knew she'd see me here today. And she's prepared to ignore me. Not that I blame her. Not after how I told her to get out of my life.

"Can I do the honors?" Arthur glances around the table.

Knox shrugs. "By all means."

"This is Priscilla Whittington, Toren Whittington's sister." Arthur nods in her direction. "Toren and I agree that the best way to resolve our family feud and join our collective fortunes is through an arranged marriage."

An arranged marriage? My heart drops into my stomach. My guts heave. No fucking way. Does he mean her and Knox? My dream woman and my brother? *No!* This can't be happening. My throat closes. I squeeze my fingers around the wineglass holding the spritzer.

"Of course, you did." Brody snorts.

Arthur ignores him. "Tor couldn't be here, but he was happy for us to go ahead with announcing—"

"To cut a long story short, Priscilla has agreed to be my wife," Knox cuts in with a bored eye roll.

There's the sound of a glass breaking. I glance down to find the water glass I was holding has shattered. Water drips down the side of the wooden table. Blood drips from my palm. I can't feel the pain. I push back from the table. Instinct draws my attention back to Priscilla. She watches me with a stricken look. Her brown eyes are filled with pain and regret. I glance from her to Knox's considering look. He tilts his head, looks from me to Priscilla, and a look of understanding comes into his eyes.

I rise to my feet and stalk off.

I take a sip from my tumbler of whiskey and stare out from the window of my living room. It's dark outside. The lights of the city twinkle in the distance.

Serene is asleep. It took hours for her to drop off. Likely, she picked up on my disquiet. I've learned how sensitive she can be to how I feel. And likewise, I'm tuned into her enough to know when she's hungry or wet or wants attention. It helps that she's already able to communicate her basic needs. But even before that, I became an expert in picking up on her unspoken cues. It's strange how quickly we bonded... Or maybe not. She's an adorable child. And I found myself falling for her very quickly.

After I walked out of the lunch at Arthur's place, I went to Saint's home to pick her up.

His wife, Victoria, and Sinclair's wife, Summer, are the only two people Serene is happy to be with. They've helped to babysit when needed, advised me on everything from feeding to changing nappies to potty training—a phenomenon I never thought I'd spend so much time obsessing about.

When I told them about my experience with the last nanny and why I had to fire her, they insisted on drawing up a shortlist of nannies for me to contact. They advised me that it was a matter of continuing to search until I found the right one.

How I wish I had someone in my life with whom I could talk these things over. Someone with whom I could share the delight in Serene's growing and crossing important developmental goals, like walking. Or when she said her first word. I miss having a confidante, someone living life with me who will understand my concerns and offer alternative viewpoints. *Someone like Cilla.* Clearly, she's on my mind because I saw her earlier. Nothing prepared me for that.

I asked her to get out of my life—and today, she showed me just how much she took that to heart by appearing in my life as my brother's fiancée-to-be. That's a curveball I had not anticipated. Damn. I feel the need to toss back the whiskey I'm holding, but with a child in the other room, I'm limiting myself to one drink. I need to savor this one.

Patience... That's what this entire gig as a parent has taught me. Perseverance. Persistence. The three Ps in my life. *And what about Priscilla?*

I shove the thought away. Since Serene came into my life, everything has become more complicated. If Priscilla were here, she'd have been dragged into the chaos too. No — asking her to leave was the right choice.

I couldn't, in good conscience, ask her to treat my problems as her own. I would never have been able to give her the kind of attention she deserved; not when I've spent almost every waking minute learning how to be a dad. But to have Priscilla turn up six months later and engaged to my brother? Fuck. That's some crazy shit.

I take another sip of my whiskey. She must have known Knox is my brother. So, why would she agree to this marriage? I'm not going to presume that it's so she could be close to me. Perhaps, she was inspired by revenge. Maybe she's trying to get back at me for asking her to leave that day—but no. My instinct tells me she wouldn't do that. Even if, after the way I asked her to leave, she probably hates me.

And I haven't contacted her since. I've been too caught up in the changes Serene has brought about in my life.

I pull out my phone and navigate to the picture of the two of us I saved from the social media feed of The Sp!cy Booktok. I did it in a moment of weakness. When thoughts of her crowded my mind and I wondered if I'd imagined it all.

Seeing us together in the picture reassures me. She may not be with me, but she's out there somewhere. That's enough. It *has* to be enough. For now. But it makes me miss her even more. *You could call her. You could explain to her...* What? What am I going to tell her?

What could make up for the fact that I asked her to leave hours after I all but hinted to her that I saw her in my life on a more permanent basis? That I was deeply attracted to her. That I felt connected to her. That... I still want her. I could explain that I haven't called her because I haven't felt ready. I was still adjusting to Serene's presence and how it changed me and my life.

I could tell her I needed time to figure things out and sort through my feelings about her. That I was still trying to work things out in my head.

I could ask her why she's engaged to Knox. I don't, for a second, believe the two of them have any feelings for each other. I saw how Knox looked at his assistant, even if he thought he was hiding it. And Arthur made it clear, it's an arranged marriage, and surely, she deserves better than that?

She deserves a man who loves her, adores her, and who'll take care of her. A man like... Me? Fuck. This is screwed up.

I take in our smiles in the photo.

How excited Priscilla seemed. I recall how thrilled she was that I'd brought her to the bookstore. How her breathing hitched when I put my arm around her and pulled her close for the picture. How her scent drove me crazy. I close my eyes and recall how she felt in my arms. All feminine curves and softness. How I had such a raging boner, I prayed it wouldn't show up in the picture.

And thinking of how much I wanted her, how hot it was when I made her come, my cock extends in my pants. It's a relief to know that, while I'm a father, I can still feel desire. My longing for her hasn't abated. And perhaps, seeing her with my brother has served as a wake-up call. The fact is, I never forgot about her. I download the photo and save it to my phone.

I might still be learning to be a good father, but maybe, that's something I'll spend a lifetime learning. I might still be trying to navigate my way through the emotions Priscilla evokes in me. But now that I've seen her again, I realize how much I miss her. How much I want her. How much I need her. Question is, what am I going to do about it?

20

Priscilla

I am the hero of my story.
-Cilla's Post-it note

"Are you okay?" Zoey looks at me over her cup of brew. "You don't look okay."

"I'm okay." I dip my head to avoid my friend's scrutiny and take a sip of the chai I ordered. We're at the Fearless Kitten, our favorite coffee shop in Primrose Hill, run by Zoey's friend Skylar, where we agreed to meet.

I'm partial to coffee, but she ordered this particular concoction for me. I took a sip and the flavors bounced off my tongue.

English breakfast tea, star anise, cinnamon, nutmeg, topped off with frothed milk, and then, something bitter, which elevates the taste to being electric. "Whoa, what is this?" I glance down into the frothy concoction like I can discern the contents. "What did you order me?"

"A dirty chai tea latte," she says in a sly voice.

"A *dirty* chai tea latte?" I take another sip. Yep, it definitely has a sting at the end. A bite which lifts my entire mouth. "How is that different from a normal chai tea?"

"It's got a dash of espresso," she says in a conspiratory tone.

I shoot her a surprised look. "A dash of espresso? In my chai tea?"

"Nice, huh?"

"That's the one new thing I learned today." I manage a small smile.

She chuckles. "I remember, you did that in university, too."

"Some habits—" I shrug.

"And you still have Post-it notes with inspirational quotes stuck all over your room?"

I shake my head. "I've restricted it to the surface of my refrigerator."

She laughs.

"I'm still the queen of self-help books, while my life is barely held together by dry shampoo and good intentions. Only, I'm in my twenties instead of my late teens."

"Oh man, I know the feeling. Sometimes, I feel like I'm making the same mistakes over and over again, instead of learning from them." She toasts me with her cup of chai, then takes another sip. "My way of dealing with it is to have lots of friends."

"I was...*am* still amazed at how many people you manage to keep in touch with. As for me? I'm better at having a few friends with whom I have deeper relationships. Not that you don't," I hasten to add.

She laughs. "I need to meet people. I thrive on the interaction."

"It's what makes you a good editor."

"Maybe." She tilts her head. "It's easier to find perspective on other people's lives than my own." She stares at me meaningfully. "This is my way of asking if you want to talk about it. I'm a good listener, as you know."

"You mean, the part where the daycare I've worked at for over two years is about to shut down—and I might lose my job?" I hunch my shoulders, a knot tightening in my chest. "And that I've had to report not one, but two child safeguarding cases, where the kids were taken from their families? *That was brutal.* I know I did the right thing, but it doesn't make it any easier. Their lives were changed in the most traumatic way imaginable." I shake my head, voice low. "God, listen to me. I'm complaining. The one thing I swore I'd never do."

"You're allowed. Working with children is not something I could do for a living. I'd be too emotionally involved with them to take care of them properly. All credit to you for doing it." She purses her lips. "Also, it's your prerogative what you decide is right for you, and whether you want to talk about it or not."

I know what she's alluding to. And *I do* want to talk about it. "You mean, why did I agree to this so-called 'arranged marriage' with Knox, only to not go through with it?"

She waves her hand in the air. "I've seen shorter engagements. Yours lasted almost a month, so there's that."

"I'll take that as a compliment." I snort.

She sets her cup on the table, then reaches over and places her hand over mine. "I'm sure you have your reasons for doing this."

I give her a grateful smile. My friends are always in my corner. Lord knows what I'd have done without them. "You're sweet and thank you for that. But I'm aware of how it looks from the outside."

"It doesn't matter how it looks to the world. You're the one going through it. As long as it makes sense to you —"

"It was Tor who suggested it."

"Toren? Your brother?" She frowns.

They've never met, because I've been on my own since I met Zoey. She and the girls have become my quasi family, in that sense.

"He's on an ambitious growth path for the Whittington Group of companies. He and Arthur Davenport, the patriarch of the Davenport Group got together and decided they wanted to bury past differences by having a Whittington and a Davenport marry. In return, the Davenports would use their business influence to support the Whittingtons, et cetera, et cetera. Get my drift?"

Her forehead scrunches up. "An arranged marriage seems to be all the fad with these moneyed families." Then she pauses. "Present company excluded, of course."

"Of course." I toss my head. "You don't have to restrain yourself on my behalf. I might still have Whittington on my passport, but I left my family and all the riches they stand for to pursue my own life when I turned eighteen, as you're aware."

Her scowl deepens. "That doesn't make sense."

"What do you mean?"

"If you don't particularly care for the Whittington name, why did you agree to this arranged marriage?"

"W-e-l-l." I squirm around in my seat, then take another sip of the fortifying chai tea. "When Tor suggested that I marry a Davenport, of course, I thought he meant Tyler."

"Tyler Davenport?"

I nod, then proceed to tell her about my almost one-night stand with him, and Serene's arrival that night, and how he then asked me to leave.

"Shut up." She stares at me with a *what-the-fuck*, expression.

I resist the urge to giggle, because unfortunately, this is my life we're talking about. I've lived it, and it wasn't fun at all. "Told ya, it's complicated. Especially since I didn't really sleep with him."

"What do you mean?" she nearly shrieks.

"I mean, I did everything but sleep with him, actually."

"Bish, he must be very talented, especially since you're still thinking of him." She leans back in her seat. "It's been, what? Six months since you met Tyler?"

"Almost seven."

She raises her hands in a I-rest-my-case gesture. "He must have made a hell of an impression on you."

"Yeah." I uncross my legs then cross them again. "I'm sorry I didn't tell you about what happened with him earlier."

"Ya think?" she drawls.

"In my defense, I couldn't even think about it without crying, never mind talking about it. It was a lot packed into one night. I'm still unpacking it, to be honest. I know it was even more stressful for

Tyler. A part of me understands why he didn't want me in his life right then. And I did want to get over him. Truly."

"Then your brother comes along and suggests you marry a Davenport, and you get excited because you think he means Tyler. But he means Knox, so you turn him down, but then you change your mind?"

I blush a little. "I know, it sounds crazy when you put it like that."

"Not crazy, just"—she hunts around for the right word—"intense."

"Thanks." I half-smile. "I figured it would be a good way to put myself in front of Tyler and provoke a reaction, discovering, once and for all, if he had any feelings for me."

"And did it? Force a reaction?"

"Oh, it was... Interesting." I chuckle.

"What's that supposed to mean?"

"Well, first, Knox's assistant, now wife, made it clear this was unexpected, and she was *not* happy about it. Meanwhile, I know Tyler was upset about seeing me with Knox. First, he crushed his water goblet in his hand, which did not go by unnoticed, then he marched out of the lunch where our engagement had been announced. After that, I kept expecting him to track me down and demand I break off the engagement, but—"

"He didn't?"

I shake my head, anger and confusion squeezing my chest. "I could have sworn he seemed like he was on the verge of marching up to Knox and punching him, but he simply left. That was a month ago."

"And you haven't heard from him since?"

I shake my head in frustration. "Nope. Nothing. Not a phone call. Or even a text message in the month since."

"That cad," she says with feeling.

I shoot her a grateful look. "Of course, I'm not about to approach him and tell him I'm tired of waiting."

"And are you? Tired of waiting?" She looks at me closely.

"Yes! Of course I am. And I want to say to hell with Tyler Davenport and move on with my life. But"—I look away, then back at her — "I keep thinking of him and Serene and wondering how they're coping. I shouldn't care. Not after how much of an asshole he's been. But something inside of me feels like there's something unfinished here. I mean, for a few hours, I thought I'd met 'the one'..." I trail off.

She nods but doesn't say anything, for which I'm grateful. I'm not expecting her to have any answers, but speaking my mind aloud helps clarify things in my head.

"So, with no reaction forthcoming from Tyler, you broke off the engagement?"

I nod. "No way was I going to follow that charade with Knox to its logical conclusion. Especially not when Knox was, clearly, in love with his assistant."

"June."

I nod. Knox's assistant is also known to Zoey, so I'm not surprised she has an inkling of what's happening. It's another reason I didn't want to share all of the gory details. I didn't want to put Zoey in the position of deciding which friend she wanted to support. But given Knox and June are getting their HEA, and I'm interested in another brother, there's no conflict of interest in sharing now.

"So, Knox and I decided this engagement wasn't working out for either of us. We agreed to break it off."

"You did the right thing. You shouldn't marry someone you don't love."

"Agreed. Which is why I'm confused that Tyler didn't react the way I thought he would. The man's possessive. I know that from the time I spent with him. But maybe I misjudged him. Maybe the emotions are one-sided."

Zoey opens her mouth, then hesitates.

"What?"

"Look, I'm not defending the guy. I think he's acted badly with you. The least he could have done was explain his actions fully, which, from what you've said, he didn't. But—" She seems to choose her words carefully. "But, and this is not an excuse, by all accounts, he's now a single dad, and a really good one. Perhaps he's struggling with doing his best by the little girl. Perhaps he's unsure what it means to bring a woman into the mix? Perhaps he does have feelings for you, but he's not sure now is the time to act on it?"

I tap my fingers on the table. "My sense is, you're right. There is a bit of his new status as a parent that's probably stopping him. And believe me, I work with kids. I understand they come first, but —"

"But you also want him to not shut down the possibility of you being in his life?"

"And of his being in mine... I'm a nanny; I can deal with having a kid in his life. She must be nearly nineteen months now." I feel myself soften thinking of Serene. "There's this pull toward her which I can't explain." I rub at my forehead. "It's another reason I can't simply just let things go."

She gives me a small smile. "Maybe he felt it wasn't fair to expect you to take on both of them in the relationship?"

To be fair, I considered and discarded that option. "That would be very noble of him, don't you think?"

She taps her fingers on the table. "I mean, all of this is supposition. Unless you meet him and talk to him, you won't understand what happened."

"Only, my attempt at getting his attention didn't pay off. In retrospect, getting engaged to Knox was a stupid thing to do. Except for the fact it helped him realize he was in love with someone else, after all. So perhaps something good came of it." I shrug.

Understanding filters into her eyes. Once again, she doesn't interrupt my train of thought, for which I'm grateful.

"So, what are you going to do now?"

I glance down at the dessert she ordered and which I've ignored so far. It looks enticing. I take a bite of the cake. "Mmm, this is heavenly. What does Skylar call it?"

"C!itasaurus, complete with the exclamation point, instead of an 'l,' so people can take a photo and tag the shop without begin dinged."

I chuckle. "It's genius to have a coffee shop inspired by Booktok. I saw the notice for the book club meetings held here. You go to them, don't you?"

"I do. And don't change the topic, Bish." She waves a finger under my nose. "You're not over this guy. Hell, you're not even one-fourth of the way to forgetting him."

"Tell me about it." I discard my fork and pick up the delectable dessert with my fingers, then take a huge mouthful. "Oh, my God," I moan as the juicy, moist morsel melts on my tongue. I chew, swallow, and all but stop my eyes from rolling back. "You've got to tell Skylar that her desserts are delish."

When she doesn't answer, I look up to find she's staring past me with a funny look on her face.

"What?" The hair on the back of my neck rises. I'm not surprised when she says, "Don't look now, but Tyler Davenport just walked in."

I begin to turn, but she shakes her head. "No, don't do that."

I slowly lower the half-eaten slab of cake to its plate, then wipe my fingers on a tissue. "What's he doing now?"

"He's heading for the counter. He's ordering something. Now, he's joking and laughing with the woman behind the counter."

Some emotion I'm not going to name squeezes my chest. What do I care if he's laughing with some woman?

"Is he flirting with her?" As soon as the words are out, I regret them. "No, don't answer that. I don't care if he is."

"Actually, it's her who's flirting with him. Not the other way around."

"What a bish." I toss my head. "Anyway, I don't care."

"Guess he hasn't seen you yet." She uses her spoon to scoop up some of the cake and eats it. Her gesture is casual. Meanwhile, she keeps a running commentary. "He's looking at his phone. Now his watch. Now he's got his coffee to go. Now he's turning— Oh no."

"What?" I ask, panicked. "What's happening?" A shiver grips me.

It's with a dawning sense of the inevitable I hear her say, "He saw you." Her gaze widens. "He went all still. And he's staring at the back of your head." She nods. "He seems to be coming to a decision."

"Don't tell me he's coming this way." I curl my fingers into fists.

"He's coming this way," she confirms.

"Oh, no. No. No." I look around wildly. "I think I'm going to leave." I begin to rise.

"Thought you wanted to talk to him and ask him why he asked you to leave abruptly."

"I did." I sink down. Not a coward. I'm not a coward. "It just seems better as a concept than when I've really been given an opportunity to do so," I confess.

Chin up. Man up. Or woman up. You can do this. What are the chances he ends up at the same coffee shop as me, huh? But he's here. So am I. Guess this is my chance to find out how it feels to talk to him face-to-face.

I'm expecting him, but it's still a physical shock to my system when he steps up to stand at our table. "Priscilla, what a surprise."

21

Tyler

She looks incredible. When I saw her, I couldn't believe my eyes. But there was no doubt, it was her. The sunlight slanting through the windows of the coffee shop lit up her auburn hair, throwing a glow around her. I recognized the slope of her shoulders, saw her face in profile, felt that familiar pull, and knew, without a doubt, I had to go over and speak with her.

"Tyler." Her voice is calm, steady. "Fancy seeing you here."

"Ah... I live close by."

She blinks. "You moved?"

"Wanted to be close to my brothers and friends who already lived in Primrose Hill. And this way, Serene has more space both in and out of the house."

A soft expression crosses her face. "How is Serene? You didn't have her at the lunch, either." She firms her lips.

That lunch. That bloody lunch which is seared into my brain, when I found out she was getting engaged to my brother. I swallow down the questions I have around *that* fiasco.

The old Tyler, the one I was before Serene came into my life, would have confronted Priscilla, demanding to know why she'd gone through that charade with Knox. But the new me, the one who's a father, the one who's more measured in his decision-making, disciplines his reaction. "She's with Summer."

"Summer?" A flicker of something crosses her eyes.

"My friend, Sinclair's wife? They have a son, Matty, who Serene has taken to. I often drop Serene with them when I have to head out for a meeting."

"A meeting?" She looks me up and down. "You mean, a date?"

Zoey—who I recognize as Skylar's friend—clears her throat. "Uh, I guess I should be leaving."

"Zoey. I'm sorry, that was impolite of me. Lovely to see you here. Hope you're well."

Zoey rises to her feet and pats my arm. "I'm good. Lovely to see you, too. But I need to be on my way. I'm…late for a meeting with one of my authors." She smiles at both of us, then indicates to Priscilla that she should call her. "Bye, Cilla. Bye, Tyler." She grabs her bag and leaves.

For a few seconds, I stay standing, while Priscilla stares down at the half-eaten cake in front of her.

"The pastries here are good," I venture, then curse myself. *That the best you can come up with, asshole?*

She stays quiet.

"Innovative names, too. Though I don't understand half of them." I nod my head like a fucking twerp. Jesus, why am I so nervous? *Because you like this woman. And you told her to leave, like a coward, without explaining yourself completely. And you haven't called her since to tell her you were thinking of her. You're a dumbass!*

"If you don't understand the names, how do you know they're innovative?" she asks in a wooden voice.

At least she's speaking to me. That's a start. "They're not names I've seen before. And the shop seems to be doing well, so—"

"Booktok." She finally raises those gorgeous brown eyes to mine. "The names of the desserts are inspired by spicy books."

"Spicy books?"

"Romance novels. With steamy scenes." She blows out a breath. "What do you want, Tyler?"

"To talk."

"You didn't do much talking at your penthouse that day." She lifts her chin in a dignified sneer. "In fact, if I remember correctly, you asked me to leave and haven't contacted me since."

I nod slowly. "May I have a seat?"

She looks like she's about to say no, then waves a hand in the air, "Suit yourself."

Well, I deserve that. I deserve everything she throws my way. But I can take it. By some quirk of fate, I'm here with her, and I'm going to make the most of this occasion.

I slide into the seat opposite her, moving the plates and cups on the table in front of me aside, so the space between us is not cluttered.

"I'm sorry."

"Huh?" she blinks. "What did you say?"

"I'm sorry. I was an arse for asking you to leave my place the way I did that day. I'm a twat for not coming out and sharing what was on my mind. I'm an ignominious wanker for not telling you what I was feeling. Truth is, I was thrown by what happened. First you, then Serene, entering my life in less than twenty-four hours. It was like an emotional dynamite exploded my life. And I'm still picking up the pieces."

She stares, not speaking. Simply stares, like she can't believe her ears, or that I'm sitting here apologizing to her.

"Priscilla," I murmur her name. I relish the sensation of forming her name on my lips. It feels like forever since I spoke her name aloud. "Cilla?" I coax her. "Say something."

She firms her lips. "You saw me with Knox, but you didn't say anything. You turned and left."

I lean back in the seat, then cross my arms over my chest. Yes, I'm feeling defensive. Yes, I'm showing it with my actions. But one thing I've learned in the past few months of being a dad? Life is an emotional minefield. And you can't keep everything locked inside. Indeed, it's okay to sometimes to share your vulnerabilities. And I'll admit, I'm hoping that by doing so, I'll get through to her, so I jerk my chin. "I did. I didn't want to do something that could come back to haunt my daughter. I didn't want my actions to make her be ashamed of me."

"Oh." She swallows. Some of the fight seems to go out of her. "You're right, of course." She looks away and swallows again. "I'm being selfish, aren't I? Thinking only of myself and my feelings, and how much you hurt me. And of course, all this time, you've been coping with being a father. You have Serene to think of now."

"Cilla…" I lean forward. "Please don't beat yourself up. It's me who's at fault. I was cruel, telling you to leave, and then cutting you out of my life like that, when you and I had a connection. I knew you were moved by seeing Serene on my doorstep that day. If you hadn't been there to help me through those first few hours with her, I wouldn't have been able to cope."

"You're stretching the truth. I didn't do anything." She tosses her head.

"You showed me how to change a nappy. Believe me, that was valuable."

She looks at me closely, then shakes her head. "I can't believe you're here. And that you live near The Fearless Kitten. When did you move?"

"About a month ago. I needed help with Serene. And when my friends' wives offered to help with babysitting, I knew it made sense to move here. Besides, it's not like I'd trust just anyone with Serene. Especially not after the experiences I've had with nannies." I wince. "Sorry, didn't mean it that way."

She half-smiles. "You're good. I know how difficult it is to find good childcare. I also know, I'm good at what I do. Although, considering the funding problems the daycare I work at is having, you wouldn't know it." She pops a shoulder. "But enough about me. How are you and Serene doing?"

She pastes on a smile on her face.

Which doesn't fool me at all. There's worry lurking in her eyes, which makes my chest tight. I scan her beautiful features, take in the shadows under her eyes. At the lunch, I was too overcome with emotion to notice, but I can see she looks tired. And she seems to have lost weight, too. Concern stabs at my chest.

"We're doing okay. As well as a single dad who holds down a full-time job and tries to take care of his kid can do." I chuckle. "Which is to say, I barely manage. My respect for single moms is sky high. Their jobs are far more difficult than being the CEO of a company. I should know; I am one, after all."

Her gaze gentles. "I'm sure you'll figure it out. Everyone does. Eventually." There's a quiet confidence in her voice.

I lean in as close as I dare, given the table between us, and without it looking too creepy, so I can draw in the subtle scent of her. I managed to sniff her when I passed her earlier, and it was enough to make my heart sigh in relief and drain the blood to my groin. That attraction between us has only intensified over the past few months. And the fact that I almost lost her to Knox? Damn, it was a wake-up call which gave me many sleepless nights.

"I'm sorry I didn't call you or make an attempt to reach out to you after that lunch."

She stiffens. The thaw I sensed in her demeanor vanishes and is replaced by a flash of anger. I almost regret broaching the issue, but I have to. I need to clear the air, to the best of my ability. I need to figure out a solution to bring her back into my life. Because I need her. I miss her. More than I can admit, even to myself.

"Seeing you with Knox and realizing I might lose you for good was my worst nightmare come true."

She frowns but doesn't comment.

"You had your reasons for agreeing to go through with that potential arrangement. And that's your prerogative. You had every reason to move on after I asked you to leave that day. I left it open. It's not like I made you any promises, either, I'm aware. But... You have to know, that connection we had when we met was... *Is* real. I still feel it, Cilla."

She folds her hands in her lap, her expression both confused and tormented. "It's true, we had a connection. But after all these months... After your silence—" She shakes her head. "I've had to try a lot of things to move on, Tyler. It wasn't easy, but I have tried."

"Did you succeed?"

She looks torn, then looks down and slowly shakes her head—it's barely perceptible—but not before I catch a glimpse of her watery eyes.

And I hate myself for it, but at the same time, a load rolls off my shoulders. I draw in a breath and my lungs burn. I feel so relieved, my head spins. That's when I know, I need to find a way to keep this woman in my life. I have to. I can't lose her again. I was a dickhead to let her go. Then... Not reaching out to her? Sure, my life has been taken over by Serene and coming to grips with being a new father, but that doesn't excuse the fact that I didn't bother reaching out to Cilla, when I *knew* she felt the same connection that I did.

Maybe a part of me assumed she'd wait for me. That when the time was right, I'd reach out to her and apologize, and everything would be fine. But seeing her almost marry someone else was a shock, a warning that I could lose her at any moment.

I still didn't reach out to her after because—I wasn't sure what to say to her. I've been putting off making the call. But here she is. I ran into her and I'm going to use this opportunity to bring her back into my life. But how?

"Your daycare is in financial trouble, you said?" I ask slowly.

"Yeah. The funding from the local council got cut off. And the donors we had are not sure if they'll renew their grants. It happens. I'm sure they'll figure something out." She doesn't look that hopeful, though.

And given the cost-of-living crisis, my sense is, it would take a miracle for any kind of funding to be renewed.

"I might be able to help you," I say slowly.

She tilts her head. "What do you mean?"

"You're likely going to be out of a job. And I... I need a nanny."

She blinks slowly.

"And you've already met Serene. I've seen you with her. You're good with her. Hell, after seeing the nannies I engaged and how much they were lacking in their childcare experience, you'd be a godsend."

"I'm not sure I follow…"

I hold her gaze, school my expression into one of earnestness. "Would you consider becoming Serene's nanny?"

Her jaw drops. "You want me to take the position of Serene's nanny?"

I nod. "I can no longer trust a stranger to look after her, regardless of their references. And I can't keep using up the goodwill of my friends' wives. But I'd trust you with her. I can't think of anyone else who'd be a better nanny for my daughter." I try to rein my excitement in. *Easy does it. Don't scare her off.* "That is, if you'd consider it?"

A flurry of emotions flashes across her face—first elation, then amazement. It shifts to confusion, and finally, sharpens into anger.

"You know what, Tyler? I can't make up my mind if you're being serious. No, I *know* you're being serious. I'm sure you think you're doing me a favor by offering me a job because you think I need it—conveniently for you. And you don't even realize how insulting it is for me that you offered me this role."

"Insulting?" I frown. "How can you say that? We can help each other this way, can't we?"

She throws up her hands. "I thought you weren't the asshole billionaire that most men in your position are. But honestly, if the fact that you told me fuck off—"

"I didn't tell you to fuck off," I protest.

"It was certainly implied." She lowers her hands to her sides. "You asked me to leave because your *tiny* brain couldn't cope with all the emotional upheaval you'd gone through."

"You're right." I take in the flush rising in her cheeks, half entranced, half falling all over again for this woman. I'm reminded why I was drawn to her in the first place. Her spirit is a siren call I never stood a chance against. And now… I know I can't let her slip out of my life.

"You'll accept the role of Serene's nanny?" I ask carefully, almost holding my breath.

She leans forward, closing the distance between us so I can make out the individual eyelashes that line her eyes.

Then she tips up her chin. "Absolutely not."

22

Priscilla

You are the author of your own reinvention.
-Cilla's Post-it note

It's been three months since I threw his offer in his face and walked out. The nerve. Sure, he apologized for not being open with me about why he'd asked me to leave his penthouse the day Serene arrived. But he didn't offer any further explanation. Damn him. What I want is for him to tell me the real reason he asked me to leave that day. My guess is, events overtook him, and he couldn't fathom making time for a relationship when he'd just found out he was a father, but I want to hear it from him. I want him to tell me how much he missed me. I want him to say he's ready for a relationship with me.

He claimed to feel the connection between us. But then, he

seemed to translate that into playing the knight in shining armor and offering me a job as Serene's nanny because I was on the verge of losing mine.

Of course, I'd love to be around Serene, but I want to be in his life as more than a caregiver to his daughter. That jerkface missed that completely.

Only, his offering me a job turned out to be prophetic because, since that run-in with Tyler, I *have* lost mine.

I found another, but the mother of the child turned out to be a helicopter parent, which drove me crazy. Nothing I did was right, according to her, so I had to quit that one. The next one, which, to be fair, I found right away, ended with the father of the child grabbing my arse. When I complained to the mother, she fired me. Refused to give me a good reference. Luckily, I had enough references to find a third position.

Only this time, it was with a single mom who got laid off within a week of my starting with her as her son's nanny. She came home, burst into tears, and I had to calm her down. She barely managed to pull herself together, and I spent the evening playing nursemaid to her, as well as taking care of her kid. After which, she told me she wouldn't be able to continue paying me. I was gutted. And frankly, the enthusiasm to find another daycare position, or one as a nanny, is waning.

I pull out my phone and stare at the screen as I have done so many times since. *You could call Tyler and tell him you'll accept the position as Serene's nanny...*

No. Absolutely not. I turned him down—and it felt good to do so. I was *right* to do so. He took me for granted. Again. And I'm not going to swallow my pride and call him. Nope.

I jump up and begin to pace the floor of my living room. I've paid the rent for the week. I have two more days to go. There isn't enough money to cover the rent for the next one. I've been living off my savings, but I haven't compromised on my lifestyle, such as it is. I was confident I'd find another role. But, in this economy, even parents are feeling the pinch, so there aren't as many childcare jobs out there—and even if there were, who's to say the parents wouldn't turn out to be creeps?

Tyler said he wouldn't trust Serene with a stranger. And I'm finding I don't want to work for a stranger, either. I squeeze the bridge of my nose. *So, call him and accept the job.*

Aargh, I really don't want to do that. Of course, I could call Tor and ask him for a loan. And my brother would give it to me. He was so understanding when I broke off my so-called engagement with Knox. Then, he told me he was taken aback—grateful but taken aback—when I considered it, in the first place. He could have told me so earlier and saved me the ignominy of that charade. But then again, I went into it with my eyes wide open.

And if I hadn't, Tyler might not have been so open when we met. Again though, it would've been nice if he'd sought me out earlier. To think the meeting at The Fearless Kitten was a coincidence. Just like how we met on the tube. Is our relationship destined to be a series of chance encounters?

I blow out a breath. I'm feeling a little dizzy with all these thoughts racing through my head. I walk into the kitchen and put on the kettle. Maybe a cup of herbal tea will help? I pull open the cabinet door and realize I'm out of tea bags. And I'd have to buy more using my credit card, which I've begun to max out over the last week. Ugh. I rub at my temple. It's crunch time, all right. I need to make a decision.

My phone pings. I look at the message and smile. It's from Aura. Or rather, Princess Aurelia Verenza. We went to the same school. The kind that rich kids go to. I was one of them at the time, after all. She got in touch to let me know she was marrying Ryot Davenport, Tyler's older brother. She'd heard through the grapevine about my short-lived engagement to Knox and decided to reconnect with me. We've kept in touch since.

It should be weird that Tyler and I have so many people in common. But considering our families move in the same circles in London, maybe not. I may have tried to leave my roots behind, but I'm beginning to realize the futility of it. One can never outrun one's past completely, I suppose. And m-a-y-b-e, one has to embrace it to move forward?

Aura: Hey you, how are you doing?

Me: All good. 😊

Aura: Don't mind my asking this, but I wondered if you're still looking for a job.

I perk up. I met Aura, along with Zoey and some other friends, a few weeks ago. I remember getting a little tipsy on white wine and regaling them with my string of recent bad luck when it came to finding nannying roles. I don't remember the details, but whatever I said must have been hilarious; we laughed all evening. It certainly lightened my mood. Except for the hangover and the looming deadline of finding a job the next day.

Me: I am, actually. Why? Do you have a lead? 😊

Aura: Feel free to ignore this, but I heard Tyler's still looking for a nanny. The man's at his wit's end. And of course, I thought of you.

Huh?

I lean against the counter and stare at the message. What are the odds, eh? Like I said, these bloody coincidences with Tyler and me are uncanny.

Aura: I'm aware there's some history between the two of you (the Davenports' family grapevine can be quite full on) so I don't want to put you in an uncomfortable position or anything. Feel free to turn it down. But it came up in conversation with Tyler today, so I thought you should know.

I read and re-read the message. Whoa. Tyler still hasn't found a nanny? He looked like he was drowning under the weight of parenthood when I ran into him at The Fearless Kitten.

He needs childcare help, like yesterday. And I need a new position. Like *stat*. It's *only* a job. I don't have to marry the guy. Ha! As if I wouldn't love that. And I can keep it professional. I mean, I can certainly try. But this is a sign, isn't it? Aura messaging me like this, out of the blue? And I'm sure I can charge a lot. The man can afford it. And I can be back on my feet in no time.

I only have to work for him temporarily. A month or two, to tide me over, and then I can leave. I wouldn't be a professional if I didn't consider all of my options, right?

Me: Thanks Aura. I think this would be interesting to consider.

Aura: Oh good. I'll send you his address and let him know to expect you. What time works for you?

Me: How about 5 p.m.? And thanks for this Aura!

She sends through the address in the next message. It's an address in Primrose Hill. That'll be his townhouse.

I set down the phone and begin to pace. I'm doing the right thing, aren't I? It's not like I have any other options. I need this job. But if he says or does something to piss me off, I'll be out of there, even if it means I end up on the streets.

23

Tyler

"Not Peppa Pig, honey. Anything else but that, please?" If I have to listen to this episode one more time, I might scream. I swear, I know all the words by heart. That's how many times I've seen it with Serene.

It's late afternoon, I'm running on fumes. I've managed to juggle two conference calls in between applauding Serene for telling me when she wants to use the bathroom to poo.

Yep, not even two and she's almost potty-trained. A miracle. I know. But Serene's ahead of the curve in a lot of her developmental goals. It's the only thing reassuring me I'm not a complete failure as a dad.

I hold up the TV remote in one hand, my phone in the other, scanning my gaze over the list of emails that never seem to abate. Goddamn. I'm clearly behind on my work again. And it feels wrong that I'm checking my emails when I'm with Serene, but given I work out of the house full time now, and I still don't have a nanny, this is the only way I can manage to do both.

"Papa. Peppa Pig. Please. Papa. Peppa Pig. Please," Serene chants and bounces on the couch.

I've propped her up with cushions on either side to make sure she doesn't slide off. Which she has in the past, and it's been completely fine, because the kid's steady on her feet and runs everywhere around the house. And she's tall for her age, so she's able to slip off the sofa or the chair and always land on her feet. But still. Best not to take chances, right?

"How about something else?" I flip to another program. "This one?"

"No." She shakes her head.

Oh yeah, we're still in the 'no' stage. That hasn't abated, either.

I flip the screen to a third program.

"Nope. Papa. Not this." She scowls. Yeah, her expressions are alarmingly grown-up. She can hold entire conversations with me and is so aware, it's almost like talking to a grown-up. A little grown-up. Mostly. Except when it comes to mealtimes, and bath times, and bedtimes, that is. As long as I'm treating little Miss Serene like a proper grown-up, she's totally fine.

I push my luck, try a fourth program. She screws up her face in what I know is a prelude to a crying jag. Shit. I give up, flipping the screen to Peppa Pig. Instantly, her face lights up. "Thank you, Papa," she says sweetly.

My heart melts. This little girl can manipulate me in a heartbeat, and honestly, I don't mind. It's probably not good that I let her get her way with me so often. But I'm only human. And my daughter means the world to me. It's difficult for me to deny her. Doesn't mean I'm going to give her everything she wants. I'm not going to risk spoiling her. But allowing her to see a kid's program so I can answer my emails is all right. I think?

I place the remote down, and she leans around me to watch the show. Yep. Dad's forgotten. I'll take that as my exit... For now. I move to the armchair not far from her and settle down to answer my emails.

The security app on my phone dings. I pull it up and find a familiar face at my door. I stiffen. *Cilla?* What's she doing here? My heart pounds in my rib cage. Is she here because she misses me? Because she wants to be with me?

She seems to be staring at the door with a half stubborn, half dreading-this look on her face. She turns to leave, walking down the steps from the front door. Then changes her mind and walks up to stand in front of the door again. She probably doesn't realize I have a motion sensor which triggers my security app.

She looks nervous, anxious, like she'd rather be anywhere else but here. My heartbeat slows. Common sense prevails. After how she turned me down that day at the coffee shop, it's not likely she's here to pick up where we left off. Not when she was so pissed off that I asked her to be my nanny... I stiffen.

Hope is a tenuous green shoot that breaks through a crack in the parched ground of my heart. *Is she here to accept my offer of being Serene's nanny?* Not Cilla; I need to call her Priscilla. After how pissed off she was the last time, I don't think she'd appreciate it if I used that nickname. In fact, she seemed to make it clear that I should keep my distance from her.

I use the opportunity to watch her, unobserved. Her thick, auburn hair is lit up from behind by the setting sun. Maybe a coincidence, but like the last time I saw her at the coffee shop, she seems to have a halo about her. Yeah, she's my angel, all right. One I seem to have a knack for pissing off. Believe me, I racked my brain for days on end, trying to figure out what I'd done wrong when I asked her to be Serene's caregiver. She threw it in my face and stormed out of there as if I'd insulted her, leaving me stupefied.

I mulled over it, ending up none the wiser. Clearly, I was missing something. I wanted to check in with my brothers on it. But most of my brothers are married and busy with their own lives. As for Connor and Brody? Given their bachelor status, I'm not sure they're the people I want to take advice from.

Instead, I settled for realizing I'd done something wrong, but I didn't have a clue what it was. I didn't try to contact Priscilla, either...not wanting to make things worse between us. And then, I spent the last month travelling and helping Ryot and Aura with security arrangements.

It meant calling on my background as a Royal Marine, and I enjoyed the groundwork. Since returning, I've thrown myself into caring for Serene and trying to function as CEO—*trying* being the operative word. I'm drowning. I need help with childcare. Desperately. But after picturing Priscilla in that role, it felt wrong to even *think* of someone else taking her place in Serene's life.

So here I am, living life an hour at a time, still trying to make sense of what I did. And now she's here. Standing at my door. Like a goddamn dream. Like the sky cracking open after weeks of rain. Like that first hit of air when you've been underwater too long.

Has she forgiven me—for forcing her out of my penthouse that day, thinking I was doing the right thing? Is she here because she feels it too—the way I've missed her, every damn day since?

My chest tightens. My pulse kicks. I swallow hard.

Is she here because she still wants this—wants *me*?

I watch her on the security feed. She shifts from foot to foot. Blows out a breath. Tilts her face to the sky.

Come on. Ring the doorbell. Please.

She glances over her shoulder. Sighs again. Then lifts her chin.

And finally, the doorbell rings.

24

Priscilla

"What are you doing here?" The impact of those mismatched eyes feels like I've slammed headfirst into an immovable object. One, glacial blue, resembles an icicle which could lance through my chest and draw blood. The other, an untamed golden-green, brims with feral energy. Taken together, they're a fierce contradiction, a clash of elements, untamed and unrelenting; a warning as much as they are a lure.

I drink in his patrician nose, the high, diamond-hard cheekbones, the angles of his jaw, the cords of his throat standing out against his skin. When he folds his arms across his chest, the biceps strain the button-down he's wearing... All of it hints at tightly leashed power.

I forgot how much of a full body impact meeting Tyler is. I clutch the straps of my handbag—the same one he rescued from being crushed by the doors of the train—for support. Then tilt my head back, and further back, so I can meet his gaze. Not that I forgot his height. Or the breadth of his shoulders that fill the doorway to his house.

Clearly, absence makes the heart grow fonder. Every part of

him seems harder and more unforgiving than when I last saw him. He's all angles and harsh edges. But something beneath those edges calls to me, deeper than it should. Except for the shadows under his eyes, and the hollows under his cheekbones. Together with his rumpled hair and the loosened tie, as well as the rolled-up sleeves of his shirts, it only adds to his sexiness. Goddamn. Tyler in his single dad era is going to be my downfall. I've never been attracted to the fathers of the children I took care of before this.

But this guy! In the year since I first met him, his appeal has skyrocketed. He was—and still is—that billionaire alphahole who has a confident, I-own-the-earth air about him. But it's tempered with something else in his eyes. Something that makes him more humane, more approachable. Something that makes me ache. A shiver squeezes my belly. My pussy clenches.

One look at him, and I want to climb him like a tree and lick him all over. *Ugh. This is bad. You should go. Pivot and walk out of here. You must be out of your mind to think about coming here for the job.*

His eyebrows knit over his nose. There's a question in his eyes, but his expression is not unkind. Far from that. He takes me in from head to toe, and back to my face, like he can't believe I'm here. Is that my imagination or... Is he happy to see me? And I don't mean in that way. Though I would be thrilled if he were happy to see me in that way too. He's looking at me like I'm something he thought he'd lost.

He's looking at me with desperation. With relief. With something very close to signaling that he missed me.

He clears his throat. "Priscilla—"

It's like someone took a pin to the bubble of hope building in my chest. He called me Priscilla. Not Cilla. The shift lands like a slap. His tone is formal. Distant. I was mistaken in what I saw in his eyes. Maybe, he stopped seeing me as the woman he once brought home? The one he said he saw a future with? Maybe, everything between us has changed since I last saw him?

My mind spins, questions crashing into each other—but even through the ache, I can't stop drinking him in. Like I always do.

He's so big, and the heat from his body is so intense, it feels like I'm standing in front of a furnace. Or the gates of heaven?

Nope, not going there. Not when I'm here to do a job as a professional.

"Can I come in?"

I'm sure he won't refuse. Still, I'm relieved when he steps aside. I walk past him, the heat of his body wrapping around mine like memory, trying hard not to breathe in deeply of that very masculine, musky scent of his as I do.

I survey the hallway, which has a table on which are keys, spare change, a soft toy. The table is high enough that it's out of reach of an almost two-year-old. The soft toy is familiar. It relaxes me further. I take in the hooks on the wall.

From one hangs a man's coat, XXL-size. Clearly, his. On the others are a couple of smaller coats. One pink. One purple with unicorn motifs. From the living room, the sound of a children's program reaches me. Peppa Pig, if I'm not mistaken.

The remaining tension drains from my body.

"I'm here for the nanny position," I declare.

Silence greets me. I turn to find him staring at me. Those heterochromatic eyes of his grow wide. His thick eyebrows draw down. That beautiful face, which has haunted my dreams for the last year, takes on an expression of hurt. One which confuses me.

It's as if he expected me to say I'm here to be your girlfriend, but I said something else entirely. His chest rises and falls. Then he shakes his head and seems to compose himself. "You're here for the nanny position?"

"I heard you're still looking?"

The groove between his eyebrows deepens. "How did you find out?" His forehead clears. "Wait. You're the person Aura referred for the childcare position?"

I nod. "You are still looking to fill the position, aren't you?"

A light seems to come on in his eyes. Bit by bit, his shoulders unclench. Huh. Apparently, he was taken aback to see me and wasn't sure why I was here.

"I know, I turned it down then, but —"

He raises his hand. "Say no more. You're here; that's what matters."

"Oh." I swallow; my throat tight. He's not making me feel more uncomfortable than I already do. There's no cold distance, no wounded pride, no trace of anger from the last time I turned down his job offer. And he's not gloating, not throwing it in my face that I've changed my mind. Instead, he's making it feel like I'm doing him a favor by asking for the role.

"You're making this awfully easy." I'm unable to keep the suspicion out of my voice.

He must catch it, for his lips quirk. "No games. I promise." He holds up his hands. "It's not an exaggeration to say that I've been drowning, trying to take care of Serene while also doing my job, and—"

"Papa." A small child toddles over to us, her little legs unsteady but determined.

His whole presence shifts—suddenly alert, protective. And then... Oh, my God. Something washes over him—love, raw and tender—and it changes everything about the way he holds himself. It steals the breath from my lungs and sends my heart stumbling in my chest.

This...this is the man I thought I knew—who I *did* know—briefly. This is the man who captivated me. This is the man I glimpsed under the harsh, unforgiving, demeanor when I first met him.

He turns and, bending down, hoists the little girl up in his arms. The sight of that little poppet in those massive arms, nestled against his massive chest, turns my insides to mush and sends my ovaries into hyperdrive. *Sweet Mother of Divine Timing.* Now I know, I really did make a mistake coming here. Seeing him hold that little child fills my insides with all kinds of weird longing.

I take in the tiny tot with the cloud of chestnut curls surrounding her cherubic face. I can spot the traces of the infant whose nappy I changed that day.

Serene looks at me with her big brown eyes which seem to have turned more golden since I last saw them. You can see through to her soul. Innocent. Nothing to hide.

Unlike his heterochromatic gaze which hints at secrets—layers upon layers. You know, there's a heart somewhere inside...but you need to chip away to get to it.

The memories of that day at his penthouse would catch me unaware, in my weakest moments; when I wondered how they were. How he'd coped. If he'd found the mother of the child. If he was together with the mother—which I learned at the lunch, he was not. If the child was definitely his? *And now, I know.*

The shape of her eyes is even more similar to his. That's what I thought the first time I saw the little girl, and the resemblance is even stronger now. Now that she's older, she reminds me of him even more. The angle of her stubborn jaw and the tiny nose... All of that is a lot like his.

She may be the cutest child I've ever seen. I can't tell you how many times I've heard parents say that about their own child, and I always resist rolling my eyes. Every parent thinks their child is the cutest one ever. But in this case, without the blinders that parents wear, I can objectively say, she's absolutely adorable.

Of course, seeing Tyler in the flesh is nothing compared to the images of him I've carried in my mind. He's bigger, brawnier, larger-than-life, than I remember. And the chemistry between us... It affects me in a way that turns my memories into pale imitations of this inferno that thrums between us.

Taking in the protective way in which he holds the child, it's clear, he loves her.

Steeling myself against Tyler's appeal was bad enough. Add Serene to the mix, and I know, I won't escape unscathed. I'll lose my heart to both of them, and I can't afford that. Not when he only sees me as a nanny. Not when I want more from him. I thought I'd be able to protect myself against his appeal but seeing him—seeing both of them together—tells me I don't stand a chance. If I have an iota of self-preservation left, I'm going to get out of here.

"Umm... *Maybe* this wasn't a good idea." I am about to step back when the munchkin lurches from his arms toward me.

25

Tyler

"Mama!" Serene dives toward Priscilla, and my heart jumps into my throat.

"No, Serene—" I cry out, but she's made up her mind.

To her credit, Priscilla opens her arms and catches Serene. She wraps her arms about the little girl and brings her close. The two look at each other—Serene with her little chin tipped up and her lips slightly parted, and Priscilla with a slightly shocked look in her warm brown eyes.

Her eyes... How they've haunted me. How they made an impact on me when I first met her.

How she instinctively trusted me, and not only because I'd rescued her purse when it'd gotten caught between the doors of the train on the tube. It was how she looked at me with openness.

How she smiled when I took her to that hidden bookshop, and she fawned over her favorite romance novels. How she came home with me. How taken I was with her that I wanted her in my house, under my roof, and yes, in my bed. How I looked into her beautiful face and knew something had shifted. And that first kiss. How it made my soul shatter and my heart stutter. And drained my blood to my groin.

Over the past year, in between the chaos that a baby brought into my life, and during the lulls that any single parent will savor... I allowed myself to think of her. The touch of her skin against mine, her scent in my nostrils, the brush of her hair against my cheek... These thoughts returned over and over, filtering across my mind like an elusive rainbow which felt beautiful but too far away to touch. A mirage, perhaps. A dream. Maybe, I imagined it all?

In between continuing to be CEO of one of the Davenport Group of companies, helping with my uncle Quentin's security firm, and taking care of Serene, my life is full. Stretched to delivering on the challenge of parenting a little girl who came into my life so suddenly, I've tried my best not to regret letting Priscilla go. *And failed.*

It all came back to me when I saw her at the lunch where Knox announced he was engaged to her. I was furious with him, then relieved when he told me he wasn't going through with it. A relief... I don't want to question too closely.

"Mama?" Serene touches Priscilla's cheek. There's a look of wonder on my daughter's little features.

"Oh." Priscilla's gaze grows big. Her chin trembles. She opens her mouth and closes it, seemingly unable to react.

"Mama." Serene nods with satisfaction. There's confidence in her voice, the kind I've never heard before. Then she grabs hold of a strand of Priscilla's hair and tugs on it.

"Ow," Priscilla says softly, still not looking away from my child.

"Mama come home." Serene squirms in Priscilla's grasp, and she puts the toddler down. Not that Serene lets go of her.

She grabs Priscilla's hand and gently tugs, trying to lead her toward the living room.

Priscilla glances down at her with a half-surprised, half-amused kind of expression on her face. I don't blame her. It summarizes how

I feel about what's happening. Does my little girl have a sixth sense about Priscilla? Is it even possible she remembers her? Or is it simply that she likes the look of Priscilla—which I can't blame her for. *After all, whose daughter is she, hmm?* But also... I'm bemused.

"Papa—" She looks at Priscilla, then back at me. "Mama?"

Priscilla shifts her weight from foot to foot. "Oh no, I'm not your mommy, Poppet. I'm—"

"Your new nanny," I cut her off.

Priscilla jerks her chin in my direction. "I... Uh, I'm not sure—"

"Thought you said you wanted the position?"

"I do..." Priscilla glances down at the child, a soft expression on her features. Her forehead is furrowed though, as if she's confused. From the tension which has crept back into her body, I'm guessing she's having second thoughts. I need to reassure her. To coax her into accepting the position of nanny. But how? As I'm racking my brain, Serene resolves it.

She pulls on Priscilla's hand. "Mommy."

Priscilla's eyebrows twist. She crouches down so she's eye level with Serene. "Oh honey, you shouldn't call me that."

She shouldn't. But damn, if that doesn't spark a coil of warmth in my chest. Damn if it doesn't make my head spin. This...is a scenario which I dared not think about. It's exactly what I've been trying to avoid since Serene arrived in my life. And it's making Priscilla feel uncomfortable.

"I'm sorry, she's never done that before." I rub the back of my neck. "If you try to dissuade her, it'll make her more insistent."

Priscilla straightens, a confused expression on her face. Serene gives her hand another tug. Priscilla holds back—until Serene juts out her lower lip in a little pout. She looks up at her with wide-eyed determination.

Priscilla's resistance crumbles. A small smile curves her mouth. Total sucker. Just like me. She lets Serene pull her toward the living room.

I lean in her wake and take a deep sniff. Apple blossoms. The scent that's haunted me all these months. My groin hardens. My chest hurts. Goddamn. She's here as Serene's nanny, and I have a hard on for her. How inappropriate is that?

I want more from her. But right now, it's more important that I find someone to help me with Serene.

I shut the door and follow the two inside. The sight of my little girl's fingers woven with those of the woman who's been my personal ghost sends a tremor up my spine. They look like they were meant to be together. My stomach ties itself in knots. My guts churn. But my heart... It relaxes. For the first time since I sent Priscilla away, my skin doesn't feel too tight.

The hurt in my chest eases. I draw in a breath—and it feels as if oxygen saturates my blood for the first time in months. Enough to make me feel lightheaded.

Serene ignores the living room and the lure of the children's program playing on the television—*a first!*—and walks into the kitchen, Priscilla in tow. She heads for her highchair and tries to climb on. Priscilla places her handbag on the counter and tries to help her, but Serene shrugs her off.

She's been independent for as long as I've known her, my little girl. Very aware. Constantly asking questions. Always clued-in to the world around her. She started talking within a month of her arrival.

She picked up vocabulary very quickly and, by the time she was eighteen months, was speaking in almost complete sentences. It meant I could hold conversations with her. Still, she's only a toddler. She needs a full-time caregiver. And I can't be by her side twenty-four hours a day. She needs a nanny. Someone smart enough to keep my kid intellectually stimulated. Someone like Priscilla would be a godsend. Assuming she's not put off by Serene calling her 'Mama' and is happy to accept the position.

"It's dinnertime," my daughter declares.

I check my watch. Sure enough, it's five-thirty p.m. My little poppet is a stickler for routine.

I head to the fridge and pull out the simple pasta dish with a tomato sauce I made earlier. I plate it into Serene's favorite dish, garnishing it with parmesan cheese. Then, I add boiled beans, carrots and corn kernels on a side plate. I place the dishes on the counter in front of Serene, along with her training fork.

"Don't you want to heat it up in the microwave?" Priscilla asks.

I shake my head. "She prefers it cold."

Serene looks at Priscilla with expectation on her face.

"You want me to feed you, honey?" Priscilla asks softly.

Serene nods. I raise my eyebrows. Serene is independent enough to want to eat on her own. I can count the number of occasions on which she's allowed me to feed her since discovering it's something she can do on her own. Yet here she is, insisting that Priscilla feed her?

Priscilla scoops up some of the pasta and offers it to Serene. Without taking her gaze off Priscilla's face, Serene accepts the food, chews and swallows, then pops her mouth open again.

I watch with growing amazement as she finishes off the pasta, as well as the vegetables. She's far better behaved for Priscilla than for me.

"Dessert," the kid demands.

"Coming up, your highness." I exchange a glance with Priscilla, who seems amused by my daughter's imperious manner.

She schools her features into a stern expression and turns to Serene. "What do you say?"

Serene blinks at her. I'm sure she's going to ignore Priscilla but instead, she surprises me by saying softly, "Please?"

"Well done." Priscilla flashes Serene a big smile.

Serene seems enchanted by it. Don't blame you, kiddo. I can barely tear my gaze off Priscilla's shining features to peel a banana and cut it up.

I place it in a bowl in front of Serene. Once more, Priscilla feeds her. And Serene finishes off every piece of fruit without demur. I bet Priscilla thinks Serene's such a well-behaved child. And she is, normally. Except for when she gets obstinate about certain ideas.

Serene raises her arms. "Bath time."

She's never let anyone else but me bathe her. Apparently, that's going to change?

Priscilla turns to me, a question on her face, hesitation in her eyes. But underneath that is tenderness and bemusement. Seems, as much as Priscilla trusted me the first time we met, my daughter trusts her.

"Her room is upstairs. The second door on the right. There's an attached bath."

26

Priscilla

Your softness is not weakness —
it is the quiet strength that holds worlds together.
-Cilla's Post-it note

I let Serene lead me to her room. As we walk away, I glance back and catch Tyler watching us, his expression unreadable.

"Aren't you coming?" I ask.

He shakes his head. "She's comfortable with you. I could use the time to catch up on my emails."

I pause.

Serene tugs on my hand, but I tell her in a firm voice, "One minute, Sweetie, I need to talk to your father." Serene's gaze widens.

I'm sure she's about to protest but instead, she stops and waits.

"You don't really know me." I shift my gaze in his direction. "You shouldn't let someone bathe your child unless you've made sure they're safe."

His tilts his head. "I know you and your family. I trust you. And consider yourself hired… If you'll take the job, that is."

When I hesitate, Serene pulls on my dress. "Bath time?" she asks in an impatient voice.

She looks so cherubic that I can't stop myself from leaning down and hauling her up in my arms.

"Okay." I smile at Serene. "Yes, I'll take the job."

I sense the tension roll off his shoulders. When I sneak a peek at him, there's a relieved smile on his lips. "You have no idea how much that means to me." He runs his hands through his hair. The way the motion strains the cuffs of his shirt makes my heart wobble. Damn. I need to shield myself against this man's appeal. Professional. I need to be professional. I'm here to do a job. And I owe it to Serene to do it well. I owe it to her to not complicate things by lusting after her father.

"I'll message you my passport details, et cetera, so you can run a background check."

"That's not necessary—" he begins but I shake my head.

"It's best we do things by the book, don't you think?"

He tilts his head. Another inscrutable look crosses his eyes. "Of course." He nods. "Once you've bathed and put her to bed, join me in the study, and we'll work out the payment terms, et cetera."

Before I can ask him if he wants to put her to bed himself, he spins around and heads off. I'm guessing he's in a hurry to get back to his work.

I fill the bathtub and help Serene bathe. She plays with her toys in the tub and obediently comes out when I tell her it's time. I have a feeling she's on her best behavior because she knows it's my first day. She probably wants to impress me. Children are more astute than one realizes. They have a sense for what's happening around them and are very good at picking up signals from adults.

When I've dried and dressed her and tucked her under the covers, I pick up the book she wants me to read from. It's *The Cat in the Hat* by Dr. Seuss. I begin to read from it, and she slides down in the bed. Every time I look at Serene, her eyelids are drooping, but she keeps propping them open. She's fighting sleep, and I can't stop a small smile from curving my lips.

When she sits up in bed, I put the book down. "Do you want your papa to come tuck you in?"

Even as she begins to nod, a voice says from the doorway, "I'm here." He walks over to her. "You okay, honey?" he asks softly.

To see this tough man acting so tenderly with his daughter brings a lump to my throat. And when Serene nods, that melting sensation spreads to my chest. To my surprise, I find tears pricking the backs of my eyes. There's no reason to feel this moved, this emotional, is there? And yet, I can't stop myself from feeling incredibly moved as I watch this man tuck his daughter into bed.

"Tell me a story." She looks at him with her big, brown eyes which, although a different color, are shaped like his. His hair is jet black, and I notice the flecks of gray at his temple, which I don't remember him having a year ago. Nothing ages you like becoming a parent, responsible for another life. Serene's hair is chestnut-colored with streaks of copper woven through them. But her features are so similar to his.

He reaches for the book I put down on the nightstand. Lying down next to her, he holds it up so she can also read.

She shakes her head. "No, read me the one about the stars."

He picks up another book from the bedside table. When he holds it up, I see the title, *Where the Stars Always Shine.*

From the packaging it looks, not like a book which was mass produced, but like one which was printed specifically for her.

He begins to read.

"Once upon a time, under a sky full of stars, a baby girl was born. She had tiny fingers, a sleepy smile, and a quiet little sigh."

Serene cuddles closer. He continues reading.

"Her mother loved her very much. But love alone wasn't enough to give her the life she hoped for her baby.

"With a heart full of hope and sorrow, she put her baby into a carrier. She said goodbye with a kiss and carried that goodbye forever."

I swallow around the ball of emotion in my throat, remembering how we found Serene on his doorstep.

"The baby girl went to a new home. There, her father was waiting, ready to give her all he had.

"She grew up in a home filled with bedtime stories, badly made pancakes on Sundays, and warm hugs that lasted a long time."

He hugs Serene, and she giggles, then throws her arm over his chest.

"She learned to ask big questions. She wondered where she came from. And sometimes, she missed someone she didn't remember.

"Her father never had all the answers. But he always listened. And he never stopped loving her, not for a second."

He kisses her forehead. She turns to him. "I love you, too, Papa."

"I know, Poppet." His gaze meets mine over the book. There's a sadness in them I haven't seen before. The air between us heats. The moment stretches. Then he looks down at the book, and it's lost. He continues reading.

"She carried two stories: The one that began with goodbye. And one that kept growing with love, every day. And wherever life leads her, some things will always be true: She is loved. She is real. She belongs."

He closes the book and lowers it. Serene's fast asleep with her head on his shoulder. He gently places her head on the pillow.

It feels like I'm intruding on a moment that's personal, something which should be shared only by father and daughter.

I back away, then head out of the room, down the stairs and into the kitchen, where I get myself a glass of water. Then, because I'm curious about his place—which is so different from the penthouse where I last visited him— I wander up the hallway. I peek into a room and, ooh, find it's a library with bookshelves lining the walls. A fire is crackling in the hearth, and it feels so inviting. I walk in, and when I draw in a breath, I can smell the spicy and very male scent of his above that of the burning logs. The desk and chair in the corner facing the room has a computer screen, a keyboard, and enough paper to indicate he must use this as his home office. I can feel his presence here strongly.

A shiver grips me. My nipples turn into points of need. Damn. He's not even here, but if I close my eyes, I can pretend I'm being embraced by him. I draw in another breath, allowing it to both arouse me and calm me, an oxymoron I've always associated with Tyler. Then, I head for the books on the shelves.

Dragging my finger down the spines, I take in the titles. *Atomic Habits* by James Clear, *Deep Work* by Carl Newport, *The Design of Everyday Things* by Don Norman… *Interesting. These are similar to the self-help books I gravitate toward.*

Then I come across *Dude, You're Gonna Be a Dad!: How to Get (Both of You) Through the Next 9 Months* by John Pfeiffer, and *The Single Dad's Survival Guide: How to Succeed as a One-Man Parenting Team* by Michael A. Klumpp.

I sense his presence and look up to find him walking into the study. "That was a beautiful story. It was about Serene, wasn't it?"

"That's her life storybook." He crosses over to the wet bar. "Would you like white wine?"

I nod, grateful he didn't take me for granted and pour it for me. For a macho alpha male, it's incredible that he doesn't order me around in real life. In bed though… That's another matter. And he's already shown me he's dominant and a beast when it comes to assuaging my wants. My cheeks heat in recollection. I pull my thoughts back to the present

"Life storybook?"

"She had so many questions about her mother… I kept as close to the truth as I could, but put her life into a story form," he explains, turning to me with a snifter of whiskey in one hand and a glass of wine in the other. "Her therapist said it would be an empathetic way for her to understand her past and deal with the trauma of separation."

"Wow, that's a great way to introduce her to her past."

He nods. "I thought so, too. This way, whenever she asks about her mother, I can pick up the book, and we read from it together. As she grows older, I can introduce more information to her in an age-appropriate manner. I hope it will help her get more familiar with her own history and eventually, help her in creating her own identity."

He walks over to his desk, places my wine in front of one of the chairs, then heads over to sit in the armchair behind the desk. He looks right at home there. From frazzled Dad who loves his daughter, to smoldering business executive who wields his power like it's an invisible whip so mere mortals bow down to him, to the demanding yet unselfish lover who made sure to pleasure every inch of my body while ignoring his own needs, Tyler Davenport is one fine man. It's going to be a challenge to keep my emotions in tow and focus on the job at hand.

I slip into the chair, take a sip of my wine, which is crisp and refreshing. "This is so good." I take another sip.

"It's the same one you had the day we met."

"Oh?" I'm not sure what to make of that revelation. Does he mean he bought it because I had it that day? "You remember what I drank that day?"

"I remember *everything* about that day." His voice turns gritty. The air between us sizzles. It's like he's reliving exactly what happened that day and night. I sure haven't forgotten it. But... The last thing I want to do is dwell on it. Not when he's the one who asked me to leave.

"What about her mother?" I ask, not because I want to know. Okay, I do want to know, but I'm already jealous of whoever she is. Which is not good. I really need to get control of myself. Besides, the only reason I need to know about Serene's mother is so that I'll do a better job of being her nanny, right?

"I tracked her down. But before I could ask her about Serene, she left the country. Her tracks proved difficult to pick up, even for my investigators. Meanwhile, the DNA tests were conclusive. Serene is my daughter."

27

Tyler

"So, you adopted her?"

"The proudest day of my life." Tenderness and joy fill my chest. "The DNA test proved she was mine. I established my paternity in court and filed for custody. But since I couldn't track down her mother, adopting her secured my parental rights. Of course, I'd have done it even if the DNA test had been negative."

Her face gentles. "That's really noble of you."

I shake my head. "No, it isn't. Thanks to Serene, I went from someone selfish and focused only on my pleasures, to realizing I am not the center of the universe. It made me grow up." I chuckle in a self-deprecating fashion. "I found myself responsible for another person. It was a wake-up call."

"Children can do that to you, huh?"

I laugh. "You know about that, of course."

She half-smiles. "Were you upset that you couldn't meet her mother?"

Her tone is casual but something in her eyes tells me my answer is important to her. "I don't remember her. Don't recognize her name. She's a stranger to me. So, no." I shrug. "I realize that answer might make me sound callous. And you're probably thinking I had a one-night stand I don't recall. I admit, I considered the possibility and discarded it. I might have been self-absorbed, but I do recall every woman I slept with. And I always, *always* wrapped it up."

She winces. I curse myself. *Why the hell did I have to talk about women I've been with?*

"I've mentioned it to you before and I'll do so again. None of them meant anything to me. After I met you, I realized how meaningless those encounters had been. And then, not having you in my life made me realize what a fool I'd been. Will you please forgive me for what I did that day?"

She looks away. Her forehead furrows. "You had a big emotional upheaval. Of course, you weren't thinking straight. And I know, more than anyone, that a child comes first. Anyway, all that is water under the bridge." She straightens and pastes a smile on her face, which tells me, she doesn't completely believe that. But for now, I let it go.

Once she joins me as Serene's nanny, I'll have time to convince her, through my actions, that I hadn't forgotten about her, even though I hadn't called her in the last year. *I hope.*

"As her nanny, you'll be entitled to £10,000 per month." Needing her to stay, I throw out triple what I paid the last nanny. "What do you say?"

She seems taken aback. "I think I'll enjoy being Serene's nanny," she says slowly. "She's such an adorable little girl. She reminds me of why I wanted to be a nanny in the first place."

"And why *did* you want to become a nanny?"

"Is this part of the interview? Thought you already offered me the job?" There's a tinge of amusement in her eyes.

Ha. This is a different side of Cilla. She seems to have matured in the last year. She was already confident but now, she's more poised.

"You do have the job. I simply would love to find out more about you."

"Oh." She digests that. "It was after I completed university and found, despite a degree, all I was being offered were unpaid internship roles. I was running out of money, had student debts, and felt like the only way out was asking my brother for a loan. And I didn't want to do that."

"Your independence is important to you."

"It is." She tips up her chin. "At twenty-one, that translated into a lot of anger against the system. I wanted to change the world, but damn, it felt like I couldn't do that without money. That really pissed me off. A friend of mine was volunteering with special needs children. I decided to do the same. It seemed like a good idea. Better than being jobless and getting upset.

"My first hour there, and my mindset shifted. It put my own life in perspective. There were these kids, taking pleasure in small things, despite the odds they were facing. And I was angry at what—? Not being able to find a job? That's when I decided I wanted to work with kids."

I look at her closely. "And you called *me* noble?"

She thinks that over. "I suppose, in that sense, I share your view. It's not me caring for the kids, which I am, of course, but it's also them doing me a favor by letting me care for them, you know? *My* life is richer for the experience. And I wouldn't trade it for anything."

There's silence. Her words sink in. The truth in them resonates within the deepest parts of me. Places I didn't know existed—hidden parts of me that react only to her.

The air between us swirls with unsaid emotions. The hair on the nape of my neck rises. I want to reach over this desk, pull her into my lap, and kiss her senseless. I want to push her onto her front on my desk and bury my throbbing cock inside her sweet pussy. I want to—not take her for granted. I want to show her the respect she deserves for being Serene's nanny. She hasn't even started the position, and I'm already screwing it up.

I give myself a mental shake, slide my phone out of my pocket, and pull up my bank app. "The position comes with the apartment over the garage. You'll also have access to the car in the garage, which you can use for both Serene and your personal needs. Are you good with starting immediately?" I glance at her to find a quizzical expression on her features.

"Is that important? That I move into the apartment?" She doesn't seem fazed that I asked her to start immediately. Score for me.

"I need you to be here all day, and also on the nights I need to be on conference calls with people in other time zones." I shrug. Not completely the truth. My partners and vendors will change their times to suit mine, but there's no reason for her to know that.

"It would save you rent money," I point out.

She nods slowly. "It would."

"You're taking care of my daughter. I want to ensure you don't have to worry about paying your bills, so you can focus on her completely."

I slide my phone to her across the desk. "Key in the details of your bank account, please, so I can transfer the money for your first month of employment."

She hesitates. "That figure you quoted is too much. Not that I don't appreciate it. Childcare professionals are undervalued for what they do. Still"—she purses her lips—"it feels like an inflated amount."

"Your role is second only to mine in her life. As her nanny, you'll not only take care of her, but you'll be responsible for her mental and emotional well-being, something I know you'll be great at."

She swallows, seemingly moved by my words. "Thank you. You're very kind."

I cut the air with my hand. "Only saying the truth. I saw you with her today. It's the first time she's allowed anyone else, other than me, to bathe her."

"Oh?" She seems taken aback.

"Not any of her previous nannies, and not even my friends' wives. You are the only other person she's allowed close enough for that. So yeah, I know you're the right person for the job."

"Oh!" She fans herself. "You're making me emotional."

Her eyes glitter. Seeing the tears in her eyes is a special kind of hell. Perhaps, becoming a father has made me more sensitive to other's feelings. But even if it were not for that, I wouldn't be able to bear causing her any more distress. I already upset her deeply when I asked her to leave my penthouse that day.

But I was too distracted with Serene's arrival to notice the impact my words had on Priscilla. Perhaps my reasons were justified. I did have to focus on my daughter. *But could I have found a way to have both in my life…?*

I push aside my misgivings. My time with the Marines has taught me to live in the present. She's here under my roof now, and I'm going to find every way possible to keep her in my life.

She refers to her phone, fills out the details on mine, then slides the device back to me. I transfer the money to her immediately. Some of the tension rolls off my shoulders. That's a done deal. She can't back out now.

Her phone pings with a notification. She glances at it, then directs a glance at me. "You paid me already?"

"You've been out of a job for a few months, I assume?"

She nods, a strange look on her features.

"You must have bills to pay. This should help."

I could have paid her a lot more, but then, she'd likely pay off her bills too quickly. And that'd mean she wouldn't need to be Serene's nanny anymore. And yes, this makes me a calculating bastard — guess I'm not completely reformed — but with this figure I'm paying her, she'll be able to pay off debts, *and* save, *and* have enough to not have to compromise her lifestyle.

She hesitates, then jerks her chin. "Thank you."

"It's me who should be thanking you for reconsidering the role. You have no idea how grateful I am."

Our gazes meet and hold. Like clockwork, that ever-present chemistry between us flares. My balls harden. Goddamn, how am I going to get through keeping up this professional façade? Especially since, I wasn't kidding when I said I was grateful she accepted the role of Serene's nanny. It's going to make a huge difference to both Serene's life and mine. I don't want to do anything that's going to upset Priscilla or scare her off. Not until she's had a chance to get to know me better. Not until she realizes I've changed. I've gone from being the person who couldn't even refer to my daughter as a child when she first arrived, to my world revolving around a smile from her.

"My lawyer will be in touch with a Non-Disclosure Agreement and your employment contract."

She laughs. "You paid me already, before asking me to sign the agreement."

"I already told you, I trust you."

She swallows, and her eyes widen. She seems both taken aback but also happy that I said that. "Thank you for saying that."

Once again, the air between us grows heavy, charged with every-thing we've said and everything we haven't. My heart pounds, loud and insistent, echoing in my ears. I drink her in, every inch of her, awash in the quiet miracle that she's here. That from this moment on, I get to see her every day. And maybe—*if I'm lucky, if I find a way*—for the rest of my life.

Color smears her cheeks. She makes a small sound at the back of her throat. One which tightens my belly. It makes me realize how much I want this woman. How I'd do anything to have her back in my life. *Get it together. Don't screw it up before she's even started the job. Show her the respect she deserves.*

I rise to my feet, indicating the meeting is over.

She interprets my move and, turning, walks out of the study and toward the kitchen. I follow her. She picks up her purse from the breakfast counter and turns to me. "Thanks again for this opportu-nity. You won't regret it."

28

Tyler

"Don't make me regret that I made you an heir to my fortune." Arthur glowers at me from under his eyebrows. "I realize, you're not happy with my condition, but in time, you'll appreciate it."

We're in his study. I received his command to come by and see him today. Not unusual for Arthur. He's known to summon my brothers when he has something of importance to discuss. It's the first time he's called and asked me to come out of the blue.

The only reason I could make it is because I have Priscilla at home with Serene. In the month since she's taken on the role of Serene's nanny, my life has regained some semblance of normality. I have a little more space during the day. The nights, though, are still rough.

"Tyler, are you listening?" Arthur's voice cuts through my thoughts. I yawn, then shake my head to clear it.

"Am I boring you?" my grandfather asks through gritted teeth.

Yes.

"Sorry. Didn't sleep much last night."

"Serene still having nightmares?" Imelda asks in sympathy.

"She's better than she was six months ago," I murmur.

It means, I have to wake up once, instead of three times every night to soothe her when she wakes up crying from night terrors. I don't say that aloud, though. I'm wary of complaining about the challenges of raising my daughter when the satisfaction far outweighs any hardship.

Tiny heaves himself to his feet. He pads over, sinks down next to my chair, and pushes his big head into my lap.

"Hey, boy." I scratch him behind his ear, and he makes a purring noise in his throat. "Serene loves playing with him. He's so good with her."

"He is." Some of the sternness in Arthur slips away. Other than Imelda, it's this mutt he has a soft spot for. As for the rest of us? I often wonder if he tolerates us only because we are the bearers of his bloodline.

"You were saying?" I prompt him.

"That you need to get married."

I scoff. It's Gramps' favorite topic. He's on a mission to marry his remaining single grandsons off.

"I put you boys in my will. And I want you to inherit your share of the Davenports' wealth. But first, you need to get married."

I fix him with a scowl. It's the first time Arthur has given me what sounds like a deadline on this matter. "You may have harangued my brothers but I'm wise to your machinations."

He pops a shoulder. "I've never hidden the fact that I'll do what's necessary to get you guys married off. Besides, Ryot married Aurelia of his own volition."

"Hmph." It's true that it was Ryot's idea to help Aurelia pay off her father's debts in return for her marrying him. But my brothers and I speculated Arthur had had a hand in setting things up, nevertheless.

"As for Quentin, Nathan and Knox, all I did was nudge them in the right direction." He looks pleased with himself.

"You told them you'd disinherit them unless they got married, which is what you're trying to tell me now, if I'm not mistaken."

"You are the most astute of the lot. I know you'll figure out a way to get married within the next four weeks—" He doesn't complete the sentence. While it's a barely disguised threat, he says it while managing to look innocent. A look which may fool an unsuspecting person into thinking he's a harmless old man. But I know the truth. He's a devious, Machiavellian bastard who'll do anything to get his way.

While Gramps was diagnosed with the Big C, the treatment was successful. He's in remission and is settled with his girlfriend. No doubt, the diagnosis made him aware of his mortality. It's why he's putting a time limit on my getting married. He wants to see me hustle. And I get that. But I resent it.

Anger knots my gut. I shove it down, digging deeply into the patience I learned in the Marines—the kind you need when you're on a mission for weeks, getting close to the enemy, waiting for the right moment to strike—and refined as the single parent of a demanding and too-intelligent-for-my-own-good toddler.

Imelda scowls at Arthur. "What your grandfather means is that he's worried about you." She turns to me. "He knows bringing up a child on your own is a lot."

"Hmm." I look between them. "Somehow, I doubt that, given Gramps hasn't a single empathetic bone in his body"—Arthur opens his mouth, but I keep going—"but giving him the benefit of the doubt, and assuming that is his motivation, why has he waited this long to bring this up? Why didn't he do it when Serene first came into my life?"

"Because I knew you were trying to find her birth mother. I thought, perhaps, you might settle down with her." Arthur shrugs. "Clearly, that's not happening."

Before I can react to that, Imelda rushes in with, "Not that you're doing a bad job. It's beyond amazing. As a single parent, you've been stellar. You've given so much love and attention to that little girl, it's clear to all of us that she's thriving."

I subside, somewhat mollified. Imelda's a tough cookie, but she has a way of playing peacemaker and interpreting Arthur's words for the rest of us so that they appear less offensive. She helps to soften his edges and make him appear almost human.

My grandfather cuts in, "And now that you have a reliable nanny..."

"How do you know that?" I ask, my hackles rising.

He waves a hand dismissively. "It doesn't matter. The point is, I know that Priscilla Whittington is Serene's nanny now. So, that frees up your time to find a wife."

I'm momentarily stunned into silence when Imelda cuts in, "The fact is, you've been pushing yourself too hard, Tyler. If you had someone to share the weight—"

"I'm not going to marry someone just so I have help with Serene," I snap. "That's why I have a nanny." And yes, I'm aware that nannies come and go. But I definitely will *not* marry Priscilla just to ensure she'll stay. She deserves better than that. Never mind the fact that I haven't stopped thinking about how quickly Serene bonded with her, and how she'd make a perfect mother for her.

"No one's suggesting you tie the knot just to get a live-in caregiver," Imelda says gently. "What your grandfather means is—"

"If you're not married in four weeks, you're out of the will," Arthur cuts in, plain and direct.

Imelda sighs. She seems like she's about to contradict him, then sighs.

Tiny raises his head and whines. "It's okay, boy." I pat his head. "Gramps needed to get that out of his system." I rub under his jaw until Tiny finally sinks back with his head between his paws.

"Thank you for being honest." I lean back in my seat. "I will not be coerced into marriage." I narrow my gaze on Arthur.

"That's what your brothers said, too. Now look how happy they are." Arthur coughs. "I'm getting on, boy. I won't be around much longer. And I fully intend to see you lot settled before I depart."

The man's health seems to improve with every passing day. I'm also aware he likes to play the victim card, if it means he can get his way. Though, hearing him cough again, I have to give him the benefit of doubt.

Imelda rises to her feet and pours him a glass of water. As he drinks it, she plumps the cushion at his back.

"Enough, woman. Stop fussing," Arthur says gruffly, but his eyes tell me he loves the attention. He proves it when he grabs her hand and kisses it before letting go. "Thanks, Im."

Imelda smiles, her face lighting up in a way that makes the decades drop away. "You're very welcome."

She begins to move away, but he pats the couch next to him. "Sit with me."

Imelda sinks down, and they hold hands. They look into each other's eyes, and it feels like a tender, very personal moment. And suddenly, I feel like I'm intruding.

"Guess I'll be off." I rise to my feet, but Arthur turns to me.

"I'm not done."

I sink back with a sigh. "You've said your piece, what else is left?"

"I'm lucky I found Imelda. And thankful she drilled some sense into my stubborn head, so I didn't let my ego stand in the way of confessing my feelings for her."

I look between them, the way she looks at him adoringly, and something like envy squeezes my chest. I admit, there have been times in the past few months when I wished there were someone else —okay, Priscilla—who could share the load of childrearing with me. It goes against every reason why I pushed her to walk out of my life. But she kept returning. Not once, but twice. And this time... It feels right. The way Serene has taken to her confirms it. But thinking of her in the same breath as my wife, simply because Arthur has demanded I marry?

Fact is, I can't see anyone else in that position. From the moment I met her, I knew she was my future. I pushed her away so I could focus on my daughter because I was sure I couldn't give her the kind of attention she deserved. I wanted her to be free of the responsibility that came with having Serene in my life. Then, I was hurt because she agreed to marry Knox. But as far as I'm concerned, she's always been the one. Now, Arthur is pushing me to marry, and I can't conceive of being with anyone else.

Only... Is it fair to Priscilla? And why would she marry me now, after how I pushed her away in the first place?

The old man's ramblings are confusing me and twisting around my thoughts.

"I understand why it might feel scary to open up your life to someone else, especially now that you have a little girl to take care of... But it's because of her that I'm pushing this. She needs a mother," Arthur says in a firm voice.

All of which is true and mirrors sentiments I've felt over the last few months. Longer than that, if I'm being honest. Especially when Serene would look at women in storybooks, point to them and say, "Mama." And she's stopped doing that since Priscilla arrived. Is it a coincidence she called Priscilla by that name?

She's never said that to anyone else. She seemed too confident, like her instinct told her Priscilla is the mother she's been looking for. And I can't deny, she's the only woman I want in my life.

I made a mistake, asking Priscilla to leave that day. Of that, I have no doubt. The problem is, how do I convince Priscilla she can trust me now?

Outwardly though, I scoff. "I call bullshit. You're pushing it because you want all your grandsons married, and you're using Serene as a convenience to get me hitched."

Arthur adopts a look of innocence which is patently false on his face. Gramps should get an Academy Award. "You wound me, Grandson. I only have your best interests at heart."

I glare at him, and he smiles back. He's enjoying himself. This is Arthur in his element, controlling the lot of us like pawns on a chessboard.

"You know how to time your demands, don't you, old man?" I lean forward in my seat. "You know, I would do everything in my power to ensure Serene gets access to the Davenport wealth. It's her due."

Which means, I need to find a way to comply with Arthur's

demands. For unless I claim my inheritance, I can't pass it on to my daughter. Only, I have no idea how I'm going to do this.

As if he can read my mind, Arthur's expression softens. But his voice stays steady. "I want Serene to have what's hers, too. But that depends on you." He taps the arm of the sofa, eyes on mine. "So, what's your move?"

29

Priscilla

"Those are some fancy moves, honey." I chuckle.

We're in Serene's room. We came up after her dinner, and she insisted she wanted to play with me before her bath.

She asked me to play nursery rhymes for her. When she grew tired of that, I switched to one of my playlists—a mix of pop and rock music. Right now, she's dancing to one of my all-time faves.

Seduced by the upbeat tune, my feet begin to move as if on their own. I glide toward Serene, and when she looks up at me and squeals, I laugh. "It's good, right?"

She nods and holds out her arms. Without hesitation, I lift her up, then dance with her. Both of us bop our chins. I do a shimmy which makes her giggle, then bump and grind which makes her cling to my shoulders.

"Dance. Dance. Dance," she says breathlessly.

"Yes, Poppet, we're dancing."

"Faster. Faster," she urges me.

I hold her tightly and twirl around. It's been two weeks since I became her nanny, and I have loved every second of it. Serene and I have this kinship. We seem to be on the same wavelength, so being with her has been one of the most stress-free experiences of my life. I've never adapted so quickly to a child's routine as I have with hers. And Serene, for her part, has been an absolute darling. Of course, I don't sleep in the house at night, so I'm not there for whenever she has nightmares. But I know when she's had a bad dream because Tyler looks exhausted the next day.

He insists that they've begun to reduce in frequency since I started taking care of her. But I'm not sure I can take all the credit.

I've read up and taken enough classes on childcare to know that, even without separation trauma or the unknown of how a child was cared for during her first year of life, sometime in their second year they begin to realize that they are a separate entity from their primary care person.

They realize they can't control the world around them. With this awareness comes the instinctive fear of abandonment by the familiar surroundings and people.

In Serene's case, she was given up by the woman who gave birth to her. Something she must realize deep inside. I have no doubt this left its mark on her. But she's a survivor. She has a zest for life which makes me feel lucky that I get to take care of her.

She moves her little body, wriggling around in my arms, so I hold onto her even tighter. I continue to shake my hips and roll them, as I do a mini twerk. She begins to giggle. Her face is alight with mirth, and that makes me chuckle and laugh. I continue to sway with her, humming the song under my breath, then begin to sing along. She looks at me, entranced. You'd think I was the most famous pop star in the world, the way she stares at me. The trust and adoration in her eyes causes the breath to catch in my throat. Damn.

I need to be careful. The way I'm falling for Serene is a slippery slope. Somewhere deep in the hidden recesses of my mind an insidious voice sparks to life. *If only she were yours. If only Tyler were yours. If only you weren't the nanny, but Tyler's* — What? I shake my head.

What do I want to be? Tyler's wife? Serene's mother? The latter seems even more unattainable. No, I am Serene's nanny. And Tyler's employee. And I need this job. I can't do anything to fuck this up. And Serene needs me, too.

I'm not egoistical, but I know I'm a damn good childcare professional. No one else can look after Serene the way I can. I'm worth every dollar Tyler is paying me. And he *is* paying me. So, our relationship is not personal.

I need to remind myself of that every time I'm attracted to him. And every time my heart stutters watching him carry his daughter like she's the most precious thing in the world.

The hair on the back of my neck rises. A shiver runs up my spine. I turn in time to see Tyler appear in the doorway. He leans a shoulder against the door frame. He must have just returned from work—today is one of the rare days when he had to head into the city for meetings.

He's loosened his tie and rolled up the sleeves of his buttoned-down white shirt. It's crumpled enough to show he's had a long day. With the five o'clock shadow, mussed hair, and muscle-bound thighs stretching the fabric of his tailored pants, he looks delectable and sexy.

He slides one hand into his pocket, stretching the material of the trousers across his crotch further. Heat arrows down my belly and straight to my clit. A throbbing need springs to life between my thighs. Why does he have to look so yummy? Why do I want to throw myself in his arms, go up on tiptoe, and lick up the strong cord of his throat.

"Papa. Papa." Serene wriggles around in my arms. I bend and let her down. She scampers over to Tyler, and he swings her up. With that lithe strength and confidence that comes with being a big man who's done this many times, he throws his daughter up in the air and catches her.

She squeals, "Again! Again!"

He obliges once more.

"Again! Papa. Again!" she says breathlessly.

"Don't want to make you sick, sweetheart." He cuddles her close and kisses her cheek. "Did you have a good day?"

"Yes, Papa." She nods vigorously.

His smile grows tender. "You looked like you were having fun dancing."

"I love it." Overcome with excitement she throws her arms around his neck. "I played with Donny the Dinosaur and had a tea party with Mama."

"Honey, I told you to call me Cilla," I correct her gently.

She thrusts out her lower lip. "Mama." She scowls at me. "Mama. Mama. Mama."

Tyler and I exchange a look. I have corrected Serene many times, but that only seems to make her more adamant on calling me Mama. I open my mouth to correct Serene again, but he shakes his head. Without saying a single word, I know he's telling me that if I do, it's only going to make her more insistent. I raise my hands in a helpless gesture.

He smiles back, his expression reassuring. I love that we can communicate without speaking. We're on the same wavelength. It's special. Unique. *Something I have only with him.* I push the thought from my head.

"What else did you do today?" Tyler turns to Serene.

Her forehead smooths out. "We played ball. Went for a walk. And made paper planes."

"Wow! Sounds like you've been busy." He looks past her face and winks at me.

My heart swoons. My belly trembles. A treacherous melting sensation seems to have taken up permanent residence in my pussy. *Get a grip, woman. You can't be so attracted to him. You can't keep wanting to jump his bones. You need to be a responsible adult.* I slap away the treacherous sensations in my body and ignore the butterflies which have taken flight in my chest. I paste my patented Mary Poppins' expression on my face, the one I've used in the past with great effect with parents, and nod.

"She's had a full day. We sketched, worked on puzzles, worked our way through name and object recognition activities, finger painted, and read picture books to build vocabulary. Then, she helped sort her toys and even counted with me up to ten. She's been so good, haven't you, Poppet?"

Serene nods and snuggles into her father's chest. Aww, the contrast of her tiny body curled up into Tyler never fails to excite my ovaries. It's the only time I wonder about the eggs I donated. I did it because I needed the money, but it was such an intrusive experience, I decided it wasn't worth repeating again, regardless of how broke I was.

Looking at Serene now, I wonder if my gesture helped someone else. I hope so. Especially if it helped create a child as adorable as this little girl.

"All that crammed into one day?" Tyler blows out a breath. "That's impressive."

I chuckle. "She's an energetic little girl. Like her father."

"Oh?" His gaze sharpens. That flare of interest in his eyes leaves me in no doubt what he's thinking about.

Heat sears my cheeks. Damn. "I... I didn't mean it like that."

He cants his head. The wolfish expression on his face causes electricity to shoot through my veins. Our gazes meet. Hold. That electricity crackles and turns into a stream of magma. My toes curl. My hair follicles tighten. The air between us spikes with something kinetic. Something which sends goosebumps spiraling under my skin. I take a step forward. So does he. It seems to wake Serene up from the dreamlike state she'd fallen into. She grabs his chin and tugs.

His Adam's apple bobs. With reluctance, and a last blistering look that I pretend I didn't catch, he glances down. "Yes, Poppet?"

"Papa. Bath time?" She looks at him with big eyes.

His expression softens. Just like that, the lethal alpha male is replaced by a teddy bear. This combination of tenderness and protectiveness he wears like the most natural shield over that big, brawny body is my catnip. No... It's Tyler who's my catnip. And my vulnerability. And my undoing. Suddenly, my skin feels too tight for my body. I glance away, draw in a breath, and compose myself.

"I think she wants to spend time with her papa," I murmur.

"Do you, honey?"

Serene nods.

"Okay then, I'll give you a bath and put you to bed, eh?" He tucks her hair behind her ear in a gesture that speaks volumes of his love for her. Again, my throat closes. *Ridiculous.*

You'd think I'd get used to seeing them together, but each time I do, it brings home how lucky they are to have each other. And how alone I am... *No. Nope. Not happening. Not going there.* I begin to tidy up the toys and put them away, mainly so I don't have to look at him.

"Leave it; you've had a long day, as well," he rumbles. That gruff voice of his never fails to pinch my nerve endings and sensitize every millimeter of my skin. Normally, I'd protest, but I'm so aware of him, it's best I get out of here. Fast.

I straighten and manage to meet his eyes with what I hope is a composed look. "Thank you. I do believe I'll take you up on that offer." I walk toward the doorway. "Have a good evening."

He seems on the verge of saying something, but to my relief, he doesn't. He steps aside. With a nod at him, and after blowing a kiss at Serene, I skitter out of there.

Back in my little apartment over the garage, I pour myself a glass of wine, then inhale it. Splashing some more of the ruby red liquid into my glass, I place it on the small table separating the kitchen area from the living room. It's such a small space; it's only a few steps to the refrigerator. I open it and survey the contents. I'm not very hungry—probably because my appetite of a different kind has been roused. I blow out a breath. Enough. I have to stop thinking of Tyler.

I should be grateful to have a roof over my head. With the money he's already paid me, I've paid down my credit card debt and begun to pay off my student loans, too. All in all, I'm in a much better space than before

I came to work for him... Except, now that I see him every day, I miss him so much. Most nights, I dream about how it was to kiss him, how it felt to have his lips on me, and his tongue inside me, and his fingers playing me like I was his favorite musical instrument.

Grr! All that work I put in, trying to forget him, was in vain. It's as if I parked the memories somewhere deep inside, and now, they insist on parading across my brain like a movie every time I close my eyes.

I shake my head, count back from ten. *I'm not falling apart—I'm rearranging into someone stronger.* No idea where I read that, but it helps me feel a little more in control. First things first, I need to eat a little something. It'll help me feel better.

I look at the ingredients I have in the refrigerator and navigate to my favorite website, where I can key them in and get suggestions for what to make for dinner. When I look at the time next, nearly an hour has passed. Damn. I got sidetracked going on my social media feeds and checking my email. And I'm no closer to finding a recipe I like. Guess I'll have to fall back on something I've made before.

I push my phone aside. Then head to the refrigerator and pull out the Halloumi cheese, along with the vegetables I need for a salad. I slice the cheese into half-inch thick pieces, heat a pan over the flame, add the olive oil to the pan, then place the Halloumi slices in the pan.

While they begin to fry, I turn to the chopping board and begin to chop the cucumber, then move onto the tomato. I lose myself in the Zen of the repetitive actions. A cucumber-tomato-mint salad will be refreshing and—I cough. Damn, I forgot about the Halloumi. It has a high protein content, and I left it too long in the pan. The cheese is charred, and smoke pours from the pieces. Even as I reach for the pan, one of the pieces catches fire. From somewhere above me, the fire alarm begins to blare.

"Oh, my God!" The noise is so loud, my ears ring. I grab the pan and thrust it into the sink. Then I open the tap, and when water hits the pan, it sizzles. And even more smoke bellows from it. Jesus. I can't believe one small hunk of cheese could cause so much smoke to arise. I cough again, grab the tea towel, and look around, trying to spot the smoke alarm. It's too high to reach.

I was hoping to fan the air in front of it to try to get it to shut off, but I guess that's not going to happen. With streaming eyes, I stumble to the window. I throw it open, shove my head out, gulping in air. My lungs burn. My eyes won't stop tearing. I keep fanning the smoke toward the window, when the door to the apartment crashes open. I look over my shoulder and, through my tears, watch Tyler burst in. My jaw drops.

"Are you okay?" He barrels across the living room and toward the kitchen area. Barefoot. Shirtless. Wearing nothing but gray sweats that hang low on his hips, clinging to that sharp V of muscle that disappears beneath the waistband.

My gaze lowers before I can stop myself. That body—God. That chest. Those abs. That line of sweat gliding down between his pecs like a lover's kiss. My throat closes. My breath catches. And it's nothing to do with the smoke in the room, which is already fading, thanks to the open window.

I haven't seen his sculpted chest since that night at his penthouse. But I've remembered. My body has never forgotten. That eight-pack has starred in so many of my dreams, I've woken up tangled in sheets and soaked through my panties more times than I care to admit.

And now he's here. Real. Breathing hard. His whole body carved from heat and tension and fear.

I look up—and my stomach drops.

His face is pinched tight, his jaw clenched, his gaze frantic. There's something wild in his eyes. Something raw. Fierce. Terrifyingly tender. Like he thought—no, knew—he was about to lose me.

Oh God.

He saw the smoke. Heard the fire alarm.

He thought the apartment was burning. He thought I was inside.

"I'm fine, the pan caught fire—"

I don't get to finish.

Because he's rounded the table, stepped up to me, and grabbed me around my waist.

I'm stunned. My mouth falls open. I don't even protest. I just hold onto him, every muscle in his body coiled with tension, every inch of him wrapped around me like I'm his most precious possession.

He lifts me off my feet like I weigh nothing. Then pivots and thunders out of there—back across the living room floor, out the front door, and down the steps leading to the garden. I'm so taken aback; my mouth hangs open. I'm too shocked to even protest.

I merely hold onto his massive shoulder as he reaches the bottom most step, jumps onto the lawn, and begins to race across it.

Only then do my brain cells begin to function. "Stop, Tyler. What's wrong with you?"

"Fire. The apartment was on fire," he rasps through gritted teeth.

"No, it wasn't. I burned the food I was making. That's all."

I don't think I'm getting through to him because he doesn't slow down. I sense the tension pouring off of him. See the sweat clinging to his bunched-up shoulders. The muscles of his body have seized up so much, it feels like I'm clinging to a stone pillar.

I pat his big broad chest. "Tyler, I'm fine."

No answer. The granite hard profile, the set to his chin, that fierce edge to his gaze... All of it is so sexy, it turns my insides to mush. But it's the way his arms lock around me, like he'd rather die than let go— That's what shatters me.

"Tyler, everything's okay," I say again in a soothing tone.

When he still doesn't answer, I realize, he's in some kind of zone. The concentration on his features gives me a glimpse of how he must have been as a Marine. Sharp. Ruthless. Unflinching in the face of chaos. My heart constricts with an emotion I don't dare name. Something that claws at my chest and makes my breath hitch.

I act on instinct. I lean up and kiss the side of his mouth.

Instantly, he comes to a stop. He turns his head and deepens the kiss.

30

Tyler

Yes, I'm carrying her under one arm. A part of me registered what she said. And my instincts have finally receded from the Op Critical mode they kicked into.

I was about to jump into the shower when the fire alarm went off in the apartment, and the security app on my phone blared a warning.

I grabbed the first piece of clothing I found, my sweats. Then I pocketed my phone, which is linked to the baby cam trained on Serene, and raced toward Cilla's apartment.

Every cell in my body snapped to attention, a red mist descending in front of my eyes and the only words repeating in my mind were that I was not going to let anything happen to her. And when she kissed the corner of my mouth, the fog broke.

In seconds, I realized three things: She was safe. Serene was back home and safe. And Cilla was in my arms, her mouth touching mine. Okay, four things. I did what anyone in my situation would have. I made the most of it.

Now, I lick into her mouth, and a moan swells her throat. Soft. Sweet. Like candy and honey and every single pleasurable thing on this planet. The touch of her lips is like a spark to a fuse of dynamite. Lust rips through me. Combined with the relief that nothing happened to her, every barrier I've tried to put up between us collapses.

I allow her to slide down until her feet touch the ground, while maintaining my grip around her waist. Then I dip her over my arm and ravage her mouth. She kisses me right back.

Her curves are plastered to me, her breasts flattened against my side. I pull her even closer. I thrust my thigh between hers, widening my stance so my legs are planted solidly on the ground. For a few seconds, it feels like everything I need is here...with me...in my arms.

Her taste on my palate, her scent in my nostrils, her essence coursing through my veins. This is heaven. This is what I've been searching for. This is what I've missed. This is it. *This. This. This.*

She wraps one leg around me, pushes her hips in closer, and with her dress around her waist, she begins to ride my thigh. The drugging warmth from her core sinks through my pants and into my skin. I'm so hard, my balls feel like they've turned into anchors.

Then she tears her mouth from mine. "Serene, is she—"

"Asleep. I have my phone, which is linked to the baby cam."

"Oh, that's good."

We stare at each other. Her cheeks are flushed, her hair wild around her shoulders. Her lips are kiss-swollen, pupils blown wide. She looks wrecked. Beautiful. *Mine.* She looks as dazed as I feel.

The air is thick with everything we haven't said. My heart's still pounding. My blood's still racing. I'm still reeling. Still adjusting to the reality that she's fine. She. Is. Fine.

"I'm, uh, sorry I kissed you," she whispers.

I'm not.

"Umm... You surprised me." She pulls away from me. I let her go and miss her already.

"I wasn't getting through to you and realized I needed to get your attention, so—" She smooths down her hair, then rubs her hands down her dress. I realize she's barefoot in the grass, and the sight of her pink-tipped nails and her narrow feet is intimate in a way that undoes me. My heartbeat ratchets up. My pulse pounds at my temples, my wrists, even in my fucking balls.

"You succeeded." My voice comes out like my throat is lined with gravel.

"It was the Halloumi cheese. I forgot how quickly it burns, and I was chopping the ingredients for the salad and forgot about it. Didn't realize the fire alarm was this sensitive. Or loud. Speaking of—" She glances in the direction of the garage. "Guess it stopped. Thank God."

My ears are still ringing—not from the alarm, but from the truth. I must find a way to have her in my life. I can't live without her. *Holy fuck*, Arthur's ultimatum provides me the perfect excuse for coercing her to marry me. *If not for me, maybe she'll agree for Serene's sake?* I know, she doesn't trust me yet, and I can't blame her for that, but if I can convince her to marry me, it buys me time to prove to her that she can trust me.

Even as I think that, I know it's wrong to do so—but also, it's not. Because it feels so right. It's why she came back into my life. At just the right time. As a former Marine, I know how much of life is about timing. It's why some people come back from missions and others don't. It's why I met her on the tube the same day Serene came into my life. It's why Arthur gave me that ultimatum, at the time *she* came back into my life. It's providence. It has to be.

"Are you okay?" She peers up at me from under her eyelashes. "You look a little shell-shocked. There was no fire." She waves a hand in the direction of the apartment "As you can see, there's no harm done."

Except to my composure. I rub the back of my neck. "I can't keep both my daughter and you safe if you live so far from the main house. I think you should move in with us."

"What?" She laughs. "You're joking."

Nope. I'm going to find a way to get you to move in with me. I don't say that aloud though. When I stay silent, her expression gentles.

"I'm all right, I promise."

Not yet. But she will be. We will be. Outwardly, I nod.

"Come back home tonight."

"Excuse me?" She blinks.

"Your dinner is burnt. Come over and eat with me."

31

Tyler

"Congratulations, I hear you hired Priscilla as your nanny, and she's lasted — what's it, almost five weeks now?" Brody, my second youngest brother tugs down the shirt sleeve on his left arm. It's to hide the scars I know cover the entire underside. A memento he picked up in the Marines. He's never spoken about what led to it, so we can only speculate as to what might have caused it. Considering he's the silent kind who prefers to limit his interactions to grunts, it's telling that he made the remark.

I grunt in response.

"We've all noticed how much you've been juggling lately — looking after Serene and running a company at the same time — so I'll admit, I didn't expect you to volunteer to host tonight." Connor deals the cards with practiced ease, his fingers moving smoothly through the deck. Two cards to each of us.

Poker night is a ritual Arthur started, and after he got sick, my brothers and I began rotating who hosts. Tonight, we're in the basement of my townhouse. I'm only able to host because Cilla's upstairs with Serene.

Nathan calls, tossing a small stack of chips into the pot. "I figured it might've been awkward, since she was once engaged to Knox. But he's happily married now. And Priscilla doesn't seem to hold a grudge. Plus, she's great with Serene—so I guess it all worked out, huh?"

"Priscilla wasn't strictly engaged to Knox," I growl. "He never bought her an engagement ring. And it was never serious between them.

"It was all a part of Arthur's ploy to get Knox to notice June, anyway." June's his wife now. And yes, they are happily married, and I don't begrudge him his happiness at all. But damn, if it doesn't feel like I'm being stabbed in my chest to be reminded of how I almost lost her.

My brothers exchange a look.

Connor shrugs. "Whatever you say, Bro." He raises, sliding in a bigger stack of chips into the pot.

He's humoring me. I'm about to tell him to fuck off, when he adds, "Guess it's a case of ninth, or is that the ninetieth, time lucky?"

I narrow my gaze on him. "What do you mean?"

"Given the number of nannies you've tried, I'm glad you found Priscilla. We were beginning to despair you'd ever find anyone to help. And boy did you need help." Connor scratches his chin. "You were drowning, ol' chap."

Brody laughs. "You looked like you were one dropkick away from collapsing into a sobbing heap in the corner." Brody fixes me with a stare. "We're glad to have you back in the land of the living."

And it's thanks to Cilla. I survey the cards I've been dealt. Then re-raise. I push forward a neat stack.

"Leave the bugger alone." James—a good friend who served with me in the Marines and is now a Michelin-starred chef—who's joined us for the first time, lounges back with a whiskey glass in hand. "He has a lot on his mind."

I shoot him a frustrated glance. "Thanks for the concern. *Not.*"

James switches his cigar from one end of his mouth to the other and smirks at me.

"He does?" Connor picks up on what James said.

It's been a week since my conversation with Arthur. A week during which Serene seems to be sleeping better at night. Other than one night when she had a nightmare, she's slept through the others. Which means, for the first time in almost a year, I feel wide awake and alert.

I'm sure it's Priscilla's presence in my daughter's life that's led to her feeling more secure. Which, in turn, has led to Serene sleeping better. My daughter seems more at ease, happier, more content. It's clear Cilla is the only person for me.

We had—still have—a connection. But so much has happened since I asked her to leave my penthouse that day. We're both different people now. How can I ask her now without seeming like I'm doing it because it's convenient? If she gets pissed off and resigns from her job as Serene's nanny, then I'll have lost her. If she feels the same way I do, and I ask someone else to marry me just to avoid upsetting her, again I'd lose her.

But if she stays—what then?

I'd be trapped in a loveless marriage, watching the only woman I want take care of my daughter, day after day, just out of reach. It would destroy me.

Arthur's decree has me cornered. I know what I want—*who* I want—but how do I get her to marry me without pushing her away?

Unbidden, my gaze strays to the app open on my phone. It's linked to the cameras trained on Serene's bedroom. I use it to keep an eye on my daughter. Parents do it all the time. And if I end up sneaking peeks at my new nanny while she's in my daughter's room, it's simply because she happens to be in the same space as Serene.

It has nothing to do with how the sight of her gives me as much pleasure as my daughter. It has nothing to do with the ring burning a hole in the pocket of my pants either. *I only need to find the right time to propose to her.* That's not what's making me nervous and jumpy and pissed off at my brothers. That, and the fact that every time one of them talks or asks after Priscilla, I want to tell them to not speak her name. That's how possessive I feel about her.

"Are we referring to the tension between him and Priscilla at her engagement to Knox? Which, by the way, did not go unnoticed," Nathan muses.

"It wasn't a real engagement." I glare at my older brother, only to find him fighting hard to stifle a smile. He's trying to get a rise out of me. Once my brothers got married, they seemed to want the rest of us bachelors settled. For men who complained bitterly about Arthur's machinations, they seemed to move over to his school of thought quickly once they got their Happily Ever Afters.

"Don't you guys have anything else to do besides worry about my personal life?" I glance around the table.

"You admit hiring Priscilla *is* linked to your personal life?" Brody tosses his cards into the pile.

"Of course, hiring her is linked to my personal life. She's taking care of my daughter." I turn on him, only to notice his eyes gleaming. "Wanker," I say mildly.

The fact that my normally reticent brother has joined in on the ribbing tells me they've, indeed, discussed me when I'm not around.

"How is it that we've been granted the pleasure of your company?" I turn on James in a bid to move the spotlight from me. "Thought you were married to your restaurant?"

"I am." James surveys his cards. "But even I need a break...on occasion."

"Anything to do with a certain member of your team?" I can't resist asking.

His features darken. "Don't remind me."

"So, you *did* come here to get away from said sous-chef?" Connor theorizes.

"I'm the boss." James glowers at him. "What I do with my time has nothing to do with my team. I needed some downtime, is all."

"And you chose to spend it with us? I'm so humbled." My voice oozes mock gratitude.

James looks at me, then places an Ace of Spades and Ace of Hearts on the table.

Brody groans.

I chuckle. "You have the luck of the devil, don't you?"

"Not always," James murmurs. There's a look in his eye hinting at shadows from his past. I know, he's referring to a particular mission that went badly for him. He sees the understanding in my eyes, and his own shutter.

He has his secrets. As do I. Neither one of us is going to betray the other about it.

I deal the next hand.

Brody looks at his and groans, then throws his cards face down and folds.

Connor, too, makes a sound of disgust and folds. Nathan does the same.

"You folding, too?" James asks, calm as ever. Man's the coolest customer I've ever met. Whether he's in the control room or out in the field, you'd never guess the pressure he's under. The way he keeps his emotions locked down is almost as good as mine. Almost.

In response, I turn my cards over. It's all four Kings, plus a Five.

"Well, glad to see the Monarchy's thriving," Brody says, deadpan.

James places his cards one-by-one, face-up. Seven, Eight, Nine, Ten and Jack. All hearts.

"Show off," I scowl.

Connor clutches his chest in mock betrayal. "I thought you loved me, man."

Brody reaches for an olive and stares at it. "Since when are we snacking like influencers?"

"Since I found out Tyler survives on processed food, which is unhealthy." Priscilla walks into the room with a couple of platters. One of which is a plate of cut vegetables and that brown stuff—hummus—she insists on plating out with it.

I stifle a groan.

Nathan levels a glance at me which I interpret as asking, *"Since when does nannying stretch to playing hostess?"*

I shrug. In the time she's been here, she's already made changes to my diet—and to Serene's diet—for which I'm grateful, and this included throwing out all the pre-packaged food I had on-hand, saying nobody should be eating those additives.

She's right, but I had enough on my plate—pun intended—with ensuring a relatively healthy diet for Serene. I stopped making any effort when it came to my own diet. So, having her step in and plan my meals is something I gratefully accepted. In retrospect, I could have paid a housekeeper or a chef to do this, but it hadn't occurred to me. Am I taking her generosity for granted by accepting this from her?

I stare back at Nathan, trying to communicate with my eyes that: *This wasn't part of the job description.* But when she offered to cater food for the poker game, I couldn't say no. Another way I've taken advantage of her thoughtfulness?

"You could try the French fries," she hastens to clarify. "Baked, of course."

"*Baked* Fries?" Brody winces.

"You can't even tell the difference." She places them on the table, not noticing Brody shooting me a knowing glance. One which I pretend not to notice.

James samples one of the fries, then looks at her with surprise. "You made these?"

She nods. The light of recognition in her eyes tells me she realizes who he is, but she doesn't make a big deal about one of the most famous chefs in the country sampling her cooking.

"They're good," he says slowly.

Her face brightens.

"It's good to see you, Priscilla." Connor winks at her.

I glare at the mofo, but he continues to stare at her with an entranced look in his eyes. Jealousy stabs at my chest. I squeeze the edge of the table, trying to hold back my anger. Asshole's doing it to provoke a reaction from me, and I'll be damned if I'll give him that satisfaction. I stifle the growl bubbling up.

"It's nice to see you, too, Connor," she says in her sweet voice.

Connor's smile widens. "I'm so pleased you're Serene's nanny. I bet Tyler appreciates the help."

"All credit to Serene. She makes it so easy. She's a wonderful little girl." She begins to gather up the empty beer glasses.

Connor jumps up to help her, but when I glare at him, he slowly sinks back, a smirk on his face. One which turns me hot under my collar.

I should not have agreed to let her bring us food. It's exposing her to the gazes of my brothers and my friend. With the exception of Nathan, they're single.

All three are watching her like she's an angel. Which I admit, she is. And dressed in that simple pink wrap dress and ballet flats, she looks almost virginal. Contrasted with the thick hair that flows down her back and her obvious curves, she exudes an allure which calls to me. It makes me want to pull her into my lap and kiss her, regardless of who's watching. I hadn't realized having my brothers and my friend look at her with interest would make me want to jump up from my seat, push her behind me so she's out of sight and growl, "Mine."

I don't like the idea of her waiting on the others at the table. In fact, I don't want her lowering herself to the role of domestic help by gathering up the used beer glasses. I realize, while I want her to take care of Serene, I don't want her to do it as a nanny, but as something more. I want her to be my wife. *And how selfish is that? Am I thinking of her as the most likely candidate because she's here and available?* No, that's not it. It's because she's the only person I can see myself with. It's been her or no one else, since I met her.

All of these thoughts run through my head, along with anger at myself for sending Priscilla away in the first place. Now, I'm nervous that when I spring my proposal on her, she's going to turn me down. If she does... *She won't. She can't.* I'm going to make it so irresistible that she has to accept it. *But if she doesn't?* Sweat breaks out on my brow. I shove aside the churning in my guts, and when I say, "Leave it," it comes out on a snap.

Priscilla seems taken aback, then manages a smile. "It's no problem. I'm heading back into the kitchen, and—"

"You don't need to do it. I already pay someone else to help with the cleaning, as you're aware." Again, my voice comes out harsher than intended. I curse myself, but the damage is done, for she stiffens. The glass that she grabbed slides out of her grasp. It hits the table, but before it can bounce off, Connor grabs it and rights it.

"Thank you," she says in a low voice.

"You're welcome." He flashes her another smile, this time apologetic—on my behalf—and I want to bury my fist in his face. *Tosser.*

She turns on me. "Thanks for the clarification." She huffs. "I'll keep that in mind for the future." Anger sparks in her eyes, making me feel like a heel. Which, in turn, makes me even more pissed off. *At myself.*

She leaves the glasses where they were, then spins around and walks out, her spine rigid. Her dress stretches across the ample curves of her butt in a way that draws my attention. I look around to find I'm not the only one who's noticed. Again, except for Nathan, who's glaring at me. The other three are watching her exit, and goddamn, that's the last straw.

"Stop looking at her like that," I bite out.

"Like what?" Connor asks in an innocent voice.

"You know what I mean!"

"You calling dibs, Davenport?" James drawls. "Because if you aren't..."

Anger squeezes my rib cage. I know he's yanking my chain, but goddamn, if I can't stop myself from taking it seriously. I throw down my cards and glare around the table. "She's out of bounds, you bastards. If I see any of you looking at her with anything other than respect, I'm going to kick your arse all the way back to whichever hole you climbed out of, you feel me?"

Brody whistles, then slowly nods.

The others, too, seem to realize I'm being very serious, for James jerks his chin. "Message received, mate."

Connor leans back in his seat. "For someone who's sweet on her, you have a funny way of showing it."

"Whaddya mean?" I snap.

"She was doing a nice thing by bringing us food to eat—food, by the way, which smells and tastes delicious." He dips a fry in the mayonnaise—bet its low fat—and pops it into his mouth. He chews and swallows, then stabs his finger at me. "If you're not going after her and apologizing, I'm going to have to assume you don't have the balls."

He's right, of course. I should tell her I'm sorry for behaving like a dickhead. I'll never forgive myself if I've spoiled any chance of her listening to my proposal.

"Fuck." I run my fingers through my hair.

Connor nods. "You did fuck that up, royally."

"Fine. I'll go." I jump up and walk out the room.

I head to the kitchen to find she's not there. Also, the counters have been wiped down. Every surface is gleaming. She didn't have to do that, either.

The cleaner leaves by six p.m., but given there's a kid in the house, I normally end the day with dishes in the sink and half-eaten takeaway cartons—none of which has happened since Priscilla got here. And I haven't thanked her for it. Not once. I kept telling myself I wouldn't take her for granted but, apparently, I have. Without even realizing it.

My blood still boils from how jealous I felt when the other men watched her or spoke to her. I might try to tell myself she's only Serene's nanny, but clearly, I was never going to be able to limit it to that when I've always seen her eventually having a different role in both my life and Serene's. I can blame Arthur for accelerating things, but the truth is, I'm glad he did.

I want this and I can't keep delaying. What if I've fucked things up too badly by allowing my frustration with myself to alienate her? I need to apologize, and I need to convince Cilla to marry me. *Right now.*

Where is she, though? Has she already left for her apartment over the garage? The thought has me racing toward the front door. I pull the door open and see her storming across the driveway.

I grab her coat, which she forgot to take in her hurry, and rush after her, calling out, "Priscilla."

32

Priscilla

I keep my head held high as I rush to my apartment, determined not to slip again. I was only trying to be nice. But instead of being grateful, he seemed pissed off.

Maybe I overstretched my role as Serene's nanny, but I can't seem to help myself. The instinct to feel needed, to feel wanted is something I feel strongly with him. I want to do more for him, to *be* something more for him than just a nanny to Serene, more than his employee. It's a feeling which grows stronger, the more time I spend with him and Serene.

You would think the year I was away from him would have helped dampen my feelings for him, but it didn't. And being this close to him daily, I find myself drawn to him even more. Attracted to him. Desiring him in a way that I shouldn't. He's Serene's father. I am her nanny. I need to get over him, to keep our relationship professional, but I'm failing at it. It still doesn't excuse how he spoke to me in front of the others. My cheeks heat even more.

I understand I may have overstepped my role as a nanny. I only wanted them to have a nice evening. And once Serene was asleep, I had time on my hands. I thought they could do with additional food. I thought I was being thoughtful when I went down with the platters. I thought he'd thank me. Instead, he told me to get lost, that jerkass.

I hear him call my name and increase the speed of my steps. Not that it helps; with his much longer legs, he catches up. "Wear your coat."

"I don't need it."

"You're chilled."

"I'm not," I lie. It's only a short walk to my flat above the garage, but the temperature has dropped enough for goosebumps to snake up my skin.

"Wear. Your. Coat. Cilla."

The command in his voice is enough to stop me in my tracks. But it's the word tacked on at the end which stops me. I turn to face him. "What did you call me?"

"Priscilla?" His forehead furrows.

"You said, Cilla."

"So?"

"You stopped calling me that when you asked me to leave your penthouse."

"Did I?" He seems taken aback. "I never stopped thinking of you as Cilla."

I blink. *That...* I did not expect to hear. "So, why did you stop calling me that?"

I allow him to place my coat about my shoulders. He smooths it down. The goosebumps intensify, not because of the cold, but because I can feel the warmth of his hand through the material.

"When you turned down the role of Serene's nanny at the coffee shop, you looked so pissed off. So angry and upset with me, I thought you wouldn't want me to call you Cilla. That you'd prefer I kept some distance between us. Then, when you agreed to become Serene's nanny, I felt it was best I address you in a more formal manner, to remind me of our professional roles. You were Serene's nanny, and having you take care of her meant some level of sanity came back into my life. Trust me, I didn't want to risk upsetting you and losing that." He chuckles, then rubs at his temple.

The act lends an air of vulnerability to him which stops me in my tracks. I'm pretty sure it wasn't there when I met him the first time, or at the luncheon or even, the time I ran into him at The Fearless Kitten, and he offered me the role of Serene's nanny.

Tyler Davenport, with his six-feet, four-inches of pure muscle, massive shoulders, and chest like a brick wall is, surely, unfazed by anything that comes his way? *Except for a toddler who has him twisted around her little finger.*

"I'm sorry about what I said in there." He cracks his neck. "I was rude to you. And in front of my brothers and James. That is inexcusable."

I blink. His apology throws me enough that I decide not to push for an answer. The very fact that he called me by my nickname tells me how far we've come in the weeks I've been here. That has to be enough, for now. Especially since, in the last few weeks since I've been Serene's nanny, he's kept his distance from me.

He's been polite and helpful in explaining Serene's routine and providing me with everything I need to take care of the little girl's needs. When his second payment came in, I realized, it's already been a month since I've been here.

The money has given me the kind of security I last had when I was a little girl and lived with my family. *Or maybe it's being this close to him that makes me feel safe?* Maybe it's because he owns the roof I live under that I sleep so well at night? My heart does a little flip in my chest.

"Will you forgive me?" His voice softens, and the look in his eyes is one of contrition. "I was very happy to see you walk in. And I didn't like the way Connor looked at you, or how James appreciated your cooking, which made me ask you to leave in such an impolite manner."

A quiver squeezes my chest. "You... You were jealous?" Another shudder grips me, and I pull the jacket closer.

"You're cold." With a hand to my back, he guides me in the direc-

tion of the staircase at the side of the garage leading up to my apartment. It's just a touch, but once again, it feels like he's branded me.
My entire body hums. Electricity crackles at my nerve endings. I'll
never get used to how my body reacts to being near him. I feel
excited, and on edge, and nervous... A bit of everything. All
emotions rolled into a ball of exhilaration which ping-pongs across
my insides. I pull forward so his hand drops away. Then walk up the
stairs and push open the door to my apartment. He walks in behind
me. I shrug off the coat, place it on the coat stand near the door, then
go straight to the kitchen area and put on the kettle.

I take two cups down from the shelf. Mainly so I can keep myself
busy. "You want a cup of tea?"

He shakes his head. "I'm good."

I make a cup for myself and place it on the tiny table.

He takes his seat opposite me. It's not a big space, but with him
in here, everything feels doll-sized. *I* feel doll-sized. I take my seat,
then take a sip, allowing the hot liquid to warm me up from the
inside.

"For the record, I prefer you calling me Cilla," I murmur.

"And *I* prefer calling you Cilla." He flashes me a smile which
lights up his face and makes his eyes gleam. For a few seconds, he
resembles the rake I thought he was when I met him on the tube.
Then, he grows serious. "Arthur gave me an ultimatum yesterday."

"Oh?" The hair on the back of my neck rises. Something in his
tone jangles my nerves. Call it a sixth sense, but instinct tells me I
don't want to hear this.

I glance around the kitchen. "Do you want a biscuit? It's not
home baked. But it's my favorite, Jammie Dodgers. Those are my
weakness and—"

"He wants me to get married."

My heart drops to my feet. My stomach heaves, and I can taste
bile on my tongue. Specks of black spot my vision, and I feel like I'm
going to faint. I look around wildly. I need to run out of here, before
I do something stupid. Like vomit all over him. Or worse, faint like a
character from a regency era romance. *Get control of your emotions.
Now.* I curl my fingers into fists and take a deep breath, then another.

It's not a surprise that Arthur gave him that ultimatum. After all, it *was* Arthur and my brother who came up with the plan for me to marry Knox. Subconsciously, I expected that Tyler might come under the same pressure. But I didn't expect it to be so soon. I manage to bring my attention back to him.

"Arthur...wants you to get married?" I manage to croak.

"It's a condition for me to inherit my portion of the Davenport fortune."

"Oh." My heart boomerangs up to my chest, then past it, to lodge in my throat.

He has to marry to consolidate his inheritance? *Of course, he does.* Marriages are important when you come from money. It's how families like mine traditionally kept control over their wealth.

But why is he telling me this? Is it because he's going to marry someone else? OMG, no! He can't be. I can't stay here and see him with someone else. Which means, I'll have to leave. But I don't want to be away from Serene. I've bonded with the little girl more than any nanny should. I'm aware of that, but I haven't been able to stop myself. So, what am I going to do?

I can't go through losing him again, even though I haven't actually gotten him back—but I was hoping we might get there in time. Omigod, omigod, omigod, I'm going to lose Serene! I'm going to lose my job. And just as things were getting back on track.

Sweat pools in my armpits. My heart races like the flapping wings of a butterfly in my chest. *Deep breaths. Don't hyperventilate.*

"Wh-What"—I swallow—"are you going to do?" My voice is barely above a whisper. I can't seem to take in enough breath.

He taps his finger on the table. "I can't say no to Arthur. I want to make sure Serene gets her legacy."

I nod; I can't speak. I take another sip of my tea to soothe the stinging sensation that's formed in my throat, but it doesn't help. I set down my cup and clutch my fingers together in my lap. I can do this. *Let it hurt. Then let it go.*

"Do you... Do you have someone in mind?" As soon as the words are out, I curse myself. What do I care who he's going to marry? Whoever it is, she'll probably be a spoiled society princess. Someone like I might have turned out to be, had I not chosen not to. Someone who'll be happy to hand over childcare duties to me. That's the best-case scenario because the thought of being separated from Tyler *and* Serene is unimaginable. I want to say something more but can't seem to form the words.

"I do." He looks straight into my eyes. "It's someone I've had on my mind for a while. Someone I have amazing chemistry with. Someone who is gorgeous inside and out. Someone, who not only has the most incredible curves, but also a beautiful soul. Someone who is kind and generous, and also quirky, and never fails to liven up the atmosphere when she walks into a room. Someone I trust. Someone who I know will take good care of Serene."

My heart bounces back into my throat, and if he says one more word, I'm afraid I'll lose it. *So, he does have a woman in his life?* I didn't think he did. I haven't seen any woman coming around, so I just assumed he was single. Given how hands-on he likes to be with Serene, I assumed there was no other woman in his life. But I never asked him. Was I wrong? And he trusts her with Serene? But I've never seen anyone else interacting with Serene. This can't be happening. Is this his way of letting me down gently? Telling me I'm out of a job? I feel like someone is choking me.

"So… You have a g-girlfriend?" I say through lips that feel numb. He certainly played the role of harassed father who had no time for anything or anyone else so well that I believed him. But all along, he's been dating someone else? *That cad.* Anger begins a slow boil in my tummy.

"This woman is…the only other person who plays an important part in my life, other than Serene. In fact, I went ahead and got a ring for her." He pulls a velvet box from his pocket and places it on the table between us.

"B-but I haven't seen anyone else around here…" I say through gritted teeth. The anger boils up, spreading to my extremities. My entire body trembles with suppressed rage while disappointment is like an anchor embedded in my chest.

I look around the space again. Can I make an excuse and get out of here? Too bad, we're in my apartment, otherwise, I'd have left already. And the place is owned by him, so I can't ask him to leave. Oh, my God. This is crazy. I can't sit here and listen to him spout praise for some other woman, can I? As for that...box? I can't bear to look at it. I can't.

"Uh... I... I think I need another cup of tea." Maybe something stronger? But I only have wine. I need...a shot of tequila, or perhaps, vodka? Yes, vodka, neat. But I can't really pour liquor and toss it back in front of the person who is, for all purposes, my employer and who's child I'm responsible for. I settle for: "Actually, I... I'm out of sugar. I need to run out of get some."

I jump up and try to inch away, when he growls, "Sit down." Then, he shakes his head. "Damn, I'm not doing a good job of this." He draws in a deep breath and seems to get himself under control. "Please?" He urges me in a much softer voice.

I sit down. And not only because he said the P-word. That dominance in his tone...does funny things to my insides. I can't refuse him. Even though, this is the last place I want to be.

He pulls the ring from the box and holds it up. The light coming in through the window bounces off the golden-brown gemstone with a silky glow that shifts across the surface. The stone is oval cut and placed in a six-pronged setting, with the band itself made of rose-gold.

"It's beautiful." I'm unable to take my gaze off of it. *It's not mine. It's not for me.* Yet... It's so gorgeous. So special. I feel like it's calling to me.

"It belonged to my grandmother."

He means Arthur's now-dead wife.

"She left behind a piece of jewelry for each of her sons and grandsons to give to their future wives." *And he wants to give it to her.* So, he feels something for her? He must. That's the only reason he'd give her a family heirloom as a ring.

My heart vacates my body, leaving an empty cavity in my chest. My pulse booms in my temples so loudly, I can barely hear myself think. *Which is strange, given I don't have a heart anymore. So how can the blood still be pumping in my body?* How can I still be alive and listening to him go on about another woman? Bloody hell. Where's your self-respect? Get out of here; leave before you say something you're going to regret.

"Can you try it on?" he rumbles.

"What?" I jerk my chin in his direction. "No," I burst out, "I can't do that."

His eyebrows knit. He rolls his shoulders, cracks his neck, then once more, fixes me with his hypnotic heterochromatic gaze, "I want to see how it looks."

What's that got to do with me? My thoughts spiral, clawing at anything that might make sense. This is…some special kind of hell he's putting me through.

If you survive this, imagine what else you're capable of?

Another self-help platitude, which seems particularly apt for this situation. Only, it's easier to read and far more difficult to implement in real life.

"Please." His throat bobs. "I wouldn't ask if it weren't important."

What the— Why does he look as desperate as I feel? Something in his voice—low, rough, full of something close to agony—cuts through the storm in my head. I swing my gaze to his and, oh shoot, that was a mistake.

The plea in those stunning mismatched eyes makes my breath catch. *What's he up to?*

The first slivers of doubt pierce the panic that grips my mind. No, surely not… He doesn't mean to… Nah. *Not possible.*

But the thought sparks, catches, spreads like wildfire. My heart pounds so hard in my chest, I'm sure it's going to crack through my rib cage. I can feel the blood rush in my ears. The world shrinks to him, to this, to now.

When I don't react, he holds out his hand. Not forceful. Not demanding. Just… Steady. Certain.

As if he did a mind-meld, I place my hand in his.

He slips it onto my left ring finger.

33

Tyler

It fits perfectly.

She stares at the ring on her finger like it's going to change into a snake and bite her any moment. The ring catches and scatters light. Golden sparks flash in the depths of the stone. It reminds me of the sparkle in her eyes. It's no coincidence that my grandmother bequeathed this ring to me. Perhaps, she already knew that the woman I'd end up losing my heart to would have eyes resembling the color of autumn leaves kissed by golden sunlight.

"I had it resized for you."

"Resized?" She tries to pull her hand away, but I hold on. She jerks her chin up, and her gaze clashes with mine. "For... For *me?* What do you mean?"

"I mean—" I try to get my thoughts in order. " I need a wife, and Serene needs a mother figure in her life. She loves you already. She trusts you. And she fell for you as soon as she saw you." *Like me.* "And we already know, we have chemistry..."

"Hold on." She pulls her hand from mine again.

This time, I release it.

"Is this… Is this…" She seems to be having trouble forming the words. The anger and hurt I glimpsed in her eyes have faded. In their place is confusion. And disorientation. And a healthy dose of disbelief. "Is this what I think it is?" she sputters.

I nod.

"You mean…this…this is…" She swallows. Her eyes bug out. She opens and shuts her mouth, then shakes her head. "No, it can't be. I'm dreaming."

"You're not. And this *is* a marriage proposal." There. It's finally out in the open.

The color fades from her cheeks, leaving her so pale, I'm worried she's going to faint. Then, her eyes flash. She leans over the table and slaps at my chest. "You… You… Asshole."

Electricity zips out from the point of contact. My heart seizes. My cock lengthens. Her touch is fucking everything. I place my hand over hers and hold it there.

"You saw how much of a shock what you were saying was to me, but you didn't clarify what you meant," she bursts out.

"Let me explain, I—"

"No, you listen to me. Were you so oblivious to my internal agony? You saw how I was stuttering, how I was making a fool of myself, but you didn't change the impression you were giving me."

"You're right." I peer into her eyes. "I realized my words were coming out all wrong. I could tell you thought I was talking about someone else—"

"You bet I was."

"But my emotions were all over the place." I infuse the urgency I feel, the nervousness gripping my insides—yes, I *am* nervous—into my words, hoping the rawness I feel will communicate itself to her. "I can't tell you how much courage it took to force out that proposal. But every time I spoke, my words came out all wrong."

"Ya think?" She tosses her head.

I draw in another breath, urging my pulse to calm down. Opening myself up this completely to another person is the most vulnerable feeling in the world. But she hasn't pulled her hand from mine. And she's still listening to me. So perhaps, I didn't mess this up completely. "I'm sorry I gave you the wrong impression. I was trying my best to correct it, but I only seemed to make it worse. I didn't mean to upset you in any way, Cilla. You have to believe me."

"Hmph." She tips up her chin, but her eyes are clear. And the tension in her features has faded. Thank fuck.

"I am so sorry for making it seem like I was talking about someone else. I only had *you* in mind. I thought, for sure, you'd realize it was *you* I was referring to."

"Well, you thought wrong," she says primly.

But there's a small quirk to her lips. My heart rate slows down. Perhaps, there's hope for me, after all?

I squeeze her fingers one last time before I let go. Then nod toward her cup of tea. "Maybe, have another sip?"

She obliges, taking a sip. Some of the color filters back onto her face.

"So, this *is* a wedding proposal?" Her voice is stronger, but her tone is cautious. It sparks a melting sensation in my chest.

"It is." I look into her eyes. "Will you be my wife, Priscilla Whittington?"

"Wow." Her jaw drops. She stares at me.

For a few seconds, neither of us speaks. We stare at each other. Me, trying to push down any hope that threatens to spring in my chest. And her, with an expression that goes from disbelief to incredulity... To anger. Shit. *I thought I was over the worst.*

"You have a nerve." Her eyes flash golden fire again. "Asking me to be your wife because it's convenient for you. Because I happen to be around, and no doubt, you have a deadline to meet, huh? Couldn't find anyone else to fall in with your plans so, of course, you turn to me."

"It's not like that."

Yes, it is. If I hadn't been here as Serene's nanny, would you still have reached out to me and asked me to marry you?"

It's a question which hadn't crossed my mind, but now that she's asking it, I nod. "Yes."

She frowns, taken aback, then leans back in her seat, her arms crossed over her chest.

"You don't believe me?"

She flattens her lips.

I drag my fingers through my hair. "I don't blame you. Because if I were in your position, I probably wouldn't believe me, either. But it's the truth."

She frowns but still doesn't speak. My heart begins to race in my chest. My words sound hollow, even to me. How do I convince her that I mean them? That she wasn't just a convenient choice; she is my *only* choice. Somewhere, deep in my mind, I hoped that if she stayed on as Serene's nanny, we'd get to know each other better, and perhaps, we could have had a slower, more organic build up—which might still end in something more permanent. Maybe. How can I convince her, when I hadn't let myself believe something like that was possible? When I tried my best to keep things professional between us? I have to try though, right? I lean forward in my seat.

"I'm aware we don't love one another, but it should be clear to you that I respect you."

"That's why you told me off in front of your brothers and James?" As soon as the words are out, she winces. "That's not fair." She looks away. "You've already apologized for it, so I shouldn't be dwelling on it."

"I was a bastard for being short with you that way. Truth be told, Arthur's deadline is weighing heavily on me and, probably, screwing up my judgment. And then, you walked into that room, looking so beautiful. And I wanted to tear out the eyes of everyone there who was seeing you. I wanted to carry you out of there and finish what we started at my penthouse when we first met."

"Oh." Color flushes her cheeks. When she meets my gaze again, her eyes flash, but this time, with something like...lust?

It turns my blood to lava, and my balls to steel. I bat aside my desire, choosing my words carefully. "I felt it was beneath you to be gathering up those empty beer glasses."

Her forehead wrinkles. "I was being hospitable."

"I know. And honestly, there's nothing wrong with what you did.

But I felt… I felt—" It's my turn to look away until my emotions are under control. "I felt, you deserved better. I felt, you deserved to be more than Serene's nanny. I felt… If you'd been doing it as my wife, it would have been fine." I glance back at her. "But you are Serene's nanny, and I worried you were demeaning yourself by clearing the glasses. That you were taking on the role of the cleaning lady."

She blinks. "If I were your wife and clearing away the empty glasses, it would have been fine. But as Serene's nanny, it felt wrong?"

The back of my neck heats. "When you put it that way, it feels illogical, but trust me, there's been nothing logical about having you under my roof and watching you with my daughter, seeing the two of you grow close in the last month."

The skin around her eyes relaxes. "I really am very fond of Serene. There's this connection between us I can't explain."

"She has that effect on people." That tightness in my chest dissolves a fraction. Talking about Serene will do that to me. It's the only time Priscilla and I have actually communicated. We see eye-to-eye when it's anything related to Serene. *We also used to see eye-to-eye when it was us, skin to skin.*

As if she senses where my thoughts have turned to, her pupils dilate. The pulse at the base of her neck speeds up. Those unspoken emotions spike the air between us. "You know, what we have is more than what most marriages are based on."

"What do you mean?"

"We both care for Serene and can offer her the stability she needs. And we know enough of each other to know we're compatible in bed."

Her flush deepens. She licks her lips, and I have no doubt, she's recalling the last time we were in bed together. A groan builds in my throat, and I swallow it away. I have to slide my legs apart to accommodate my raging erection.

I realize now, my trying to keep things professional between us would never have worked out. It's a blessing in disguise that Arthur's deadline forced things into overdrive.

I never would have been happy for things to progress organically between us. My patience would have run out before that. At some point, I'd have taken things into my own hands. Come to think of it, I've already been doing that on a daily basis. But the fact is, not even the possibility of risking upsetting her enough to leave her position as Serene's nanny would have stopped me. Perhaps, my grandfather wasn't entirely wrong in his actions. *Am I giving the old coot credit?*

I shove those thoughts aside, bringing my focus back to her.

"The chemistry between us only built over the past year. Since you came to work for me, I've been aware of you in a way that's intruding into my thoughts and taking over my dreams. There hasn't been a single day I haven't woken up without having dreamt of being inside of you."

"Oh, my God." She squeezes her eyes shut. "I can't believe you said that."

"It's true," I say softly. "I understand it feels inopportune, even crude and opportunistic, that I'm asking you to marry me now, but believe me, I mean it. And to show you how much, there won't be a prenup."

Her eyes fly open. "No prenup?"

"I know it's unheard of, especially when you think about the billions that I stand to inherit if you marry me. It means everything I have is yours. You'll have access to the Davenport fortune. You won't have to worry about paying your rent or debts. Of course, if you want to hold down a job, or even start your own daycare, I won't stop you."

"You'd be okay with me working?" She frowns.

The fact she asked that question reveals she's at least considering the option. I release the breath I wasn't aware I was holding. It's too early to celebrate, though. "Of course, if that's what you want. I'll never stop you from following your heart and doing what you need to do to feel fulfilled."

She swallows. "That's unexpected."

I frown. "It shouldn't be. I'd never do anything that would make you feel insecure or unhappy. I'd never make you feel like I'm taking advantage of you. I'd never stop you from reaching your full potential. Being a single father has taught me how important it also is to maintain perspective. Which means, having some kind of link to the outside world. It was—still is—tough, managing both a kid and a job, but there have been times when the job has also been my sanity, know what I mean? After the unpredictability of dealing with a child, the discipline of a conference call and the petty bottom line-related arguments between team members is almost a relief to defuse."

She half-smiles. "That's very insightful of you. In fact"—she looks at me closely—"since you walked into The Fearless Kitten and offered me this job, I'm often amazed at how self-aware and reflective you've become."

"Having a child can do that to you, huh?"

Her forehead smoothes out. Some of the tension leaves her body.

"What do you say? Everything I have will be half yours. You'll have financial stability. You'll be independently wealthy, without being beholden to anyone."

She leans back in her seat. Her eyes show surprise. Her gaze signals she's digesting everything I've said.

"If money were that important to me, I wouldn't have left home when my father told me he'd disinherit me. Or I might have put my emotions aside and married Knox, which I didn't."

"This is different." I tilt my head.

"How's that?"

"You turned your back on your father's money to prove to yourself you can make it on your own. Which you have now."

"But—" She begins to speak, but I interrupt.

"As Serene's nanny, you make enough to live comfortably. You don't have to prove anything to yourself, on that count."

Her forehead wrinkles, but her expression tells me she's paying close attention to my words.

"As for Knox—you'd never have gone ahead, knowing he had feelings for someone else. Knowing"—I look deeply into her eyes—"you had unfinished business with his brother."

"Unfinished business, huh?" She tips up her chin. "Thought that was done when you didn't reach out to me for almost six months."

"But I did—I admit, it took me time to get my head out of my arse and work out my feelings. But I did reach out to you."

"To ask me to become Serene's nanny. It wasn't to ask me to be your—" She firms her lips.

"Wife?" I supply.

She shakes her head. "That's not what I said."

"I'm saying it now." I walk around the table and go down on one knee in front of her. She looks at me, flabbergasted, her eyes wide with shock.

I take her hand in mine. "Marry me, Cilla. Help me raise Serene. Make the three of us happy by agreeing to be my wife."

34

Priscilla

The answers you seek aren't out there.
They've been whispering from within…
-Cilla's Post-it note

The man of my dreams is on bended knee, asking me to marry him. Everything he's said so far is perfect. If only it'd happened a year ago, when I was a little more naïve. When I believed if I wanted something badly enough, I'd draft a manifestation statement with my self-help books, and the universe would, in time, give it to me. *Which is kinda, sorta, happening now.*

And it's freaking me out. Or rather… I can't really get my head around the fact that he really wants me —*Me!*— to become his wife.

All of his reasons make sense. And it's not like he's making me feel cheap by offering me money in return for marrying him.

He's being so reasonable, so gentlemanly—so logical. *Maybe I simply need more convincing?*

Pulling my hand from his, I rise from the table and walk over to the sink and place my almost empty cup of tea on the counter. Then I turn and lean a hip against it. "You're good at coming up with convincing arguments."

"Have I convinced you yet?" Far from being deterred that I didn't give him a yes, he rises to his feet with an expression of determination on his face.

I lock my fingers together. "I'm not sure."

"What else can I say to help persuade you?"

By rights, he should feel nervous that I might say no. He should be impatient that I haven't decided yet. After all, it's his entire fortune on the line. But he stays calm. Resolute. There's a steely tenacity in those mismatched eyes. It warns me he's going to try everything possible to make me agree to his proposal. And damn him, but I'm so tempted. It really is what I want, on many levels.

I *do* like him. A lot. More than a lot. I'm half in love with him. Have been since I saw him the first time. And even more so, now that he's Serene's father. And then, there's Serene, herself.

I begin to pace, arms locked around my waist. "So, while this is a marriage of convenience, it's also a real marriage?"

He nods. "There's too much of a connection between us for it not to be."

I pause, looking at him. "And once we're married, Arthur will hand over your share of the inheritance?"

He nods again. "It would be *our* inheritance."

Our. Ours. The word sends a pleasant thrill up my spine.

"We'd be husband and wife. Sharing a house. Sharing Serene. You'd share everything I have."

"Including a"—I lick my lips—"bedroom?" What's making me ask this? Do I want him to spell things out about us sharing the marital bed? *Maybe.*

"You already know the answer to that." He takes a step in my direction. The heat in his eyes elicits an answering flurry of delight deep in my belly.

"I'm very attracted to you. And you're attracted to me, too. Once we share a bed, I can promise you, neither of us is going to be doing much sleeping. Not for a long time." He takes a second step. Another. And another. Until he's standing in front of me.

I lean my head back, taking in his proud features. That jut of his cheekbones, which could, likely, cut glass. That mouth of his, which screams sex. The strong column of his throat. The breadth of his shoulders that I itch to touch. The expanse of his chest, which draws me toward him. It makes me want to bury my nose in the skin exposed by the lapels of his shirt and breathe deeply of that drugging scent of his. My thighs tremble. My pussy clenches. I feel myself begin to thaw, and struggle to hold onto the remnants of resistance to his proposal.

"The main issue I have with what you're suggesting is that it sounds so coldhearted."

"Coldhearted?" He frowns.

"Maybe that's the wrong word." I shuffle my feet. "It sounds too calculated. Too carefully thought out. It's not very romantic." I wave my hand in the air.

A small smile quirks his mouth. "Is that what you want? Romance?"

"Every woman wants romance." My gaze flickers to the floor before finding his again. "Not that I'm the kind who wants a big wedding."

"Neither do I," he says with something like relief.

We're talking about the nitty gritty details. *Which implies I'm thinking about this seriously.*

He must realize the same thing, for his shoulders relax. He's a smooth operator, that's for sure. He's addressed my doubts before I can even raise them. I could just say yes, I suppose, but I can't resist testing him one last time.

"There *is* one thing." I tuck a strand of hair behind my ear. "There's someone I met in the past month. Someone I'd like to continue to see, after the wedding."

There isn't anyone. Because I never got over Tyler. He's haunted my dreams. Occupied so much of my waking thoughts. It's annoying and embarrassing that I'm not over him. It also feels so right that he's asking me to marry him. It also feels wrong, because he hasn't yet told me that he loves me. And I feel like a fool for even thinking of the L-word.

My emotions are in such a turmoil, when he snaps, "No," it takes me a moment to understand what he's referring to. Then, I connect it to our previous conversation.

"So, even though ours would be a marriage of convenience, I can't see anyone else?" I stare.

"That's out of the question." His jaw hardens. "That would negate the impact this announcement has on Arthur. Besides, didn't I make it clear enough that this is a real marriage? My proposal was real and this"—he takes my left hand and holds it up—"is a real ring."

His gaze locks on mine—unyielding, furious, and laced with a possessiveness that scorches. Lust simmers beneath it, thick and undeniable, until every nerve in my body hums, and my insides dissolve into liquid heat. Being the focus of that raw emotion—his desire, his hunger, his claim—sends a rush through me so fierce, it steals my breath. The way he looks at me, like he's two seconds from throwing me over his shoulder and making me his, lights up my chest with sparks and turns my blood electric.

I manage to get my hormones under control and tip up my chin. "That would also apply to you."

He rolls his shoulders. "Since Serene came into my life, I haven't had time for women or for love. I've made up my mind that she is my focus. I've dedicated my time to her. Besides, I wasn't interested in being with anyone else but you."

I swallow thickly. "You're saying you haven't been with another woman since—"

"You." He nods. "Of course, I've had to take myself in hand a lot —and jerk off to some very X-rated images of you in my head, to keep myself going."

"Whoa..." *That's hot.* Not only the picture of him holding his dick in his hands, which is strangely erotic. But also, the fact that he hasn't slept with another woman. I hadn't allowed myself to think of it, but had secretly been almost certain he must have had sex with other women in the interim. Because he might be a dad, but he's also so virile, he literally oozes testosterone. And just seeing him would cause women to spontaneously climax. "You really haven't been with anyone else since that...night?"

He shakes his head. His expression is stern, his gaze intense. Every angle in his body is hard and tough and screams that he's deadly serious when he rumbles, "You were it for me. How could I have ever taken anyone else to bed when I'd already tasted how completely sublime it would have been with you?"

Now, that's the kind of romance I was thinking of... The band around my chest dissolves. That last barrier standing between me and saying yes to him vanishes. I want to throw myself at him and climb him like a tree, but something makes me ask, "And love? What about love?"

He hesitates. "That is something I hope will come, eventually."

Just like that, the hopeful part of me deflates a little. Was I really expecting him to come right out and proclaim his love for me? "You did say that I was it for you."

"You are." He nods. "On the few occasions I thought of being with a woman, I couldn't fathom it being anyone else but you."

"But you don't think you love me?" *Why am I belaboring this point?* Clearly, he hasn't sorted out his feelings on that yet. Why is it such a big deal for a man to admit he's in love? Based on everything he's told me today; I can't help but think he's more than halfway there. I mean, the man hasn't slept with anyone else in almost a freakin' year. That's not something that would have been easy for him, right? So, it must mean something.

He shuffles his feet. "Over the last year, I poured all of my energy into Serene. All my emotions are invested in her. In all honesty, I don't think I have anything left over to give to anyone else."

Ah, okay. I force my muscles to unwind, take a deep breath, and will my shoulders to relax. "You realize that loving a child opens your heart to more love, not less? Loving a child increases your capacity to feel emotions. To love."

He considers my statement and nods again. "I believe you. Perhaps, I'm all loved out with what I've had to pour into bringing up Serene?" He looks uncertain, in a way that makes my breath catch, and my heart to stutter, because Tyler being uncertain...is not something I've seen before. Not even when he found Serene in a carrier on his doorstep.

He was pissed off and defensive, maybe, but he still carried that unshakable confidence — the kind that screams former Marine.

This version of Tyler, though? He's tough and wears his dominance like a shield... But there are chinks in the armor. Enough for the tenderness that he holds inside him to show through. He may not yet be in love with me, but I'm going to make sure he will be.

Of course, once again, I seem to be headed for a non-romantic partnership. Only this time, I'm confident my future husband has feelings for me. He simply has to come to terms with them. *And doesn't every woman think she can tame the alpha male and make him fall in love with her? Am I falling into that trap, too?*

I curl my fingers into a fist, feeling the metal of the ring warm against my palm. I look down at the beautiful stone.

"It fits you perfectly," he murmurs.

"I haven't accepted your proposal yet," I warn him. *What are you waiting for? What's stopping you?* Damn if I know.

I try half-heartedly, again, to pull it off.

"Leave it," he orders.

I scowl at him. "So bossy."

"You know that already." He smirks. "And *you* like it."

Our gaze meets, and instantly, I'm so turned on. I'm clutching at straws here. I'm trying to find excuses to turn him down and, honestly, I'm running out of them.

I shake my head to clear it. "Can I have some time to think about this? It's a big decision. One that's going to change my life."

His features fall.

Sure, his arguments were very persuasive, but did he think I'd make such an important decision in the spur-of-the-moment?

Then his expression hardens with purpose.

"I understand. You need to be sure. But don't take too long. The sooner I tell Arthur we're married; the sooner I can secure Serene's inheritance."

He pauses. His gaze sharpens.

"And I don't want to wait, either."

He must mean sexually. He's already said he's not ready for love…yet. But the need in his voice is unmistakable.

Heat rises to my cheeks. My breath catches.

The thought of calling him *my* husband. Of being with him. It sparks something low in my belly, something shaky in my chest.

I swallow. "How long do I have?"

35

Waiting for certainty is just fear in disguise.
-Cilla's Post-it note

"He gave you a week to think things through?" Zoey picks up a bunch of daisies and pays for them before sliding them into her bag.

We're at the Columbia Road flower market, which is open only on Sundays. Tucked away in a corner of the East End behind a row of bustling city cafés, this place is a gem. Florists, vendors, and artists set up shop under twinkling string lights, selling the most stunning flowers. It's one of my favorite corners of the city to come to when I want to think. Something about being surrounded by flowers is so up-lifting.

"Yep." I pick up a peony and smell it. "Flowers improve mental clarity. I read it in *The Power of Presence*. And right now, I can use all the thinking help I can get."

"Whoa, look at the size of that rock." Harper grabs hold of my wrist. Her gaze is trained on the ring I haven't been able to take off.

"It's nothing." I snatch my hand back, and she lets me.

"That's not nothing. It's a massive Tiger's Eye engagement ring,"

"Hmm." Harper shoots me a strange look. "These are great inspiration for the edible flowers I need to bake into this new concept cake I'm planning. Though that's not the only reason I'm here."

"I know." I send her a grateful look. When I sent Zoey an SOS message, she called up her best friends, whom I also know from university. I've kept in touch with all of them, Zoey more than the others. I'm grateful to have them here, though. In the five days since that conversation with Tyler, I've turned into a nervous wreck. Who knew that mulling over whether I should accept a wedding proposal from this hotter-than-Hades man I've never gotten over would be so agonizing?

Grace hands over a one-hundred-pounds note to a flower seller and picks up a bunch of roses.

"Those are gorgeous, honey, but don't you think a hundred quid on a bunch is a tad too much?" Harper murmurs.

"It's worth it." Grace buries her nose in the flowers—a mix of red, pink and yellow, and they are spectacular, I have to admit. But a hundred bucks for the lot? Blimey. I rub at my temple.

It's not cheap living in this city. Not having access to my father's money brought home how challenging it is to pay your bills, despite having a fairly decent job. Maybe Tyler has a point. I may not place that much importance on money, but not having it certainly made me appreciate how much it can cushion the effects of the cost of living.

We continue walking between the flower displays. The air itself is filled with the scent of myriad blooms. I keep drawing it into my lungs. Normally, it would help me calm down, but this time, it's not helping. I sigh and stop in front of a florist. This one specializes in wedding bouquets. It feels like a sign. *No, it's not. Stop reading meaning into random things.* I'm about to move on when Zoey stops next to me.

She glances at a particularly enticing bouquet made of lilies, tulips and eucalyptus. "This is gorgeous, hmm?"

When I don't answer, she shoots me a sideways glance. "You okay?"

I manage a nod, unable to tear my eyes off the wedding bouquet, but also wanting to move on.

"These are gorgeous, right?" The woman selling them smiles. The sign above her pop-up stand says, *The Tilting Tulip.*

"That's an interesting name," I murmur.

"Can't take credit for it. The owner came up with it," she says cheerfully.

"Inspired by Don Quixote?" I hazard a guess.

She laughs. "You're right. We specialize in tulips." She nods at the assortment of flowers in front of her. "Are you looking for wedding bouquets?" She picks up one made with roses, tulips and baby's breath, and holds it out. "It's gorgeous, isn't it?"

I stare at the flowers in fascination.

"Go on, you can hold it. Are you getting married? We specialize in flowers for weddings."

"Umm... What?" I shake my head. "No, I'm not. Uh, thank you, but I have to go."

I spin around and walk off like I've been stung.

"Priscilla, hold on." Zoey catches up. She tucks her arm though mine, "Are you okay? You seem perturbed."

I stay silent.

"Was it the wedding bouquet? Did it remind you of the possible outcome of your deliberation."

When I don't say anything, she takes it as assent.

"I assume, you're no closer to making your decision?"

"I've been reading through my self-help books, trying to get guidance on making this decision. But so far none of the strategies they've suggested have helped." I shake my head, feeling defeated.

"It's understandable." Harper walks over to bracket me from the other side. "This is for the rest of your life, after all." Harper hesitates. "It is, isn't it?"

"Well..." I keep walking. "It *is* a marriage of convenience. This way, he gets to fulfill his grandfather's requirements that he get married, and I get to be in Serene's life. And of course, marrying him means I never have to worry about paying a bill for the rest of my life."

"These Davenports sure do love their marriages of convenience. Why can't one of them keep things simple and come right out and say they love the woman and want to marry her and woo her?" Grace grumbles.

"What do you mean?" I glance her way. "Did his other brothers have similar arrangements with their wives before they got married?"

"Nathan and Skylar, then Quentin and Vivian, not to mention Knox and June, and recently, Princess Aurelia and Ryot. All their marriages started as an 'arrangement.'" She uses air quotes. "We've had a ringside view of their love stories. And they are love stories," Grace concedes. "They are, all of them, sickeningly in love—despite how they started out."

"Hmm..." I stop in front of a florist selling gardenias. I can't stop myself from purchasing a bunch. I slide them into my bag, and we inch forward. "Did all of them also decline to have a prenup before they married their wives?"

Silence descends. I glance around to find them watching me with expressions that vary from curiosity to surprise to downright disbelief.

"Bish, is that what he said? No prenup?" Grace finally asks.

"Umm. Yes? And he kept insisting the marriage is for real. Which I suppose it is. I mean the ring is definitely real, right?" I stare at it again, and sigh.

"Did he put a timeline on this marriage at all?" Zoey tilts her head.

"Nope. By all accounts the proposal is genuine."

"So, the man insists he wants to marry you for keeps. And that there's no prenup?" Grace blinks.

"Yeah, it seems too good to be true, right?"

She searches my face. "Is that what you think? That it all feels too good? You do have feelings for this guy don't you?"

I nod. "But he hasn't said he loves me. Not yet, at least."

"Men." She rolls her eyes. "They wouldn't know love if it bit them in the arse. You know that, right? Not that I'm pushing you to marry him or anything, but by all accounts, it seems to me, he really wants to marry you. I mean, the timing is a little inconvenient, because he needs to marry to inherit, but other than that"—she shrugs—"it seems like he really means what he said."

"Maybe you should flip a coin? It's as good a way to decide as any." Harper offers.

Zoey looks at her in surprise. "I would not have guessed for you to be this...*flippant?*"

"Cute." She snorts. "When I'm faced with a choice, I'm often paralyzed, I find a coin has often helped me make a choice which, in retrospect, has always proved right." She pulls a coin from her purse and holds it out. "Want me to toss?"

I stare at it in fascination. I'm tired of going around in circles. Of having my thoughts loop in on themselves. Of feeling like I'm in stasis. I need to make a choice soon... May as well be by tossing a coin.

"Do it." I nod.

"Heads, you marry him. Tails, you...walk away?"

"Tails, I walk away from his life. And being nanny to Serene," I say slowly.

"Does it have to be all or nothing?" Zoey frowns.

"Of course, she can't stay there if she has feelings for him and the little girl, and then, she has to watch some other woman take her place," Harper bursts out, then reddens. "Sorry, didn't mean to phrase it like that and make you feel like you're caught in a bind."

"It's true, though." I won't be able to stay on and watch him marry someone else. Because marry, he will. He won't risk losing Serene's legacy.

"Here goes." Harper starts to toss the coin, but I grab it from her. "Don't. I know what I have to do."

36

Tyler

"Are you busy?"

I glance up from where I've been engrossed in the latest paper-work related to a takeover the Davenports are planning. I lean back in my seat and beckon her to come inside.

She walks in and comes to a halt behind a chair. She doesn't sit. Instead, she clasps the back of the chair. My gaze is drawn to the ring on her left hand. She hasn't taken it off. Each time I spot her wearing it, my heart feels lighter. As does the tension in my shoulders. I have managed not to remind her to give me her answer over the past five days. Only one more day to go. Tomorrow is the deadline for her to let me know, though I'd prefer not to wait until then. By the look on her face, I'm pretty sure she's come to a conclusion. My muscles seize up. My shoulders turn to stone. Fucking hell, if she says she's not going to marry me... I... I'm not sure how I'll get over it.

I'm not sure I'll ever be able to love her the way she deserves to be, but I also can't let her go so she can marry someone else.

Seeing her with Knox brought home how much I hate that idea. I'm being petty and selfish in keeping her for myself, while unable to put her first because Serene will always be first.

The money, I hope, will help take the sting off my proposition. I can only hope she sees the benefit in what I proposed. And then, there's Serene and their relationship.

She grips the chair with such force, the skin stretches across her knuckles. She looks so tightly wound up, sympathy squeezes my chest.

"I'm sorry I put you in this spot. If it weren't for the fact that this is what's best for Serene, I might have talked myself out of it. But I know this will benefit Serene the most.

She nods. "It's why I'm saying yes."

"You're agreeing to my proposal?"

She tips up her chin. "I'm agreeing to marry you. To be a mother to Serene. But not to any of the money that'd come with being your wife."

I still. Place my fingertips together, slowly. "You don't want access to my money?"

"When I marry you, I will no longer be her nanny. I become a mother to her. And your wife. And you said the marriage is real. And for it to feel real for me, I don't want any money in the equation, at all. Which means, yes, I don't want access to your fortune. You should leave it all to Serene."

Something hot slices through my chest. This woman—she can strike me dumb. Not something that normally happens.

"So, you'll marry me. And you'll take care of Serene. But you don't want my money?"

"I'll be living here under your roof. No doubt, you'll be taking care of all living expenses. I'll ask for a monthly allowance, so I have my independence and am not dependent on you." She names a figure that's a little over what I'm paying her as a nanny. "This is more than enough for me to take care of my spending needs and also, saving. In no time at all, I'll have enough set aside that I won't need to be dependent on anyone else. The vast amounts of money you mentioned?" She lifts a shoulder. "What would I do with that?"

I realize, she's serious. What she's saying is not what I expected at all. I rise up from my chair and walk around to stand next to her. I hold out my hand, and she slips her palm in mine. Overcome by an emotion I can't quite put a name to, I bring her fingers to my mouth and kiss them.

She draws in a sharp breath. "What was that for?"

"You're spectacular." I look into her eyes. "You're the most genuine person I've ever met. I knew there was a reason I couldn't forget you. And it wasn't only because you were the subject of many X-rated dreams."

She flushes and tries to pull her hand from mine, but I hold onto it. "There was something so authentic, so real about you, it hit me right away. It was your heart, your soul, which stood out. And of course, your beauty."

Her lips curve. "Are you saying that I'm beautiful?"

"You know I am. And to be clear, whether you want my money or not, you will have access to everything I own. What's mine is yours, you feel me?"

Her entire face softens. "You're stubborn."

"I am."

"And bossy."

"You bet. You should also know that I think you're ravishing, and irresistible, and curvaceous, and stunning."

"Don't overdo it." She tosses her head. "I mean, I'm aware that you like my figure. You made that clear the first time we met."

I chuckle. Damn, I love that she never puts down her curves. I love how comfortable she is in her own skin.

"Like? I *love* your figure," I growl with vehemence.

"I do, too." She tips up her chin. "Despite the fact that, even the years I was surviving on ramen didn't help me lose them."

"Thank fuck." I twine her fingers with mine. "I should also say thank you!"

There's a question in her eyes.

"For agreeing to marry me. For agreeing to become the mother Serene needs so desperately."

"Papa?" Serene pushes the door open and pads in, dragging her favorite soft toy — Donny the dinosaur — with her.

"Serene, what are you doing out of bed, honey?" Priscilla exclaims.

Serene walks over to stand between us. Letting go of her toy, she holds up her arms.

Priscilla and I look at each other, then together, bend and pick her up. My arm lines up above hers, my skin brushing against hers as we hold the child between us. My chest seizes up. That melting sensation that invaded it when Serene called Priscilla 'Mama' seems to pervade my entire body. If I needed any further proof that marrying her is the right thing to do, here it is.

"Did you have a bad dream?" Priscilla asks her softly.

Serene nods. "It was a tiger." Her breath hitches. "I'm scared."

"Don't be, baby. The tiger's not real," I say in a soothing tone.

Serene's chin trembles. Another tear drop squeezes out from the corner of her eye, following the trail left by the others. My chest hurts something fierce. Between these two, I'm going to turn into an emotional wreck. I reach up to brush away her tear at the same time as Priscilla. Our fingers brush against each other. Sparks zip out from the point of contact. She must feel it too, for her cheeks turn pink. She pulls her arm back, and I clasp Serene to my chest.

The little girl places her head under my chin and sucks on her thumb. She contemplates Priscilla with that seriousness I've known her to have from the day she arrived. I swear, Serene feels everything more deeply than any kid her age does. I personally theorize it has to do with being separated from her birth mother so early in life. I hope the therapist I've consulted will help Serene deal with her trauma. I'm also confident Priscilla's love and care is going to do a world of good for her.

Serene holds out a hand in Priscilla's direction. Priscilla takes it, and Serene urges her closer. Then she yawns hugely. "Can I sleep in your bed today, Papa?"

"She's asleep." Priscilla closes the book she's been reading, then stifles a yawn.

"You're tired," I say from the other side of Serene.

All three of us are in my bed, where Serene insisted on bringing us. Then, she wanted Priscilla to read a specific story to her, over and over again. Until finally, on what felt like the hundredth read—but was only the fifth one—my daughter's eyes finally closed. I rise to my feet and scoop her up in my arms.

Noting Priscilla's worried expression, I reassure her, "Once she's out, it'll be a few hours before she wakes up. But when she does sleep, it's deeply. She won't be disturbed if I carry her to her room." I walk across the hallway and into Serene's room, then place her in her bed. I cover her gently, making sure her star projector night-light is on so the ceiling of her room is speckled with stars. Then, I kiss her forehead. I straighten and turn to find Priscilla watching me from the doorway. She steps back, and I shut the door. She follows me down the hallway, down the stairs, and back to my study.

I pour a drink at the bar for myself and a glass of wine for her. Then, I walk back and hand it to her.

"I shouldn't be—"

"She's asleep. She'll stay asleep for a few hours. And if she does wake up?" I point to the baby monitor I have on my desk.

"Okay. I guess there's no harm in one glass." She takes a sip, then licks a drop from her lips.

It draws my attention to her gorgeous mouth. And damn, if I don't want to kiss her and capture her breath. I force myself to glance away. She's agreed to marry me. I'm not going to screw this up... Not until the papers are signed, and she's mine. I walk around to my desk, pull out a few sheets of paper and place them on the desk.

"This is the paperwork needed to apply for a marriage license."

"Oh." She sets her glass down. The apprehension on her face makes me feel sorry for having disturbed her enjoyment of the wine.

But it's best that we get through this paperwork while she still seems open to the idea of the marriage.

She sinks into the chair and leafs through it, then reaches for a pen. She signs the papers and places her pen down. "Now what?"

I slide the papers into my drawer, then round the desk to her. I hold out my hand, and she places her much smaller one in mine. I urge her to her feet.

When I look into her eyes, she meets my gaze. I only see clarity in hers. That beguiling honesty which appealed to me from the beginning. Then there's her beauty. Her luscious curvy body. Her responsiveness to me — as confirmed by the way her breathing speeds up. I run my thumb over the ring on her finger, and a fierce possessiveness fills me. One I don't question too closely. She's mine. She's going to be my wife. I'm going to tie her to me. I'm going to take care of her. Cherish her. Protect her. I'm going to make love to her. I'm going to fuck her. I'm going to ensure she never lacks for anything. And perhaps, in time, that will compensate for the fact that I might not be able to love her. Perhaps, everything else I offer her will be enough? I bend my knees and peer into her eyes. "You won't regret this."

37

Priscilla

You are enough, exactly as you are.
-Cilla's Post-it note

"I now pronounce you husband and wife." Edward Chase, former priest, officiant at our wedding, and Tyler's half-brother smiles at us. "You may kiss the bride."

We are on the patio in Tyler's backyard. It overlooks the garden which, in turn, looks out on Primrose Hill. Using his considerable clout, Tyler sped up the process and here we are, within forty-eight hours of my having signed that agreement, getting married.

By mutual consent, we decided to keep the wedding low-key. It's us and Serene. Tyler didn't mention it to any of the Davenports. He's going to call Arthur right after, and then the entire clan will find out, he said.

I messaged my friends. No way, could I not inform them. Harper and Grace are traveling and couldn't make it. Zoey is here and agreed to be one of our witnesses.

We asked the gardener to be our other witness, and he was very happy to oblige.

When Tyler and I told Serene we were getting married—and that it meant she could call me Mama—she barely looked up from her toys.

"You already are my mama," she said. Then she went right back to playing.

Tyler and I just stared at each other, a little stunned, a little amused. Serene had already arrived at the conclusion we were still trying to wrap our heads around. To her, we were already a family.

I'm wearing a new dress I picked out from Karma West Sovrano's bridal collection online. It fits like it was made for me. I also ordered the wedding bouquet I came across at Columbia Road flower market from *The Tilting Tulip*. It's owned by Theresa Sutton Sovrano, who's married to one of the Sovrano brothers and related to Karma. Imagine that?

I also ordered a dress for Serene, and a corsage she wears around her wrist. She had a wonderful time spinning around in the dress like little girls love to do, then proceeded to watch the ceremony unfold with a curious look on her face. She was so very well behaved. She clapped when Tyler placed my wedding band on my finger and smiled hugely when I did the same for him. Tyler's is a simple band. Mine is another family heirloom, which fits perfectly with my engagement ring.

Tyler lowers his chin, and I'm lost in his mismatched gaze. I'm drowning in those sparks that flare in his eyes. Then his lips touch mine, and I flutter my eyes shut. Hard lips, firm, authoritative. A tingle spirals down my spine. My thighs clench. My pussy flutters. Then he licks into my lips, and I part them on a sigh. Instantly, he sweeps his tongue in over mine. My pulse rate ramps up. Goosebumps shimmer on my skin. My entire body feels like it's on the verge of catching fire. He wraps a strong arm around my waist and brings me in closer. Heat from his body surrounds me, corrals me in place. All of my senses are focused on his kiss. A syrupy, drugging sensation fills my bloodstream.

When he finally lifts his head, my eyelids feel so heavy I can barely drag them open to meet his gaze. He looks serious, jaw set like stone. The intensity radiating off him is staggering—fierce, focused —and it sends my heartbeat into overdrive. My stomach flips, a flutter of nerves and want.

He opens his mouth, but before he can speak, a voice calls out.

"Did you really think you could get married without us catching wind of it?" We turn in unison to see Brody headed toward us. "Congratulations." He slaps Tyler on the shoulder and shoots me a smile. "I hope the two of you are very happy together."

I hope he comes to love me one day, the way I know I already love him.

"Thank you," I murmur.

"How did you guys find out?" Tyler glares at Brody, then turns on Edward. "You told them?"

We hadn't asked Edward to keep it a secret, strictly speaking.

"Guilty as charged." He tilts his head.

"Thank you for conducting our wedding." I nod in Edward's direction.

"The pleasure was all mine... *Mrs.* Davenport." His smile widens.

Mrs. Davenport? Jeez. That...sounds...strange.

Brody leans in, apparently, to kiss me on my cheek, but Tyler steps between us. "What do you think you're doing?"

"Kissing the bride?"

"Fuck off. She's mine," Tyler growls, just low enough that Serene doesn't hear.

The raw possessiveness in his voice ignites a wicked thrill that coils up my spine.

"Tyler as a jealous bridegroom? Who'd have thought?" Connor pipes up. "And you thought we wouldn't find out about it?" He shakes Tyler's hand, then turns to me. "I hope you know what you're getting yourself into. If this wanker doesn't live up to your expectations, don't forget to call me."

"I won't." I laugh.

"Uncle Connor." Serene tugs on his jacket.

Connor scoops her up. "Hey, princess! You look beautiful."

"Did you bring me a toy?"

"Hmm, let me see." He pretends to search one pocket, then the other, before pulling out a soft toy.

She grabs it from him and clutches it to her chest.

"What do you say?" I touch her cheek.

"Thank you." She smiles shyly at him, then she kisses his cheek.

"You're welcome, Poppet." He laughs.

"That was a beautiful wedding." Zoey steps up and wraps an arm around me.

I hug her. "I'm sorry I didn't give you more notice. It all happened so fast. I barely had time to catch my breath."

"Don't worry about that." She gives me a gentle squeeze. "I'm just so happy for you, babe."

"I'm glad you came," I say, voice catching. Having her here means more than I thought it would.

When Tyler suggested we marry this quickly, I felt nothing but relief. No time to think. No time to fall apart. But it also means I haven't told Toren. Or any of my brothers. I've been avoiding it.

I press my lips together. "I need to call my brother and let him know."

"Want me to come with you?" Tyler asks.

I shake my head. "I'll be fine."

He studies me for a moment, then gives a small nod. I turn and head into the house, making my way to Tyler's office. Once inside, I close the door behind me. My phone is still where I left it, charging. I pick it up and dial Toren's number.

He picks it up on the first ring. "Pri, you okay?"

My brother's voice brings a warmth to my chest. Perhaps, it was a mistake I didn't invite him here? I walk over to the chaise in the office and sink down into it. "I have something to tell you."

There's silence, then his voice comes over the line, "You're getting married?"

I chuckle, not surprised at all. Toren has a sixth sense, which serves him well in business, and otherwise.

"No, actually—" I pause. "I'm already married."

There's silence again. This time, it stretches for a few seconds. When he speaks again, his voice is neutral. "Tell me it's someone I'm going to approve of."

"It's someone you will approve of. In fact, if father were alive, he'd approve of my husband," I mumble.

"Someone father would have approved of?" His voice is surprised. I sense him thinking this through, then he snaps, "It's Tyler Davenport, isn't it?"

My jaw drops. I pull the phone from my ear and stare at the screen. What the—? "How did you guess that?" I place it against my ear again.

"I heard how badly he reacted at the lunch when your engagement to Knox was announced. Then, within weeks, you broke off that proposal. It's not rocket science to piece things together from there."

I don't know whether to be thankful or shocked that my brother is this insightful. I laugh a little. "You're scary, you know that?"

"It's a useful skill to have in my position. And you're right. Father would have been over the moon. I'm not unhappy, either."

"This will help in rebuilding your relationship with Arthur, I assume?"

He hesitates. "It won't hurt it. But that's not the only reason I'm pleased for you. It's a good family to be marrying into."

I wince. Damn. I spent my life rebelling against the rules my father imposed on me, yet I ended up marrying exactly the kind of person he'd have picked.

At my silence, Tor continues, "You don't have to make life more difficult for yourself, Pri. It's okay that you did something the old man would approve of. That *I* approve of. Even prodigals come home someday."

I chuckle. "Thanks, I guess? Though you should know, I did it because I wanted to. I did it for myself."

"Good for you. You are as headstrong as me and the rest of our brothers. I've always supported you living your life your life on your terms. If this also meant finding someone who made you happy *and* who our father would have looked kindly upon, then it can only help our family as a unit." His voice is sincere.

My brother has this loyalty toward the Whittington name that I've often struggled to understand. Maybe it's easier when you're a boy and the oldest son, groomed to take over the family fortune. As for me, I think I'll always hold our father responsible for the accident that killed our mother. I was five then, but I remember Toren breaking the news to me, then holding me while I cried.

With time, I realized, logically, it was not my father's fault... But combined with his distance from me during my growing years, a part of me will always feel my father had a role to play in it.

It's another reason I empathize with Serene so much. No one should grow up without a mother. And if I can fill that gap in Serene's life, it will make me very happy.

"I suppose it doesn't hurt that it would have made our father happy," I finally admit.

I sense him smile. "That's my girl. When am I going to meet you and your new husband?"

"We're headed off on our honeymoon. Maybe after that?"

38

Tyler

"She's exhausted from the excitement." I look over to where the little girl is asleep with her head in Cilla's lap.

We're in my private jet, heading to Bali, where I booked us into a private villa at a resort with kid-friendly activities. It also boasts childcare facilities, though that's, perhaps, me being overly optimistic that my daughter will be open to spending time away from us. Still, it's worth a try if I can get some alone time with my wife.

My wife. I still can't believe I get to call her that.

This gorgeous woman is *my* wife. Mine. And I intend to hold onto her. I intend to make up for the fact that I might never be able to love her the way she deserves by using the physical attraction between us to give her so much pleasure that she won't be able to think of any other man but me.

"Poor little mite." My wife runs her fingers through my daughter's hair. Seeing the two of them together, realizing Serene will never be without the love of a mother, makes my throat feel like it's lined with sandpaper. I reach for the bottle of water tucked into the arm of my seat and take a long pull. Capping it, I put it down, then rise and scoop Serene up in my arms.

"I'm going to put her to bed."

Cilla follows me into the bedroom at the back of the jet. This one boasts a smaller bedroom adjoining the main one. I installed a single cot with guardrails here, and I place Serene in it. She's developing enough body awareness that, soon, she won't need the rails. My kid's growing up fast. I already miss when she was a baby. Not the sleepless nights, but that complete innocence which surrounded her like a halo and which, with every passing month, I find changing to one of childish consciousness. I'm enjoying this phase of her life too, of course, but I realize, now, I was so caught up in simply surviving those early months that I, perhaps, didn't treasure them as much as I should have.

I pull the cover over her, then turn on the camera positioned on her. It's linked to the baby cam app on my phone.

I take my wife's hand, pull her into the next room, and shut the door between us. I make sure to lock it, then turn to her.

"But Serene—" she begins.

I cut her off by placing my mouth on hers. She instantly melts into me. I grip her under her thighs and boost her up. She wraps her legs around my waist, and feeling the heat of her pussy over my crotch sends the blood draining to my groin. I deepen the kiss and absorb the moan swelling her throat. Then, I walk over to the bed and drop her on it. She gasps, bounces once, then stares up at me.

"Will Serene be—"

"She'll be fine. Once she falls asleep, nothing can wake her up for a few hours. And if she does, we'll hear her." I pull out the phone from my pocket, and place it next to the bed, with the screen showing the feed from the camera trained on Serene.

"A few hours?" She swallows.

I turn to face her. "Does that make you nervous?"

"Nervous?" She tosses her head. "Why should that make me nervous?"

"Oh?" I shrug off my jacket and toss it to the floor.

Her gaze widens. "Wh-what are you doing?"

"What does it look like I'm doing, Wife?" I reach behind me and pull off the T-shirt I changed into before we left home.

Her gaze drops to my chest and stays there. "Whoa." She opens her mouth but seems at a loss for more words.

And because I can't stop myself from preening under the weight of her admiration, I flex my chest muscles. Her eyes grow so big, they seem to fill her face. Her features flush. She pushes up on her elbows and follows my fingers as I slide them down my bare chest.

A frown wrinkles her forehead. She stares at the tattoo over my left pec. "This looks different. You didn't have those Roman numerals the last time I saw you."

"It's the day Serene came into my life. The day *you* came into my life."

"Oh." Her expression changes from surprise to gentleness. Her whole demeanor softens. "You didn't have to say that. I know Serene means a lot to you."

"And you," I bend my knees and look into her eyes. "I never say anything I don't mean."

Her lips part. Her throat moves as she swallows.

I reach for my belt. The jangle of the buckle, then the hiss of the zipper as I lower it, fills the temporary silence.

My cock springs free.

She bites down on her lower lip, and fuck me, I want to feel her mouth around my dick. But...not before I feel her warm, wet pussy milking me first.

"You're even bigger than I remember." She clears her throat.

And I'm hornier for you than I was that time.

Again, I'm unable to share that with her because... I'm not sure what it means that I want her even more now. Also, I'm done analyzing my response to her. My balls are so hard, they seem to weigh as much as cannonballs. My dick is so thick with blood, I'm sure I'm going to come any moment. And when she reaches forward and touches the swollen head with her fingers, I can't stop the groan which rips out of me.

"If you do that, I'm not going to last very long."

She peers up at me from under her eyelashes, then wraps her hot, little fingers around my cock. Before I can protest—not that I would —she's leaned in and licked up the column.

A thrill squeezes my lower belly. My thigh muscles turn to stone. "Fucking hell." I slide my fingers into her hair, wanting to stop her. Wanting to guide her so she takes me down her throat. Wanting to... fuck her mouth, but knowing I'd never last. And the first time we're together, I want to be inside of her.

"I need to be inside you," I say through gritted teeth. Sweat beads my forehead. My heart is racing so fast, I'm sure it's going to burst out of my rib cage. This is a moment that I've dreamed of. That I've simulated in my mind so many times, I can't believe I'm actually here with her, and about to make her my wife in every sense of the word.

I gently tug on her hair, so she pulls back.

"You don't want me to blow you?" she asks softly.

F-u-u-c-k, my wife talking dirty to me strikes differently.

"I want to fuck your face more than anything, but first—" I drag my thumb across her mouth. I remember how much the sight of my dick terrified her the first time and caution myself to slow down, but goddamn, all the pent-up desire and lust and need and want from over the last twelve months seems to have broken through the dam I built around them. There's no stopping me now.

"I want to bury myself into that tight little pussy, and stuff my tongue inside your mouth, and when you're about to come, I want to slide my finger into that little knot between your arse-cheeks, so when you go over the edge, it'll be with me filling every fuckable hole in your body. And your mind will be full of me, and your blood will sing with my touch, and every cell in your body will echo with the need to be dominated by me."

A shiver grips her. I step back so her hand falls, then sink to my knees before her. I push her dress up so it's around her waist, then I tear off her panties.

39

Priscilla

"Wha—?" The shock of that primal gesture has my insides twisting. My pussy threatens to melt; my bones feel like they've turned to rubber. And when he sinks between my thighs and throws my legs over his shoulders, I gasp.

He leans in and drags his nose up my slit. Desire is a lit trail of gasoline that punches its way through my bloodstream. My head spins. My pulse rate goes through the roof. My nipples are so hard, and I'm so turned on, I collapse back on the bed. "Oh. My. God."

He begins to lick up my pussy in earnest. I dig my fingers into his hair and hold on. "Ohgod. Ohgod. Ohgod." *Who gave the universe a performance bonus?* It feels like I'm going to shoot out of my skin and toward the stars any moment, that's how incredible what he's doing to me feels.

He stabs his tongue inside my weeping hole, and a trembling seizes me. He continues to eat me out, and it feels so good. So incredible. I've relived the time he did this before, but it's nothing compared to the reality. It feels like he's consuming me. Drawing my very essence inside of him as he sucks on my pussy lips, and when he nips at my clit, my entire body jolts. My spine curves, and I writhe under him as he pins me to the bed with his tongue. Then he pulls back. The cool air flutters over my pussy. I glance down to find him watching me.

"Don't take your eyes off me," he warns. Then he slaps my pussy.

I instantly orgasm. The climax sweeps through me and crashes behind my eyes. I cry out, then slap my hands over my mouth to stop making so much noise. Serene's next door. She's asleep, but I don't want to risk her hearing me. I continue to shudder and shake as I come down from the high. That's when he crawls over me. He circles my wrists, twists my arms over my head, and pins me to the bed. He positions himself at my entrance, then stills. "Should I use a condom?"

He begins to pull back, but I wrap my legs around him. "I'm on birth control."

His eyes blaze. The lust in them reaches out to me and lights a thousand fires in my blood.

"You sure?" he asks in that growly voice of his which makes my insides quiver. He could keep speaking, and I'd probably orgasm from listening to him.

I nod. "Very."

Without another word, he fits his cock against my slit. He feels so big, so daunting, so very gigantic. The thought of him penetrating me with his monster dick sends another shiver up my spine. I should be scared that he could hurt me with that XXXL-sized organ, but given how turned on I am, how every part of my body seems to be on fire, how my pussy seems to have turned into one throbbing mass of need, which in turn reminds me of how empty I am, of how much I yearn to feel him inside of me, how I've dreamed of this moment for months, sends my need, soaring to seismic proportions. Anticipation digs its claws into my belly and slides down my inner thigh.

My nipples tighten, and my breasts begin to hurt. I twitch under him, curve my back, wanting to get closer to him. Wanting to crawl inside him and live there.

As if he understands the urgency in me, he kisses me firmly on my lips. "Shh, it's going to be good, I promise."

He continues, kissing the tip of my nose, each cheek, then back to my mouth where he nips on my lower lip. "I'm going to fuck you now."

His words spark a fuse which sizzles up my spine. Then, I cry out again, for in one smooth move, he impales me.

My entire body jolts. He feels even bigger than I imagined. So thick. So everything. As he presses against my inner walls, I whimper. He presses his forehead into mine and stares into my eyes. Those hypnotic heterochromatic eyes of his hold mine. He seems to be communicating to me without words. Telling me to trust him. Telling me this will only hurt for a minute. Telling me how much he wants me. He cups my face and kisses me softly, so gently. A tremor grips me. My insides relax. The tension in my muscles fades. That's when he slips in further.

A soft moan escapes my lips. He absorbs it. He drags his palm down my neck to wrap his fingers around it. And it should feel weird, but somehow, it calms me down further. "Good girl," he mutters in that low, thick voice, which in turn, ramps up the lust inside me further. Another whimper spills from my lips.

A bead of sweat slides down his temple. His jaw is so hard, a muscle flicks above his cheekbone. The tendons of his throat stand out in relief. His shoulders are fixed, the planes of his chest formed into bricks. He's so strong, so viral. So *mine*.

A tear squeezes out from the corner of my eye.

He stills. "Am I hurting you?"

I shake my head.

"You sure?" His gaze settles on me, then he brushes his lips over mine again, and again, as soft as the flutter of a butterfly's wings. A complete contrast to how hard he is inside me. It turns me on even more.

The gentleness of his kisses has me melting into him further. He releases his hold on my throat, only to cup my breast. He pinches the nipple, and I yelp. My pussy clenches in response. A groan rumbles up his chest. He licks into my mouth, and when I part my lips, he sweeps in. His tongue tangles with mine, then he swipes it over my teeth, against the walls of my mouth, filling it up, mirroring the way his dick pushes against the sides of my pussy.

The kiss seems to go and on, drugging me with his need, filling me with his taste, and when he bites on my lower lip, I shiver. He pulls back and surveys my heated cheeks. "You're so tight, it feels like I'm your first."

Oh, shoot. I glance away, but not before he sees the guilt in my eyes. He inhales sharply, then pinches my chin so I have no choice but to look at him. He studies me, and his forehead furrows. "It's not possible," he says softly.

"It's nothing." I bite the inside of my cheek. "I didn't meet anyone I wanted to sleep with." *Not before you. And not after.*

"All these months—" He shakes his head. "Was it because—"

"—I wasn't waiting for you." What a lie. I absolutely was— subconsciously, at least. But it feels stupid to say that aloud.

His gaze softens. "Honey, I haven't wanted anyone else since I met you, either."

"Oh!" He told me as much when he proposed to me, but somehow, hearing him say this when he's inside me makes it feel even more real.

"Well," I offer, "I'm not a virgin anymore." I smile as if this isn't the most momentous event in my life.

In response, his cock pulses inside of me.

"You should have told me." He slides his palm down my stomach to cup my hip. "I would have been gentler."

"I... I didn't want that."

He looks at me, disbelief evident in his expression.

"Just because I was a virgin doesn't mean I'm innocent. I was simply discerning in who I wanted to sleep with." I jut out my chin. "But I've read enough books and watched enough stuff to know what I think I'll like."

"I know you like being held down," he says in a considering voice, "but that doesn't mean you're ready for the rest of me."

"What?" I gape at him.

"I'm only half in."

Shock steals over me. "O-only... H-half of you?"

As if to illustrate his point, he nudges his hips forward. His cock slides in another inch. I was right when I thought I'd be able to feel him all the way in my throat.

He lowers his head and, once again, kisses me on my mouth. His kiss is even more gentle. "Let me in, baby," he says in a soft, coaxing voice. He slides his fingers between us and rubs my clit. Sensations spiral out from the contact. My stomach trembles. My scalp tingles. I tilt my hips up, and he slips in further. He groans; so do I. He pinches my clit, and it's just painful enough to light up pinpricks of lust through my bloodstream. The pleasure fills in the gaps, and the mix is so heady.

My breathing grows shallow. I tug at his grasp again, and when he releases me, I wrap my arms about his neck and push my breasts up into his chest. "Fuck me, Husband."

40

Tyler

When she calls me that... When her body writhes under me, and her curves beckon me, and her clit throbs under my ministrations, I can't refuse her. I pull back, but instead of fucking into her again, I slide my fingers into her. I weave them in and out of her. Her thighs clench, and her pussy seems to melt further around my digits. She squirms but pushes up, so my fingers sink further into her. And when I twist them, I hit a spot that makes her jerk.

"Oh, my God." She digs her fingers into the sheet on either side of her and gasps loudly.

I pull out my fingers and hold them up. Seeing the blood on them turns my chest into a burning furnace. She really was a virgin. Not that I doubted her word, but seeing the proof is another level. I bring my fingers to my lips and suck on them.

She breathes in sharply. "That's...filthy."

I trail my fingers over her lips, and she flicks out her tongue and licks them.

"Now you're filthy, too." I bring my fingers back to her cunt and begin to ease them in and out of her. Each time I slip them inside; I make sure to brush against that hidden spot deep inside of her.

She shivers, wraps her fingers about my wrist and holds on. I lean in so I can kiss her breast. I suck on her nipple, and she shudders. I give the same treatment to the other, and she moans aloud. I don't let up finger-fucking her. I want her so wet that when I enter her again, there's no pain. The fact that I'm her first makes me want to take care of her. It also makes me want to ensure the experience is so beautiful, she'll remember it forever.

I continue to weave my fingers in and out of her. In and out. All the while, I kiss up her throat, to her stubborn chin, the creamy skin of her cheeks, her gorgeous lips, her nose, her forehead. I rain kisses on her, and she sighs. But her body wriggles under me. I can sense her climax building, for she begins to vibrate. The scent of her grows more intense. It goes straight to my head. Any remaining blood drains to my groin. I grit my teeth, forcing myself to hold back. I need her to come first. I increase the pace of my movements. Pushing my fingers in and out of her again. Then I press the heel of my hand into her clit. I rub with enough friction that her body bows off the bed.

She opens her mouth to scream, but I lean down and close my mouth over hers. I capture the sounds she makes as she twists under me. Her climax crashes through her. She jolts and jerks and finally, slumps, her body twitching. I release her mouth and look into her face. "Open your eyes."

She flickers her heavy eyelids open. The brown of her irises is almost golden. I wrap my fingers around my cock and position it at her cunt. "You ready for me, baby?"

When she nods, I slip inside her. She's so wet, so relaxed, I push in all the way to the hilt.

A groan rumbles up my chest. "Jesus." I slap my hand into the mattress next to her and hold myself there. I allow her to adjust to my size, then slowly begin to move. I pull out, then back in. And again, watching her closely for any sign of distress. Any discomfort.

Sensing my perusal, her lips curve. "That feels good," she says in a husky tone.

"You're so damn sexy, Wife."

Her pupils dilate. She loves me calling her that as much as I cherish her calling me her husband. *Tell her that.* I open my mouth to do so, but the words don't come. Instead, I close my mouth over those pink lips and kiss her deeply.

She melts into me completely, locks her ankles about my waist and pushes up so I slip in even deeper. "You feel incredible," I mutter into her mouth.

"I want you to fuck me, hard." She bites on my lower lip, and my cock twitches inside her.

"You don't know what you're asking for," I say through gritted teeth. "I'm trying to go slow."

"Don't. I'm not made of glass. And I want you. I've waited to be here with you, under you, for so long. I need you, Ty. Please." She peers into my face. "Please, please fuck me like—" She cries out as I slam into her with enough force that the bed shudders.

She gasps and her eyes roll back inside her head. And she feels so good, so perfect. She feels like she was made for me. I continue to pump into her. Each time I sink inside her, I hit that spot that ratchets up her pleasure. It sends shockwaves of sensation up my spine. My groin turns to stone. My muscles throb with need, with a primal drive to possess her.

She arches under me, her hips undulating as she pushes up to meet my every thrust. Each time I push into her, I angle myself so I can brush up against her clit. "Tyler," she huffs.

"Come with me, baby." I dig my knees into the bed for leverage, then thrust inside her. This time, I slide my palm under her to play with her puckered hole.

Her eyes grow wide in surprise, then she opens her mouth, this time, in a soundless scream as she convulses. I kiss her as she falls apart under me.

Then I fuck her through the jolts of aftershock sweeping through her. Seeing the ecstasy on her face sends me over the edge. I release her mouth, only to bite down on the curve where her shoulder meets her neck as I empty myself inside her. She shudders. I hold myself up until her body stills, then I slump into her, making sure to keep most of my weight off.

For a few seconds, I lay there, reveling in the aftermath of our lovemaking. Oh yeah, it's lovemaking, even if I can't bring myself to say it aloud. That went way beyond fucking. It was never going to be fucking with her. Not the first time I brought her to bed in my penthouse. And not now. I raise my head to check she's okay when a cry reaches us through the baby cam.

41

Priscilla

I pry my eyelids open. "Serene—"

"I'll get her. You take a nap."

"But—" I begin to protest, but he kisses me deeply. My already fried brain cells give in to the sweetness, the firmness, that mix of comfort and arousal that is him. It's always been him. *Always. And now I'm here with him.* I loop my arms around him and kiss him back. Tasting that maleness of him, reveling in the strength of his arms as he gathers me close. Feeling small and delicate against that wall-like chest of his. As delicious as licking chocolate ice-cream. As comforting as being wrapped in fallen leaves in autumn. As warm as sunlight on bare skin. Another cry from the baby cam has us pulling apart. We're both breathing heavily.

He eyes me with intention. "We're just getting started."

Then he kisses me again and rolls off before I can react.

He heads into the en suite—and I ogle that perfect arse of his, marveling that this man is my husband. I hear the water running as he washes his hands. He reappears, and again, I can't take my gaze off those powerful thighs of his as he pulls on his pants. Then his T-shirt.

With a last smoldering look at me, he slips into the next room. Over the baby cam, I hear him croon to his little girl. I watch as he picks her up, holding her against his chest as he rocks her. I hear him talking to her gently. I close my eyes, and tiredness pulls me under.

When I awaken, I'm alone. The shift in the plane's sound tells me we've started our descent.

I head into the en suite bathroom—flying on a private jet still blows my mind. It's nothing like commercial travel.

After freshening up, I get dressed and peek into the next room. It's empty.

I step into the aisle and walk toward the front of the plane. Serene is sitting beside Tyler on one of the club-style seats that span the rear cabin. He's focused on his phone. She's playing with a handful of toys in her lap.

The moment she sees me; her whole face lights up. She lifts her arms.

I sit beside her and pull her into a hug.

"Did you sleep well, baby?"

She snuggles into me and pushes her nose into the curve of my neck, the exact place where her father bit me a few hours ago.

I look up to find Tyler watching me with a searing look in his eyes. It's as if he read my mind. I can't stop the blush stealing over my cheeks. His mouth quirks. He takes in his daughter, then me, and his features soften. "You look good together," he murmurs.

"It feels good to hold her, especially now that I—" I hesitate, wondering how to word it."

"Now that you're my wife." He nods. "How do you feel about adopting her?"

"Adopting her?" I still. The thought hadn't occurred to me. But it makes sense. In many ways, I feel like Serene's mother, but adopting her would mean I'd also be so in an official capacity.

As if reading my thoughts he nods. "That way, you'll have legal guardianship over her."

Emotions press at the backs of my eyes, but my chest blooms with something fierce. Something very much like happiness. A certainty. "Yes." I nod. "That feels right."

I rub slow circles over Serene's back. This connection to her I felt from the moment I first met her is something I can't explain. It's like it was coiled under my breast, lying in wait, and sprang to life as soon as I saw her.

Serene wriggles in my grasp. When I let her go, she flops down on the seat between us and begins to play with her soft toys again.

"We're landing." I glance past my husband to where the sea is now visible.

"We are." He reaches over and snaps the seat belt over Serene, who doesn't stop playing. Then he nods at me. "Buckle up, baby."

"Why do you call Mama baby?" Serene says without looking up.

I exchange a look with Tyler.

"It's a term of affection," he finally says.

"It's because you love her." She nods.

"Um... I'm not sure that's what it means," I demur.

I look in his direction to find he's staring at me with a strange expression on his face. He doesn't protest what she said. That gives me hope.

Mind you, it may be that he doesn't protest because he wants us to project a strong, loving relationship to Serene, but I prefer to think it's because he's coming around to the fact that he does love me.

No, he hasn't yet told me so. But there's the way he took care of me when he took my virginity, the way he kissed me, the way he's always been tender toward me... And caring, and putting my comfort first... All of which confirms to me that he feels something for me. He has to. It's why, the first time we made love, felt so special.

Of course, it could be because I'm more than halfway in love with him. He and Serene are everything to me. I can't even remember what my life looked like before them. And I'll always be in her life, which is a comfort. An assurance. I wish he'd give me the same confidence when it comes to him, but there's something stopping him from committing fully, and I'm beginning to wonder what that is.

"Fasten your seat belt." He nods at me.

I do as I'm told. Then, needing comfort, I place my hand on Serene's back.

"Mommy." She abandons her toys and places her head in my lap.

"I'm here, honey." I slide my hand over hers and squeeze, then start when a much bigger, wider, brown palm settles over both of ours.

"I'm here for the both of you. Always," he rumbles.

Sometimes, I think this man can read my mind. Tears prick the backs of my eyes, and I blink them away. I shouldn't be this emotional... But perhaps, the wedding affected me more than I realized. Not to mention, making love to him and feeling a connection that seems like more than he promised. Slowly, it's sinking in what it means to be this man's wife... To share his bed, and his life, and his daughter...but not have him declare his love aloud for me. Perhaps, he never will. I need to face up to that.

"You all right?" he asks in a low voice.

I sense Serene stiffening and force my muscles to relax. *No, he will. I'll convince him.* My daughter is very sensitive to changes in emotions. I've noticed how her gaze always homes in on Tyler in a room... And how she seeks me out constantly when I take her to the park. But while she's happy to spend time with me, she only truly relaxes when both Tyler and I are with her. She, no doubt, notices that my thoughts are in turmoil. I push away all my apprehensions and flash Tyler as genuine a smile as I can muster. "Of course."

He doesn't seem convinced but nods slowly.

I take another deep breath, forcing the tension from my body. Only then, does Serene reach for one of her soft toys and begin to play with it.

I exchange glances with Tyler, and he mouths, *"We'll talk later."*

I nod, then glance past him—toward the deep blue of the Indian Ocean, its edges brushed with white sand. Beyond that, the paddy fields stretch out in rolling green rows. Then the runway comes into view.

"Auntie Summer!" Serene drops my hand and races toward the pink-haired woman who holds out her arms. Serene jumps into them, and Summer laughs up at the little girl. "Hey, Ser, those are some great braids."

"Mama did them for me." Serene kisses her cheek, then wriggles to be let down. Serene bounces toward the little boy with big blue eyes who's been watching her.

"Mama?" Summer mouths silently. A big smile wreathes her face, and she flashes me a thumbs up.

The tension I hadn't been aware of in my shoulders slips out. Guess I was apprehensive about how Tyler's friends would react to Serene calling me Mama. I'm relieved Summer is enthusiastic about it.

"Matty!" Serene hugs Matty.

"Serene." The five—going on fifteen—boy stands stiffly before patting her back. He steps back just as quickly.

"Uncle Sinclair!" Serene throws herself at him. Sinclair lifts her up and tosses her high. She squeals.

By the time Tyler and I reach her, I'm grinning. I glance at Tyler to find his lips are curved in a soft smile.

Remember what I said earlier about Serene only relaxing when she's with me and Tyler? Add Summer and Sinclair, as well as their son, to the list.

Summer flashes me a grin. "I've heard so much about you."

I hold out my hand, but Summer steps forward and hugs me. "It's lovely to meet you."

"You, too." I hug her back. Her *joie de vivre* is infectious.

She squeezes my shoulder. "I'm sorry we weren't there at your wedding, but we'd already booked our villa and were en route to Bali. When we found out Tyler was getting married, we suggested he bring you down here for your honeymoon. This way, we can watch Serene while you newlyweds get a chance to spend time together."

I shoot Tyler a look. He arches a brow, non-committal. "I should have mentioned it to you on the flight, but I was, uh...distracted." His eyes gleam, and his lips kick up in a roguish smile as he puts his arm around my waist and pulls me close.

Summer looks between us, and her already incandescent smile seems to grow even more sparkly. "Oh, you two look so good together."

"Clearly, you got the better end of the deal, Davenport," Sinclair booms.

He's as tall as Tyler, and broad. A couple of gray hairs at his temples give him a distinguished look. As do the lines that radiate from the corners of his eyes. The man's yummy. Dressed in a T-shirt and jeans, he radiates a confidence similar to Tyler's. The two nod at each other.

Something draws my attention from the corner of my eyes. I glance sideways to find a woman staring at Serene. Then, she looks at Tyler, and the color drains from her face. She catches me looking and glares at me.

What the...? I turn to point her out to Tyler, but when I look back, she's gone. Weird. I want to dismiss her as a hotel guest, but something about how she'd seemed so angry with me raises my hackles.

I decide to ask Tyler about the woman later.

Serene grabs Matty's arm. He looks faintly bored but doesn't protest. "Mom, can I show Serene the playroom?"

"There's a playroom?" I arch my eyebrows.

"This resort has childcare facilities, which is why we chose it. It's also very romantic." She looks between us. "Sinclair and I are more than happy to keep Serene overnight whenever you want more privacy."

"Oh, Serene's no bother at all," I protest.

"M-o-m." The boy frowns up at Summer. "Can we go to the playroom?"

"Yes, M-o-m, pl-e-a-s-e." Serene says, imitating Matty while she looks at me with big eyes.

My heart skips a beat, like it always does when she refers to me as her mother. She's been doing it since I arrived at Tyler's doorstep and saw her, but it means so much more to me, now, when I'm going to adopt her. When I'm married to her father.

I bend and kiss her forehead. "Of course, honey. If—" I glance at Tyler, who nods.

"I'm Matthew." The little boy jerks his chin in my direction. "Pleased to meet you." He doesn't hold out a hand though.

"And you, Matthew." I reach out to pat him, but he sidesteps me.

He looks at me. "You don't have to worry; I'll keep Serene with me at all times. I'll see you in an hour, Mom." He nods at Summer. Then walks off spine erect, with Serene holding his hand.

"He can be a little eccentric." Summer chuckles. "Give him time. He'll warm up to you once he gets used to you."

"He has such good manners." I watch the two kids head down the steps at the far side of the reception area and toward a smaller building off to the side. It's brightly painted and looks like exactly the kind of place any kid would want to go.

"You're being polite." Sinclair rubs his neck. "I'm afraid I'm getting a dose of my own medicine. I was a bit of a wanker before Summer came along. I fear little Matty is a chip off the ol' block." He looks both proud and disapproving.

"Is it safe for them to walk around on their own?" I nod in the direction of the kids.

"The entire area is a walled complex, and Matty has a sense of direction that never fails. Plus, he's very responsible. Not to mention, we'll be sitting there." She points to a bar on the other side of a lawn which separates it from the one-story building the kids entered.

"We'll keep an eye on them and bring Serene by soon as they're done playing. I'm sure they'll be joining some activities, and that'll take a few hours. It'll keep them busy until dinner time, at least."

"But—"

"Serene already had her nap. They'll be fine." Tyler pulls me close again. "There's security around this resort. And a very limited number of villas. If there's any place we can relax, it's here."

"Are you sure—" I study him, trying to read his reaction. "I would love to spend time with Serene."

"And I want to spend time with my new wife. *Alone.*"

My face warms. Under his burning gaze, I feel all of my arguments dry up. My brain cells, once again, melt into a mass of quivering jelly; I lose the connection between my brain and my mouth.

"We're in villa number thirteen." He nods in Summer and Sinclair's direction. "See you in a bit."

42

Tyler

"That was rude," my wife whispers as we head in the direction of our villa.

"Sinclair and Summer won't be offended." I twine my fingers with hers, and it feels natural. We step onto the path that winds through the gardens and toward our temporary home for the next week.

"It's wonderful that Serene trusts them so much."

"When I realized I wouldn't be able to manage on my own and that Serene doesn't do well with strangers, Summer and Sinclair stepped in, as did the rest of the Seven."

"The Seven?"

I chuckle. "That's what they call themselves—friends of mine who met in elementary school and went through some significant challenges that bonded them for life. Edward is one of them. They're at the heart of our community in Primrose Hill. It's why I moved there. I now have a support network in place."

Her forehead is furrowed. "A part of me will always wonder why you didn't ask me to take on the role of Serene's nanny the day she arrived on your doorstep. It might have meant that you didn't have to expose her to so many strangers in her short life."

I slow my steps and turn to her. "Meeting you, then Serene, within the same day overwhelmed me. First, this intense attraction to you, which was a surprise. I was falling for someone I just met, which was totally out of character. I knew we had something special. I knew I had feelings for you, even though you were virtually a stranger. I knew the connection I felt for you was powerful. I was trying to accept it, but before I could come to grips with it, we found Serene on my doorstep."

I shift my weight from foot to foot.

"Saying my mind was blown doesn't even come close. It hit me — back-to-back emotional punches. I didn't stand a chance. I was gutted. Spinning." I let out a breath and try to smile, but it comes out crooked.

"One day, I was a playboy with nothing more to worry about than how to make my next million and possibly, some easy sex on an upcoming date. In less than twenty-four hours, I met someone who I knew was significant *and* found out that I was, possibly, a father."

I roll my shoulders.

"My instinct told me that, even though I didn't remember who Serene's mother was, chances were good, the baby was going to be part of my life. I would have to devote myself to being a father. It felt like, in an instant, all the familiar goalposts in my life had collapsed. I felt unmoored. Detached. Incapable of thinking clearly. I needed to do something — anything — to regain a sense of control, some measure of sanity. I couldn't exactly ask the child to leave and —"

"So instead, you asked me to?" She lowers her chin, hurt flickering in her eyes.

"I knew I had to focus on Serene first. And I wanted you to have the kind of attention you deserved, which I couldn't give while I tried to make sense of everything else." I glance off to the side, jaw working. "Even in that confusion, I knew that if you stayed, I would have gladly handed Serene's care over to you and passed up the chance to be a real father to her." I drag my fingers through my hair, trying to organize my thoughts. "And I was afraid the connection between us would turn into a situation where I ended up trapping you."

Her brows draw together. "Trapped? I was a nanny. Helping you take care of her was literally my job. Why would I have felt trapped?"

"Exactly." I nod. "You were already forming an attachment to Serene. If you'd stayed, I would've taken the easy way out and relied on you. I would've used your ability to care for her as a crutch."

She rubs at her temple. "You've lost me. How would that be taking advantage of me if it's something I would've enjoyed doing?"

"Don't you see? I would've off-loaded my responsibility and let you take over without even realizing I was doing it. I wouldn't have used the opportunity to learn how to be a father. I'd have used you—and you wouldn't even have known."

She stares at me, frustration building. "So, this wasn't about me. This was about you worrying you wouldn't be a real father unless you did it all on your own?"

"That's part of it, although you did a much better job of explaining it." I chuckle. "A part of me felt like I'd been given this chance to step up. After leaving the Marines, I was drifting. With Serene, I had the chance to find a purpose. And that stubborn part of me—the Marine in me—believed I had to do it on my own."

She chuckles, not unkindly. "If only you'd realized that no one can take care of a child alone. You need all the help you can get. It's not a cliché when they say it takes a village."

I bark out a laugh. "I know that now. Back then, I was drowning. My thoughts were a mess. Life as I knew it was slipping through my fingers. Part of me wanted more than anything to ask you to stay. But I knew if you did, my attention would be split, and that didn't feel right. You deserved my full focus. So did Serene. I felt torn, and I had to prioritize. It had to be Serene."

"Which I completely understand. Of course you should put your daughter first. But—" She presses her lips together. "You didn't have to cut me off completely."

"You're right. I should have handled it better. But I wasn't in the right headspace. I had a lot going on and couldn't ask you to stay when I wasn't capable of being committed to a relationship with you. And a part of me truly believed I might end up trapping you — tying you to me by making you fall in love with Serene. If I'd kept you around to care for her, and if I continued the relationship, I thought we could have... You might wake up one day and wonder if you were with me for me or, for Serene. You might resent me for springing a ready-made family on you and putting you in the position of being a mother to a child who wasn't yours."

She firms her lips, like she doesn't trust herself to speak.

"I know. I should have talked to you about it, but I was afraid I might subconsciously, try to convince you to stay." I take a step closer, needing her to understand. "I didn't want you to stay and then end up resenting us for taking your freedom. I needed to face this on my own. Prove I could do it. I thought I had to set you free. I needed time to get my head together. Space to figure things out. That's why I asked you to leave."

"Oh, my God, you were thinking like a typical man." She throws up her hands. "You were feeling hemmed in. You panicked and did the easiest thing possible — you pushed me away. You took away my choice, thinking you knew better."

Heat suffuses my neck as I realize, she's right. But I don't look away. "You're right. I wasn't thinking straight, at all."

"You bet your gorgeous tush, you weren't." She snorts.

I allow myself a small smile at that. "Damn, I've missed your spirit. There have been so many times over the past year when I'd find myself in a particularly difficult situation with Serene and wonder what you'd have done. It's what got me through."

She swallows, blinking rapidly, as if overcome by what I've told her.

"Asking you to leave was a knee-jerk reaction. It was the obvious thing to do; so obvious that my instincts warned me not to. But I ignored them." I swallow around the ball of regret in my throat. "I was numb. Closed off. Trying to assert some semblance of control over my situation. Little did I know that I was going into parenthood where the default position is a lack of control."

Her soft brown eyes turn bleak. "It was so hard to walk away. You seemed so cold, so uncaring. It was as if nothing we'd talked about mattered anymore. You just wanted me gone, and I couldn't understand it."

I cup her cheek. My heart expands until I'm sure it's going to burst out of my rib cage. "I'm sorry; I wasn't trying to hurt you. I felt like I was unraveling; I was incapable of explaining my thought process. I needed time. But Cilla, you're the most incredible woman I've ever met. The most gorgeous, beautiful, kind-hearted, sexy-as-fuck woman. I knew when I met you, I was not going to escape unscathed. And maybe that's why I had to send you away that time. The assault of emotions on my senses—between you and my daughter coming into my life the same day—was too much. I see that now."

So, tell her how you feel. Confess your feelings for her.

What am I waiting for? Why do I not feel ready to confront the depths of my longing for her? How right she feels in my arms. In my life. With my daughter.

I shake my head to clear it of the buzzing thoughts. I have her with me—and for a few hours, at least, we're alone, and I'm going to make the most of it. I'm going to show her, with my body, how important she is to me, even if I'm unable to use my words to express my feelings for her yet.

I bend and scoop her up in my arms.

She laughs breathlessly. "Tyler!"

I laugh and quicken my pace, following the path that winds through the gardens until I reach our villa. The pool backs onto a private beach—just like I asked. I tap the contactless wristband the hotel gave us against the reader, then shoulder the door open and step into the cool, quiet air inside.

The living room of the villa is a seamless blend of comfort and nature. Soaring bamboo ceilings and floor-to-ceiling glass doors let in streams of golden sunlight. At the center is a deep, oversized linen sofa, its soft white cushions made for sinking into. A low teakwood coffee table holds a tray of fresh tropical fruit.

Against one wall is a custom-built, wooden bookshelf that holds a mix of books. Nestled beside it is a handwoven, rattan reading chair, draped with a soft cashmere throw, perfect for getting lost in a story during a lazy afternoon. Next to it is a table.

"That reading nook is divine," she exclaims.

Directly in front of the living room, stretching toward the ocean, is the infinity pool. Beyond it is a private beach which can be accessed via a short, wooden staircase. Wrapping around the back and side of the bungalow is a lush tropical garden providing privacy.

"Wow," she breathes.

I walk toward the floor-to-ceiling doors that open onto the pool. Lowering her until her feet hit the floor, I slide the doors open, and the wall between the inside and the outside disappears. The scent of frangipani blossoms drifts in on the warm breeze. The muted sound of waves in the distance adds to the impression of paradise. The polished teakwood floors are cool beneath my feet, while woven jute rugs add a touch of warmth.

"This is gorgeous." She sighs.

I pull her close, and she leans into my chest.

"Thank you for bringing me here."

I kiss the top of her head. "I'm glad you like it. How about a dip in the pool?"

I lean back against the side of the infinity pool. The water is just the right temperature. My wife, on the other hand...is smoking hot in the white bikini I bought for her. I reached out to Karma West Sovrano's team at her atelier. She was one of Europe's most famous designers, until she passed away three and a half years ago.

Of course, there's some mystery surrounding her death because Michael, her husband didn't let anyone see the body. Nor did he hold a funeral. He then whisked away his children to Italy and has since turned recluse. Summer was—and still is—heartbroken. She lost her sister and her sister's children, all at once.

There have been reports in the media that Karma is still alive, but that's probably wishful thinking. All the speculation has added to her mystique and contributes to the label's popularity. Because of my relationship with Summer, my needs were prioritized by the atelier.

I gave them Cilla's measurements, then told them to deliver everything she'd need for our honeymoon. They delivered it to the plane, and it was delivered to our room without Cilla's knowledge. She was shocked when I had her open the trunk—which she was convinced had been mistakenly delivered to the wrong room—and she saw all of the goodies inside. When I saw the bikini, I insisted she wear it, and I have to admit, her curvy figure in that bikini puts my most erotic dreams to shame. It also turns up my need to a fever pitch.

She swims slowly toward me. At the last moment, she changes course and heads toward the edge of the pool a few feet away. She leans back and looks at me from under her spiky lashes. "You're staring" she says in a low voice.

"You're beautiful... And a coward."

"A coward?" She scoffs.

"Come 'ere." I crook my finger at her.

"Oh no." She bites down on her lower lip, and of course, my cock wishes her teeth were digging into a completely different part of my anatomy.

"Like I said. Coward." I tilt my chin up in her direction.

"No, I'm not." She frowns.

"Then come on over." I allow a smirk to curve my lips.

She seems entranced by it, then shakes her head. "No, thank you."

She steps up and out. I watch her squeeze the water from her hair. Her bikini sticks to her body. It's one of those barely-there bikinis: triangles of fabric held up by insubstantial ties. She's a wet dream... Literally.

My dick lengthens, and a pulse springs to life in my balls. Fuck. It's as if my brain has descended to my cock. When I'm with her, I retreat to the most basic of my instincts. I haul myself up onto the ledge of the pool. When I straighten, the water pours from me and splashes to the ground.

She looks at me over her shoulder. Draws her gaze down my chest to where my cock tents my swimming trunks. Her cheeks turn pink, and it's not just from the sun. I stalk toward her...slowly... slowly.

She lifts her gaze to mine, and whatever intent she sees in them has her drawing in a sharp breath. She slowly lowers her arms, and her thick, auburn hair falls in ropy strands down her back.

I stop when I'm less than a foot away from her by the sun lounger. I pick up the bottle of sunscreen and take another step in her direction. She freezes. Her lips quiver. Wearing an almost transparent bikini, she resembles a pagan sacrifice.

My muscles tense. My nostrils quiver as I draw in a breath, the scent of her mixed with that of chlorine from the pool and the sunscreen lotion. Hunger digs its claws into my belly. And it's not for food. *Her. I must have her.*

Something in my stance must make my intentions clear to her, for she straightens and sets off for the villa.

43

Priscilla

He hasn't said a word. He doesn't need to. The tension radiating off him hits me like a blowtorch — raw, searing, impossible to ignore.

The narrowing of his gaze, the way he stalked toward me, everything indicating he's the hunter. And I'm the prey. My stomach bottoms out. Fear pinches my nerve endings. Excitement pumps through my veins My hind brain insists I put distance between me and that large, lethal predator who's eyeing me like I'm his next meal. The woman inside me who wants to hold her own insists I not show any hint of fear.

I deliberately slow my pace, moving forward, very conscious of him watching my every move. I reach the entrance to the villa and dry my feet on the rug. It's meant to be functional, but under his gaze, it turns into a seductive slither of skin against bamboo fibers. A shiver runs up my spine. I purposely raise my arms above my head, stretching and making sure to push my butt out. I'm conscious of his gaze burning into my back. Conscious of the increase in tension radiating from his big body. Suddenly, I'm so hot that when I step over the threshold and under the fan oscillating on the ceiling, I shiver.

I hear his footsteps—measured, deliberate—drawing closer. When they stop, so do I. Something in the silence presses against my spine. I turn.

He's watching me, satisfaction radiating from every inch of him. There's a dangerous gleam in his eyes, and my heart stutters like it's lost its rhythm.

I've done exactly what he wanted. Walked straight into a trap—one set by him.

"Run," he growls in a low voice.

I tremble. I don't understand what he's saying, but my instincts, stretching back to when men and women lived in nature, leaves me in no doubt what he intends. Still, I shake the hair back from my face and scoff, "What do you mean?"

"Run." His lips twist in a smirk. "For when I catch you, baby, I can't promise that I'll be able to stop until I've had you over and over again. Until I've stamped my name in every cell of your body. Until I've kissed every inch of your delectable curves. Until I've tasted every dip and sampled every fold. Until I've violated your every hole."

"That's...very explicit," I say primly. *Is that why I'm so turned on?* My cheeks feel like they're on fire. Every inch of my body is on edge. Ready, primed, and waiting for him. But damn, if I'm going to make this easy for him. That primitive, instinctive part of me urges me to, at least, attempt to escape.

"Nothing compared to how explicit it's going to be when I get my hands on you." He takes another step forward. I notice absently that he's holding a bottle of sunscreen in his hand. He takes another step in my direction. Adrenaline spikes my blood. My pulse rate shoots up. I yelp and skitter back.

He cracks his knuckles, then rolls his neck as he advances on me.

I frown. "You're trying to intimidate me."

He smirks again. "Am I succeeding?"

I glance around, grab one of the folded towels on the table near the door and hurl it at him. With a speed that makes me blink, he snatches it out the air, then tosses it aside.

Of course, he's a former Marine who keeps in shape. His reflexes are far sharper than mine. I spin around, then race deeper into the room. I sense him behind me. My heart leaps into my throat. A giggle rises, but I stifle it. My stomach twists. The thrill of being chased, combined with excitement of trying to evade him, and then the anticipation of what he's going to do when he catches me, laces my blood. I sprint to the far end of the living room. Breath coming in short pants, I turn to find him stalking toward me.

"You can't escape me." When he lunges for me, I bend low and evade him. A triumphant laugh bursts out of me as I put on a burst of speed and run past him. The adrenaline in my blood ramps up as I scoot forward. *Made it!* Then I yell as he grabs me around the waist.

He spins me around, swinging me up and over his shoulder.

"Let me go!" I writhe in his grasp, kicking out with my legs while bringing my fists down on his back.

Then a flash of pain bursts across my senses. "What the hell!" He slapped me across my butt! He follows up with another one across my other butt cheek. Then the first. He alternates between both sides, and I'm so stunned, I forget to react. He's spanking me. *Jey-sus! He's. Spanking. Me.* He reaches the handwoven, rattan reading chair I admired earlier and swings me down, so I'm bent over it.

I'm on my feet with my hair flowing down to block my vision, my arse up in the air.

I try to straighten, but he plants his thick arm at the small of my back, holding me in place.

"What are you doing?" I ask, breathless. I am so turned on. Something about this position that makes me feel helpless and at his mercy—not to mention the fact that I can't see what he's up to next—is strangely arousing. I'm also a little scared of what he's going to do next, and that ramps up my desire further.

In reply, he plants the bottle of sunscreen on the nearby table. The audible thump sounds ominous. Goosebumps pepper my skin. And it's not from the air conditioning. With a single flick of his fingers, he unties my bikini bottoms which fall to the floor. Cool air assails my pussy.

My thighs tremble. Then he plucks at the knots which hold my halter top in place, and suddenly, that's off too. I'm completely naked. And when he kicks my legs apart, I shudder. My desire builds to fever pitch. Moisture trickles down my inner thigh.

Heat covers my back as he leans over me. He pushes my hair aside and peers into my eyes. "Are you okay?" The concern in his expression is combined with naked lust. The vein at his temple stands out in relief. He's holding himself back. Waiting to make sure I'm okay. My heart stutters. My already soaked pussy threatens to turn into a river of need.

I look into his eyes and nod.

"You sure?" His forehead furrows. "If not—"

"I'm good, I promise. Now, can you shut up and do to me whatever you had planned?"

His mismatched eyes flash. Then he laughs. He kisses me hard. "Your wish is my command." He licks into my mouth. "Remember, you asked for it."

Before I can ask him what he means by that, he spits on his fingers. My heart somersaults in my rib cage, and when he fingers the forbidden knot in the cleft between my arse cheeks, my entire body turns to fire. It's a mixture of lust packed with a healthy dose of fear. "Wh-what are you doing?"

"I'm going to take your remaining virgin hole. I'm going to own you, baby. Possess you. I'm going to make you mine."

That's so filthy. And forbidden. And so *everything*. It detonates a line of fire to sizzle through my blood and straight to my core. My pussy contracts, as does my back hole. He must feel it, for a groan tumbles from his lips. "You're so tight, baby. So perfect."

Then he pulls his fingers out and slaps my butt with enough force that I rise up to my toes. I squeal. I can't help it. That was so sudden, and it stings, just enough to cross that threshold into pain which doubles as arousal. Enough for my thighs to clench. And when he rubs his palm across the smarting skin, goosebumps pepper my skin.

"Oh God." I allow my head to hang and grab the cushion placed on the seat of the chair for support. Then, just as suddenly, he snatches up the sunscreen. I hear the crackle of the bottle being squeezed, then something cool trickles down the valley between my butt cheeks.

"Tyler," I gasp.

"It's going to be good, I promise." I hear the whisper of cloth against skin and know he's kicked off his swimming trunks. He slips a finger inside the tender hole between my arse cheeks. It stings a little, but that soon gives way to a sensation that shouldn't feel pleasurable, but oh, it does. He adds a second finger, and when he curls them inside me, my entire body jolts.

"Oh God. Oh God." I squeeze my eyes shut, unable to keep pace with the sensations that crowd my senses. I feel like I'm burning up, every cell in my body filled with combustible material that spreads the flames faster than tinder in a forest fire.

He saws his fingers in and out of me, opening me up. And when he adds a third finger, spreading me wider, I groan. He hits a spot inside of me that pings waves of awareness into hidden corners of my body that I never knew existed. My skin vibrates, and my toes curl.

"Tyler," I cry out, seconds before a climax squeezes my body. I shudder and whimper as I float down. My muscles relax. My arms and legs feel heavy. He pulls his fingers out of me, and I feel empty. I begin to protest, but the next moment, he replaces it with something much bigger. Much blunter.

Some corner of my brain tells me I should be alarmed, but I'm too drugged on pleasure. He grips my hips to hold me in place and thrusts into me.

I moan. He fills me up in a way I didn't think was possible. All of my senses are focused on where we're joined. On where he has me well and truly pinned down with his cock. Then he leans over me, pushing my hair aside to kiss the side of my mouth. "You okay?"

"Mm-hmm." It's all I can do to gather my energy and nod. But it must satisfy him, for he straightens. Another push, and he slips into me further, then again.

"F-u-c-k," I hear him growl. "You feel incredible."

I'm too taken in with the strangeness of the sensations building inside me to answer. He pulls back enough to stay balanced at the rim of my forbidden hole. Then he punches forward and, this time, slips all the way in.

His balls slap against my slit, and a surge detonates deep inside me. My clit throbs. My nipples tighten. My whole body sharpens. Every nerve, every breath, every thought — on fire.

And when he hits that secret spot inside of me, I feel like a rocket ready to go off. The pressure inside me builds, tightens, begins to spill over to my extremities.

Like I want to. The pressure coils tighter, reaching my fingertips, my toes, my soul.

He grabs my breasts, squeezes, pinches — sending tremors through me. Then his fingers slip lower, rubbing over my clit.

It's not just sensation anymore — it's lightning. Every touch ignites me. I moan, breath stuttering. I'm unraveling.

I'm right there. Right at the edge.

Then he leans over me, his voice low, rough, his command anchoring everything that's about to break.

"Come with me."

And I do.

I splinter apart in a perfect storm that claims every part of me.

I'm dimly aware of screaming his name as I tumble over the edge. And then, his groan as he follows me over. Unable to hold myself up, I slump, but he wraps his arm around my chest and holds me up. He pulls out of me and liquid trickles down my thigh. A mix of both of us.

Then, he scoops me up in his arms and kisses my forehead. My eyelids flutter down, and darkness pulls me under.

When I awaken, I'm under the covers. Dim light slants through a crack in the curtains. I stretch, and my muscles protest. I savor the soreness that comes from being well used by my husband. Which, in turn, reminds me of how exactly he delivered on his promise to do very scandalous things to my body. I sit up, wincing when unmentionable parts of my body twinge. Yet, I also feel rejuvenated. Energy courses through my veins. It's like I've stuck my finger into an invisible source of vitality. *More like he stuck his source of vitality into me.*

I chuckle to myself.

"What's so funny?"

"Wha—" I whip my head around to find he's seated in a chair next to the bed. He's wearing a pair of sweats and a T-shirt.

Dusk fills the room with a silvery light, but his face is in darkness. *Did I sleep the evening away?* I must still be recovering from the intensity of what happened between us earlier. The intensity of it. The jet lag. It all must've knocked me out.

"Uh—I was, uh, thinking that—" I shake my head.

"Is that a flush?" He stands and moves toward the bed, settling beside me. His gaze lingers, slow and deliberate. "It *was* a flush." There's a hint of satisfaction in his voice.

His words make me blush deeper. "It's nothing."

"Were you thinking of what we did earlier?" he rumbles.

I nod. "What were you doing sitting in the dark."

"I was watching you sleep."

I tilt my head. "Creepy much?"

"Nothing creepy about watching my wife sleep after I've fucked her properly. Nothing creepy about me marveling that I have you back in my life."

His look is so intense, so needy, my throat closes. I can sense that invisible connection that binds us together and stretches between us as it tightens and grows stronger. He has feelings for me. He has; from the moment he met me. And in time, he will come to express them. I remind myself to be patient. *I need to give him time to recognize his feelings.*

I know this with a certainty that comes from a place deep within. One I don't question.

He cups my cheek and leans in for a long kiss that has me turning into a puddle. When he pulls away and places his forehead against mine, we're both breathing heavily.

"See what you do to me?" He takes my hand and places it over the crotch of his sweatpants.

The throbbing column underneath it makes my mouth water. I crawl into his lap and fit my already weeping core over his swollen shaft. Through the thin layer of fabric separating us, I can feel the heat, the length of him. I wrap my arms around his neck and fit my lips to his. Instantly, he takes control. With his hands on my hips, he fits me even more snugly over that tent in his pants.

44

Tyler

She feels so good in my arms. So perfect. The taste of her lips. The softness of her curves. The scent of her filling my senses and provoking the caveman inside of me—all of it fuses with my heart, thumping a cadence of *mine, mine, mine.*

I squeeze the flare of her butt; she gasps into my mouth. Then, reaching down between us, she pushes down the waistband of my sweatpants.

I rise up enough that she's able to tug the sweats down. My cock springs up. Ready. Thick. Long. The crown bulbous and swollen with need. Precum clings to it. I lift her, positioning her right over my aching shaft. She sinks down, taking me fully inside her. I groan. So does she. Both of us look down at where we're joined, at where we're wedded to each other in flesh.

"That's so hot," I say through gritted teeth.

With my palms on the flare of her hips, I urge her to move, to grind down on me, to move those lush hips in a circular motion that threatens to drive me to the edge faster than I want. She throws her head back, showing off the column of her creamy throat. I run my nose up to the jut of her chin and nip on it. She moans. I press tiny kisses down to one plump breast, marking the circle of her areola with tiny bites, before I suck on her nipple.

She digs her fingers into my hair, pressing me closer. I lick my way to her other breast, laving her nipple. And when I close my teeth around it, her pussy contracts around my cock. I squeeze her butt cheeks, massaging them, urging her to tilt her hips and take me in even deeper. She pants and shudders, the pulse at the base of her neck beating in tandem with the boom of my heartbeat.

How could I have allowed her to walk out of my life? How could I have not seen that she is as much a part of me as I am of her? I lick my way up to the curve of her shoulder and bite her in the same place I did earlier. I need to mark her again. I need to imprint myself in her, on her, inside of her. I need to draw her scent into my body, ingrain the slither of her curves against my skin. I need her—so fucking much.

I close my mouth over hers and thrust up and into her. I absorb her groan, her tiny noises of pleasure as she takes all of me inside her. I piston up and into her, over and over again, until she shudders, and digs her fingers into my shoulders, and her spine curves. Her body jolts, and her pussy chokes my cock. I feel her shatter around me, but don't stop fucking her. I continue to lunge up and into her, until my balls draw up, and I follow her over the edge. When I soften the kiss, she whimpers and slides down to rest her head on my shoulder. I rub circles over her back, rubbing the sweat into her skin. Our skin sticks with the evidence of our exertions. Her belly flutters against mine.

"You're so beautiful, Wife."

"Hmm." She kisses my shoulder. I sense her lips curve. "You're beautiful too. Inside and out."

"Thank you." I kiss the top of her head, then rise to my feet with her in my arms. I carry her into the bathroom, then into the adjoining outdoor shower suite where I put her down.

We're surrounded by tropical plants that afford us privacy. It's like being enclosed in your own private forest. I enjoy the luxuries of life; have never apologized for that. And my stint in the Royal Marines made me appreciate them even more.

When Serene came into my life, I was grateful I could use the resources at my disposal to track down her past. So, I have answers for her when she asks. So, I can give her the best care and therapy and ensure she grows up into a happy adult. I'm even more grateful I can share these luxuries with my wife.

A butterfly flutters over a flower nearby. A bird, which I can't identify but whose plumage proclaims it to be an exotic species, darts from one branch of a tree to the other. With the sunlight fading, hidden lights are turned on, illuminating the scene in an ethereal glow.

"It's so beautiful," she breathes.

"It is," I murmur.

She looks up at me, and blushes. I kiss her softly, then pull her close, and bend her over my arm. This need, to brand her in a way that ensures every male who comes within a foot of her knows she's taken tightens my chest. I need…to rub myself into her, to proclaim to the elements that she belongs to me. I follow an instinct that comes from somewhere inside and deepen the kiss.

When I pull back, and straighten, she stares down between us as if not quite understanding the trickle of liquid making its way down her thigh, her calf, and to the floor.

"You—" She shakes her head. "Did you pee on me?"

"I did."

"That's…just filthy."

I nod.

"And obscene."

I tilt my head.

"And indecent."

I chuckle.

"And so, so, primitive." Her pupils dilate though, telling me she isn't as put off as she's trying to come across.

"It's me." *It was the only way I could show you what I'm feeling without putting it into words.*

She seems to sense my unspoken emotions; she leans up on tiptoe and raises her chin. "I should feel disgusted, but I'm not. I should feel revulsion; instead, it feels like—" She swallows. "It feels like this binds me to you in a way that's unshakeable."

I turn on the shower. Then grab her under her butt and pick her up. She locks her legs around me.

I kiss her again, and don't stop kissing her, not even when I step with her into the stream of water.

The water flows over us, drenching us, making her hair stick to her forehead. I nudge it aside with my nose, rain kisses on her eyelids, her nose, her cheek, her sweet mouth.

"Are you sore?" I whisper against her mouth.

She shakes her head.

"Are you sure? I can wait if—"

She reaches between us and positions my cock against her slit. A growl boils up my throat.

"I'm sure." She bites down on my lower lip.

It's all the urging I need. I position myself at her opening and, in one smooth thrust, I enter her.

She cries out, and damn, that noise is the rhythm of my soul. The soundtrack to my life. I hold her in place, not moving. Giving her time to adjust to my size. And when she arches back, I bend and take one nipple in my mouth. I suck on it, and she moans. Her pussy clenches around my cock. I still don't move. I lick her nipple, then move to the other, bite it, and treat it similarly. She begins to pant. Her nipples are almost as sensitive as her pussy. It makes me ravenous. It makes me want to bite her, and kiss her, and not let go of her until I've wrenched every possible drop of pleasure from her body. It makes me want to crawl inside of her and stay there forever.

I lick the stream of water flowing down her throat. Draw in the scent of wet woman which is so uniquely hers. Then I kiss her again and, when she parts her lips, slip my tongue in between them. I slide my tongue over hers. She whimpers. Her thigh muscles contract, and her pussy flutters. She digs her fingers into my hair and tilts her hips up, so I slip in even deeper. I groan into her mouth. Then, unable to hold back, I begin to fuck her.

45

Priscilla

Wet inside and out. The slide of my fingers through his hair. The sound of skin slapping against skin. The sound of our fucking. Our moans. His grunts as he tunnels into me, trying to get in so deep, it feels like he's blasting through any barriers I may have thrown up against the world, burrowing his way under my skin. He's occupying every part of me. Imprinting himself into my cells, until everything in me is tuned into him. Until I know I belong to him. Something I knew from the moment I met him.

And now... It feels fated. It feels real. It feels so right. And when he pulls out and lunges up and into me and hits my G-spot, I shatter. The noises which emerge from my throat feel more animalistic than human. And so raw. And then, he follows me and, with a rough groan, empties himself inside me. My body shudders with after-shocks, as does his.

His cock pulses inside me, reminding me how thoroughly he's

ravaged me. He reaches out and flicks off the shower, and the sound of water cuts out.

I slowly raise my head and look into his eyes. "Wow. That was—" I shake my head. "Something."

A pleased smirk plays around his lips. "Yeah?"

I resist the urge to roll my eyes. There's a reason this man's ego is bigger than any room he walks into. And after that orgasm—correction, multiple orgasms over the past few hours—I feel more than kindly disposed toward him. "Yeah, and you know it."

The skin around his eyes relaxes. The look in his eyes is tender, protective. It's like how he regards Serene—but there's something else layered beneath it. Possessiveness. Hunger, held in check. As if I'm his, and he knows it. And the way that makes me feel... It's too much. Like I matter in a way no one else ever has.

I lean in and kiss him hard. "Thanks."

"For what?"

"Everything. For bringing me here. For letting me be part of Serene's life. For allowing me back into both of your lives."

His expression grows serious. "There was never anyone other than you who could have played this role in her life. I was wrong"—his throat moves as he swallows—"wrong to push you away."

Something inside me settles at his apology. He hasn't said those three words... But this makes up for it in a big way.

He kisses me hard, and soon, we are panting. I feel him thicken inside me, and when we break apart, I stare at him. "Again? So soon?"

"Mama!"

Serene darts toward us, all windblown hair and sunshine, and launches herself into my arms. I catch her with a soft grunt—she's heavier than I remember. Denser. Like childhood is slowly giving way to something else. Something taller, bolder, more her. She's growing, in front of my eyes. And I get to witness all of it.

The ache in my chest is fierce and golden.

"Hey, honey. Did you have fun?" I press a kiss to her cheek, breathing in the warmth of her.

She nods, breathless. "I played with Matty. Pirates and Cowgirls. I beat him."

"You did?" I look past her to where Matty stands, flanked by his parents, arms folded across his chest like he's thoroughly unimpressed. But there's a softness tucked in the corners of his eyes that gives him away.

"She was better than me." His tone is matter of fact.

Sinclair ruffles his son's hair. "Proud of you, Son. Takes a man to give credit where it's due."

Beside me, Tyler lifts his brows. "My own daughter forgets I exist."

I turn to him quickly. "Oh, no. Serene would never—she's just still finding her footing with me in the picture, and—"

I take in the teasing glint in his eyes and relax. *Love isn't about losing yourself in someone else; it's about discovering the parts of you that were always meant to shine.*

I'm not sure which self-help book I read that in, but it strikes a chord. This man seems to bring out the best parts of me, with very little effort.

Then, Serene backs me up by taking a flying leap into his arms. It's how she landed in mine that day when I turned up at Tyler's doorstep. And my, how things have changed since then. I shake my head. If I hadn't lived through it and found myself here, married to Tyler and on my honeymoon, I wouldn't have believed it.

Serene hugs her father and kisses his cheek. "Missed you, Papa."

"Missed you too, honey."

She looks at him with those big melting eyes. I can see Tyler's entire body relax as he smiles at her. "Can I stay the night with Matty and his parents?"

Tyler turns to me, a *what-do-you-think* expression on his face.

The fact that he consults me when it's something to do with Serene when, really, he could have decided for both of us, turns my pathetic heart to Jell-O. I feel a familiar ball of emotion in my throat and swallow it down.

"Oh no, honey" — I touch her cheek — "we can't be bothering Matty's parents like that."

"But you're newlyweds; you need alone time," Matty says in that grown-up voice which should sound incongruous but coming from him — and despite my suspicion that he's simply repeating what he heard his parents say — it doesn't seem wrong at all.

Tyler's expression turns almost pleading. The weight of his attention sends a flicker of heat low in my belly. I look away and shake my head at Matty. "We can't impose on your parents — "

"Yes, you can." Summer flashes us her trademark, sunny smile, and bounces toward us with a spring in her step. "And Matty's right. You guys need, at least, one night on your own. And we enjoy having Serene with us." She holds out her arms, and Serene goes to her right away.

"Are you sure?" I look from Serene's smiling face to Summer's. Serene definitely is very comfortable with them.

"Absolutely."

Serene wriggles to be let down. Summer obliges. As soon as her feet touch the ground, Matty walks over and takes her hand in his. "Do you want to play football?"

She makes a face. "I'm a girl."

"So? Girls play footie too." Matty scowls.

"Oh." Serene thinks about it, then nods. "Okay, but you'll have to teach me."

Matty leads her to Sinclair. "Dad, will you set out the practice cones for us?"

"Yes, but tomorrow."

"But D-a-d," Matty begins to protest, but Sinclair shakes his head.

"It's dinnertime. You two need to eat and then have your baths."

"Eww." Matty makes a face and, suddenly, he looks like the five-year-old boy he is.

"And once you're both tucked into your beds, I'll tell you the new story I made up."

"I prefer to listen to my audiobook." Matty sniffs.

Sinclair looks at Summer with a *"can you believe this boy?"* look on his face.

Summer laughs. "Better go rescue my husband before our five-year-old gets the better of him. See you two tomorrow, post brunch."

The four of them troop off in the direction of the restaurant.

"That was unexpected." I turn to Tyler. His expression tells me he's not surprised.

"You planned this, didn't you?" I ask with sudden insight.

"Did I?" He smirks.

"Why do I bother asking?"

He scoops me up in his arms. I flush, glancing around to see if anyone's watching us, but there are no guests in the lobby, and the receptionist is looking at her computer screen.

"What are you doing?" I hiss.

He heads to the steps leading down from the reception area and toward the path that takes us to our villa.

"Taking my wife back to our room so I can make love to her again."

46

Tyler

I watch her as she sleeps.

We came back to our villa, and I made love to her—this time, taking her from behind. We napped. I ordered dinner, and we ate on the patio overlooking the pool. Then she climbed into my lap, pulled down my sweatpants, and demanded I fuck her. I told her it doesn't work that way. That I set the pace. She pouted prettily, but didn't demur when I pushed her onto the table and proceeded to eat her out until she came. The taste of her pussy and the sweetness of her cum were the best dessert I ever had. Then I fucked her right there, ensuring she came again before pouring myself inside her.

Her eyelids were closing, fatigue pulling her down, when I carried her inside and put her to bed. Unable to sleep myself, I stretched out next to her and settled for watching her. Next to watching my daughter sleep, watching my wife is my new favorite pastime. Those long, thick eyelashes of hers flutter as her eyeballs move behind her closed eyelids. Then, she settles down again. Her breathing grows deeper. Her chest rises and falls. I pull the cover down so I can watch her plump breasts. Yes, I'm gawking. And perhaps, this is stalker-like behavior, but surely, I'm allowed?

We're legally married, and I'm in love with her— I pause. It still feels foreign to say that to myself. I'm still getting used to these feelings crowding my mind and my chest every time I think of her. I'm still reeling from how right it feels to have her in my life. How it feels so natural to have her by my side, sharing the burden of parenthood. She's my partner. My other half. My beautiful wife.

As if she feels my scrutiny, she turns toward me, then opens her eyelids. For a few seconds, she stares at me, her expression filling with warmth. Then she drags her gaze down my naked chest, and lust steals into her eyes. She places her palm on my abs and drags it toward my waistband. I place my hand on hers and stop her.

"You must be more than sore."

She smiles. "I still want you."

"You need to recover."

"Hmm." She pretends to think. "I could still deep throat you."

For a second, I'm taken aback, then I bark out a laugh. "Have I created a sex monster?"

"Not my fault you're so good at it, Mr. Davenport."

"Not my fault that your pussy is so delectable I want to live between your legs, Mrs. Davenport."

Her cheeks flush. So fucking adorable. I lean in and kiss her deeply. My cock instantly thickens. Sparks of lust ignite in my blood. I'll never not be turned on by her. I release her hand, and she slides it under the waistband of my sweats and then around my dick. I hiss into our kiss. And when she squeezes me from base to crown, those same sparks turn into flames. She climbs between my legs, and without taking her gaze off of me, she slides down and closes her mouth around my cock.

"Fuck." I slide my fingers into her hair, not to direct her as much as support her, as she begins to lick up my shaft. Then, she curls her tongue around the rim of my crown, and it's such an erotic sight. It's so very titillating, so seductive, all my attention coalesces onto my cock.

True to her word, she pushes up on her knees and ensures the angle is such that she takes me down her throat. I wrap my fingers around her throat and feel my cock stretch the inner walls. Seeing her mouth stretched around the width of my shaft, spit running down her chin, tears squeezing out from the sides of her eyes, is the most lascivious sight I've ever seen. She swallows, and the pressure at the base of my spine spikes. And when she gags, it feels like she's sucking my soul through my cock.

"You're the most beautiful woman in the world," I hold the hair back from her face with one hand. The other, I slide down to squeeze her nipple. Then I bring up one knee between her thighs and grind up into her clit.

Her gaze widens, her breathing growing choppy. The pulse at the base of her throat beats rapidly. I know she's close, as am I. I'm not leaving her behind. I continue to rub her clit, tweak her nipple, and when she bites down on my cock, the pain lends an edge to the pleasure which shoots me over the edge. "Come with me." I pour my cum down her throat.

With a muffled moan, she shudders and jolts and digs her fingers into my thigh as she shatters. I pull out of her, bring her up, and kiss her, tasting myself in her mouth. It's symbolic of our joining. A mix of me and her. And it's mind-blowing. I soften the kiss, frame her face, and simply look.

"You're staring." Her flush deepens.

"Can't I look at my wife? And after that blow job—" I laugh. "I don't think I'll ever be the same again."

Her smile widens. "If that's all it takes to reduce the big mean CEO and former Marine into putty, then I'll have to put a blow job on the schedule more often."

I slide my fingers around the nape of her neck. "Ah, but it's a schedule that'll have to be dictated by me, baby."

She pouts. "Does it always have to be with you in control?"

"When it comes to sex, yes."

"That's arrogant."

I stare at her.

"And very dominant of you."

"Is that a problem?"

She holds my gaze, then slowly shakes her head. "Actually, it's rather hot."

"It's my turn to return the favor." I tap my chest.

She stares, then shakes her head. "I don't think so."

"You don't want me to eat your pussy?"

"I do...but—" She looks away.

"But what?"

"Uh, I might be a bit too heavy for you?"

I stare at her. "Too heavy. For *me?*"

She finally turns her gaze on me. "I'm proud of my curves. They suit me." She tips up her chin. "And it's not like I have a body positivity issue but...I'm not exactly made for, uh... What you're suggesting."

"How dare you insult my wife?"

A big smile blooms on her face. And that makes me happy.

"In case you haven't noticed, I'm strong enough to handle you. Besides, you are perfect. I love the flare of your figure. And the handfuls I can take of your thighs when I spread them. And to be able to squeeze your hips when I dive into you from behind, and—"

"Stop." Her cheeks turn pink.

In response, I grip her hips and coax her up, until she's positioned over my face. Her juicy pussy is close enough that when a fat drop of her cum slides down her inner thigh, I lick it up.

She shivers and tries to pull away. I squeeze her hips and hold her in place, then drag my whiskered jaw up her pussy lips.

She cries out. Her thigh muscles tremble and, were it not for my hold on her, she'd have fallen. I support her weight, and stare at her core.

"Oh, my God, you're embarrassing me."

"You should be proud of your beautiful cunt." I lick up the cleavage between her pussy lips, and she whimpers. Her sounds of pleasure spark an inferno in my veins. I slide my tongue inside her slit, reveling in her sweetness. And when I close my lips around her swollen nub, she moans. Her entire body shudders. She grips my hair and tugs on it. The pinpricks of hurt traveling down my spine turn my pulse into a drumbeat of pleasure. I lick and suck and slurp on her pussy like it's the tastiest dessert I've ever encountered. And when I slide my fingers down the cleavage of her arse cheeks to play with her forbidden hole, she moans. I slide a finger inside her back channel and push three inside her cunt.

That's when she throws her head back, and with a long, low groan, she climaxes. Her cum coats my tongue and sinks into my blood, adding more fuel to the fire raging in my veins.

Quickly, I lower her to the bed on her back. I settle between her thighs, angle my cock at her opening, and impale her. She's so wet, I slide all the way in and brush up against that spot inside her I know drives her crazy. Sure enough, she shivers and grabs at my shoulders. The next time I thrust into her, her entire body jolts. The bed moves, and it seems, so does the room; I'm still not used to the way her pussy strangles my cock.

"You're so fucking hot. So beautiful." I bend and kiss her, and look into her eyes as I fuck into her. I pour my entire being into my actions, this need to bury myself in her.

I try to get as close to her as possible, until it's my skin and hers, joined together. Until I don't know where I stop, and she begins. One body. One soul. *My heart is hers.* I only need to tell her so.

I push into her again while I cup her breast and squeeze her nipple in that way which sends her out of her head. Then, I wrap my fingers around her throat. I squeeze gently, and a flare of lust lights up her eyes. She locks her ankles around my waist, tightens her inner walls around my cock, and I'm a goner.

"Fuck," I breathe into her mouth. "Come with me, baby." She holds my gaze, her pupils so dilated, there's only a ring of golden brown around the irises. "Come. Now." I piston into her, wanting to please her, knowing I can satisfy her, confident this is going to be the best fuck of her life. And she doesn't disappoint. She opens her mouth in a silent scream, and I make sure to inhale it as she climaxes.

I fuck her through her orgasm, and when her body jolts with aftershocks, I join her in that place where it's only us. Where no one can hurt what we've become to each other.

47

Cilla

Your past does not define your future.
-Cilla's Post-it note

"Mommy, wake up." Little fingers dance over my face. The
breathless little girl's voice brings a smile to my face. I know it's
Serene. Know I need to open my eyes. Sense the light pouring in
through the window and filtering through my closed eyelids. But
every bone in my body feels tired. My muscles are sore—in a good
way. I feel more than well-fucked. I feel satiated. Well taken care of.
There's a warmth that suffuses my being. I've never felt this
contented.

The days on this idyllic island have been the happiest of my life.
We collected Serene from the Sterlings yesterday after brunch and
took her on a walk through the paddy fields which the resort orga-

nized. Followed by snorkeling in waters so clear, you could see the fish in all their glory. Then, it was back for dinner at the villa. Serene fell asleep very soon after. Tyler wasted no time in carrying me off to bed, and proceeded to fuck me senseless. The man has an insatiable appetite, and the stamina to match. Lucky me. I feel so fortunate to have him and Serene in my life.

"Mommy." There's a tug on my arm. "I want brekkie."

"Let your mother sleep. I'll get you breakfast," Tyler's voice rumbles.

"But, Papa, I want to eat brekkie with Mama." The disappointment in her voice urges me to crack open my eyelids.

I wrap my arm about my daughter and bring her in for a kiss. "Hello, pumpkin." I pretend to bite her cheek.

She giggles. "Mama, you're awake."

"I am." I beam at her, then spoil it by yawning hugely.

"Give your mom a chance to wake up fully." Tyler walks over to sit next to me on the bed. "How are you feeling?" He scans me with quiet intensity. "You were sleeping so deeply; I didn't want to disturb you."

"I was…knackered," I murmur. There's a knowing look in his eyes, which makes me flush. I bite down on my lower lip and am gratified when those hypnotic eyes of his flare. He leans in and kisses me firmly. As always, that goes to my head. My heart feels like it's galloping in my chest. I can feel my pulse at my wrists, at my ankles, at my temples.

Then Serene giggles. I try to pull away, conscious our daughter is watching us, not that my husband lets me. He kisses me thoroughly and at leisure. When he finally releases me, there's a look of satisfaction on his face. He rises to his feet and hauls Serene into his arms. She squeals, locking her arms about his neck. Both of them look at me with twin grins of delight. Warmth squeezes my chest. This… feeling of being complete… I hold it close to me. I tuck it away in that corner of my chest where it will continue to warm the rest of me.

"Get dressed, we're meeting the Sterlings for breakfast."

"There, honey, have some fruit." I place a few slices of mango on Serene's plate, then help myself.

We're seated by the main pool in the resort having breakfast with the Sterlings.

I bite into the fruit, and the sweet-tart juice fills my palate. "This tastes so good. *Everything* tastes so good."

"It's the appetite you worked up." Tyler smirks.

Summer laughs.

Sinclair arches an eyebrow.

"Did you work out, Mrs. Davenport?" Matty asks me in that solemn, grown-up voice of his which I'm still getting used to.

"Oh, she did." Tyler puts his arm around me. "In fact, we worked out together."

"Tyler." I dig my elbow into his side.

Tyler's smirk turns into a grin.

Summer coughs.

To my relief, Matty loses interest in the conversation and focuses on his pancakes. I shoot Tyler another scowl, then look past him to find a woman at the next table staring at us. It's the same woman I noticed at the reception when we'd checked in. I almost forgot about her. But here she is and, once again, she's staring at Serene.

Something in her expression makes the fine hairs on the nape of my neck rise.

"What's wrong?" Tyler must notice my expression, for he looks her way. His entire body goes still. His muscles bunch. That's when I know, my instincts are right at being alarmed.

"Who is she? Do you know her?"

He doesn't reply. His hand tightens around mine. I sense the tension bouncing off of him. "Tyler? "

His jaw hardens. A vein at his temple pops. I glance at the woman, only to find she's gone completely pale. Her throat moves as she swallows. Then, she rises to her feet and walks toward our table.

She comes to a stop before us, looking from Tyler to Serene, then back to Tyler.

Something in the rigid set of her body, the edge of desperation in the way she looks at me — and that flicker of hope, fragile and raw —

triggers alarm bells in my mind. All of my instincts scream. I should move. I should grab Serene and protect her from this woman. I try to move, but my arms and legs don't seem capable of functioning.

"Don't do this," Tyler growls.

The woman's lips twist. "You know who I am, don't you?"

"You are Lauren Bolton, the woman who dropped off Serene at my doorstep," he says softly through gritted teeth.

She nods slowly. "I'm Serene's mother."

At that, Serene stops eating. She looks up at the woman and frowns. "You're not my Mama." Serene clutches at my arm. "*This* is my Mama."

The woman's features crumple, then she seems to get a hold of herself. "No, sweetheart, I'm your mother. Your father probably hasn't told you, but I dropped you off with him when you were only a year old. But I *am* your mother."

She grabs Serene's arm, who tries to shake it off, but the woman doesn't let go.

"Stop that, you're scaring her," Tyler says in a low voice.

Summer, Sinclair and Matty are watching the woman in stunned silence.

As for me? I'm unable to get my brain to function. She's Serene's mother. Her *biological* mother? *This is the woman who Tyler slept with?* I shove that thought out of my head.

Then, Serene makes a sound of distress, which snaps me out of my fugue state.

"You should realize how confusing all of this is for Serene." Tyler glares at her. "She has no concept of you, since you dropped her off when she was so young. And by coming so suddenly into her life, you're going to cause her a lot of distress. Surely, you don't want to do that, do you?"

The woman looks at Serene, and something in her posture loosens, gentles. They lock eyes—blue meeting brown.

I always assumed Serene's eyes came from her birth mother, but clearly, that's not the case. The woman's hair is a light, golden blonde, nothing like Serene's deeper, darker strands—so much more like her father's.

And yet, despite the differences, despite the fact that Serene shows no recognition of her, my chest hurts.

"I'm sorry, I didn't have the courage to bring you up alone." Lauren bows her head. "I was convinced you'd do better with your father. But you should know, I regret dropping you off that day. I've spent so many sleepless nights thinking about my decision."

Serene goes still, her whole body tight with unease. Tears well, then spill silently down her cheeks.

"Papa." Her chin trembles. "I want my papa."

Tyler snaps to attention, his whole body coiled tight like a wire pulled to its breaking point. His fingers clamp down on the edge of the table until his knuckles bleach bone white.

"You don't belong here," he says, voice low but razor-sharp. "And you sure as hell shouldn't be unloading all of that onto Serene—not here, not like this. You're upsetting her."

He stands, slowly, deliberately—like he's approaching a wild animal that might bolt or bite if provoked.

Across from me, Summer's face drains of color. We lock eyes, and I see the same thing reflected in hers: dread, and the sharp, rising awareness that something fragile is slipping out of our control.

Sinclair's jaw is hard. His forearms flex, and when I glance down, I realize his fingers are flying over his phone. *Is he calling security?* His gaze, though, is focused on the woman.

"I am going to calm down my daughter." Tyler rounds my chair, reaches Serene, and places his hand on her shoulder. "Don't worry, Poppet. Everything is going to be okay."

"I… I didn't mean to upset you." The woman swallows. "I promise, Serene. I'm here because I knew I had to put things right by you."

"It's a little late for that. You can't just undo your actions," Tyler growls.

The woman looks genuinely distressed. "You don't know what it is to be pregnant on your own. I didn't have any emotional support."

"You could have come to me," he says through gritted teeth.

She shakes her head. "The circumstances of her birth were complicated. More than you can imagine."

I frown. *What does she mean by that?*

"And her birth was not easy." She swallows. "Then I had post-partum depression. I couldn't deal with it. That's when I dropped her off. I regretted it right away. But it was too late. It's not like I could walk back to you, say it was a mistake, and ask for her back."

"You had the opportunity to come to me and explain your actions."

She jerks her chin in his direction. "And be judged by you? No, thank you. I... It's why I decided to leave the country. I thought, putting distance between Serene and me would help."

Clearly, it didn't, because here she is. I can't help but feel a tinge of sadness for this woman. How messed up must she have been to drop off the baby she gave birth to with a stranger. Then, seeing the child and realizing how much you missed of her early years, would be heartbreaking.

"I understand this cannot be easy for you—" I begin.

"It's not. But you wouldn't know that. You think you've taken over my place, haven't you? You're trying to be her mother. But you're not. You never will be."

A thickness squeezes my throat. My chest tightens. Her words are my worst nightmare come true. A fear I've never articulated, even to myself. Subconsciously though, I realize, I've wondered what I would do if Serene's birth mother turned up one day and asked for her daughter back. My stomach drops to my feet. *Not her mother. I'm not her biological mother. I never will be.* So what, if Serene took to me right away? So what, if I fell for her the moment I saw her. We don't have a blood relationship. That can never be replaced. It's not my blood running in Serene's veins.

The pressure in my chest spreads to my head and presses down behind my eyes. I blink away the tears. Tyler must sense my distress, for he flicks his gaze in my direction. Whatever he sees there has his face turning to stone. "You're causing a lot of pain to both my daughter and my wife."

She fixes her attention on me, sharp and unflinching. "I'm sorry. I never meant to hurt you. But that doesn't change the truth."

Then she turns to my daughter, her tone shifting, gentling. "Do you know how you got your name, Serene?"

Serene looks up at her, wide-eyed. There's confusion on her face. She shrinks into the chair and closer to Tyler, who squats down next to her. "It'll be okay, princess. I promise."

The woman goes on as if she hasn't heard him. "I called you Serene because, though your birth was traumatic, when you came out, you didn't cry for long. You fell asleep as soon as they placed you on my chest. And you looked so much at peace. For a few seconds, it felt like it had all been worth it. That's why I named you Serene."

"You're not her mother; Mrs. Davenport is." Matty looks at her steadily with his piercing blue eyes.

"I gave birth to her. She didn't." The woman twists her fingers, growing agitated. Summer places her hand on Matty's shoulder. The boy scowls but falls silent.

"I'm your mother, Serene. I promise you—"

"Enough." Tyler rises to his full height. "You should leave."

The woman's face falls. "I need to talk to you. I need to tell you about—"

"We can talk about it later. You should leave now. You're upsetting Serene and my wife." Tyler stabs his finger in the direction of the doorway leading away from the pool.

She wrings her hands. "But you need to listen to what I have to say, I—"

Serene darts forward.

"Serene!" I jump to my feet in such a hurry, my chair falls back.

She runs past the woman and toward the pool.

My heart is a wild thing, battering my ribs like it's trying to escape. "Serene, stop!" I race after her.

She looks at me over her shoulder, tears in her eyes. "I'm scared, Mama, I—" Her feet slip from under her. She screams as her head hits the cement with a resounding crack. Then, she rolls into the pool.

48

Tyler

"Serene!" I race past her mother, then overtake my wife and reach the pool. A part of me notes the red that stains the water and panics. My breath seizes. Then my training as a Marine takes over. I push back my thoughts and dive in. She's already underwater so I grab her and swim to the surface. By the time I reach the edge of the water, Cilla's there. I hand Serene over to her, then haul myself over the edge.

"Serene!" Cilla is on her knees next to my daughter.

"Serene!" I crawl next to her. "Serene, can you hear me?"

There's no response. Her eyes are closed. Why is she not breathing? Surely, she wasn't in the water long enough to swallow too much?

My heart gallops so hard, it feels like it's going to sprout hooves and break through my rib cage. My throat closes. My arms and legs feel numb. *Calm down. What would you do if you were on a mission and one of your team was hurt? You need to find that core of calmness inside. You need to draw on all your reserves of strength. Serene needs you. Your daughter needs you.* I cannot... I will not fail her.

But before I can reach for her, Cilla takes over.

She turns Serene on her side and pounds her back. Water oozes out from my daughter's mouth.

She leans in, ear close to Serene's lips. Her fingers press gently under the jaw, searching. She waits—too long. Her lips firm. That's when I realize. My daughter isn't breathing on her own.

I've faced enemy bullets without flinching but seeing my little girl pale and motionless on the ground...has me frozen.

My blood pressure spikes. A high-pitched ringing starts in my ears. My hands shake. My legs feel like they're sinking through the floor. I can only watch as Cilla moves with terrifying calm. She lays Serene flat again, tilts her head back slightly, and lifts her chin to open the airway.

I force my hands to obey. I press two fingers to the side of her neck, to her wrist. Nothing. I can't feel a heartbeat.

A sound tears from my throat. I start compressions. Lock my hands, heel to sternum. Rhythm sharp. Precise. Desperate. Yet gentle. I hold back, reminding myself how easy it would be to crack a rib on a toddler. Thirty compressions. Then sixty. Ninety.

Cilla breathes for her.

We fall into sync—mechanical, relentless. I don't stop. I can't.

Again, compressions. Again.

I let her chest rise fully. Another thirty compressions.

Still no breath.

Cilla and I exchange a look and switch positions. I slide beside Serene's face, pinch her nose closed, and make a tight seal over her mouth. Two breaths. Watch for the rise of her chest.

Another two breaths.

Nothing.

Two more.

Please. Come on, Serene. Two more. *Come back to me.*

My wife's voice cracks. A whisper at first, then a sob. "Serene, please."

Another two breaths. Then Serene coughs, sputtering out more water. My heart leaps in my chest. Relief has my limbs going weak. My stomach folds in on itself, and I taste the bile on my tongue. I gather her in my arms and fight back tears.

I realize how close I was to losing her. And all because I wasn't fast enough to protect my daughter from that woman. She might be Serene's biological mother, but that doesn't give her the right to upset my daughter like this. How dare she scare my daughter so badly that she ends up hurt? *How dare she put Serene's life in peril?*

The thoughts race through me as I hold my daughter in my arms.

"The EMTs are here. I called them as soon as I saw Serene fall into the pool," Sinclair announces. He, Summer and Matty joined us at some point.

I lower my daughter to the ground but am unable to let go.

"You need to step back so we can examine her," one of the men tells me.

There's a touch on my shoulder, then Sinclair coaxes me to my feet. Summer helps my wife up. I reluctantly take a step back.

I watch as they check her vitals, hooking an oxygen mask to her. I want to cry and scream at them to leave her alone, but I fold my fingers into fists, forcing myself to bite the inside of my cheek.

"She's going to be fine." My voice sounds so harsh, I barely recognize it, and I feel Priscilla shrink next to me. I wrap my arm around her and pull her close.

Serene's mother, meanwhile, watches the EMTs with an anguished look as they take Serene away. She turns to me and mouths, *"I am so sorry."*

"Tyler, can I talk to you please?" My daughter's mother stands in front of me, wringing her fingers. We're in the waiting room in the hospital. Cilla insisted that, as her legal guardian, I ride with my daughter in the ambulance. I didn't protest. She followed with Sinclair.

Summer stayed behind with Matty.

They ran tests on her. The doctor told us she was suffering from a concussion and lost a lot of blood. Serene has a rare blood type, so they took blood samples from me and my daughter's mother to test for a blood match. I suppose, it's good thing she's here, so if the blood matches, she can provide a blood transfusion. On the other hand, if she weren't here, Serene wouldn't be in this condition.

I run my fingers through my hair, glancing down at the scrubs someone loaned me. They're tight around the shoulders and chest and short in length, but they'll have to do for now. The doctor returns. She's wearing a puzzled expression.

I rise to my feet, Priscilla with me. "Is everything okay?" she asks.

The doctor looks between the three of us. "Neither Mr. Davenport nor Ms. Bolton's blood is compatible with the patient's blood type."

"Is that a problem?" I frown.

"Serene's blood type is AB. One of the parents should be compatible with hers, but neither are."

My heart begins a slow thud. "I had a DNA test done; I'm definitely Serene's father," I point out.

"I gave birth to her. I have the hospital paperwork to prove it." Lauren's mouth pinches into a thin line.

"Uh, I… My blood type is AB," Priscilla offers. "I'm sure, it's only a coincidence, but this should help, right?"

"Yes." The doctor's face shows her relief. "If you'll come with me, Mrs. Davenport, we'll test your blood and make sure you're compatible."

Priscilla squeezes my arm, then follows the doctor down the corridor.

I stare after them, trying to piece together this new information. "Neither your blood nor mine is compatible with Serene's, but the genetic testing confirms that I'm Serene's father." I turn to her. "Which means… You're not her mother."

Lauren swallows. Something in her expression has the hair on the nape of my neck rising. She sits down heavily one chair down from me. "I gave birth to her; I didn't lie about that."

"But?"

She shakes her head. "But nothing."

I rise to my feet, knowing I'll loom over her. Knowing I'll come across as threatening when I stand opposite her. "Don't lie. You've done enough to disrupt Serene's life. The least you can do is come clean now."

Sinclair, who's been on the phone at the other end of the corridor, walks over to join us. "Everything okay?" he asks in a low voice.

"Lauren was about to explain why she's not Serene's biological mother."

"I... I did give birth to her," she says, hunching her shoulders. "But it was through IVF."

"What do you mean?" I jerk back.

"You have to understand, I have wanted to be a mother since I was sixteen. I always thought I'd end up with a brood of them. That I'd have a family of my own. But when I turned thirty and broke up with my long-term boyfriend, all of my hopes of becoming a mother seemed so far away. I decided to go ahead on my own. That's when I discovered I couldn't conceive naturally. My eggs weren't any good. I was desperate. I had to find a way. I had a successful career, I was making good money, but my life was so empty. I knew if I didn't find a way to have a child I would never be happy." She wrings her hands.

"Is there a point to this story?" I ask through gritted teeth.

"I arranged for donor eggs and donor sperm. I bought them about five years ago, but I kept putting it off." She looks away. "Eventually, I went through with it. They created the embryo and transferred it into me. First try, I was pregnant."

"You used my donor sperm?" I force the words out, my throat burning like it's full of glass.

She used my sperm. Goddamn.

I knew it. I knew I'd remember every woman I ever slept with. I'd been driving myself crazy, trying to figure out if I'd met Lauren before — and coming up blank. A weight I didn't even know I was carrying slides off my shoulders.

"You donated sperm?" Sinclair asks.

I nod shortly. "Yeah. When I was twenty-one. Two of my buddies and I saw an ad while we were on a break from bootcamp."

"And *you* did it?"

I rub the back of my neck. "They did it for the money. I did it to keep them company. Figured maybe it would help someone." I drop my hand. My voice hardens. "How did you even find me?" I glare at her. "It was supposed to be anonymous."

She pops a shoulder. "Amazing the kind of information money can get you."

No one knows that better than me. But being on the receiving end of this kind of action—the kind I'd normally initiate—makes me so very angry.

How dare this woman violate my privacy? She was entitled to use the sperm. I donated it, hoping it would help someone in need. But that she broke the confidence guaranteed when I made the donation is unforgivable. On the other hand, it's because she did so that Serene came into my life. Something I don't regret at all. If she thinks she can take Serene away from me now, she's mistaken. I curl my fingers into fists.

"You are not her biological mother," I snap.

She lowers her chin to her chest. "I carried her inside me for forty weeks. I almost died giving birth to her. I *am* her biological mother."

I want to have empathy for this woman. I do. My sources confirmed she gave birth to Serene.

"You may have carried her, but you share no genetic material, no bloodlines, with my daughter. You allowed me to believe I slept with her mother and was unable to recollect who that was. You made me feel guilty and ashamed all this time"

"You did donate to the sperm bank and sign the waiver papers," she points out.

"It was meant to be confidential. You broke that agreement."

She looks like she's about to protest, then some of the fight seems to go out of her. "I was desperate. I thought I would be able to bring up my child on my own. But I lost my nerve." She hunches her shoulders. "I had been so sure all I wanted was to have a child. But then I held Serene in my arms and knew I knew I couldn't do it alone. I was overwhelmed. All my courage deserted me. Can you imagine how difficult it was to realize that I was mistaken?" She swallows. "That the one thing I wanted my entire life... I couldn't go through with it. I knew I had to find a home for Serene. I had to find someone else to take care of her. I looked you up, I discovered how well off you were. I knew you'd make a good father. That she'd be better off with you."

"Yet, you decided to come back into her life?"

"Because"—she looks away—"I missed her. I found I couldn't just simply walk away. Not when I'd spent so much of my life wanting a child." She swallows hard. "I did not intend for things to become this messy. I did not intend to turn my daughter's life upside down."

Tears begin to roll down her cheeks. She looks miserable, yet I can't find it in myself to sympathize with her. "You're the reason Serene is in the hospital."

"I'm aware"—she sniffs—"and I'm sorry. I truly am."

A thought which has been eating away at my subconscious since I first saw her breaks through. "How did you find out we were here?"

She blinks rapidly. "Would you believe me if I said it was a coincidence?"

I snort. "Not likely."

She looks down, and I have to strain to hear her. "I paid a private investigator to find out where you'd moved. Then paid him again to track where you were headed."

That anger that gripped me intensifies. I don't broadcast where I live, but I also don't take pains to hide it or what my travel plans are. There was no need to do so. *That changes now.*

This woman has maintained an unhealthy interest in the whereabouts of me and daughter. This goes beyond an invasion of privacy. Her actions are downright illegal.

It resulted in my daughter getting hurt. I tamp down on the rage that churns my guts. I need to keep control of my emotions. Serene needs me. My wife needs me. I need to understand Lauren's motivations better, so I can find a way to keep her away from my family.

"You seem to have a lot of money to spend tracking my movements. You could have used that to take care of Serene, instead."

Her shoulders dip. "I'm not a billionaire. But yes, I make enough to afford IVF and to get details on your whereabouts. I will not let you guilt trip me for that. Nor for my actions. Only I know what I went through. Only I know how difficult it was to decide to get pregnant on my own, and then realize I needed to give up my daughter so she could have a better future."

"She's not a toy that you can give away at will, then decide you want back when you miss her," I snap.

"I merely wanted her to know who her mother is. Surely, I have a right to that?"

"You lost all rights when you left her with me. And because of that, my daughter will always suffer the consequences of knowing that the woman who gave birth to her abandoned her."

This woman's choices are the reason for the trauma my daughter has experienced in her short life.

"And finding out you're not even her biological mother? That's just another betrayal she'll have to live with."

She hunches her shoulders. Her expression deflates. A shadow runs through her eyes. She opens her mouth to speak when Priscilla walks over to join us. Noticing the charged silence, she looks between us.

"Everything okay?" She slips her fingers through mine. "Are *you* okay?"

Something twisted inside me unfurls. The chaos inside me settles, just a little. Seeing her, having her by my side, feeling her softness against me, grounds me. Reassures me I can find my way out of this mess. I need to keep the faith. I have her with me. Serene is going to be okay. Serene has to be okay.

I wrap my arm about my wife's shoulders and pull her close.

Lauren seems to shrink further into herself. She looks miserable, but she's not getting any sympathy from me. She's responsible for the upheavals in my daughter's life. I can't forgive her for that.

My wife urges me to the side, out of earshot from the other woman. "I don't understand or agree with any of her actions." She reaches up and cups my cheek. "But it doesn't change the fact that she gave birth to Serene. Our daughter will want to know that. She'll likely want Lauren in her life when she's older."

I want to deny it. I am tempted to use all the power I have to ensure this woman has nothing to do with my daughter. But I know my wife is right. She has more perspective on this situation. She understands how important it is for Serene to have contact with all three of us. Overcome by emotions I can't quite put a name to—and don't want to, at this stage—I settle for lowering my chin and kissing my wife, hard. I take comfort from her nearness. Her scent. How she opens herself and allows me to take from her. How she feels like a rock in this shifting landscape that my life has become.

The sound of someone clearing their throat cuts through the turmoil in my mind. I lift my head and turn around to find the doctor waiting. This time her expression is one of relief.

"Mrs. Davenport's blood type is compatible with Serene's."

49

Priscilla

"Mama?" She searches the room until she finds me. "Mommy." Her lips tremble.

It's the first time she's calling me Mommy. She must be really upset.

The doctors stitched her up and completed the blood transfusion with the blood I donated. They also conducted a few tests on her. They told us she's going to make a complete recovery. Thank God. *Thank you, universe, for showing up for my daughter.*

"I'm here." I sit down in the chair next to her bed and carefully put my arm around her. "How are you, baby?"

She sniffs; tears roll down her cheeks. My heart squeezes in on itself.

"Oh, honey." I kiss her forehead. "Does it hurt?"

"A little." She cuddles closer.

I use a paper napkin to wipe off her wet cheeks.

She sniffs again. "I'm tired."

I take in the dressing on her forehead. It seems innocuous enough, but the doctor told us the cut was deep. Enough for her to have lost a significant amount of blood, and to receive fifteen stitches. They promised us that they were careful when they stitched her up and that the scar should, hopefully, fade with time. Also, it's close enough to her hairline that it shouldn't be too noticeable.

Though she didn't fall from a great height, she lost enough to warrant a transfusion. I'm so glad I was on hand to help. I take her hand in mine. "I'm not going anywhere."

She looks into my face. Whatever she sees there seems to reassure her. "I love you, Mama." She yawns, then closes her eyes.

"I love you too, sweetheart," I whisper. My heart swells so much, I'm sure it's going to burst out of my rib cage.

In a few minutes, her breathing deepens. I cradle her hand gently between both of mine. Her skin is cool, her complexion washed out, and deep shadows bruise the delicate skin beneath her eyes. My chest tightens at how fragile she seems—like the smallest gust of wind might carry her away.

And that fall she took, I swallow. When she hit her head against the edge of the pool, my heart seized up. And when she fell into the pool, my entire body froze. My brain couldn't begin to comprehend what had happened. But my body was already reacting. My feet didn't even seem to touch the ground as I raced toward her.

And seeing her lifeless body made me feel like I was about to die. I recovered quickly enough to begin to resuscitate her. And thankfully, Tyler was able to revive her. I am so grateful the EMTs reached us so quickly, and that I could save her by donating my blood.

Thank God, our blood types are compatible.

Serene's going to be fine. Tears squeeze out of the sides of my eyes. My poor baby. She *will* be fine. I place my head on the bed next to her, and for the first time in hours, allow myself to relax.

The next thing I know, a hand on my shoulder has me snapping my eyes open. I look up into the gorgeous, mismatched eyes of my husband. He urges me to my feet.

"You look exhausted." His gaze lingers. "Are you okay?"

I nod. "And *she's* going to be okay, thanks to you." I glance toward our daughter. "If anything had happened to her—" I tremble. He pulls me close, and I let him draw me into that wide chest of his. Pressing my cheek into the warmth of that solidness, I continue to look at her features.

"It's my fault. I should have ensured there was more security who would have stopped that woman from approaching us." His Adam's apple bobs.

"It's not your fault. We're in Bali. The last thing you could've anticipated was for her to turn up here." I look up at him. "How did she find us, anyway?"

A shadow crosses his eyes. Without looking at me, he rumbles, "We need to talk."

"Okay"—I frown—"but can't it wait until Serene is awake?"

"The doctor says it might be hours before she's fully awake. For now, she's out of danger." When he finally meets my eyes, there's something in them which makes the fine hair on the nape of my neck rise. "Is everything okay?"

He doesn't reply. Instead, he urges me toward the door.

"Tyler, you're worrying me."

He sends me a lopsided smile. But his eyes are serious. "I'm sorry about that." His voice softens. "There's something I needed to talk to you about, and it's best we do it now."

I nod, somewhat mollified by his words. But the dread which crept in earlier intensifies into a knot in my chest. "Does this have to do with her birth mother showing up?"

He guides me down the corridor and into an empty waiting room. I take in the couch, the comfortable chairs, and the window from which I can see the sea in the distance. The space is air-conditioned, and my feet sink into the thick carpet. It's a tastefully appointed room. I realize, we must be in a private hospital.

I'm grateful my daughter is getting the best care possible.

For the first time, I appreciate that my husband has money. For the first time, I don't knock the fact that I grew up surrounded by luxuries. I've spent all my life running from it. I felt compelled to rebel against the kind of lifestyle my father afforded me and my brothers. I wanted to be more 'normal.'

I felt it was wrong that I had access to wealth when there were so many people in this world who had nothing. It's what made me turn my back on my family. And I concede, it was so I could get more attention from my father. Becoming a mother has made me more appreciative of how difficult bringing up a child is. For the first time, I empathize with how much stress I must have caused my family.

When Tyler coaxes me to sit down in the comfortable settee, I don't demur. He walks over to the nearby counter, then makes me a cup of tea and an espresso for himself before he returns.

He hands the tea to me, and I accept it with gratitude. I cup my palms around the cup and let the heat seep into my bloodstream, then take a sip. Feeling better, I glance at him. "So, it does have to do with her birth mother showing up?"

He nods slowly, tosses back the espresso and sets the cup down on the coffee table.

"You already know that neither Lauren's blood type nor mine were compatible with Serene's."

"That's not unusual, is it?" I frown, wondering what he's getting at.

He shakes his head. "Not in itself. But then it turned out that your blood type was the same as hers."

"So?" I tilt my head. "I'm aware my blood type is rare. I didn't realize Serene's would be the same."

He nods. "That in itself is, again, not uncommon." He hesitates.

And that's so unusual for this man. He's always so confident. So in control. The only time I saw him shaken was the day Serene was left at his doorstep. And then today, when Serene was hurt. I sink back in my seat. That nervousness which gripped me earlier tightens into a ball of apprehension in my throat.

"Is it about Serene?"

He nods. Then he sees the panic in my eyes and squeezes my hand. "You heard the doctor. She's going to be fine."

Some of the tension drains from me. "What is it then?"

"Because her blood and yours are uncommon, and because the doctor wanted to be extra careful, I agreed to them cross-checking genetic markers to ensure there are no underlying conditions that could impact clotting or immune response."

I rub at my temple trying to make sense of the words. "You wanted to verify her blood type against mine for safety reasons?"

He nods.

"I assume it's normal protocol to do so?"

He nods again.

"So, what's the problem?" I half-smile. "You had me worried."

He doesn't return the smile. "When they ran the genetic markers test, they found a maternal match."

My heart seems to stop in my match. "A maternal match?" I croak. Surely, he doesn't mean—I shake my head. "Not sure I'm following."

He presses his lips together. "The tests indicate you're Serene's biological mother."

50

Tyler

"What?" Her mouth gapes open. She looks shell-shocked. As taken aback as I was when the doctor told me this news. It's not possible. That's how I felt then. That's how I still feel now.

"For a moment, I thought you said—" She shakes her head, then chuckles. "Nah, I must have heard you wrong."

"You didn't. I said you're her biological mother."

"I didn't give birth to her. The first time I saw her was when she was dropped off on your doorstep."

"The genetic markers don't lie. Lauren may have carried her to term, but you're her mother."

She stares at me, then pulls her hand from mine. I release her.

"This is a bad joke." She jumps to her feet. "It can't be possible." She locks her fingers together. "I have often wished I was Serene's biological mother, but surely, this can't be possible?" She shakes her head, a dazed look in her eyes.

"I agree this seems very far-fetched. And when I first heard about it, it seemed like the doctor had mixed up the results. But I had the reports forwarded to a friend of mine who's a well-known doctor in London. He confirmed that you are Serene's biological mother."

She tosses her head. "I really don't see how that's possible—" She stills. "Unless—"

I nod. "Unless you donated your eggs, and somehow, it's your eggs that were used during the IVF process."

She opens her mouth, then shuts it again. A look of comprehension flashes in her eyes.

I know then what she's going to say. And I'm not surprised when she stutters, "I... I did donate my eggs. Right after I left university and was drowning in debt. I couldn't find a job. I had no money so —" She exhales loudly.

"Do you remember which fertility clinic you donated to?"

She reels off a name which I recognize as the one Lauren used for her fertility procedures. When I tell my wife that, she looks stunned. "So, she used my eggs and—"

"—my sperm." I rub at the back of my neck. "I donated sperm during a shore leave from the Marines." I narrow my gaze on my wife. "What are the odds that you and I would meet, and that she'd drop off the child conceived of our genetic material when you were with me?"

"Umm, I'd say impossible. There are too many coincidences here. It's"—she wraps her arms about herself—"incomprehensible that something like this would happen."

I agree. There is definitely no earthly way this list of incidents would line up so precisely. "If it weren't for the fact that I saw the results of the genetic markers myself and heard it from the doctor—" I shake my head. "I'm still getting my head around it too."

"That's—" She laughs nervously. "It still seems impossible."

"It's a one in a million—or perhaps a billion—chance of that happening." I lower my chin. "Just as unlikely as my riding on the tube the day I met you."

She tilts her head.

"I had never taken the tube before that day. And never after. It was on that particular day, at that time, I decided to use it because my car was being repaired. There were no alternate chauffeurs or cars available from any of the services the office uses, no cars on the various ride-hailing apps. And I was late for my date. So, I decided to take the underground." I lean forward. "The fates conspired to bring us together that day. And they played an even bigger role in bringing Serene into my—into *our* lives."

She half-smiles, but her eyes still carry the bewildered expression I suspect I had when I first found out. "I want to believe it; I do. I never thought I would be Serene's mother, not by blood." She rubs at her temple again.

"Do you have a headache?"

"It's a tension headache. With everything that happened, I guess I'm struggling to keep up."

"When did you last eat?" I tuck a strand of hair behind her ear, noting how exhausted she looks. "You should go to the resort and rest."

"Not until Serene is discharged. When she wakes up, she'll want to see her mother." A determined look comes into her eyes when she says that. Her throat moves as she swallows. Her eyes glisten.

"Oh, baby, come here." I gather her close. And when she sinks into me, the world feels right again. I lift her onto my lap. She makes a protesting noise, but when I lay back with her and encourage her to stretch out next to me, she sighs. I turn her on her side away from me. Then I begin to massage her shoulders.

"That feels so good," she moans.

My cock instantly stands to attention. Given her sweet curves are pressed against mine, I'm not surprised. I squeeze the tense muscles of her back, dragging my knuckles down her spine.

She groans, and the sound is so fucking erotic. I'm aware the tent in my crotch is making itself known to her, but I ignore it. I continue to dig my fingers into the knotted muscles, and when they unwind, she sighs. Her body relaxes against mine. "Thank you," she mumbles, then yawns widely.

"Take a nap," I coax her.

"But, Serene—"

"Will be fine. There are nurses monitoring her. If anything changes, they'll find us."

That seems to satisfy her. She closes her eyes. Her body twitches, and I know she's already asleep. I tuck her head under my chin and breathe deeply of her scent. As always, it soothes me. Some of the tension drains out of me. I'm tempted to sleep but shove that aside. All of that training in the Royal Marines means I can school myself to go days without shut-eye.

I allow my mind to mull over the revelations which have come to light. What does it mean for us? Once my wife has had a chance to digest the news, how will she feel about it? It's a good thing, right? I married her without being aware she's the mother of my child, but I could sense their bond right away. This simply means, she's also Serene's biological mother. What does it mean for Serene? When do we tell her?

Likely, it won't make a difference to her now, as she's too small to understand the nuances. But we can add more details to her life storybook as she grows older, and share her past with her in an age-appropriate fashion.

As for Lauren? Well, that's something I need to discuss with my wife when she's awake.

As if she senses my thoughts, Cilla's eyelids flutter open. "How long was I asleep?" she asks in between yawns.

I check my watch. "Almost an hour." I'm surprised so much time has passed.

She turns in my arms, then lifts those gorgeous eyes to mine. Her eyes are still tired, but clearer than before.

"I should get you something to eat." I begin to rise but she puts her arm on my chest.

"Stay a little longer."

I sink back, then urge her upward until we're almost nose to nose. I gaze into her eyes, marveling at the golden sparks within them. "You're beautiful," I whisper.

Her lips curve.

I lean in and kiss them. "And so sweet." I deepen the kiss.

She whimpers, sliding in closer. I hook my arm about her waist, drawing her in until we're plastered from chest to thigh. I slide my thigh between her legs until the warmth of her core sinks through my clothes and into my skin. I continue to kiss her and, with my hands on her hips, urge her to ride me. I grind up and into her center, swallowing her sharp exhale. I slide my palm down her back to squeeze her ample butt. She shudders. I continue to raise and lower her against the hard muscle of my thigh, while massaging her butt and thrusting my tongue inside her mouth. I dance it over hers, and she jolts. I continue to kiss her, looking deeply into her eyes. Pulling her dress up, I slip my hand inside her panties to squeeze her backside.

Her gaze widens, and when I increase the pace of my movements, her entire body hums. She begins to vibrate and, with a soft sigh which I swallow, she falls apart. I hold her as she shivers and climaxes, the scent of her orgasm seeping into the air and turning my cock to a column of concrete; it feels just as heavy, too. I hold her and continue to dry fuck her through her orgasm. When she finally slumps, I tear my mouth from hers, pull her close and hold her. Her eyelids flutter down, and while she naps, I put her clothes to right. I hold her for a few minutes, until she rouses herself. She looks up at me from under her eyelashes, "That was—incredible."

"Feel better now?"

She nods slowly.

"Your headache—"

"—is gone." The smile starts in her eyes and reaches her mouth. "Thank you. I feel almost human now."

I kiss her hard. Then roll off the bed and rise to my feet. I hold out my hand. "Let's get you something to eat."

"This is not what I expected a hospital canteen to be." She looks around and shakes her head. "But then, the hospital itself is quite luxurious."

We checked with the nurses, who assured us that they'd watch over Serene. Then, I brought my wife to the cafeteria to get a bite to eat.

"It's the best one in the country." I look around the space with the wooden tables and chairs, and a counter at the far end well-stocked with juices, water and refreshments. Considering the waitstaff who took our orders and brought us our food in minutes, the place resembles a luxurious airport lounge, rather than a typical hospital canteen. I'm grateful for that. While patients need the best care in hospitals, their near and dear also need to be looked after, so they can find the strength to keep going.

"Sinclair has contacts here. Enough for the hospital to prioritize us. And the surgeon who operated on her is known to Arthur. It's why she took up the case personally."

She toys with her food. "I'm glad she got the best attention."

"You should eat." I nod toward her plate. "You need the sustenance."

She obediently takes a couple of bites from her plate. A fierce satisfaction fills me. The fact that she obeyed me and that she's eating the food I ordered and paid for... It's the closest I'll come to hunting and procuring food for her. I've always been dominant, but she brings my caveman tendencies to the fore. I try my best not to be too overbearing around her, but don't always succeed. She's smart and knows her mind. She's gorgeous and sexy, and has proven she can take care of herself. But a part of me is unable to hold back from protecting her. From taking care of her. From wanting to shield her from the world. It's a primitive instinct I can't contain. Which is why, when she puts down her fork, I use it to scoop up more food from her plate and offer it to her. She half-smiles, but doesn't decline. After a few mouthfuls, she shakes her head. "I'm full."

"Have some more."

She chuckles. "Any more, and I'll burst. I've eaten as much as I can, I assure you." She smiles. "Thank you for taking care of me."

I put down my fork, then reach over and place my hand on hers. "You're my wife. Of course, I'll always take care of you. I'll do anything to keep you and Serene safe." I swallow, then look away. "I failed her." I begin to pull my hand back, but she catches it.

"You couldn't have known Lauren would track us down here."

"I should have been more careful. When I found out she left the country, I figured she didn't want anything to do with Serene. I assumed she was Serene's biological mother and that I didn't remember her." I blow out a breath. "And when the DNA testing came back positive, I accepted Serene as my daughter. It didn't occur to me to investigate that further; which, in retrospect, was naïve of me." I drag my fingers through my hair.

"If I had... I'd have tracked you down earlier. As it was, I was embarrassed. You had reacted poorly to finding out I'd slept around, and I felt like Serene being dropped off at my door was confirmation of my indiscretions. I couldn't face you, knowing what you'd think of me. If I'd known... Of course, it would have surprised me to find out you were her biological mother, but it would've meant you'd be a part of our lives earlier. We'd have become a family much sooner." I cradle her smaller, slimmer palm between mine.

"You're being too hard on yourself. I can understand your embarrassment; I reacted with jealousy, when I barely knew you. I had no right to judge you for what happened before we met. Then, you found out you had a daughter. And naturally, she became your priority," she says softly.

I shake my head. "If I had been thinking clearly, if I had been more alert, I'd have found out that Lauren had conceived through artificial means. I might have tracked her down and found a way to stop her from getting close to our daughter. I would have protected her better. I'd have stopped Serene from getting hurt. If I'd done more research, I might have discovered you were her biological mother, and we could've been together..."

"You can't blame yourself for that. Who'd have thought she'd have access to my eggs from the one time I donated them." She places her free hand on top of mine. "What matters is that Serene's safe now."

"Because of you," I say, voice rough. I look at her—grasping for the right words. "If you hadn't been here — God, I don't know what would've happened."

"Don't think about that, I —"

"There you are —" A new voice has us both turning in the direction of the doorway to the café.

51

Priscilla

"What are you doing here?" Tyler frowns at his brother.

Connor cuts a path through the tables and toward us. I notice every woman in the café is watching his progress.

He's as tall as my husband, as broad. But where Tyler has a wild untamed air about him, Connor—who's wearing a suit, without a tie —resembles an off-duty spy. I wouldn't be surprised if he were one. Although Tyler tells me he spends a lot of time away on research expeditions.

Until now, I hadn't realized that many of the other tables in the cafeteria are occupied. I was too caught up in my husband and what he revealed to me.

Connor reaches us and pulls out a chair next to Tyler before seating himself. "How is she?" His voice is worried.

Now that I look closer, I realize his eyes are bloodshot, and there are shadows under them. He looks like he hasn't slept much. His next words confirm it.

"The Sovranos loaned me their jet. I got here as fast as I could."

"You shouldn't have—" Tyler begins.

"I absolutely should have. You shouldn't be going through this on your own. Neither of you." He looks between us. "Also, since you're sitting here in the restaurant instead of in the waiting room"—his eyes turn speculative—"I assume she's out of danger?"

Tyler nods. "The nurses are watching over her. They promised they'd call when she wakes up."

He relaxes a little, and a server approaches him. "What can I get you?" she asks without taking her gaze off his face.

"A coffee. Black. No sugar," he says without looking at her.

Her face falls, but she walks away.

Tyler and I exchange a glance. He chuckles.

"What's wrong?" Connor's brow wrinkles.

"Nothing." Tyler shakes his head. "Seriously, you needn't have come. You had to fly halfway around the world to get here."

"It was worth it." He surveys my husband and me with a piercing expression on his face, the one indicating there's little that escapes him. There's more to this man than meets the eye. Secrets lurk behind that exterior. People would do well not to underestimate him. With his gorgeous features and movie-star build, it would be easy to get distracted and not see him to what lies deeper.

"How are you two holding up?" he asks.

"We're better, now that Serene is out of danger." Tyler wraps his arm about my shoulders.

"What happened?"

Tyler looks at me. I see the question in his eyes and interpret it correctly. He's seeking permission to share some of what happened. I half nod, trying to tell him without words, I prefer to keep the details to us... For now.

Tyler hesitates, then lets out a sigh. "The woman who dropped Serene off at my doorstep showed up."

I relax a little. He's not giving away all of the details of how Serene was conceived. I feel almost ecstatic that we could have a silent conversation, and he understood what I was trying to signal him. It makes us feel like more of a unit. More of an us-against-the-world feeling I never thought I'd have.

Connor's jaw drops, then he seems to gather himself. "Thought she'd left the country."

"She did. But then she tracked us here. Said she realized how much of a mistake she'd made by giving up Serene," Tyler says slowly.

He rubs my upper arm in a soothing gesture. Which, I admit, feels very good.

"Took her only a year to realize that, huh?" Connor asks in a wry voice.

"It must have been difficult for her—both to give up Serene because she thought it'd be best for her, and then to admit to herself that she'd made a mistake," I say in a soft voice.

Both Tyler and Connor look at me in surprise.

"I know. I'm not supposed to empathize with someone who could theoretically be a rival for my daughter's affections. But as a mother —" I swallow. It's the first time saying those words makes me realize, I'm Serene's mother by blood. And truthfully, I should be ecstatic about it, but all I feel is a sense of befuddlement. It's like the events have been unfolding on the other side of a curtain, and I'm watching the shadows move, but can't quite tell what they're up to.

"—as a mother, I can't help but feel for what she's going through."

Tyler stares at me.

"What?" I draw down my eyebrows.

"You're a better person than me, though that doesn't surprise me at all," he confesses.

The waitress brings Connor his cup of coffee. He murmurs thanks, takes a sip, and sighs. "I needed that. So, the woman who dropped Serene off with Tyler shows up, and it leads to Serene being injured?"

Tyler's body stiffens. A ripple of tension runs through him, then he seems to get a hold of himself. "I've complained to the security about the incident and had them escort her off the premises. I've also asked my lawyer to apply for a restraining order, so she's not allowed near Serene again."

I whip my head in his direction. "When did you do that?"

"While you were with Serene." His features gentle. "Meanwhile, I've asked for additional security to be allocated to you and Serene while we're here." Then he studies me closely. "I hope you agree that it was the right thing to do?"

I purse my lips. "She is Serene's—" I hesitate. What should I call her? She's not her mother. She's a surrogate. "She thought she was Serene's mother. I don't condone her actions, but cutting her out of Serene's life seems heartless."

My husband's expression grows disapproving, then considering. "After what happened, I can't let her be alone with our daughter. I will not risk anything that could hurt Serene."

"Me neither." I place my hand on his. "But it seems coldhearted to not allow her to see Serene."

My husband hesitates. I see the conflict in his eyes—the father in him warring with the humane part of him I'm trying to appeal to. Because time and time again, Tyler has proven to me that, while his persona might be that of a cold and calculating billionaire business-man, what he is at heart is the former Marine who'd sacrifice himself for the greater good. It's what I sensed about him when I met him. It's what I admire most about him. Despite the fact he asked me to leave that day Serene was left at his doorstep, without giving me a valid reason why, I know he's a good man. He cares about his daugh-ter. He cares about me. I know, he'll do what's right.

"What if you don't let her meet Serene alone?"

Tyler scowls. Connor holds up his hands. "If I were in your shoes, there's no way I'd want that woman anywhere near my daughter. But your wife's argument is hard to brush aside. So, my suggestion is, what if one or both of you are always present when she meets Serene? And we can make sure there's security as a backup."

Tyler's forehead knits. He seems to be struggling with his thoughts. When he begins to pull his hand out from under mine, I hold on. I beseech him without saying anything, counting on that unspoken connection we've established, where I hope he can read my thoughts. Where I hope he realizes that I understand him. "I'm upset by what happened with Serene, but she already saw Lauren and is bound to wonder about it. I don't want to lie to our daughter about who Lauren is. Of course, we'll need to explain it to her in an age-appropriate manner and ensure she's comfortable with it. We can't just cut Lauren out of her life, but we can make her wait until Serene is ready."

Tyler's jaw hardens. But I'm still holding his hand, and he hasn't pulled away, so it gives me the encouragement to keep going. "Again, it's not an excuse, but what happened was an accident."

My husband glares at me. A part of me quivers at the anger in his gaze. It borders on eroticism for me. A part of me loves that I'm at the receiving end of his attention. And the other part of me wonders how I could be so selfish to think of myself and my needs when our daughter is lying wounded upstairs. But it's also thoughts of her and her future which has me holding his gaze. My heart flutters, and my pussy quivers, but I don't look away.

For a few seconds, we're locked in this battle of wills, and the chemistry between us spikes. The very air between us heats. Then Connor clears his throat. It breaks through the tension building between Tyler and me.

Tyler's eyes gleam. I read his expression correctly as promising me retribution. I shouldn't feel excited by that, but tell that to my pussy, which melts in anticipation. Then Tyler nods. "Let's talk to Serene's therapist and see what she suggests."

My heart soars. Being willing to consider my opinions when it comes to Serene means more than he can imagine. "That sounds like a great idea. Thank you."

Tyler merely tilts his head.

That's when his phone vibrates. Without taking his gaze from mine, he pulls out the device, listens to the voice at the other end, then rises to his feet. "She's awake."

52

Tyler

"I want to go home, Papa," Serene whispers.

I kiss her fingers. Then, when that doesn't seem like enough, I rise to my feet and, making sure not to disturb the IV she's hooked up to, I slide onto the bed with my daughter.

The bed's narrow and too short for me, so I'm perched on the edge, almost curled around our daughter. She snuggles in, and my heart squeezes in my chest.

My daughter feels so little, so fragile. And each time I take in the bandage on her forehead, my guts churn with anger. I hold her close. "As soon as you're well enough to travel, I promise, we'll head back."

She sniffs, then nods, and her eyes close. I rub my finger over her soft cheek and promise to myself I'll never allow myself to slip up like this again. The only reason I agreed to allow that woman to see my daughter again is because my wife asked. I can't deny Cilla. That's the kind of power she holds over me. And it's because I trust her more than anyone else in my life that I agreed to her idea. That, and the fact she guessed rightly that there's a decent man hidden inside me. The one she brings to the surface because she makes me want to be the kind of man she'll be proud of.

"She's asleep," my wife murmurs from the chair across the bed.

When I don't move, she walks over and sits on the other side of Serene, bracketing her between us.

She rests one hand on Serene's shoulder, the other cradling her face. "What are you thinking?" she asks quietly.

"That I'm lucky to have both of you in my life. That I'd do everything in my power to protect both of you. That I'll never let anything hurt either of you."

She smiles and her eyes glow with warmth. "I believe you."

"How do you feel about everything that's happened?"

Her forehead wrinkles. A haunted look comes into her eyes. I already miss the tender light in her eyes, but it would have been remiss of me if I hadn't asked her that question.

She looks away. "I haven't had much time to absorb everything. I'm still taken aback by it. A part of me can't believe this could happen. Another part tells me, of course, this is why I was so drawn to Serene from the beginning. And yet, another part is having trouble accepting it. It all feels like a lot."

"It is." I place my hand on top of where hers rests on my daughter. "And you should take all the time you need to adjust to it."

"Thank you." When she looks at me again, her eyes are sad. "I should feel ecstatic about this, but it all feels like a dream. I feel more than a little disoriented."

"It's natural. You went from thinking you were her stepmother to realizing you're her biological one. It's a big change."

She half-smiles. "You're good at being understanding."

I hold her gaze. "I lost you once. Didn't think I'd ever have you back in my life. So, when I opened that door and saw you standing there, I felt I'd been given a second chance. I'm not going to screw things up this time."

Her chin trembles, and her lips part. She leans in at the same time as me. I press my mouth to hers. Softly. Gently. Ever so carefully. Savoring the sweetness. Feeling the tenderness well up in me.

Becoming a father and a husband has shattered the armor I once wore to protect my emotions. It's shorn me of the barriers I put up against the world. Gone is the man who was focused only on himself. I might have been a Marine, but the money and privilege I came from gave me a false sense of security. Perhaps, it even made me feel invincible in ways I wasn't aware of.

Serene coming into my life shattered those illusions. It made me painfully human. It stripped me of all illusions and showed me what life is really about. The reality of being responsible for another human being who can't take care of herself, one who's completely dependent on me for everything, made me realize how vulnerable I am. While I went through life with confidence, feeling essentially untouchable, overnight, I turned into someone who feared the world was not a safe enough place for my daughter. And the incidents of the past twenty-four hours have, in a way, confirmed it to me.

Life is fleeting. It can change in an instant. Seeing my daughter's prone body, finding out she wasn't breathing, and then resuscitating her, was more traumatic than every encounter I faced on a mission as a Marine. And now that she's alive and safe, I'm humbled and grateful. While I never gave much thought to a higher power, having my wife and daughter near me makes me appreciate this chance I've been given. And the fact that Cilla is biologically Serene's mother completely blows my mind. In a good way. It feels right. Like it was meant to be. After that initial surprise, it made so much sense, I can't think of a reality where anything else could be true.

I lean back and look deeply into her eyes. "I love you."

Her eyes grow wide. She seems stunned. Maybe it's too much? Maybe I should have waited to tell her? Should I have given her time to assimilate her relationship to Serene before I launched this at her? But I wanted her to know as soon as it dawned on me. Surely, there's nothing wrong with that?

"I have loved you since I first saw you struggling with your handbag and trying to get it free from the train doors."

I take in the shock on her features, which turns to surprise and pleasure. She opens her mouth, and I'm sure she's going to tell me those three words back, when the door opens and a nurse walks in. "I need to check her and make sure everything is fine."

"Of course." My wife pulls her hand from under mine and rises from the bed. She straightens her crumpled dress, pushes the hair off her face, then smiles brightly at the nurse. "I'll be outside." She leaves without looking at me. I take my time straightening, push aside the rejection coiling around my heart, and bend and kiss my daughter. Then, I nod at the nurse and follow my wife through the connecting door into the room next door.

I could tell myself she's upset about our daughter, which is why she didn't return the sentiment I express to her. I'm confident she has feelings for me. I sense it when I hold her in my arms, when I look into her eyes and kiss her. When I make love to her. When I see her with Serene. I felt our connection from the second we met. And while I might have messed up when I asked her to leave that day — I don't believe it was enough to kill her feelings for me completely.

She must love me still. She must have feelings for me. So why didn't she tell me so when I professed my love for her?

I follow her into the adjoining room. I asked the hospital to place my daughter in this suite when she came out of recovery. It meant we could spend the night in relative comfort. It has two single beds, but I can't complain. The suite itself is outfitted more like the room of a five-star hotel, with carpets and curtains, soft lighting, and an en suite bathroom. There's even a kitchenette and a small seating area. It softens the reality that we're in a hospital. And the fact that we're so close to Serene is indispensable.

I shut the door softly and walk over to where my wife is standing by the window.

"Are you okay?" I stand next to her.

She nods but continues to stare out the window. My heart sinks a little. This isn't looking good. I shove my thoughts aside and focus on her. "Serene's going to be fine. She's in good hands."

Cilla nods again.

"And I already agreed to give that woman a chance to see her."

My wife turns to face me. "It's been a lot. I never thought I would turn out to be Serene's biological mother. Not in a million years." She tries to smile but her chin trembles. "It's overwhelming."

A flurry of unease prickles my spine. But I manage to keep all emotions off my face. Everything she says is right. And it must be a shock to find out she and Serene are mother and child.

"I have feelings for you, Tyler. A lot of powerful feelings." She swallows.

I nod again. The hair on the back of my neck rises. "But?" I manage to force out.

"But I am still getting my head around the fact that I'm Serene's mother." The expression on her face turns beseeching. "I know, it shouldn't be so. After all, this is the best possible outcome of the situation. But it seems, I'm much better at giving than receiving." She half-smiles.

"What do you mean?" I'm trying to make sense of what she's saying, and perhaps I have an idea, but I need her to spell it out for me.

"Turns out, when you get everything, you desire, you're so in over your head, you need a little time to get used to the new reality." Her gaze is pleading. "Can you give that to me please?"

53

Priscilla

You are not lost; you are choosing your path.
-Cilla's Post-it note

I love you. Those three words I've hoped to hear from him. And now that he's said it, I find myself doubting him. *If he really loved me, wouldn't he have said those words to me when he asked me to marry him?*

Is he saying this to me because he found out I'm Serene's biological mother? Does he feel obligated to do so now?

I wasn't lying when I said that I felt blindsided by the revelation of being Serene's biological mother. First, being denied by him, then tentatively accepted, and now, faced with this revelation makes me feel like I'm drowning. That is the only explanation I have for my inability to accept what he's saying.

And why can't I ask him these questions? Why do I feel so

tongue-tied? My brain feels exhausted, as does my body. I feel like I've run a marathon and now, I've run out of energy. My shoulders sag a little. I must sway, for his expression changes to one of concern.

"I'm being selfish, thinking only of myself at a time like this."

Before I can protest, he bends and scoops me up in his arms. I stare—surprised, bemused, and also, relieved for the weight to be taken off my feet. I should protest, but really, it feels so good.

"You're tired." He doesn't wait for my response before he walks to one of the beds in the room and places me on it. Then he pulls off my shoes and covers me. "You should get some more sleep. We can talk tomorrow." He turns to leave, but I grab his hand.

He glances my way. There's disappointment in his eyes but also, understanding. His hair is mussed up from having run his fingers through it. His face seems leaner, almost gaunt. Those cheekbones that were sharp enough to cut glass seem more pronounced. There are new lines around his eyes, and I swear, there are flecks of gray in his hair I never noticed before.

Naturally, it just adds to the whole package. Even the scrubs work for him—hell, they worship him. Tyler Davenport in medical gear still looks like a runway model for *Sexiest Man Alive: Surgeon Edition.* And like fine wine, he's only going to get better with each day —richer, darker, more intoxicating. And *I* get to enjoy all of it. "Sleep with me?"

He stiffens. "You sure?"

I nod. "I want you next to me."

He studies my face like he's memorizing it—like he won't settle until he's sure I'm okay.

Then, wordlessly, he toes off the disposable hospital-issue footwear and climbs onto the bed beside me. The mattress dips with his weight.

He coaxes me onto my side, then slides in close. His arm glides under my neck, so my neck rests against the solid curve of his bicep. He wraps his other arm around my waist, anchoring me to him.

He fits himself against me, chest to spine, breath to breath.

His heat seeps into my skin, wraps around my ribs, melts the last of the tension I didn't realize I was still holding.

A breath slips from my lips—half sigh, half surrender. I snuggle in closer.

"Comfortable?" His voice rumbles up his chest.

I nod. I sense him hardening against my thigh. And that's reassuring. It's a sign of life. It tells me more than words that things are going to be fine.

"Close your eyes," he orders.

When I open my eyes next, the silvery light outside tells me dawn is breaking over the horizon. I also hear the chirping of birds; it's soothing. I haven't stirred from the position I fell asleep in. And neither has Tyler. His chest rises and falls. The thickness which prods at my waist seems to have grown in size. Despite the air conditioner in the room, Tyler's body is so hot, I'm sweating. At some point, I must have thrown the covers off because of that. My dress is bunched up around my waist, and Tyler's thrown one muscular leg over mine, pinning me in place. I feel refreshed though. His breathing is even, so Tyler must still be asleep. I lay there and watch the sky lighten outside the window.

At some point, his muscles ripple, and I sense he's awake. His arm tightens around my waist. "You awake?"

Without waiting for an answer, he lowers his leg from over mine and urges me to turn. Now, I'm face-to-face with him. Nose to nose. Our mouths within kissing distance. I survey that pouty lower lip and want to dig my teeth in and suck on it. His warm breath singes my cheek. His arm on the dip of my waist is heavy. He slides his thigh between mine, the ridge of it pushes against my core. The breath whistles out of me. My nipples pebble. My thighs tighten.

He flattens his thick fingers over my butt cheek and squeezes. A soft moan spills from my mouth. One side of his lips kicks up, like he's pleased by my response. And when I raise my gaze, his pupils are dilated. He's as aroused as I am. His nostrils flare, a nerve popping at his temple. I raise my hand and trace the line of his jaw.

His morning scruff is rough, the look in his eyes tender. A study in contrasts, like him.

He maneuvers me closer, holding me in place so my melting pussy is positioned exactly at his crotch.

"Take me out," he murmurs.

I glance toward the door. "We shouldn't."

"We absolutely should." He squeezes my butt cheeks with just enough pressure that my pussy responds. My clit throbs. My breasts grow heavier.

"Do it," he says in a low, hard voice.

My nerve endings crackle. I reach down, slip my fingers under the waistband of his scrubs, and pull out his cock. I automatically drop my gaze and find the crown swollen, almost purple, with beads of precum clinging to it. My mouth waters. I wrap my fingers around him, swipe from base to crown, and squeeze.

A groan rumbles from him.

A thrill squeezes my lower belly. I continue to massage him, watching as he grows even bigger, thicker, until I can barely keep my fingers wrapped around his circumference.

"Fuck, baby, just like that."

A shiver cascades down my spine. His approval sets off a chain of need deep inside me. I continue to stroke him, continue to get wetter, hornier, more needy.

He pushes aside the gusset of my panties, then positions me so I'm straddling him, with the crown of his dick teasing my opening. Placing one hand on his chest for leverage, I stay there for a second, then I push down and impale myself. *So good. So filling.* I groan. So does he.

His cock throbs inside me, pushing at my inner walls. I throw my head back, allowing my senses to coalesce at the place where we're joined. He seems even bigger than before. I'm fuller, somehow. Or maybe, it's because I feel closer to him. Knowing Serene is our daughter—has both of our blood running through her—knowing we share her, and everything that's happened in the past twenty-four hours makes this feel even more intimate.

I look into his face to find he's gritting his teeth. His mismatched eyes are filled with lust. With desire. With need. And love. It adds another dimension, turning our lovemaking into something on the verge of being soul-shattering. Gaze locked with his, I pull back until he's balanced at the rim of my pussy, then lower myself again.

His shoulders ripple. His hold on my butt cheeks grows almost punishing. The pain accentuates the spirals of pleasure coursing out from where we're joined.

"You feel so good, baby. Your pussy is so tight. So wet. It has my cock in a choke hold."

His words are filthy and turn my blood into molten lava. My desire peaks. My breath comes in pants. I'm so turned on; my thighs turn to jelly. He seems to understand my inability to move effectively, for he takes charge. He holds me in place, then punches his hips up and buries himself to the hilt.

I gasp, hold onto his biceps as he pistons into me. Each time he thrusts into me, he hits that spot deep inside. My desire escalates. My heart clatters against my rib cage. He lunges up and into me, seeming to grow even bigger. The sensations are so intense, they seem to vibrate through my body to my extremities. I hold onto him, unable to do anything but take his pounding, riding that wave that gets higher and higher, unable to close my eyes, for he has me locked in the tractor beam of his gaze.

It's intense, and hot, and sexy, and somehow, so very emotional. My throat closes. A pressure builds behind my eyes. And when he pistons up and into me and growls, "Come," the tears squeeze out from the corners of my eyes, and I shatter.

54

Tyler

She begins to cry out. I release my hold on her and slap my hand over her mouth to muffle the sounds. Normally, I'd want the entire world to hear how well I satisfy my wife, but I don't want to disturb Serene. As her body shudders in the aftermath of her climax, I flip her over so she's under me. She stares at me with lust-filled eyes as I plunge into her, fucking her through the shudders jolting her body. Until, with a final thrust, I pour myself into her. I keep my weight mostly off her, so as not to crush her, reveling in the tiny flutters of her pussy around my cock. Then, unable to stop myself, I lower my head and kiss her deeply. She winds her arms about my neck and kisses me back. The taste of her is drugging. It goes straight to my head and to my groin.

I feel myself get erect again and force myself to pull out. She needs her rest. But I can't stop myself from kissing her. Falling onto the bed next to her, I gather her close. For a few seconds we lay there, skin plastered to slippery skin, her heart pounding against mine.

"Wow." She turns her head into my chest and presses her lips there. "That was…something." She looks down between her legs. I follow her gaze to find my cum dripping out of her.

On instinct, I reach down, scoop up my cum, and push it back inside her.

"What are you doing?" she gasps.

"Making sure you take every bit of what belongs to you." I tilt her chin up and kiss her again. "You belong to me. This pussy is mine. This mouth. These lips. These breasts." I squeeze her nipple. "All of this belongs to me. Only me. You feel me?"

She nods.

I kiss her again, wishing I could bury myself inside her once more, but knowing we need to become parents again. With a resigned sigh, I release her, pull up my scrubs, swing my feet over the side, and rise to my feet. I hold out my hand and help her up, then put her clothes to rights. There's a knock on the external door leading to our room.

"Come in," I call out.

Connor pushes the door open and walks in with two backpacks, which he places on the closest chair. "Clothes for the both of you. Summer packed yours." He nods in Cilla's direction. "Your phone is also in there."

"Thank you," she murmurs.

He turns to me. "And there's a replacement one for you." If he guesses what we've been up to from our disheveled, state he doesn't mention it.

"I'll wait outside for you."

We get dressed quickly, then peek into Serene's room. There's a nurse on duty next to her, so we walk over to Serene and, together, we watch our sleeping daughter.

"She slept through the night. The doctor should be here to see her shortly," the nurse tells us.

After confirming she'll call us when our daughter is awake, we exit through the door to the corridor and join Connor.

"How is she?" He nods toward Serene's room.

"She had a peaceful night. We'll have to wait for the doctor to examine her to let us know about her condition."

By mutual consent, we head down to the cafeteria again for breakfast.

After we've ordered, Cilla busies herself with her phone, no doubt, answering messages which must have come in. There are a lot of unopened messages and emails on my phone too, but they'll keep.

"Arthur's worried about all of you. He wants you back in London ASAP." Connor takes a sip of coffee.

"Me too."

Connor's phone vibrates. He pulls it out and makes a face. "Speak of the devil." He answers the call and listens, then looks at me. "He's here."

He holds the phone out to me.

My grandfather is the last person I want to speak to. When I hesitate, my wife takes the phone from Connor. "Hello, Grandad."

I frown. I've never called Arthur that. It's always Arthur or Gramps.

She listens, and nods. "Yes, she's better. The doctors said she's out of danger. But we're waiting for her to be examined to find out when she'll be discharged."

I hear the old man's voice at the other end of the line. I'm too far away to make out the words though. She listens intently, then nods again. "Yes, of course, I'll call you and let you know when we've taken her back to the resort."

She listens some more.

"No, no. There's no need for you to come. Tyler has it under control." She shoots me a glance.

I frown, a question in my eyes, but she shakes her head, indicating she'll tell me about it after the call. At least, that's what I assume. I accept this telepathic connection we seem to have formed somewhere along the way.

"Of course, Grandad, nice to speak to you too." She disconnects the phone, hands it over to Connor, and levels a glance at me.

"What?" I growl.

"Didn't think you'd be afraid to talk to Arthur."

I scoff. "Not afraid, simply discerning. The man has a way of getting involved in things he has no business being involved in."

"He was worried about Serene."

The knot of discomfort in my chest eases a little. "He does love Serene," I confess.

"He wanted to know if there was anything he could do to help, is all."

"You told him I was handling it." I lower my chin.

"I meant it. There's no man more capable than you, Tyler Davenport."

Yet, she hasn't told me she loves me. I can't stop the frown that filters across my forehead.

She leans forward in her seat. There's a plea in her eyes which I could claim I don't understand except, with this damned intuitive thing going on between us, that would be a lie.

She wants me to give her time to figure things out. To come to terms with everything that's happened. The way I needed time to process everything when she and Serene came into my life at the same time.

I forced the space between us then. The good thing is, unlike me, she hasn't asked for physical distance. If she did, I'd agree out of respect for her wishes, but it would be bloody difficult. And to be honest, I'm not sure if I'd be able to comply.

Our gazes meet, and the air between us heats. One thing she can't deny. Our bodies are tuned in to each other. As if sensing the invisible pull between us, she sways forward. I grab the arms of her chair and haul her closer. She raises her chin; I lower mine and brush my lips over hers. She opens her mouth; I sweep my tongue in. The moment my tongue touches hers, my blood heats, and my groin hardens.

I begin to deepen the kiss, when I hear a loud throat clearing. Connor. I ignore him, until the nurse's voice reaches us. "Serene is awake and asking for you."

55

Priscilla

Healing isn't linear, but it's always progress.
-Cilla's Post-it note

This morning, two days after the incident at the pool, the doctor discharged Serene. He confirmed she was well enough to travel, and we made the decision that it would be best to move Serene back home as soon as possible. With that in mind, Tyler hired a doctor and nurse to accompany us on the flight back. He also sourced a private aircraft already kitted out with everything needed to transport our daughter.

The main bedroom on the flight is equipped with a medical bed to ensure Serene's comfort. There are IV poles on hand, as well as an adequate supply of medical-grade oxygen with an easily accessible mask. Tyler insisted on adding medical monitoring equipment, a defibrillator, and an emergency kit. The pilot confirmed there's sufficient power sources for medical devices, as well as a backup power supply. The filtration system was upgraded to ensure her immune system is not compromised. And of course, there are extra blood units of the correct blood type—mine—as well.

There's an additional bed in the room for one of us to sleep in, as well an adjoining bedroom where we can retreat to for some privacy. Tyler's attention to detail is astonishing. He personally supervised everything. It's a testament to just how involved he is in Serene's well-being.

Sinclair, Summer and Matty, as well as Connor, are traveling with us. The grown-ups have insisted on relieving us by taking turns spending time with Serene. Serene trusts all of them. And she's happy to have Matty with her. The boy marched in with his books and toys and hasn't left Serene's side since we took off. With the presence of the doctor and nurse onboard the flight, I feel reassured that Serene will be fine.

We're halfway through the flight home. Sinclair, Connor, and Matty are with Serene. Tyler and I are seated in one of the double club seats, and Summer is in the one next to us across the aisle.

I left Serene smiling and enjoying Matty's company. Sinclair and Connor are keeping watch over them. With my head pillowed on my husband's shoulder and a soft blanket covering me, I feel warm and secure.

My phone buzzes with an incoming FaceTime call. It's Zoey, so I answer it.

"Oh, my God, there you are, finally! We were so worried." Zoey's face fills the screen. "How is Serene? And are you okay?"

"Serene's doing much better. And I'm fine." *And it's all thanks to Tyler.*

As if sensing my unspoken words and confirming to me again that he can read my mind, Tyler lowers his chin and presses a kiss to my hair.

"Is that Tyler? Oh my gosh, you guys are so cute," she cries.

I pull the phone back so Tyler can smile at Zoey. "How are you doing?"

She flashes him a smile. "I'm good." Then she sobers. "I'm so pleased Serene is better."

"She's a survivor. She'll pull through, and hopefully, there won't be any lasting damage from what happened, neither physically nor emotionally." His jaw tightens.

"I'm going to step aside and talk to Zoey, so I don't disturb you and Summer, okay?" I kiss his cheek and rise to my feet, walking to the far end of the aircraft where there's a meeting area, complete with a bar, a couch, and a coffee table. I sink onto the couch and look up to find Tyler's eyes are on me across the length of the plane. He responds to something Summer asks, but his gaze is fixed on me. There's no mistaking the possessiveness or the love on his face, even at this distance. He's sprawled in the club seat, and the solidness of his body seems to take up all the oxygen in the space. With those broad shoulders, his arm flung over the seat, and his long legs kicked out in front—he's an impressive specimen of male virility. And warmth. And sexiness. An apex predator at rest.

One side of his mouth kicks up. There's a teasing glint in his eyes. A combination of affection and possession which makes me blush. Damn, I don't think I'll ever get used to seeing the lust in his eyes and realizing it's for me.

I hear the low murmur of Summer's words as she says something else to him. With a last heated glance, he turns to her. My muscles slump. I feel like I've broken free of a riptide I didn't know I was caught up in.

"Priscilla, you there?" Zoey frowns.

"Yes, of course. What were you saying?"

"Harper and Grace also want to join the call. Is that okay?'

"I'd love to talk to them."

She brings them on. Harper and Grace appear in their squares on screen.

"Hey bish, I'm so happy to see you," Harper cries.

Grace looks at me closely. "How are you holding up?"

I smile, grateful for my friends' concern. "I'm not bad, considering."

"So sorry you had to cut your honeymoon short. But Serene's fine, and that's all that matters, right?" Harper's eyes soften.

"She's a trooper."

"And she has the best parents in the world. She's going to be fine," Zoey says with so much confidence, it makes my heart swell in my chest.

Grace, who's been eyeing me with growing intensity, interrupts, "What's up with you? Tell us everything."

I glance away, wondering how much to confide in them. Yes, they're my friends, but these details feel so intimate. On the other hand, I feel like I need some perspective on what happened. And help in understanding my panicky reaction to Tyler's declaration of love. So, I pop in my earbuds, then sink down on the couch, so I'm no longer in direct line of view with Tyler. Mainly, so I can concentrate on what I'm saying. Then, in a low voice to make sure I'm not being overhead, I tell them everything that happened.

From Lauren showing up, to Serene hitting her head and falling into the pool. Tyler saving her, the scramble to the hospital, and then finding out my blood type matched Serene's. And then, of course, the big reveal of my turning out to be Serene's biological mother. And then, Tyler's confession that he loves me.

When I finish, there's silence. Even the normally unflappable Grace is staring at me, open-mouthed.

Harper is the first to recover. "You're her mother. That's great. It's what you wanted all along." She grins at me.

Grace widens her gaze. "It's not that simple, is it? It's mind-boggling when you think of the odds that something like this could take place."

"But he loves her; he told her so," Harper addresses her comment at Grace. "It may have not happened in the conventional fashion, but she has her family. Isn't that what matters?"

"I think it's more complicated than that," Grace says again.

I watch her intently. It feels good to hear her say what's on my mind, but I've been unable to voice.

"Why not?" Harper scowls. "He loves her. And she certainly has feelings for him. And they have a beautiful child. They found each other. It's a ready-made family. And they all lived happily after."

"But did he tell her he loves her because he found out that she's Serene's mother?" Grace's eyes wear an astute expression.

"Is that what you're worried about?" Zoey tilts her head.

"Partly," I admit. "Also, it might be that it all feels too new? That I'm Serene's biological mother, and that Tyler loves me?" I rub at my temple. "Maybe it's because I've wanted to hear these words from him for so long, and now, doing so is making me run scared?"

"Perhaps, you need time to accept it, is all," Harper says slowly. "I mean, you do love him, don't you?"

I nod. *Of course, I do.* It's why I've never gotten him out of my mind, since I met him. And yes, I want to be with him. So why am I unable to come out and tell him how I feel?

"Is it because he didn't tell you he loved you when he asked you to marry him? And with you turning out to be Serene's biological mother, it feels too tidy to tell him about your feelings?"

I rub at my temple. "I'm sure that's part of it too. It's confusing, to be honest. On the one hand, nothing matters because I am where I'm supposed to be, regardless of the drama that came before it. And yet... A part of me tells me I need to wait. For what, I don't know." I look into the screen and recite from memory. *"The desire for a more positive experience is itself a negative experience. And paradoxically, the acceptance of one's negative experience is itself a positive experience."*

"Is that from one of your self-help books?" Grace's voice is amused.

"I forget where I read it, but it seems to ring true right now." I lean back against the cushions of the couch. "It might feel like the world is collapsing around me, but on the positive side, I have Serene. And I'm her mother. Her biological mother. And then, I'm in a luxurious private jet, married to the man I thought I'd never have, talking to my friends, and surrounded by people who care for me. So, you know, it's not like I've come out so badly."

"Exactly." Harper brightens. "You just need to go with the flow. Give yourself a chance to accept everything, until things feel normal."

She's right, of course. And everything I've said rings true. If not for that tiny niggling something in the corner of my subconscious, a bit like how the pea gave the princess a backache — I'm actually good. "What do you think, Zoey?" I ask my friend.

She gives me a small smile. "I think you should follow your instincts. No harm in making the man sweat a little before you tell him the words, I'm sure he wants to hear."

56

Tyler

"Hold still, Papa," my daughter admonishes me.

I find a more comfortable position, spread my legs wider, fold my arms across my chest and sigh. "How much longer?"

"Until I finish painting your face." She shakes out her coloring pen and draws a line down my cheek, then up the other way, drawing what I assume is a circle. Then she begins to fill in the space, her tongue between her lips as she concentrates on the task at hand. With her brows furrowed, and golden sparks flaring in her eyes, she looks so like Cilla, I wonder why I didn't spot it earlier. A person sees what they want to, I suppose. Before Priscilla, I'd look at my daughter and be sure I saw myself in the curve of her chin, the high cheekbones, the nose. And every time I was reminded of Priscilla, I dismissed it as something my mind had conjured because I regretted sending her away. Now, I look at Serene and I see Priscilla, especially in many of her expressions, and I know it's not my mind playing tricks on me.

She crosses over my lap to stand on my other side. We're on the couch in the living room where the football game is on. Arsenal is playing Man-U. The rest of my brothers decided to meet at Sinclair's place to watch the match. I turned it down to stay home with Serene and Priscilla.

Priscilla offered to cook dinner, but I insisted on getting it catered tonight. I wanted to spend the night with us on the couch doing absolutely nothing. And if I'm secretly hoping Serene will eat the food and go to bed soon so I can steal a few hours with my wife alone, that doesn't make me a bad father, does it?

The food arrived, and Priscilla busied herself plating it out in the kitchen. I suggested keeping a chef who'd come in on a daily basis to cook for us, but Priscilla refused. She prefers to do the cooking herself, and I help her out, too. Our domestic help is restricted to the cleaner and the gardener.

Other than that, I have my uncle Quentin's security team monitoring the house. I have faith in him. And it seems to be working. So far, Lauren hasn't contacted us or shown up, which I take as a good sign. Some instinct tells me, she's not going to give up. She's not going to wait patiently for us to contact her. She might try to find a way to meet Serene. But I shove that aside. That's why I have the restraining order in place. I doubt she's going to break that and jeopardize her chance of having a future relationship with Serene.

Ensconced in my living room with the television showing the game, my daughter next to me on the couch, and waiting for my wife to join us, I've never felt more content.

"Look that way." Serene steers my face so my chin points to the side. I manage to keep my eyes glued to the TV screen and the game in progress.

She's taken it into her head to paint my face. Something I couldn't say no to. It's been nearly a month since we returned from Bali. Serene recovered quickly from her ordeal. The bandages and stitches came off within a week.

Within the next day, she was on her feet and insisting she wanted to go to the playground. She's also wanted to go swimming, which is a relief. It means her ordeal hasn't put her off from using the swimming pool.

Connor, who returned home after his last research trip, decided to stick around and help me out. For now. My other brothers, Nathan and Knox, have pitched in, too. Brody offered, but I refused his help. That man's a workaholic. He already works eighteen-hour days, I wasn't going to ask him to spend more time behind a desk. Nathan and Knox have a better work-life balance, being married. And they know when to switch off so they can have a life outside of work. As for Connor, I know it won't be long before he heads off on another of his mysterious trips, which he seems to relish.

I've spent every free second possible with Serene. Priscilla, too, has devoted herself to her. The result? Serene had made a full recovery. Except for the scar on her forehead, which will fade with time—I hope. She hasn't mentioned the incident to us. By mutual agreement, Priscilla and I haven't brought it up with Serene either. At some point, we'll have to decide how to introduce Lauren to Serene, but that won't happen for a few more months, at least. Not until Serene is completely recovered. Meanwhile, I've increased security around the house and ensured Serene and Priscilla don't go anywhere without someone watching over them.

"Papa, close your eyes." Serene frowns.

"I'll miss the football," I protest.

"Pl-e-a-s-e," she begs me.

Of course, I oblige her. She begins to paint under my eyes, and I have a feeling I'm not going to like how I look when I open them. But I can't refuse this girl. Or my wife. I love both of them so very much. Only Serene tells me so; Cilla still hasn't. I thought it wouldn't be long before she shared her feelings for me. But it's been weeks since I first told her, and she hasn't ventured there yet.

If anything, we're closer as husband, as wife, and as a family. Since we returned, I've made love to her every night after Serene is asleep. The intensity of emotions I feel every time I fuck her has only grown. I've told her I love her when I'm inside her, hoping she'll tell me what I want to hear in the heat of passion. I swear, she's even come close to saying it to me, but so far, it hasn't actually happened. Still, I don't give up hope.

It's only a matter of time. I'll wear her down. She does love me. I can feel it in the absolute harmony there is between us, in this feeling of what I can only call bliss every time I come inside her. If only she'd say those words to me.

The football commentator's voice rises in excitement. The cheering of the crowds reaches me. *It's a goal.* I groan. Damn, I missed seeing that.

Serene stops painting. I sense her shift on the couch. "Can I open my eyes?"

"No," she yelps. The couch dips as she steps back to the other side of me, then she touches my cheek. I realize she's pasting something on my face. I grimace, but don't protest. It's fine. I can wash it off, right? A few more minutes of this, then she moves to my hair. Grabbing at the short strands, she bunches them, then uses a band to tie them together. Her fingers get caught in the strands, and when she tugs on them, I wince but don't move.

I still have my eyes closed, but I hear footsteps approaching and realize Cilla is walking toward us. Then I hear her giggling. "Oh, my God, you look—" She seems to have difficulty forming the words. "You look adorable."

I sigh again. Not the kind of word I want associated with me. But if it makes my daughter and my wife happy, I guess, I can put up with it. For a little while.

"Can I open my eyes now?" I ask Serene.

She touches up something on my chin, then jumps off the sofa. "Okay."

I open my eyes, snapping my gaze on the television, but the game is already over. I sigh, switch it off, then grab my phone, open the camera app, and look at myself. My face is a blur of colors—yellow around my eyes, blue on my cheeks, and the tip of my nose is painted purple. My lips have been painted a bright red, and there's more of it on my chin. Various stickers featuring different kinds of fruit are stuck to my face. And the band around my hair has a pink flower stuck to it. "I look—"

"So cute!" My wife clasps her hands together. "I need to take a photo." She pulls out her camera and points it at me. I grab Serene, and she shrieks and wriggles in my arms. I hold her close, then press my cheek to hers.

She shrieks, "Ugh, Papa, you're making my face dirty!"

I stare at her, dumbfounded. "Why you little—"

She giggles and squirms in my hold, then kisses my cheek. *Awww.* My fingers loosen, and she darts free, jumps down, and races to her mother, hiding behind a laughing Cilla. "You can't catch me, *na—nana—na-na.*" She sticks her tongue out at me.

When I rise to my feet and stalk toward them, she yelps and grabs hold of Cilla's blouse, plastering herself to her mother, as if that's going to hide her from me. I reach them, swipe out my hand, but she evades me. Giggling madly, she releases Cilla and makes a run for it. But I'm faster. I snatch her up, and she shrieks again.

I hold Serene over my shoulder, and she begins to giggle even more. Her entire body shakes so much with laughter, it's infectious. And I find myself grinning at Cilla, who's doubled over chuckling to herself. Very aware that Serene's only recently recovered from her injury, I slowly lower her to her feet.

She instantly darts away and through the open door into the garden. "You can't catch me," she yells over her shoulder. Her footsteps recede.

Cilla continues to grin at me. "You do look rather dashing, Mr. Davenport."

"Is that right?" I take a step in her direction.

She's still laughing, so I take her by surprise when I grab her by her waist and haul her up so her feet are dangling off the ground. Then I bend my face and kiss her, smearing her face with the colors on mine in the process. She squeals, tries to arch her face this way and that, trying to evade me, but I'm stronger and faster. I drag my cheek against first one of hers, then the other, then rub our noses, before kissing her deeply again. She melts into me, wrapping her legs about my waist and her arms about my neck. The phone slides down my back and bounces off the floor. I ignore it, heading toward the wall next to the door leading outside. The one Serene rushed through moments ago. I push my wife into the wall, making sure my throbbing cock is positioned exactly against her pussy, so when I thrust my hips forward, I hit that sweet spot in her center.

She groans, "Oh, my God, how do you do that so well?"

"I'm good at finding my mark, baby." I piston forward, gathering speed, knowing we might have a minute, maybe two. If we're lucky, three. The only time we had more time for each other was during the early days of our honeymoon.

When you have a kid around, you make the most of the limited time you have and draw as much satisfaction as you can from it. So, I squeeze her thighs, holding her in place as I dry fuck her. I kiss her deeply, grinding down as deeply as I can with the barrier of our clothes between us. She digs her heels into my back, and when her body arches, and she shudders, and her breathing grows rough, and I can hear her heart thundering against mine, I bite down on her lower lip, making her jolt. Then I tear my mouth from hers, look into her eyes and growl, "Come."

Instantly, her body vibrates as she shatters. She opens her mouth to scream, but I place my mouth on hers, absorbing every sound, continuing to grind my cock into her clit which I can feel throb through the clothes. I feel the warmth of her pussy sear my length. Feel her flutter as she comes. I continue to rub up against her as the aftershocks grip her. I soften my kiss, until she raises her eyelids.

The dazed expression in them is my badge of honor. My heart feels so full, like it's growing bigger by the second. It fills my chest and overflows, turning my body into one pulsating organ beating out the rhythm that says: "I love you. I love you so fucking much."

Her eyes fill. She opens her mouth, and I'm sure she's going to say those three blasted words back to me, when there's a scream from the garden.

57

Priscilla

"Serene!" My heart slams into my rib cage. My pulse rate shoots through the roof. I have just enough time to take in the flash of comprehension, followed by terror, on Tyler's features. A look I'll never forget. The next second, he lowers me to the floor and races through the door. I follow him, running into the garden. I scan the grass that slopes down to the boundary wall separating the property from the rest of Primrose Hill, the trees that line the space near the walls, the garden shed...but don't see her.

"Where is she?" I pant. "Serene?" I call out.

There's another scream, and this time, it's clear the sound comes from the space behind the garden shed.

Tyler takes off in that direction, and I follow. By the time I reach the shed, he's disappeared behind it. I round the side of the shed into the space between the shed and the wall and careen to a halt.

Serene's standing there, her back to us. And a few feet away, facing her, is Lauren. She's at the far side of the shed. She holds up her hands, palms facing us. "Please don't scream, Serene. I only wanted to see you."

Tears streaming down her cheeks, Serene turns and rushes past Tyler, throwing herself into my arms. I scoop her up and cradle her close. "There, honey. Don't worry. We're right here. Everything's going to be okay."

Ahead of me, Tyler's shoulders seem to swell. He seems to be getting bigger, broader, as if he's going to jump out of his skin like The Incredible Hulk. Anger radiates off of him. I sense his patience has snapped. That he's regretting not putting her behind bars, so she wouldn't come face-to-face with our daughter without warning again. Or perhaps, he's thinking he should have upped the security even more? How did she get in, anyway?

It's not like the security from the Davenport's security agency isn't exceptional. And he mentioned to me that his uncle Quentin, who runs the agency, assured him he'd put the best men on the job. Lauren must have been very determined and resourceful to have found her way onto the grounds.

"How dare you come here and scare my daughter?" he growls. His voice is tightly leashed, like a whip ready to flick out, and even a touch will be enough to draw blood.

I can't help but be grateful I'm not at the receiving end of it.

Lauren winces. Some of the fight seems to go out of her. She lowers her chin. "I'm sorry. I know it's wrong. I know I shouldn't have come here."

"No, you shouldn't have," he snaps.

She locks her fingers together. "I needed to see my—to see Serene."

Serene stirs and peers out from under her eyes and over her shoulder. She sucks on her thumb, a clear sign she's upset. But she's not crying. She seems curious.

"Are you okay, baby?" I ask softly.

She nods without looking away from Lauren.

There's no recognition in her eyes. The shock that she faced after being hurt and falling into the pool wiped most of her memories of that day. The doctor told us it wasn't unusual, given what she's been through.

The details might come back in time, when she's ready. It might also happen that she never remembers.

But seeing a stranger who she wasn't expecting must have upset her...*again*. Which is why Serene must have screamed.

She's so young, and she's been through a lot already. I'd be lying if I said that I don't want to shield her from further shock and tell Tyler I agree with him. That I don't want her to meet Lauren again. But Lauren is a part of her past. Part of Serene's history. She should know that she was conceived via a surrogate. That it was Lauren who gave birth to her. When she's ready to know about it.

And perhaps, I remember what it felt like to be on the other side of that door from Serene. How it felt like my heart was breaking when I had to walk away from her. And how it feels now, like I've been given an unexpected reward with her being back in my life.

How I felt so grateful to the universe and so immensely lucky that I have her in my life. A miracle I still don't think I deserve. How my entire being resonates when I'm with Serene. How I'll never take for granted the fact that I have her in my life. And how I sense Lauren's pain—I can't claim to understand the complexity of the feelings that led her to wanting to give up Serene and then changing her mind. But I see the regret on her features. The desperation. The helplessness that led her to seek out Serene again and again.

But she can't be allowed to shock Serene like this again. Which means, it's best to have this conversation with her and come to an understanding. If a restraining order doesn't stop her, there's nothing to say she's not going to try to see Serene again, despite all the legalities we throw at her. Instinct tells me the soft touch here will work better, for all of us.

Tyler's biceps twitch. He curls his fingers into fists at his sides. He's wearing a T-shirt that exposes his forearms, and the veins stand out in relief. His entire body is an ancient pillar of stone guarding the entry to a sacred space. He looks threatening and ferocious, every inch of him a protective barricade. Under the rage thrumming off him and saturating the air with menace, Lauren seems to shrink in size.

"I'm sorry. I didn't mean to cause her any distress." Her chin quivers.

"You broke the restraining order. I'm going to sue the hell out of you. I'm going to make sure you lose everything, you—"

"Tyler," I murmur.

He freezes, taking a deep breath. I sense him gathering himself, then he shoots me a glare over his shoulder. Those heterochromatic eyes blaze at me. I'm not at the receiving end of that rage; nevertheless, it makes me flinch. His face still wears the remnants of the paint and the stickers Serene stuck on him. The paint is smeared because some of it is on my cheeks. I flush slightly, but not in embarrassment. More because it feels like a badge of honor to be linked to my husband and my daughter in this way. It marks us out as a unit. A tribe. I love the feeling.

And when I look at Lauren, I see the bleakness on her face. How much of an outsider she feels. How much of an outsider she always will be. And a part of me curses my soft heart, but I cannot, in good faith, allow Tyler to go through with the retributions he's lined up for her in his head.

"I think we should go in and talk, honey," I say softly.

His gaze is piercing as he holds mine. Once more, we communicate without words on that wavelength which connects only the two of us. He blinks. Once. Twice. Some of the anger seems to fade. Once again, he understands what I'm trying to tell him. He doesn't seem too pleased about it but gives me a jerk of his chin.

Then, he turns to Lauren. "I don't want anything to do with you. I don't want you in our lives. But my wife thinks otherwise." He rolls his shoulders, seeming to force more of the rigidity from his muscles. "You'd better come in."

58

Tyler

"You stowed away in the back of the gardener's van and crept out and hid yourself in the shed when he wasn't looking?"

She got past Quentin's security team? That's no small feat. *This woman is more desperate than I realized.* And Quentin needs to fire his entire security staff for letting it happen.

I rub at my temple trying to take in what she's told me. My fingers come away streaked with color. The same color which is also smudged on my wife's features, and on my clothes and hers. I love that it connects the two of us. I'm proud that it shows what we were up to before we were interrupted.

Cilla is seated next to me on the settee in my office. I weave my fingers through hers, knowing the paint from my fingers is going to stain her hand, but needing the contact.

The intruder who broke in and scared my daughter—again—is seated in the chair across from us. I can't bring myself to think of her as the woman who carried my daughter to term. But it's an unshakeable fact; something my wife has already recognized. It means, there will always be a link between her and Serene. One I might want to forget but can never erase.

I called Summer to stay with Serene. Then asked Connor and Brody, to act as backup security while Cilla and I deal with Lauren.

"Add breaking and entering to your list of misdemeanors. Combined with your having broken the restraining order, it's enough to put you away behind bars for a long time."

She pales. Despite the early spring chill in the air outside, she's also sweating. She locks her fingers together and hunches her shoulders. "I'm truly sorry." She swallows. "I know I shouldn't have come, but...I couldn't keep away. It's been hell since I saw Serene hurt herself and fall into the pool. And I never got to see her afterward."

"She's fine." I snap. "She doesn't need you. She has her parents."

Cilla squeezes my hand, and I bite back the rest of the words threatening to spill out. On some level, I'm aware it's not right for me to feel this level of animosity toward someone else. But I can't forget that it's because of this woman that my child has been hurt, repeatedly.

Anger squeezes my chest. My every protective instinct is on alert. I feel like I want to hide my child away in a place where the likes of Lauren can never hurt her. But the mature part of me, the person I've become since meeting my wife, knows better.

I'm doing Serene a disservice by shielding her from her history—one she's going to have to come to terms with, at some point.

If only I could go back in time and fix things so Serene would have had a more ordinary start in life. Every fatherly instinct in me wishes I could wipe the slate clean and have Serene be born as our child, with Cilla carrying her to birth. But that's not going to happen. *'What if'* won't change anything. *'What's next'* will. A quote Cilla shared with me—and it couldn't be more fitting now.

Meanwhile, I'm going to do everything in my power to protect Serene and shield her from the events that led to her birth.

"I wanted to...make sure for myself." Lauren dips her chin. "It's not about your ability to take care of her. It's clear, the two of you love her and will do anything for her. Serene is lucky to have both of you. But then, I always knew you would be a good father. It's just" — she raises a hand — "there was this physical need in me to see her. That's all. I couldn't stop myself. I thought, I'd go mad if I couldn't see her and tell her I'm sorry."

"You said you knew I'd be a good father. What do you mean by that?" I demand.

She flushes. The color stands out on her face in blotchy patches, making her look worse than before. "I, uh, researched you online."

I stiffen. Was she planning to blackmail me?

She must notice my expression, for she holds up her hands. "I merely wanted to make sure you were the right person to leave my daughter with. Everything I found out about you confirmed that."

"Oh?"

She nods. "You are from a well-known family, so you have the pedigree. You're a former Marine, honorably discharged, so I knew you wouldn't shy away from your responsibilities. And you are a CEO, so you're financially well-off." She shuffles her feet. "Everything confirmed to me that my daughter would be better off with you."

"One thing I don't understand—" My wife leans forward. "You had—still have—money. You have resources. You could afford the fertility treatments and employing the PI. And the resort we were in isn't cheap. So, you had the means to take care of her. Why didn't you?"

Lauren seems taken aback by the question. "You mean, why did I choose to drop her off, in the first place?" she asks in what I recognize as a tactic to buy herself time.

My wife nods. "Why did you do that? Surely, you had the resources to find help?"

Lauren shifts in her seat, then lets out a shaky breath.

"I wanted to be a mother. I wanted it for so long. But when I held Serene…I froze. I didn't know how to take care of her. I still don't. I had no one. No family, no friends. No one to help me." She swallows hard. "That's why I'd never try to take her from you. I can't. I'm not a threat. I never was."

She laughs. The sound is brittle enough to break.

"All I'm asking is to be able to see Serene and apologize to her for everything. I want to tell her how sorry I am for my actions, which have only hurt her, every step of the way."

Cilla lowers her chin. "I want to tell you that you can — "

I whip my head in her direction and am about to protest, when she smiles at me and pulls my hand into her lap. "But in this, I have to defer to Serene's therapist. According to her, Serene's been through a lot. It's best to wait until she's older and mature enough to understand the circumstances surrounding her birth before she meets you."

Lauren's features crumple.

My wife blinks away her own tears. "This is not easy for me either. As a mother, I understand what you must be going through. You gave birth to Serene. Nothing changes that. But she's so young. Everything that's happened is confusing to her. She needs to grow up, become stronger, more resilient."

Lauren locks her fingers together. The skin stretches tight over her cheekbones.

"I'll reimburse you for the cost of IVF and the surrogacy," I growl, the words scraping past my throat like sandpaper. Not because I don't mean them — but because they are the result of all the stress, the tension, the uncertainty I've carried since the moment I first saw my daughter.

Cilla glances at me with that steady, grounding look that's held me together more times than I can count. We hadn't discussed this. But I see no hesitation in her eyes — only quiet resolve.

"I think that's a good idea," she says softly.

Of course, it is. We're always in sync, even when the world is fractured around us. It's that certainty between us that gives me the freedom to speak my truth without fear of rejection. She meets me where I am, every time.

"I also think it'd be a good idea to share pictures of Serene every year with Lauren." Her voice is gentler now, turning toward me like a warm breeze. "She'll be able to watch Serene grow…without disrupting her world."

I hold her gaze. There's a softness there — a compassion I'm still learning to emulate. She's better than me. Always has been. She forgives quicker. Feels deeper. And standing beside her…makes me want to rise to that level. For her. For Serene.

A current of silent agreement passes between us, steady and unshakable. I let my shoulders drop, forcing air into my lungs.

Cilla's so considerate. And she's right. This way, we keep Lauren updated on Serene, and hopefully, it satisfies her enough, so she's not compelled to burst in unannounced, again, in Serene's life.

"I think that's a good idea," I echo, quieter this time.

My wife's lips curve in a soft smile. She squeezes my fingers. It steadies the storm inside me.

"We'll make sure Serene knows who you are." She turns to Lauren. "We'll be honest about how she came to be. That you were the one who carried her. That you brought her safely into the world."

I tear my eyes from my wife—her strength, her steadiness—and focus on the woman who gave birth to my daughter. "And when the time is right," I tell her, voice steady, "you'll meet her. You'll tell her your version of the story."

Lauren's throat bobs as she swallows. "And…when would that be, do you think?"

"Serene's therapist says we can't put a timeline on it," I say, measured, deliberate. "We can't raise your hopes. It depends entirely on Serene—on her emotional readiness, on the kind of person she becomes, on how her life unfolds."

Lauren's breath catches. "So, I might have to wait until she's eighteen?"

"Ideally, no," Cilla replies. Her voice falters just for a second. "Maybe sooner. Maybe when she hits puberty. But we can't make promises. Again, her therapist says every child is different. And ultimately—it's our decision. Ours and her therapist's."

Lauren's shoulders curl inward. Her presence seems to dim. "Until then—?"

"Until then," I cut in, my voice clipped, "you stay away from her. No contact. No attempts to reach her. No watching from a distance. No uninvited visits. You stay away."

The room falls still.

"If not —" I square my shoulders. "If not, you don't get to see her at all, not for the rest of your life."

Lauren draws in a sharp breath. A shudder grips her. She squeezes her eyes shut and takes another few deep breaths. Then she squares her shoulders. When she opens her eyelids there's a determined and fatalistic expression on her face.

"I deserve that. I shouldn't have turned up at the resort the way I did. I will never forgive myself for what happened next. As long as I live, I know, I'll never get over the sight of her hurting herself and falling into the pool. And I shouldn't have come here today. I'm sorry, I scared her. I really am."

She keeps saying she's sorry but keeps doing things to be sorry for. I have a feeling this is a pattern that won't change, but I keep my thoughts to myself.

I pull my hand from my wife's, then wrap my arm about her and draw her close. I take comfort from her warmth, her scent, the familiar curves which I know as well as my own body.

"Meanwhile, why don't we exchange contact details?" Cilla says gently.

Lauren swallows, then to my surprise she offers a small smile. "I did choose well, didn't I? I'm glad Serene has you as parents." She wipes away a tear.

I see Cilla do the same as she smiles back.

Even *I* feel a bit of empathy, which I didn't think was possible. Maybe Lauren just needed the reassurance that we appreciate what she did for Serene, and we can handle it from here?

"Brody," I call out to my brother, who I know is waiting right outside the door of my study. "Can you please see Lauren out?"

59

Priscilla

"Thank you." I turn to my husband.

"For what?"

"I know how incredibly hard it must have been for you to stop yourself from turning her into the police. But you did the right thing. We did the right thing. It's best to engage with her and explain our point of view to her. And as she said, she doesn't want to take Serene from us."

"No, she only wants a relationship with Serene," he points out.

I gnaw on the inside of my cheek. "I realize that. And believe me, it's difficult not to feel threatened by that."

"You shouldn't be. You're my wife and much more than Serene's biological mother. You take care of her. And you care for her."

"She did give birth to her."

"And you thanked her for that. Which I think is part of what she needed to hear. But you're the one who's here for her, day in and day out. A parent isn't defined only by who gave birth to a child, or even who donated the genetic material. We're her parents because we're the ones who see to her needs and love her." Tyler gathers me close. "Are you okay?"

I nod.

"Are you *really*, okay?" He peruses my features closely. The way I love. The way it makes it feel like I'm the cynosure of his life. The focus of his attention. Serene will always be first, for both of us. But I'm right there with her when it comes to having my husband's attention. And I thank the universe and the fates every day for having brought him and my daughter into my life. And for having brought us into his life on the same day.

"I'm more than okay," I cup his cheek. "I'm in love with you."

He stills.

"I love you, Tyler. So very much."

His eyes gleam. Something like relief flashes in his eyes and is replaced with that look which is a combination of love and devotion and lust, all rolled into one. To be desired for how I am. For more than my body. For who I am. For my mind. My emotions. My soul. It's an all-encompassing, unselfish love which feels huge and monumental and never-ending. And when I bite down on my lower lip to stop my emotions spilling over, his gaze is drawn there. Just like that, the air between us heats. The desire never far from the surface bubbles over.

Oh God. I'll never take this...carnal need I have for him, this draw toward him, this animal attraction which binds us together, for granted. With a low noise he pulls me into his lap, then kisses me deeply. Our lips fuse together. Our teeth clash. His tongue tangles with mine. I'm burning up, my skin on fire. My core is so wet, surely, I've stained my clothes. I wind my arms about his shoulders and hold on as he devours me. The kiss is everything I've dreamed of. It's as if confessing my love for him has added another dimension. The way he holds me is more possessive. More tender. The way he kisses me is both more demanding and gentler. The way my body molds itself to the planes of his feels charged with this growing craving to have him inside of me.

"I love you so fucking much," he growls into my mouth. Then

kisses me all over again. My breath grows choppy. My head spins. The sensations crowding my body and my soul are overpowering. I—

Someone clears their throat.

I flush to the roots of my hair. I try to pull away, but Tyler doesn't let me. He continues to kiss me. But I'm very aware that Brody or Connor must have walked into the study. Summer left earlier, and Tyler's brothers took charge of putting Serene to sleep.

I almost forgot they were here.

"Uh—Serene wanted to say goodnight to both of you before she falls asleep," Connor murmurs from somewhere in the direction of the entrance to the room.

This time, when I pull away, Tyler lets me. He groans and pushes his forehead against mine, seemingly for support. His massive chest rises and falls. The musky scent of his skin is laced with desire. I take another deep breath, storing it to tide me over, then push off of him and to my feet.

"I... Uh... I'm going to Serene."

Tyler slumps back against the couch. "You go ahead. I'll be there as soon as I, uh...put myself to rights."

I take in the tent at his crotch and stifle a chuckle. Then walk past Brody, who's walking back toward the study, presumably after having seen Lauren to the door. "Kiss Serene goodnight from me," he says.

I nod, then take the steps up to Serene's bedroom, my cheeks still on fire. By the time I walk into Serene's room, I've managed to get myself together. Serene's under the covers, clutching her favorite soft toy, a bedraggled dinosaur. When I sit next to her, she opens her eyes. "Mommy." She smiles.

"I'm here; go to sleep, baby." I kiss her forehead.

She sighs, then rolls over onto her other side, still clutching the doll. I push her hair back from her face. This burst of activity is typical for her. I've learned it signals that she's comfortable and ready to go to sleep. Still clutching her toy in one hand, with the other, she grips my hand and tucks it under her chin.

My heart swells. Warmth coils in my chest. That absolute trust she places in me is humbling. It makes me want to take care of her. Makes me want to do everything in my power to protect her. Makes me wonder... How could Lauren have given her up? Makes me realize, she must have been very scared by the situation she found herself in. Enough to break so many rules to track down Tyler, then go so far as to walk away from her own daughter. The thought of it is incomprehensible to me.

It makes me so grateful that I found her and Tyler all over again. I bend and kiss Serene's forehead, staying with her for a few more minutes as her breathing deepens.

Then, I rise to my feet, turn, and still. He's propped one arm against the doorframe, with his broad shoulders taking up most of the space.

He looks from me to his daughter's face, then back at me. There's so much warmth and tenderness in his eyes, it flips my stomach. That feeling of knowing my husband loves me is the most incredible, most comforting feeling in the entire world.

"She fell asleep before you could wish her goodnight," I whisper unnecessarily.

His lips quirk. "I can see that." With his other hand thrust into his pocket, he straightens. His hair is tousled, softening the strong planes of his face. His shirt has a few buttons open, enough for me to see the demarcation of his pecs. The planes of his chest stretch the shirt and the rest of the buttons. Then, there's the way he's folded up the sleeves of his shirt. It exposes his hair-roughened, veiny forearms, and oh God, the sight is like sex-come-to-life. He's sex-come-to-life. Adonis and Eros combined. An erotic dream. He's hot and dominant and has such presence, he takes my breath away.

Heat flushes my skin. Sparks simmer in my bloodstream. I take a step in his direction, and they turn into little tendrils of fire. He watches me closely, not moving as I float toward him. The very air between us turns into a lasso of need. It settles around my shoulders and tightens with every inch I close between us.

My pussy clenches. My stomach stutters. My nipples are so hard, I'm sure he can see them through my blouse.

I stop in front of him, and he looks down at me from his great height. He must have stopped to wash the colors off of his face, for some of the strands of hair lining his forehead are wet. And his face is free of colors. Mostly.

"You missed this." I reach up and rub off a dab of color at his temple. The skin of his face is cool—as a result of washing up, no doubt—but the rest of his body feels like a furnace. A cloud of heat spools off of him and crashes into my chest. I gasp. My head spins. His nearness, his scent, the sheer force of him presses in from all sides.

Combined with that tender look in his heterochromatic eyes, it's more potent than an aphrodisiac. I begin to withdraw my arm, but he catches my wrist, presses it close to his cheek, then he turns his face into the palm of my hand and kisses it.

I shiver. The touch of his lips on me alerts every single nerve ending in my body. And when he drags his five o'clock-shadowed chin against the soft skin in the center of my palm, every pore in my body seems to open with need. I make a soft sound at the back of my throat, and he snaps his gaze on me.

"You're beautiful," he says in a low, hard voice that shivers over my skin, draws more moisture from my core, and makes my toes curl.

"So are you," I whisper.

He chuckles. And the sound is so sexy. So male. So, everything. I go up on tiptoe, push myself closer to him. He plants his big hands on my hips and hauls me up, so my feet lift off the floor. I wrap my legs around his waist, so my core is pressed into that thick column at his crotch. He feels so hard, so heavy, so perfect... My throat closes. My mouth dries.

At the same time, I'm so wet between my thighs, I'm sure I'm staining his pants. He slides his hands down to cup my butt cheeks, and a ripple of delight runs up my spine. I never imagined that part of my body could be so responsive, but whenever he touches me, wherever he touches me, it turns my entire body into a miasma of sensory delight.

He turns away from our daughter's room, managing to pull the door shut behind him. Then he walks to our bedroom, kicks the door shut behind us and drops me on the bed.

I bounce once, looking up at him in shock and bemusement. It quickly turns to delight when he first, straightens the cuffs of his sleeves, undoes a few more buttons, then reaches behind himself. In one smooth move which has his biceps bunching, he pulls off his shirt.

I stare greedily at the expanse of skin, the dog tags in the dip between his pecs, the tattoos. I run my fingers over the roman numerals. *The date I met him. The date I first saw my daughter.*

He toes off his shoes.

The clink of his belt buckle, and the r-r-r-i-p of his zipper being lowered sends a flurry of anticipation up my spine. He shucks his pants, his briefs and his socks in one go. When he straightens, his heavy cock juts out from the thatch of neatly trimmed hair. I know how that feels against my skin. His shaft is a work of delight. Crafted with great precision, it's beautiful, gorgeous, and tastes so good. Like it's mine. Like he's mine. He stands, elbows tucked at his sides, allowing me to look my fill. Then, he walks over to stand in front of me.

"Touch me," he orders.

I need no further prompting. I wrap my fingers around his throbbing dick. When he groans, a flourish of satisfaction, of power, surges through me. I bend, closing my mouth around the swollen crown.

"Fuck." He bunches my hair away from my face, holding it back. I look up to find him staring at how my lips are wrapped around his dick. I hold onto the outside of his thighs, then dip my head and close my mouth around his cock.

"Jesus," he swears.

My jaw already aches, but the look of absolute rapture on his features is worth it. I pull back, until he's balanced at my lips, then once again, angle my chin. I take him down my throat.

"Bloody hell." Holding my hair back with one hand, he wraps his long, thick fingers around my throat from the back. The tips meet, so

I'm wearing them like a necklace — or a collar. Like I belong to him. I do belong to him.

"I love you." The sound emerges muffled. He must understand what I mean though, for the look in his eyes turns even more possessive. And more tender. And more dominating.

"I can feel my cock down your throat. Do you know how much of a fucking turn on that is?"

He squeezes gently, not enough to hurt me or cut off my air, but with the right amount of pressure for me to feel every individual finger of his against my throat. With his dick blocking my windpipe, I should feel like I'm choking, but instead, I feel like I'm possessed by him. I feel weighed down by his presence. I feel grounded, like I'm wrapped in a weighted blanket. And with his gaze on me, being at the center of his focus, I feel strangely secure.

Tears leak from my eyes, and I try to breathe through my nose.

He tugs on my hair enough for me to release my hold on his cock. Then, he takes control and begins to steer me. Without removing his fingers from around my neck, he maneuvers me back and forth, back and forth, so his cock slips out then back in, then again. He takes charge so seamlessly, with so much confidence, I have to hold onto his thighs for support. Each time he slips down my throat, he fills me up in an imitation of how his cock would feel inside my pussy.

My core clenches, and moisture pools between my legs. My nipples are so hard, my breasts so heavy… His gaze holds mine, the connection growing stronger. More intense. The air between us grows heavy with our chemistry. It pushes down on my shoulders, causing sweat to pool under my armpits. Causing my thighs to clench, and my toes to curl. I'm so turned on, I know I'm going to come any second.

As if he can read my mind, he releases his hold on me and pulls out. He applies just enough pressure on my shoulders, that I lay back. He unfastens my jeans and pulls them off, along with my panties. Then, wraps his fingers around my ankles and pulls them apart. He stares at the flesh between my thighs so intently, a blush swooshes up my body.

"Tyler," I protest. "What are you doing?"

"Looking at my pussy, do you mind?" Then he drops to his knees, throws my legs over his shoulders, and lowers his face to the tender flesh.

60

Tyler

I bury my nose in her pussy and draw in a deep breath. Her feminine scent goes straight to my head. And when I lick up the cleavage of her pussy lips, she cries out.

"Tyler!" She digs her fingers into my hair and tugs. The pain zips from my scalp, down my spine, and straight to my balls. My lust spikes. My pulse thuds at my temples. I lick into her slit, so her taste fills my senses, then swipe my tongue to her swollen nub. I flick my tongue around it, sucking on it as she moans, trying to wriggle away. I place my arm across her lower belly, holding her in place, then continue to lick and tug between her pussy lips. I thrust two fingers inside of her, weaving them in and out of her, feeling her grow even more wet, until her cum slithers down my wrist. Then I curve my fingers inside her, crushing up against that spongy, secret spot deep inside of her.

She cries out, her body curves, and her hips rise off the bed. She shatters around my mouth, her juices running down her inner thighs.

"That's it, baby, let yourself go; just like that." I continue to lick the evidence of her climax, until her body slumps, then rise up to plant my hips between her legs. I grab either side of the lapels of her blouse and tug. The delicate material tears to reveal the slopes of her breasts spilling over her bra. She gasps, looking at me with lust-filled eyes.

I unhook her bra and pull it off, then cup both of her breasts. I massage them and push them together, then bend and take one nipple between my lips. The sensations swirl inside me, thrumming against my skin, coiling in my chest. I sip on her other nipple, reveling in the shudders gripping her.

Then straightening, I reach down and position my cock at her opening. I look into her eyes and push inside her.

She opens her mouth in a silent scream, and I fit my tongue in between her lips as I begin to fuck her. Sweat beads my shoulders, and heat pours off of me in waves. Our skin sticks together, then makes a sucking noise as I pull back and it releases. I'm inside her, with her tight, hot, pussy milking my cock. I groan into her mouth, grip her hip, and plant my other hand next to her to keep my weight off of her, then continue to piston into her. Again and again. And again. My cock thickens, and my balls draw up.

I sense her trembling, her pussy tightening in a way I didn't think was possible. And when I sense her close to the edge, knowing I'm almost there, I tear my mouth from hers and growl, "Come."

She climaxes at once, her cry in my ears as I grunt and empty myself inside her. I collapse with my face in the curve of her neck, then manage to turn on my back and pull her onto my chest.

Her heart thunders against mine, her body twitching as she comes down from the high. I draw in a deep breath, and the scent of sex fills me, arousing me, yet also filling that space inside me I didn't know was empty. I run my fingers down her spine. She cuddles closer, her cheek pressed to my chest. She draws circles around my nipples, and I groan. "I do need a few more minutes."

She chuckles. "Mr. Hot and Sexy Davenport admits to needing recovery time?"

I slap her butt playfully. "I'm the first to admit, I'm not perfect."

She looks up at me, then crawls up my body until she's nose to nose with me. She looks deeply into my eyes. "I love you."

I was sure that's what she said earlier, but hey, I had my cock down her throat, and no way, was I going to stop her from blowing me by asking her about it.

"I love you so very much," I growl.

Her lips curve in a beautiful smile, then she presses her mouth to mine. "I think I loved you from the moment we met."

"I know, you did." It might sound arrogant of me to say so, but I'm sure of it. She couldn't have looked at me the way she did when we met and not felt something for me. I was sure she felt the attraction between us. Only, I thought I might have crushed it when I sent her away. And while I held out hope that she'd come to love me again, I admit, I wasn't sure.

"I'm sorry I didn't say it earlier. I knew I loved you. But...I needed a little more time before I could form the words." She presses her chin into my chest. "Can you forgive me for that?"

"There's nothing to forgive. You're with me, here in my arms, and that's what matters." I cup her cheek. "I love you as much as I do Serene. You're both a part of me. I'm incomplete without either of you. I'd never be able to live without either of you. I'll never forgive myself for sending you away the day she arrived at my doorstep. I'm so sorry for all the time I wasted. I'm sorry I couldn't sort through my feelings enough to realize I needed you so much then. I thought I'd lost you. And when you appeared again at my doorstep — something inside me was clear that I couldn't let you go again."

She frames my face with her small palms. "You did break my heart. And yet, all the time I was away from you and Serene, I also knew my life would be incomplete if I didn't see you again. I kept telling myself you didn't want me, but it wasn't enough to stop myself from hoping that we could be together some day. And I couldn't explain to myself why I felt so powerfully drawn to Serene. But now we know."

"What I didn't know was how empty my life would be when you left. How, while it was so busy and so full on one hand with Serene, something was missing. How, even as I didn't have a moment to breathe while taking care of Serene, my instinct told me there was more. This wasn't everything. I was losing out on something vital. An unshakable sense of absence gnawed at me. Something crucial was slipping away. I had let you slip away."

"You have me." She rubs her nose against mine. "You have me completely."

"I love you." I kiss her lips. "Only you. You have me body, mind and soul. All my emotions, my feelings, my thoughts, my yearning… It's all for you. I'd give my life for you."

"And Serene," she murmurs.

"And Serene." I flip her so I'm arched over her, my lower body fitted to hers, my weight pressing her into the mattress. Her curves, the feel of her gorgeous body, her softness — all of it drains the blood to my groin.

"Whoa." Her eyes grow wide. "Is that —"

"It is." I allow myself a smirk of satisfaction. "Are you ready for —"

A plaintive cry reaches us over the baby monitor on the table next to the bed. I groan and press my forehead into hers.

"Serene," she says breathlessly.

"Serene." I push myself off my wife's gorgeous body and roll to my feet. "Stay right there." I point at her. "I'll be back."

EPILOGUE

Priscilla

Receiving is an act of courage. Trust it. Honor it. Allow the universe the pleasure of giving to you. Accept it.
-Cilla's Post-it note

"Tiny, stay still." Serene places another sticker in the center of his forehead, then begins to line more over the curve of his eyebrow. The big dog has his tongue hanging out from a corner of his mouth, and a long-suffering look on his face. He makes a whining sound of protest deep in his throat but obeys Serene.

We're at Arthur's place for the weekly lunch. He's seated by the fire in his comfortable armchair. It's warm in the room, but when Imelda places a blanket over his legs, Arthur doesn't protest. Fighting the Big C has left its mark on him.

Every time I see him, he seems older, frailer, more dependent, and hence, more accommodating of Imelda fussing over him. When we walked in here after lunch, Tiny flopped on the floor between them, but as soon as Serene entered the room, he switched loyalties.

"She has that dog wrapped around her finger." Tyler puts his arm around my shoulders and pulls me close. We're standing by the window, watching our daughter pull out one of her face paints and begin to paint the Great Dane's face. The dog's expression turns even more agonized, but he, gamely, stays in his place.

Nathan and Skylar are seated on a settee facing the fire, at a right angle to Arthur and Imelda. They're talking to Knox and June, both of whom are sprawled against the cushions on the carpet and in front of them. Knox has an espresso next to him, and June is sipping from an herbal tea. They look so happy together, and I'm glad we didn't go through with our ill-conceived plan. Though we had dessert after lunch, trays of fruit have been laid out on the coffee table.

Connor, who normally skips these lunches, as he's often away on one of his research trips, is the surprising addition. And Brody, too, is present. The two are at the bar close to us, with espresso cups in front of them.

Ryot is traveling with his wife.

Sinclair and Summer were invited, but they skipped the meal to take Matty to football practice and then, to martial arts. Summer tells me her son has so much pent-up energy, it's important to channel it into sports.

I love being here with the Davenports. There's a feeling of family at these meals which fills me with contentment. I look around at my husband, my child, my extended family, and allow a small smile to curve my lips. *I didn't manifest a life. I became someone who could hold it.* It's amazing how, when your dreams come true, you become more confident in yourself. In your ability to manifest. In your ability to receive, so your dreams become inseparable from you. Is this what all those self-help books meant by vibrating on the same wavelength as what you want so you could attract it? I might never know, although I think so. But the how seems inconsequential, compared to the reality of *today. Now.* When I'm happy. At peace.

Toren took the news of his new niece with surprising calm and a lot of excitement. He can't wait to meet Serene. One thing I know about my brother? Even if Serene wasn't biologically connected to me or him, he'd have accepted her right away.

"She seems fully recovered." Connor nods in my daughter's direction.

Behind me, Tyler stiffens, as he often seems to do whenever the topic of Serene's encounters with the woman who carried her comes up. I pat the arm he has wrapped around me, and some of the tension eases out of him.

"She's doing well," he concedes. "She didn't even have any nightmares after...what happened in our garden."

"She's thriving." I smile without taking my gaze off Serene. "She's started preschool and made new friends. Her teacher says she's a happy child who's inquisitive and loves drawing."

"It's thanks to you." My husband kisses the top of my head. "You're wonderful with her. You know when to be gentle with her and when to be firm. More than anything, your continued presence is a source of great comfort to her. She's secure in the knowledge her mom is here to stay."

"And, she has you too." I turn in his arms and wrap my arm about his neck. "You've come a long way from the man who didn't know what to do with the baby who was deposited on your doorstep."

His smile dims a little. I know he's thinking of the fact that it was also the day he asked me to leave him. I'm sorry for having reminded him of that. "What happened in the past doesn't matter; it's that we found ourselves again which does. That we're a family. That's a miracle I'll never take for granted."

"I'll never take you for granted." He bends and captures my lips with his. I push the fact that his brothers are watching and that the rest of his family are in the same room out of my mind and respond. Within seconds, my heartbeat accelerates, and my pulse begins to pound. That familiar melting sensation curls in my lower belly. He releases my mouth to whisper, "Perhaps we should—"

"Mama. Papa." There's a tug on my dress.

He groans, a frustrated look in his eyes as he releases me.

"Yes, Poppet." He looks down.

"I want to go out and play with Tiny. Can I?"

"Of course." I bend and kiss her forehead.

"I'll take her." Connor approaches us.

"Are you sure?" I frown.

"Yes, he is." Tyler picks up the little girl and pretends to eat her arm. She giggles. "You be good for Uncle Connor, okay?" He hands her into Connor's waiting arms. Connor heaves her up to sit on his shoulders.

She squeals, grabs hold of his hair, and tugs. "Horsey. Horsey. Giddy-up, Horsey."

Connor chuckles and walks toward the door on the side of the room that leads out onto the patio.

"I'll go keep an eye on them." Brody winks at us. "You two, carry on."

I flush. Tyler huffs out a laugh, then kisses me again. "There's a guest room upstairs which is free. We could—"

"Nope! Absolutely not. You can control yourself until we reach home."

"Can I?" His eyes heat. "I'd rather use the little free time we have to be inside you with your hot, wet pussy milking my cock."

My flush deepens. I slap at his chest. "Keep your voice down; the others will hear us."

"They're too busy catching up." He bends and kisses my lips again softly. "What do you say? An after-lunch quickie?"

"You're never quick," I remind him, half amused.

"Only because I want to pleasure you thoroughly before I come inside you."

My cheeks turn to fire, which elicits a delighted laugh from him.

Our gazes meet, hold. That indescribable something flares between us again. His arms around me tighten. "I love you so fucking much."

"I love you," I say without hesitation. The more times I say it, the deeper the emotions I have for him grow. The more time I spend with Serene, the more the both of them become a part of me. What I feel for them is woven through my DNA, coiled in my cells, laced through my bloodstream. I am them, and they are me. We are a unit. It's us against the world. I've found my safe space, and I'm so thankful to the universe for bringing me here.

The door at the far end of the living room opens again. A draft of air blows through before cutting off. There's a shift in the air behind me. Enough for me to look over my shoulder.

Connor walks over to Arthur, a worried look on his face. He's holding his phone in his hand as if he just took a call. Something in the tense lines of his body tells me he's upset. Tyler must feel the same way, for he slides his hand down to mine, then leads me toward where Connor has stopped in front of Arthur.

"I have to leave. Something came up."

"Everything all right?" Tyler asks as we reach them.

I look past him through the glass door and find Serene and Brody tossing a ball, with Tiny lolling on the grass next to her.

"My best buddy called." Connor hesitates. "He's away on a trip and won't be home for another month. He wants me to go over and check on his sister."

"Is she in trouble?" I ask.

He slips the phone into his pocket and rubs the back of his neck, seemingly choosing his words carefully. "She's been through a lot, and he's worried about her. The last time he spoke to her, he got the impression she wasn't herself. He wanted to go to her right away, but he can't leave his mission halfway through. He called to ask if I could go in his place. Of course, I said yes."

Tyler nods. "Best thing you can do is put his mind at ease. If you need help—"

Connor shakes his head. "I'm good. I'm sure she's fine. He admitted he might be overreacting, but it's best I go check up on her and let him know." He turns to Arthur. "Sorry, I need to cut out, Gramps." He nods at Arthur, then bends and kisses Imelda on her cheek. "Thanks for keeping an eye on this one."

"I'm still here," Arthur says in an irritable voice, but his expression indicates he isn't averse to Imelda watching out for him. In the little time I've known him, he's definitely mellowed.

"You behave for her, you hear me," Connor says in a mild voice.

Arthur scoffs, then a gleam comes into his eyes. "And you'd better not behave, if the opportunity arises."

Connor stares at him. "Do I even want to know what you mean by that?"

Arthur tries to look innocent and fails miserably, "All I'm saying is, with Tyler married, it's your turn next. And you know the deal."

"Do I?" Connor knits his brows. "And I'm the youngest so shouldn't it be Brody you should set your sights on?"

"It's not about age but opportunity." Arthur looks him up and down. "You'd better be married within the month, if you want me to confirm you as one of my heirs, so you can claim your inheritance. You feel me?"

To find out what happens next read Connor and Phoenix's story in The Wrong Husband. Scan this QR code to get it

How to scan a QR code?

1. Open the camera app on your phone or tablet.
2. Point the camera at the QR code.
3. Tap the banner that appears on your phone or tablet.
4. Follow the instructions on the screen to finish signing in.

READ AN EXCERPT

Connor

"Is that a threat?" I ask slowly.

"Consider it a forewarning." Arthur, that old coot, tilts his head. "An admonition, perhaps."

"Consider me admonished." I draw myself up to my full height. My phone buzzes in my pocket. I pull it out, and a message pops up on the screen. It's a name and an address

I message back.

Me: On it.

Then I delete the message string, pocket my phone, and turn to my grandfather. "I don't need your money. I have enough of my own."

Arthur leans back in his chair, then places his fingertips together. "Don't forget who holds majority shares in the company of which you're CEO; the company which also happens to own the patents to your various biochemical discoveries."

I stiffen, "The patents are—"

"Not on your personal name, because the Davenport Group filed them on your behalf," Arthur adds in a silky voice.

The old man is...right. I'd done that on purpose. But now's not the time to reveal that. I set my jaw, pretend to be upset at this revelation, then curl my fingers into fists for good measure.

"I'm simply pointing out the reality." Arthur lowers his chin. "Of course, you could choose to walk away from your patents but—"

"What he means is that he's worried about you." Imelda stares at Arthur, who surprisingly subsides.

She rises to her feet and walks over to me. "You travel a lot and work so very hard. Arthur feels you don't look after yourself enough. He only wants you to meet the right woman, so you'll settle down. He wants you to be as happy as your brothers are." She levels a look at Arthur. "Isn't that right, dear?"

Arthur looks like he's about to protest. Then, with a disgruntled expression, he jerks his chin. "I do worry...about all of you." He looks around the room. "It's why I helped all you find your soulmates and look how happy you are."

Tyler coughs. "I think the credit for finding the women we love and want to spend our lives with goes to us. Mainly."

"I played a role, didn't I? If I hadn't put the condition to have you all get married in order to inherit, I wager, none of you would have taken the final step needed to seal the deal."

Tyler's lips quirk. He exchanges a glance with Nathan, who shakes his head in an imperceptible motion. Probably warning Tyler not to say anything which might antagonize the old man further. Not that I care.

Arthur thinks he's responsible for my brothers getting their happy endings. But I'm too wise. I'm not going to fall prey to his machinations. It's one of the reasons I've managed to stay away as much as possible from the family. Also, because I've been busy carving out my career. I'm determined to be independent. So far, I've succeeded. The only reason I stayed on this long is to help Tyler. I could never turn down my brother when he needed my help.

But Tyler's settled now. His daughter Serene walks into the room, followed by Brody, with Tiny on their heels. She heads straight for her mother, who picks her up. Tyler wraps his arm around both of them in a protective gesture. Serene leans up and kisses him on his cheek, and his entire face lights up. He pulls both of them close.

My heart stutters in my chest. My chest hurts a little. It's wonderful to see Tyler so content. But is that burning sensation in the pit of my belly jealousy? *Nah, not possible.*

I don't begrudge my brothers their happiness. But I'm not going to fall into the same trap. I'm not going to give up my freedom. Besides, I'm too busy focusing on my job. Unlike my brothers, I didn't become a Marine because I've always felt I could do more for my country on the outside.

And now, thanks to my buddy James, I have a new mission. It's time for me to move on. I've never been good at being in one place.

I've always felt smothered when my family show their concern for me. Perhaps, it comes from being a nerdy kid who got bullied at school. Whose older brothers always had to rescue him from being pounded in the playground. It's when I swore to find a way to show the world that I could take care of myself.

I knew, even then, I could use my brains to outwit anyone. But I also realized I needed the physical strength to go with it. I focused on building up my body, focused on being so strong that no one would dare bother me. Paired with my high IQ, I'm virtually invincible when it comes to the kind of career I've forged. One where I can use my intelligence to come to the aid of those who need it most. It's what led to my becoming a private contractor for the government. I can serve my country, but I can choose the missions I go on, like the one I am taking on now.

With what I can only describe as relief that I have a reason to leave, I nod in my grandfather's direction. "I appreciate your being concerned on my behalf, but there's no need. I know what I want."

"Do you?" My grandfather frowns but doesn't say anything else.

I pat Imelda's shoulder. "You take care of yourself. Don't let the cantankerous old coot get you down."

Arthur makes a noise of protest which I ignore. I kiss Imelda's cheek. Nod toward Nathan and Knox and their wives, then head over to Tyler's family. I ruffle Serene's hair, clap Tyler on his back and smile at Priscilla. "I'll see you guys soon."

"Thanks for your help." Tyler lets go of Priscilla and his daughter long enough to squeeze my shoulder. "Anything you need, don't hesitate to reach out."

"I won't." With a last wave at the group in the room, I head out of there. Nodding at Arthur's butler Otis, who holds out my coat for me, I shrug into it, then leave through the kitchen using the back door. Cutting through the garden path, I head out toward the door behind the garden shed which leads out onto Primrose Hill. It's locked.

I use the code Otis, Arthur's butler shared with me to let myself out. I step out onto the grassy knoll and jump down from it onto the walkway that leads down to the entrance to the open space. The London skyline, made famous by scenes in so many movies, stretches out in front of me. I pause for a second to take it in.

Thankfully, I'm not jaded enough to not appreciate the beauty of the afternoon sun which bathes the scene in a golden glow. Cyclists overtake me. A couple holding hands walks past me, lost in each other. A family sits on a blanket in the grass having a picnic.

Everyday sights and sounds surround me. The breeze ruffles my hair. I draw in a deep breath, and smell freshly cut grass mixed with fragrant flowers. More tension slips from my shoulders.

Why am I more comfortable when I'm on my own? I don't hate my family. Far from it. Despite my impatience with my grandfather's tactics in trying to get me hitched, I know, deep down, he only has my best interests at heart. He was there for us when our own father was too self-absorbed, and our mother too preoccupied with her society life.

It was Gramps who brought us up. His methods might have been more befitting that of an army sergeant who expected complete discipline from his troops. But even then, his love for us came through. Which is, perhaps, why my brothers and I put up with his meddling antics.

Not that Arthur has any military experience, but his father did. Our uncle Quentin was the first to enlist in the Royal Marines, following in his grandfather's footsteps. And later, so did my brothers. I decided to follow my own instincts. Even then, it felt more natural to strike out on my own.

It took a few false starts, but here I am. The CEO of a biochemicals research company which I built. It did have seed funding from my grandfather, but everything else is mine. I'm the one who raised money for the IPO from the stock market. I'm the one who decides which initiatives we'll focus on. I've kept the team small. Kept my own hours.

Kept a low enough profile that it's a perfect cover for the missions I take on for the government. This one, though, is personal.

I exit the park, pull the hoodie of my sweatshirt over my head, hunch my shoulders, and do my best to blend in. With my six feet six inches height, I'll always stand out. But wearing everyday clothes helps. Ensuring I keep my chin lowered so my features aren't caught on any closed-circuit cameras is another.

I head to the nondescript white van with the name of a building company stenciled on the side. A bit predictable, but the best way to mask my presence. I asked one of my team to have it delivered so I could use it.

I take the key fob from the glove box, after keying in the code to open it, then drive off. A half-hour drive brings me to a quiet borough.

Not as well-heeled as Primrose Hill, but also, not as gritty as the East End. With its tree-lined streets and green spaces, Archway is quickly becoming sought after, in real estate terms. Given its proximity to Whittington Hospital, which is where the subject of my interest works, it makes sense that she lives here.

I double-check the address that James sent me, then shoot off a message to the investigator whose part of my team, asking him to send me a full background check on her.

I park the car a few houses down from the address I've been given.

I don't have to wait long before the door to the house opens. A woman dressed in scrubs, which mark her out as a medical professional, steps onto the pathway.

Even under the shapeless clothes, and despite the distance, I can make out her hourglass figure. She wears them with the panache of a princess wearing a gown, and glides like she's wearing not sneakers, but stilettos. The pathway in front of her seems to resemble a catwalk; that's how arresting her gait is. Thick chestnut hair flows down her back. I can make out her high cheekbones, the sweep of her nose, the evenly spaced features of her face. Though I can't make out the details, I see enough to tell me she's striking. Enough to send a sizzle of awareness down my spine, and for the hairs on the back of my neck to rise to attention. Next time, I'm getting a camera with a high-powered lens so I can watch her closely.

When I received my best friend James' message to look out for his little sister, I wasn't sure what to expect. But his message was urgent enough that I headed here right away. That, and the fact I felt at loose ends.

I spent the better part of the last month helping my brother Tyler with his division of the Davenport Group, so he could spend more time with his wife and daughter.

Now that he's resuming his duties, I'm ready for a new challenge. And the woman in front of me represents the kind of task which is both intriguing and feeds into my sense of responsibility. I owe James so I'm more than happy to help out. If I'm honest, the fact that his sister has something indefinable about her which draws me could be a complication, but it's also alluring. Besides, I'm here to watch her, so I'm not doing anything wrong, right?

The object of my attention pushes open the waist-level gate—it's more a demarcation than a deterrent, something which is a red flag among the many other red flags I've already spotted in terms of her security—and steps onto the sidewalk.

She hefts her backpack more securely, pulls out her phone and fiddles with it. She walks up the road in the other direction from me, head bent, seemingly occupied with whatever she sees on screen. Then her steps slow. She seems to stiffen and glance around.

Good instincts.

She looks over her shoulder. I'm parked far enough that I'm sure all she'll make out is an indistinct figure behind the wheel. A food delivery person cycles by.

He stops at a house between us, gets off his bike, walks to the front door, and rings the bell.

It seems to ease her nerves—she turns away and walks on. I release the handbrake, ease off the brake pedal, and let the car roll forward. She rounds the corner. I follow, keeping a careful distance, shadowing her on the fifteen-minute walk to the hospital.

Despite a couple of times when she stops and turns to look over her shoulder to survey the area before she continues, I'm far enough away, and with more vehicles on the road, there's no way she notices me.

She's more alert, more aware than I expected her to be. It makes me respect her more. It makes me *want* her even more.

I wait until she's safely inside the hospital, then turn the van around and head back to her home. I'm tempted to go in, but damn, that would be an infringement of privacy. I respect James too much to do that. And it wouldn't be fair to her either. I satisfy myself by doing another drive-by around her house to familiarize myself. Then, I head back to the hospital and park a little way down the road. My phone vibrates, I check the screen and answer the FaceTime call.

"James?"

"Connor, did you see her?" James' worried features appeared on the screen. "Is she okay?"

"I did, and she's fine. I'm headed back to the hospital to wait for her to leave; I'll follow her back home."

He heaves a sigh of relief. "Thanks, man. I'd keep an eye on her myself, but if she'd spotted me, I'd get an earful. She wouldn't be happy." He makes a face.

"Something tells me, she's not going to be much more appreciative when she finds out you've asked me to fill that role." I jerk my chin at him.

I haven't spoken to her, but given the stubbornness I'd glimpsed on her face, I'm sure she's the kind who won't take too kindly to her brother hovering over her. Or any other man, for that matter. Not that I'm going to let myself be found out. I push that thought aside. "What's this all about? Why do you think she needs to be watched over?"

James rubs at his temple. Then he nods to someone I can't see out of frame. Behind him, I hear the sounds of his kitchen and spot some of his staff dressed in chef's jackets and aprons scurrying about. He heads away, and the noise recedes, presumably because he stepped out of the kitchen. He heads into another room, where he sits down at a desk and places the phone on it. Then he leans back. "It might be nothing but—"

"But you don't think so."

He shakes his head. "Phoenix is the youngest of us eight siblings."

"Big family." I grew up with five brothers, plus a half-brother I discovered later, so I'm no stranger to having multiple siblings. But eight sounds excessive, even to me.

James laughs. "Growing up, it was quite competitive between us, as you can imagine. She's the quietest of the lot. As the youngest, you'd think she would've been the most spoiled, but she's always been too independent for that. She put herself through medical school on her own merit, refusing to take money from any of us to help."

My esteem for her increases. It's not cheap to get that kind of education, and she stuck it out on her own.

"She's always been reticent, but over the past few months she's withdrawn even more into herself. She doesn't come to family get-togethers or our weekly dinners — not that I blame her. My family can be a little full-on. But she also doesn't answer our calls. She checks in with our mother, and me on occasion, but that's only through text messages. She refuses to share her thoughts with us. And if she knew I was concerned enough to contemplate following her to make sure she's okay, she'd — " He shakes her head. "She'd be pissed off, and that's putting it mildly."

"So, you want me to be the one tailing her?"

"I get the impression she's going through something personal. Something she doesn't want to share with us. And that's fine; it's her prerogative. But it's also my prerogative, as her brother, to watch out for her and make sure she's okay."

I nod slowly. "If you want security, you should speak to Quentin or Nathan."

"They're too busy to take this on personally. Whereas you — "

"Have no such commitments." I twist my lips.

He half-smiles. "It's the truth."

I blow out a breath. I should be amused that he thinks my lack of a personal life or a family means I have the time to take this on. Instead, something inside me resents it. Not that he wants me to help; I'd do that in a heartbeat. It's more the fact that I don't have anything resembling personal commitments or people I care for that clears the way for me to do so. Which is bizarre.

Perhaps, it's the fact four of my brothers have settled down in the last year and walk around looking happy, that's making me wonder if Arthur isn't perhaps right in having given them deadlines to get married?

If you'd told me that a few years ago, I'd have laughed. Now, I have the evidence in front of my eyes, and a part of me is envious. On the other hand, I'm happy in my bachelor state.

"This won't be cheap," I warn.

He barks out a laugh. "I didn't expect it to be."

"I'm turning down another assignment to do this." It might cost me my career, but that doesn't seem as important as ensuring I watch over Phoenix.

His features soften. "I appreciate this. My sister is important to me."

And to me.

Perhaps, something of my thoughts shows on my face, for a flicker of something sparks in his eyes. "I'd do anything for her. And if anyone hurts her"—he sets his jaw—"I won't hesitate to punish whoever it is."

Phoenix

"I don't love you." I look into my boyfriend's face. "I care about you, but I don't think I was ever in love with you."

He winces. His lips turn down.

"This is so difficult for me to say, but I believe it's best to be honest."

The light in his eyes dims, and my heart seizes up. "I don't mean to hurt you, but it would be wrong to ignore how things are between us, don't you think?"

He hunches his shoulders, then turns and walks out of the kitchen, past the living room, and into the bedroom. The door slams shut.

I stare at the remnants of the breakfast on my plate. My heart somersaults in my rib cage. My stomach seems to bottom out. The food I tried to eat rushes up my throat. I swallow down the bile, then rise to my feet and place my plate in the sink. I fill a glass with water from the sink and drink it slowly. It settles me a little.

I've been building up to that; I kept putting off the conversation with Drew. But the lack of sleep and general exhaustion must have lowered my barriers, for when I sat opposite him at breakfast today, I was unable to hold back. The words I'd rehearsed for days come tumbling out of my mouth. And the result is far worse than I expected.

I pull out my cellphone as I step out of my house. Locking the door behind me, I head down the path, push open the gate which leads to the road, then stop. A prickling at the nape of my neck makes me pause. I glance up and down the tree-lined street. There are cars parked on both sides of the road, common in most residential areas in London. It's quiet, except for the chirping of the birds. It's a sound I love, which led me to buy my apartment in this building. It's only seven a.m. I should be in bed, but the ER at the hospital is short-staffed. I got a call on my day off and was asked if I'd come in and cover the shift. I jumped at the opportunity. Anything to keep working so I wouldn't need to spend time at home. So, I wouldn't have to think about what a mess my personal life is.

I look around my neighbors' homes—curtains drawn, no lights. Most likely, they're still asleep. The milkman left a bottle on the porch opposite mine. Thanks to my job I'm not home that much, so I don't know my neighbors. But I bet whoever lives in the house opposite mine believes in recycling and saving the world, which is why they're buying their milk, the old-fashioned way.

I used to be that way. I used to believe in fighting for a cause. That I could do my bit to make the world a better place. It's why I became a doctor. My parents were so proud of me.

My father wanted to pay for my education, but I refused. I was young and hopeful. I wanted to make it on my own. Idealistic. Naïve. Thinking if I worked hard enough, if I believed enough, I could manifest everything I wanted. And for a moment, for a few months even, I thought I had. Then, everything turned upside down.

I step onto the sidewalk and begin to walk toward the hospital. I love that I live so close to my place of work that I can walk there. At least, I used to, until a few days ago, when I had this sensation of being watched. I turn and glance over my shoulder.

Nothing different. Same chirping of the birds. Same parked cars. Same white van at the end of the street. I've noticed it's presence over the last three days. Strange. Someone must be getting renovations done to their place. Strange that that the workmen arrived before dawn? I shrug. It's not unusual I suppose?

I shake off the feeling, hook my EarPods into my ears, and flick on the podcast I'm listening to on my phone.

It's an interview with a medical researcher who's expounding on the last paper he published. I get immersed in his findings, until I reach the hospital. Once I'm in, I deposit my stuff in a locker. I'm already in my scrubs, so I can dive right into my first case in the Emergency Room. An older gentleman who's having breathing problems. A little girl who's suffering from high fever which refuses to come down. A leg fracture. A man who fell while getting off a bus and hurt his chin. The list goes on.

I manage to take a break to get a cup of tea and a chocolate bar. Then head back to where patients have been triaged and are awaiting examination. I pull aside the curtain to the first cubicle and pause. The man seated on the clinical table looks straight at me.

Blue eyes so pale, they seemed to reflect my image. Like I'm drowning in his eyes. Like he's drowning in mine. Thick hair cut so short, there's barely an inch on top of his head. So short, I can see the brown of his scalp which, for some reason, I find appealing. Intelligent forehead, currently bisected by a cut on his temple with blood trickling down. Long eyelashes, thick enough for me to be envious of them. High cheekbones, sharp enough to double up as scalpels. Straight nose, stern upper lip. All planes and angles. All austere. And stern. Features almost verging on being labeled mean, but for that sensuous lower lip. One which is currently cut. And which only adds to his rakish appeal.

I should be thinking of how to fix his wounds, but I can't seem to get past the shape of that mouth. It's pillow-like puffiness—accentuated by the cut— hints at forbidden pleasures. And long steamy nights. And wicked things he could be capable of. Things which could bring me a lot of gratification. And there's that chin, with a hint of a dip in the middle. Something lush and luxurious and luscious. Something expansive. And passionate. Those beautiful cords of his neck, which lead to the flesh that peeks above the T-shirt he's wearing.

A leather jacket hugs the breadth of his shoulders. Shoulders so massive, they block out the room behind him. The sleeves outline the powerful muscles of his biceps. So thick, he must have struggled to pull it on. His blue jeans have seen better days. Worn at the knees, pulled apart over those powerful thighs, between which is a substantial tent. He's packing. Which explains the confidence radiating from him. He looks powerful. Like someone used to being obeyed.

I'd place him as someone who'd be at home in a boardroom, except, there's a ruggedness to him telling me he doesn't drive a desk. That, and the massive hands, fingers splayed. One palm relaxed on a thigh. The other on the bed next to him. He has scuffed leather boots —big boots. Size thirteen? Maybe fourteen. Which means—my gaze swings back to the space between his thighs. The zipper is tight and stretched and, surely, that tent is more substantial than before.

My breathing grows rough. My nipples under my scrub tighten into points of need. I'm aware, I'm close to panting and can't understand it. Sure, he's good-looking. More than good-looking. And yes, there's something about him that's vital. And real. And commands attention. And charismatic. But he's only a man. A stranger.

So what, if the pheromones pouring off of him saturate the air between us? And so what, if the heat from his body seems to reach across the space to me, spirals around my shoulders, loops around my waist, tightens and holds me in thrall? I don't know him. So why am I so drawn to him?

My legs shiver. My toes curl. My scalp tingles. I still haven't taken my eyes off that triangle of promise between his legs. So, when he clears his throat, my cheeks flame. I jerk my chin up, meet his eyes, and see the amusement in them. His lips curl. He's caught me in the act, as it were. But when he speaks, he doesn't let that on.

"Doc." He jerks his chin in my direction. Gravelly voice—like he swallowed pebbles, and his voice has to rake over the rough surface to reach me. Dark edge—like thick, hot chocolate that you have to dig out with a spoon.

My mouth waters. I have to swallow to stop the moan that whips up my throat.

"Doctor Hamilton," I manage to croak out. "Seems you got into a fight?"

"You should see the other guy." He smirks.

The uptick of his lips is the hottest thing I've ever seen. My already sensitized nerve endings flare. My ovaries do a little dance.

Every cell in my body seems to have woken up and is locked onto him. Where's my professionalism? I'm a doctor. He's my patient. He needs urgent care. That's why he came in here. So why the heck am I not examining him, instead of ogling him like he invented the cure for an incurable disease?

"Bar fight?" I guess. Only because I want to get information that will help me treat him. That's all. It has nothing to do with finding out more about him.

"A *fight*," he agrees, but doesn't add anything more.

Okay, then. I stare. He stares back. Our gazes hold. Once more, that thrum of anticipation zips up my spine. Damn. This is not good. I need to get on with treating him. Need to do my job.

"Take off your clothes."

He arches an eyebrow.

My flush deepens. "I mean, please take off your jacket and T-shirt so I can examine your wounds."

He tilts his head.

"There's blood on your T-shirt, under your jacket. It doesn't look like it dripped there."

He glances down at himself, then unfolds his body and rises to his feet. And keeps rising. The promise of the breadth of his shoulders and of the width of his palms is borne out when I have to tilt my head back, then further back, to see his features. He's tall. As tall as my brother James who's six-feet-four-inches. The man shrugs off his jacket, dropping it on the treatment table.

I have a brief impression of the blood which blots the side of his T-shirt. Then he reaches behind him—winces—and pulls it off.

I draw in a sharp breath at the sight of acres of golden-brown skin, tanned by the sun. His pectoral muscles are well developed enough to warrant a dip between them. Very male nipples, and corrugated abs form an eight-pack. Yep, an honest-to-life eight-pack, marred only by a tattoo of what seems to be the wing of a raven curling up from the left. On the right side is an ugly bruise over his ribs. The skin is mottled and turning purple. Blood from the cut has splashed onto his jeans and dried at the edges.

My gaze slides down to take in the mouth-watering iliac furrows on either side that swoop down to the waistband of his pants. He flicks open the button, lowering his zipper. The r-r-r-i-pping sound ricochets off the walls of the room and seems to hit me in my chest in tandem to the beating of my heart. My pulse shoots through the roof. I want him to shuck off his jeans so badly. It's the hunger in me which brings me to my senses.

"Stop," I croak.

He pauses, a puzzled look on his face.

"Are you hurt anywhere else, other than your torso?"

He shakes his head slowly.

"You can keep your p-pants on then." I stumble over the word like I'm fifteen, instead of a qualified trauma specialist. I need to get a grip on my emotions.

"Whatever you say, Doc," he drawls.

That last word feels like a caress coming from him. Another shiver squeezes my lower belly. Ridiculous. I close the distance toward him. With each step I take, expectation pitches in my chest. I am conscious of the fact he's watching me closely as I inch toward him.

His scent intensifies. Under that sharp astringent hospital smell is something dark, smoky, like distant campfire on a star drenched night, with a hint of leather, perhaps, from his jacket. And something else unique. Intoxicating. The scent of his skin, perhaps?

My knees tremble. My scalp tingles. Just as I'm congratulating myself on completing what feels like a walk of shame as I near him, I stumble and pitch forward.

Connor

I hold out my arms, and she falls into them. Against my bare chest. On the wounded side. Pinpricks of shock shudder up my spine to my brain. The pain is nothing compared to the sensations hurtling out from where she's placed her palms on my chest. Slim fingers, so pale against my skin. Unvarnished nails. Cut short. Unadorned. Yet, I've never seen anything so beautiful.

I hold her close, take full advantage of the proximity to bend and sniff her hair. Flowers. Cherry blossom. Roses. With a touch of vanilla. It's feminine and light, yet packs a punch, enough to gut me. Undressing for her was a most pleasurable experience. Watching her hips sway as she walked away from me each day, as I watched her come out of her house every morning over the past week, has been agonizing. By that I mean, it gave me so much pleasure, I had to find a way to find relief afterward each day.

I watched her house closely, imagined her under the sheets of her bed at night, obsessed over how it would be to hold her in my arms... But it's nothing compared to the reality. Soft, curvy, with a waist so slim, I could span it with the width of my palm. And those gorgeous hips. I'm tempted to run my fingers over the swell, to squeeze their thickness, to massage them, to find out if they're as soft yet firm as they seemed.

But that would simply piss her off, I have no doubt. She just met me. While I feel I know her, after the vigil I've kept over her since her brother asked me to, this is the first time she's meeting me. I couldn't afford to upset her, no matter how much I want to swing her up in my arms, walk out of here, and lay claim to her.

All in good time. I swallow down my impatience and set her aside. "You, okay?"

She blinks. "Must be the new clogs. Not used to them yet."

I glance down at the yellow, closed-toe sandals with the thick, rigid sole. They should look ugly, but they only emphasize the delicateness of her feet. Toe-to-toe, she barely comes up to my chest. I'm at least a foot taller than her. I've always been a big guy. Only Tyler, my older brother, is taller than me. But I have broader shoulders. Not that Tyler will ever admit that. I've learned, over the years, how to relax my body so I appear non-threatening. But I'll always appear like a giant next to her. I sink back onto the examination table.

She avoids my gaze, picks up the paperwork the nurse left, and scans through it.

"Connor Davenport. Thirty-two year. You were in a bar fight?" She levels a look at me from under her eyelashes.

I pop my shoulder. The triage nurse was thorough. I don't see the need to add anything more than what's written there. It would mean I can avoid lying to the do.

When I stay silent, she continues reading, "You might need stitches." She sets the paperwork aside.

I slide my thighs apart in an invitation. She hesitates. Then, because that's the best way to examine the bruise I sport, she steps between them. Her cheeks flush. But her fingers are confident when she pulls out a flashlight and shines it in my eyes. Blinded, I blink, then manage to keep my eyes open. She makes a humming sound which could mean anything, in the way that doctors often do. She moves her finger in front of my eyes, and I follow the direction.

"No concussion," she says shortly. "You'll need stitches for that though." She nods toward the wound on my forehead, and that—she glances at the wound at my side.

Movements brisk, she touches the skin next to the dried blood on my forehead. My muscles jump. Sensations zip up my spine. It takes everything in me not to groan. I curl my fingers into fists, press my feet into the floor, and will my body to relax. Impossible, when every tendon in my body seems to have turned to steel. And the muscle between my legs to granite.

She presses down on the skin, and pain shudders out from the point of contact. Still, I make no sound. She frowns, presses around a little more. "Does it hurt?"

Yes.

I shake my head. I'm not lying. I can bear it.

She shoots me a disbelieving look from under her eyelashes. Then presses down harder. This time I hiss out a breath.

"So, it *does* hurt?"

"Just do what you need to," I say through gritted teeth. Sweat beads on my brow. She *is* hurting me. Just not where she imagines. It's her touch turning my blood to lava, and kicking up my pulse rate, and bringing visions of how it would be to lift her up and divest her of those shapeless scrubs that do nothing to disguise the lush curves of her body and throw her down on the examination table.

But I don't do that. Obviously, I hope nothing of my thoughts shows on my face. But she must hear something in my words because her movements speed up. Some more digging in with her fingers, which sends little points of pain racing under my skin, and she nods. "No ribs broken; only bruised. So, you won't need an X-ray. You do need stitches for this, too, however."

Then she reaches over to grab the antiseptic spray from the counter. The curve of her waist brushes my thigh, and I'm so turned on I could come from the contact. Damn.

Then I'm gasping for air, this time for real, as she sprays antiseptic on my wound.

I manage to not cry out. Which means, hopefully, I don't dispel the notions of my macho attitude and pain thresholds which I've struggled to impress her with.

Then she straightens. "Close your eyes."

I do, and she sprays the antiseptic on the cut over my eyebrow. Then on the one on my lower lip. The resulting burn is barely a twinge.

Eyes still closed, I sense her walk around and over to one of the shelves. I open my eyes in time to see her bringing over a steel tray with tools. I assume she's going to stitch me up. I'm proven right when she asks me to lay down. I stretch out and continue watching her, using the time to survey her features.

After the days of watching her from afar, I can't believe I'm this close to her. She bends over to inject an anesthetic to numb the space around the cut on my eyebrow. I inhale her scent—cherry blossoms and roses, with a hint of vanilla. It's heady and further exacerbates the lust lancing through my veins. My fingers tingle with the need to touch her, but I manage to keep my hands to myself and let her get on with the job of stitching me up. She finishes stitching my forehead, then turns toward the gash in my side.

When she touches the abraded skin around the wound with the cotton, I can't stop the groan which boils up my throat.

"Sorry," she murmurs without looking up. Goosebumps pepper her skin. Interesting. And reassuring to know she feels this connection between us. That though her touch is professional the impact on her is far from.

I sense her breathing roughen. Then she gets ahold of herself and begins to clean the wound. She follows the same protocol, numbing the space before she stitches it up.

All too soon, she's done. Cutting off the thread, she steps back.

"Keep the stitches dry. They should start dissolving within ten days. You'll have a scar, though." She pulls off her disposable gloves and drops them in the bin. "It's only going to add to your good looks, I'm sure."

"You think I'm good looking?" I swing my legs over the side and sit up.

She stiffens, then rubbing antiseptic onto her hands, turns to me. "You know you are."

"It still means a lot to me to know that you think so too."

Her expression turns cautious. "Why is that?"

"Because I think you're, possibly, the most beautiful woman I've ever seen."

She flushes, her eyes grow wide, then she tosses her head. "It's probably gratitude for having stitched you up that's kicking in." She pulls out a tablet from her pocket and her fingers fly over the surface. "You're going to need to use a prophylactic antibiotic. A prescription has been sent to the hospital pharmacy. You can pick it up there. Make sure you apply it daily until the wounds are healed." She pockets her device, hooks her stethoscope around her neck, and moves toward the curtains drawn around the cubicle.

I should let her go. This is totally unprofessional, but I can't stop myself from snaking out my hand and wrapping my fingers around her wrist. "You never told me your first name."

She stiffens, then stares down at my fingers, before looking up at me. "You're overstepping the doctor-patient relationship."

"You've treated me; that relationship is now over." I hold onto her for a few seconds more. Then, I slowly retract my hand. "Your name"—I soften my tone—"please."

She hesitates, then a small smile curves her lips. "You're a resourceful man, Mr. Davenport. I'm sure you can find it out another way."

To find out what happens next read Connor and Phoenix's story in The Wrong Husband. Scan this QR code to get it

How to scan a QR code?

1. Open the camera app on your phone or tablet.
2. Point the camera at the QR code.
3. Tap the banner that appears on your phone or tablet.
4. Follow the instructions on the screen to finish signing in.

HERE'S AN EXCLUSIVE BONUS EPILOGUE WITH TYLER & PRISCILLA

Priscilla

You deserve to be happy.
You deserve for all your dreams to come true.
-Cilla's Post-it note

"Honey they'll be home any second," I try to pull away from my husband, but he leans the weight of his lower body onto mine. He pins me in place. His large shoulders block out the sight of the room. His chest rises and falls. I can feel the cut of his sculpted muscles because my breasts are smashed against them—and I'm loving it. I'm loving the way the heat from his body surrounds me and how his scent is thick in the room, mixed with that of sex, and how a bead of sweat slides down his temple and stays there trembling, poised, ready to fall. I reach up and scoop it up, then wipe it down the cleavage between his very defined pecs. My fingers brush his dog tags. I curl my fingers around them and tug. He lowers his head, until his nose brushes mine. His breath flows over my cheek. I shiver. "Connor must be returning with Serene as we speak." I remind him again.

"Not for another fifteen minutes, if we're lucky." He urges me to wrap my legs around his waist. Then he begins to move. Slowly. Carefully. Inch by inch he sinks his massive cock inside me. So slowly I can feel every millimeter of his ribbed length push against my inner walls. "You feel so good," I breathe.

"And you feel—" He looks deep into my eyes. "You feel like the hottest, sweetest, tightest hole." He pulls back and thrusts into me again.

"You feel beautiful, and moving, and incredibly soft."

Thrust.

You feel like..." Another thrust that has him burying his shaft balls deep inside of me. "You're mine."

A trembling starts from where we're connected and spirals up my spine. This man is a wordsmith. He showers me with the most endearing compliments. And makes me feel like a princess. Like his queen. Like I can do nothing wrong in his eyes. It took me a while to accept it. For a while I couldn't believe my luck. Could this Norse god of a man who seemed like a cross between Thor and Maverick want me so much? For someone who likes to portray herself as being externally confident, I sure have a difficult time accepting that everything I wanted has been given to me. A husband who loves me. A gorgeous daughter. A home I love. And yes, I'm having to turn to my self-help books to learn how to accept it. I'm getting better at it though. I promise. With every passing day I'm learning to receive what the universe has sent my way. I am open to miracles. I am open to taking what is mine and not feeling guilty for it. I am as open to receiving as I am to giving. Especially when it is from him. He squeezes the curve of my butt, pulls out until he's balanced at the rim of my slit. The muscles of his shoulders bunch. His impressive biceps swell, as he stays there supporting the weight of his body so he's not completely crushing me, though I confess I like when he does that too.

"You ready for this baby?" he asks in a low growly voice that instantly has my pussy turning even more wet.

When he gets into this mood, I know he's going to spring a surprise on me. My husband can be a beast between the sheets. And terribly innovative. Loving and tender one minute, demanding and bossy and dominant the next. A shiver of anticipation squeezes my insides. But I know I can trust him. He wouldn't hurt me. Oh, he loves to edge me. To keep me on the razor's edge of arousal until I feel like I'll go out of my head with need.

"Darling?" He rumbles. A furrow appearing between his eyebrows. A query in those gorgeous mis matched eyes which makes my heart flip-flop every time he looks at me as he is now. "If you want me to stop?"

"No," I tilt my hips so he slides in, just enough that that massive head of his monster cock breaches me. I'm so sensitized, electricity seems to zap up my body a moan spills my lips. His Adam's apple bobs, and I know he felt that too. Damn. "Don't stop," I beg him.

The doubt on his features recedes. A sly look comes into his eyes. I shiver again. Then gasp when he pulls back so I'm forced to lower my legs. Then he flips me over. "Tyler," I cry out.

He maneuvers me so I'm on my knees, arse in the air, with my cheek pressed into the pillow. Then he pushes my thighs apart, so I'm completely bared to him. "Ty," I swallow. "What are you—" I cry out again for he's spanked my arse cheek. Tiny shock waves sizzle to my core. My clit throbs. He doesn't stop there. He proceeds to slap my other cheek, then the first, and the next. I count ten in total. When he stops, my backside smarts. I swear I can feel every fingerprint branded into my skin.

Ripples of energy crackle under my skin. It's like he's electrocuted me and now my entire body is ablaze with a breathless need. An anticipation. An expectation for more. *More. More. More.*

As if he hears me, he rubs his big palm across my stinging cheek. The pain multiplies, coalesces into this strange pleasure which hooks into my clit. A yearning fills me. A deep yawning echo chamber at the bottom of my belly. I whimper, pushing my butt up and out in his direction. Wanting him to touch me, to fondle me, to lick me right where I need him.

In response he squeezes my arse cheeks and pulls them apart. Cool air skims over my rim and my quivering pussy. I'm aware of him staring at my flesh. Feel the blush coat my cheeks and extend to my extremities. I'm one big mass of longing. Vibrating with this hunger that assails me to the bone. He's fucked me so many times, but each time is like the first. Perhaps with time it might settle into a calmer sea instead of the twister which seems to erupt inside of me every time he touches me—but I'm sure given the chemistry I share with this man it'll never fade completely. It'll never be a calm gassy sea where you can see through to the depths. He'll always surprise me. Always offer me a fresh insight into myself every time I receive him into my body. Making love with my husband will always be a religious experience. And I have the universe to thank for that.

Then he blows on my pussy. I shiver, then shudder for he's licked up my pussy lips. Oh, my God. Every time he eats me out it's like all my affirmations are finally being delivered on. He does it slowly, thoroughly, like we have all the time in this world. He starts with a wide, flat tongue and soft, gentle movements around my clit. My insides melty. My pussy stutters. It feels luxurious. Like honey has replaced my bloodstream. My muscles relax. Then he begins to circle my clit, clockwise. Round and round. My head spins. My clit throbs. The blood rushes to my center. My nipples are so hard they're digging holes into the bedclothes. Then he slips his fingers inside my channel and twists them and my thighs quiver. I almost collapse but his hold on my hips holds me up. He continues to lick up my pussy lips, while moving his fingers in and out of me. In and out. He adds a third finger, stretching me and it feels so good. But it also makes me yearn for the width of his cock. His massive monster shaft that is the instrument of so much pleasure. "Tyler please," I whine, try to glance at him over my shoulder.

In response he spanks my arse sharply. "You're not in charge."

"Oh." I swallow, even more turned on. But also, I can't stop myself from whining, "But I want."

He pulls his fingers out of my pussy, and I feel like crying. "No. No. No. Put them back in."

"Hmm." He sits back on his haunches. "What do you say?"

I blink, trying to compute what the hell he's talking about, before it dawns on me. "Please?"

He nods. "Good girl." Then he slaps my cunt.

Tyler

Her entire body jerks. Her back bows off the bed. Then with a choking sound she shatters. To see her writhe as the orgasm takes her is the most incredible sight. As for the red of my handprints on her arse—it's a mark of possession which appeals to my inner cave man. She's my woman. My wife. Mine. And I'm going to give her so much pleasure she's going to forget her own name and remember only that of her husband's.

I rise up between her thighs, grip her hip with one hand to hold her in place. Then I fit my cock to her weeping slit. I punch forward and in one smooth move I impale her. She's so wet, despite my considerable girth I slide right in.

She flutters around my shaft and sensations coil in my balls. "Jesus, honey you feel so good," I groan.

She mewls in response. And when I place my hand in the small of her back urging her to raise her hips she follows. I slip even deeper inside her, feel her warm wet channel envelop my throbbing length and almost come. I grit myself, draw in even breaths, force myself to hold back. I need to make her come again first. I reach around and squeeze her swollen slit. She cries out. "Tyler," she says in a broken voice.

"I'm here, baby." I pull back and thrust back in. Slowly. Making sure she can feel every centimeter of my possession. I continue to circle her clit as I fuck into her. She moans, and tries to pull away, but I hold her in place. Then I piston my hips forward and bury myself in her again.

My balls slap against her pussy. She whimpers. Begins to squeeze down on my cock, which is how I know she's close again. I pull out of her. Flip her over, then gently squeezing her thighs apart, I lower my chin and lick her from puckered hole to clit.

"Oh, my God," she cries out. Brings her legs together to lock her knees around my neck. Not that I'm complaining. Being stifled by my wife's thighs is a privilege. I flatten my tongue and swipe it up her pussy lips. She whines. I curl my tongue around the swollen bud between them and she mewls. She's so fucking responsive, it's driving me crazy. My balls seem to have turned into titanium. My cock is so hard it feels I've attached cement blocks to it. I wrap my hand around my shaft and squeeze it from crown to base. My other hand I bring up to her breast and squeeze her nipple. She throws her head back and moans, loudly. So fuckin' erotic.

When I groan into her pussy she shudders. Looks down to find my eyes on her. Holding her gaze, I eat her out, aware of her juices dripping from my chin. Her pupils dilate further until there's only a rim of brown around them. Her cheeks are flushed, her hair in a halo around her face. Her lips are swollen from my kisses. In that moment my chest feels like I've been punched. This feeling that connects me to her grows even more stronger. I feel like I've been gutted inside. Like my heart has been pulled out and all that remains in its place is an empty space with her name written on it. I have so much love for this woman.

I'd bring the stars down to earth for her. Go to battle with anyone in this entire world to protect her. Slay monsters for her. I curl my tongue inside her pussy, and she pants. And when I bite down gently on her clit, her spine arches, her thighs tremble, her entire body convulses, and she comes again.

Moisture flows out of her slit; I lick it up. Savor the sweet-tart taste of her cum which turns me on further. Then I crawl up her body and kiss her deeply. She wraps her arms about my shoulders and pulls me close. I reach down between us, position my cock at her opening and slip inside her. She groans into my mouth. I swallow down the sound and begin to move. Once-twice-thrice, I thrust into her. Each time I sink into her the entire bed moves. The headboard slaps against the wall. Good thing there's no one at home. I love nothing more than making love to my wife, in our bed, and with no one around so we can be free to be ourselves. I urge her to lock her legs about my waist, dig her heels into my back as I continue to thrust into her. Each movement, slow precise. As I hold her gaze, look deep into her eyes, and while my tongue mirrors the impaling movement of my cock. Then I slide my fingers over her butt, to caress the calyx between her buttcheeks. At the same time I release her mouth long enough to growl. "Come."

Her body bucks. With a silent cry, she shatters. I continue to fuck her through her orgasm, and only when her body slumps do I pour myself inside her. My orgasm seems to go on and on. And all through it the connection of our eyes hold. When the telltale tingle creep into my balls—signaling they're finally empty—I begin to pull out her. But she shakes her head. Pulls me close, clinging to me with her arms and legs around me like a burr. I lower some of my weight onto her, press my nose into the curve of where her neck meets her shoulder and breathe deeply. Apple blossoms and honey. The scent of my wife. Of love. Of lust. Of home. My muscles relax on cue. I slump further into her. "I'm too heavy."

"You're perfect." Her voice is husky like she's been screaming—which she has. I made her scream, with pleasure. And fuck if that doesn't make me want to thump my chest and announce it to the world.

She turns her head and kisses my cheek. "I love you."

"I love you," I turn to face her so we're almost nose to nose. "I love you so fucking much."

Her eyes are soft. Her features relaxed. A rush of tenderness fills me. I rub my nose against hers. "Happy?"

She chuckles. "That's an understatement."

"I want to give you everything. Anything you want. I want to make sure you're always happy, baby."

"You do?"

I nod slowly. "I'll give you anything you want, anything."

"Anything?" There's a peculiar look in her eyes.

"Anything," I search her features. "What is it? What do you want from me?"

A small smile curves her features. "A baby."

I blink. "A baby?"

She nods. "A little peanut that I could grow inside and swell with and bring into the world. A brother or sister for Serene."

"Wow," I breathe. To say I hadn't thought about it would be an understatement. I've been so busy first with Serene, then ensuring she and Cilla were comfortable with each other and watching their relationship blossom. Seeing them bond has been the most satisfying experience. They're mother and daughter, there's no doubt of that in my mind. And to have another kid, with my wife. To watch her carry the child, to be there for the birth and those early months. To see her feed our child. "Wow."

"You seem stunned." Her forehead furrows. "If you don't think it's a good idea—"

"Oh it is." I flip over on my back and pull her on top so she can use me as her mattress. The position I love best. When I can feel her curves against my planes and angles, and carry her sweet weight and feel her body adjust to mine. "I'm just...surprised."

"You mean you hadn't thought about it?" She looks up at me.

"I admit it hadn't crossed my mind, but it's something I'd have gotten to thinking about, you just beat me to it."

u hold me and kiss me, this need inside me grew. I realized I was ready. I realized I had to bring it up with you."

"I'm glad you did," He hauls me up so my face is poised an inch above him. "I want nothing more than seeing you pregnant with our baby." He kisses me softly. I open my mouth, he sweeps his tongue inside. Prickles of heat stab my chest. My toes curl. My pussy clenches. I dig my fingers into his shoulders, loving the feel of my nails against his skin. Love that I'm marking him. Love that he's already growing erect against the curve of my thigh. I tilt my head, deepen the kiss and a growl rumbles up his chest. "Fuck, baby, what you do to me."

He wraps his thick arms about my waist and hauls me even closer. Continues to kiss me until I'm breathless. And my heart is thumping against my rib cage. And my ears are ringing. *Buzz. Buzz. Buzz.*

"Is that—"

L. STEELE

"My phone," he groans against my mouth. Damn. I, too, want to ignore it. But when you have a child, they always come first. And a phone call could be something to do with them. He reaches for the phone and places it against his ear, and breaks the kiss long enough to snap, "Hello."

"Papa, we're almost home." I can hear Serene's excited voice over the phone.

"That's wonderful, honey. Mommy and I are waiting for you."

"Can I have ice cream for dinner, Papa?"

He looks at me.

I shake my head.

He frowns, hands the phone over to me. He's such a big teddy bear he can't say no to his daughter. So invariably I'm the disciplinarian. It's not easy, but I seem better at saying 'no' to Serene. I know how important it is for Serene to know and respect boundaries too.

"Honey, you need to eat your vegetables first."

"But Mama—"

"And then you can have some ice cream for dessert, what do you say?"

"Oh." I hear her thinking, then she blows out a breath. "If you insist."

I stifle a chuckle. You never know where kids pick up the grown-up sounding phrases from. Likely from one of her uncles. She loves spending time with Brody and Connor especially. They make time for her always and are happy to babysit Serene giving me and Tyler some alone time."

"I do," I say gently.

A very grown-up sigh then she mutters, "Okay, Mama." She already sounds like an irritable teenager and she's not even five. Damn.

Tyler takes the phone from me. "I'll see you at home, honey."

"We should be there in five—ten minutes at the most," I hear Connor say on the phone. "Called you guys to give you enough advance notice to make yourself decent."

Tyler disconnects the phone and tosses it aside. "You heard the man. They'll be ten minutes." He rolls me onto my back, positions his cock at my entrance and in one thrust breaches me.

I gasp. That familiar heat surges through my veins. My pussy feels so good. So full. "Oh God."

"That's oh, Tyler."

I chuckle, then moan when he thrusts into me again. "They'll be here."

"We have time for a quickie."

❊ ❊

"And then Uncle Connor let me ride the pony."

"You let her on a pony?" Tyler glares at Connor.

"I was holding onto her all the time," Connor reassures him.

"He checked with me." I hook my arm through Tyler's trying to reassure the big guy. He can be so overprotective of our daughter.

Tyler continues to glower at Connor.

"She's two, Tyler."

"Only two," my husband growls.

"And Connor is very responsible. He'd have made sure Serene was safe."

"I did. I held onto her all the time." Connor lifts Serene in his arms. "You had a great time didn't you you, Poppet?"

Serene nods vigorously. "I loved the pony," She look at Tyler with her big brown eyes. There's a plea in them which Tyler can never resist. Neither can I. But Tyler is far more indulgent of her. He's a girl dad. He's allowed I suppose.

After he made me come two times and fucked me breathless all within ten minutes, we'd dressed and come downstairs just as the doorbell rang. Connor had walked in with a very excited Serene who couldn't stop telling us all about the great time she had with Uncle Connor.

"Can I get one of my own?" Serene flutters her eyelashes at Tyler.

Connor and I exchange amused glances.

Tyler of course nods. "Anything you want."

"Oh Papa." Serene does one of those flying-leap thing which she's so adept at and jumps into his arms. He cradles her close to his chest. She throws her arms about his neck and kisses his cheek. "I love you, Papa."

"I love you too, honey."

Connor shakes his head. "To think we started this discussion with you getting pissed off at me for letting her get on a pony."

Tyler narrows his gaze on his brother. "I still think it was a risk, but since it made her so happy, I'm willing to forgive you."

"Thanks?" He smirks. His phone pings. He pulls it out, reads the message and his forehead furrows.

"Everything okay?" I ask.

"Of course." He says absently. His fingers fly over the screen as he replies back. Then he pockets his phone. "I guess I have to go."

"Thanks for taking care of Serene." I rise up on tiptoe and kiss his cheek.

My husband makes a sound of displeasure at the back of his throat, which I ignore. He can be very possessive, this man. No matter that my kiss was very sisterly.

"You're a great uncle to her." I beam at Connor.

"She's a wonderful niece." He pats my shoulder, then turns to Serene. "Can I get a kiss, Poppet?"

"Hmm." She frowns. "Depends."

"Depends?" He blinks "On what?"

"Can we go to the aquarium?"

He chuckles. "You little wheeler, dealer." He bends and presses a kiss to her forehead. "Of course I will."

"Thank you, Unca Connor." She hugs him, and plants a noisy kiss on his cheek.

"Anytime." Connor steps back, a soft smile on his face. The Davenport men don't have a hope of resisting my daughter's charms.

"You headed back to the hospital?" Tyler asks.

"Hospital?" I look at Connor with concern. "Everything okay?"

To my surprise he seems uncomfortable. "Of course, it's all good."

"So why are you going to the hospital?"

He and Tyler exchange a look. Tyler shrugs, an apologetic look on his face.

Connor's forehead furrows. He doesn't seem happy, but then he turns to me. "Remember my buddy James Hamilton's sister? He wanted me to watch out for her?"

I nod.

"Well, she's an ER doctor. I made sure to see her safely to the hospital where she works. She'll be safe while she's there. I left to take Serene to the playground. But it's almost six p.m., and she'll be wrapping up her shift anytime now, so—" He pops a shoulder.

"You're going to pick her up and bring her home?"

"Not exactly." He sticks his hands in his pockets and looks so guilty my jaw drops.

"She doesn't know you've been watching her, am I right?"

He shuffles his feet, then squares his shoulders and nods. "You're right. She's not aware I'm looking out for her. But James felt if she found out that he'd sent me to watch out for her she'd be pissed off."

"You've been tracking her to and from her place of work, but she's not aware that you're doing so?"

"I keep my distance. She doesn't even know I'm there." He holds up his hands. "I know how this sounds, but I promise I'm only doing this to keep her safe."

I fold my arms across my chest. "Why Connor Davenport, you know this is a gray area. And I don't feel comfortable about what you're doing."

"I mean her no harm. This is only until I make sure she's fine and report back to James." His eyes sharpen. "Or should I introduce myself to her and see what happens?"

To find out what happens next read Connor and Phoenix's story in The Wrong Husband. Scan this QR code to get it

How to scan a QR code?

1. Open the camera app on your phone or tablet.

2. Point the camera at the QR code.

3. Tap the banner that appears on your phone or tablet.

4. Follow the instructions on the screen to finish signing in.

*READ SUMMER & SINCLAIR STERLING'S STORY **HERE** IN THE BILLIONAIRE'S FAKE WIFE BY L. STEELE*

READ AN EXCERPT FROM SUMMER & SINCLAIR'S STORY

Summer

"Slap, slap, kiss, kiss."

"Huh?" I stare up at the bartender.

"Aka, there's a thin line between love and hate." He shakes out the crimson liquid into my glass.

"Nah." I snort. "Why would she allow him to control her, and after he insulted her?"

"It's the chemistry between them." He lowers his head, "You have to admit that when the man is arrogant and the woman resists, it's a challenge to both of them, to see who blinks first, huh?"

"Why?" I wave my hand in the air, "Because they hate each other?"

"Because," he chuckles, "the girl in school whose braids I pulled and teased mercilessly, is the one who I —"

"Proposed to?" I huff.

His face lights up. "You get it now?"

Yeah. No. A headache begins to pound at my temples. This crash course in pop psychology is not why I came to my favorite bar in Islington, to meet my best friend, who is — I glance at the face of my phone — thirty minutes late.

I inhale the drink, and his eyebrows rise.

"What?" I glower up at the bartender. "I can barely taste the alcohol. Besides, it's free drinks at happy hour for women, right?"

"Which ends in precisely" he holds up five fingers, "minutes."

"Oh! Yay!" I mock fist pump. "Time enough for one more, at least."

A hiccough swells my throat and I swallow it back, nod.

One has to do what one has to do... when everything else in the world is going to shit.

A hot sensation stabs behind my eyes; my chest tightens. Is this what people call growing up?

The bartender tips his mixing flask, strains out a fresh batch of the ruby red liquid onto the glass in front of me.

"Salut." I nod my thanks, then toss it back. It hits my stomach and tendrils of fire crawl up my spine, I cough.

My head spins. Warmth sears my chest, spreads to my extremities. I can't feel my fingers or toes. Good. Almost there. "Top me up."

"You sure?"

"Yes." I square my shoulders and reach for the drink.

"No. She's had enough."

"What the — ?" I pivot on the bar stool.

Indigo eyes bore into me.

Fathomless. Black at the bottom, the intensity in their depths grips me. He swoops out his arm, grabs the glass and holds it up. Thick fingers dwarf the glass. Tapered at the edges. The nails short and buff. *All the better to grab you with.* I gulp.

"Like what you see?"

I flush, peer up into his face.

Hard cheekbones, hollows under them, and a tiny scar that slashes at his left eyebrow. *How did he get that?* Not that I care. My gaze slides to his mouth. Thin upper lip, a lower lip that is full and cushioned. Pouty with a hint of bad boy. *Oh!* My toes curl. My thighs clench.

The corner of his mouth kicks up. *Asshole.*

Bet he thinks life is one big smug-fest. I glower, reach for my glass, and he holds it up and out of my reach.

I scowl. "Gimme that."

He shakes his head.

"That's my drink."

"Not anymore." He shoves my glass at the bartender. "Water for her. Get me a whiskey, neat."

I splutter, then reach for my drink again. The barstool tips in his direction. This is when I fall against him, and my breasts slam into his hard chest, sculpted planes with layers upon layers of muscle that ripple and writhe as he turns aside, flattens himself against the bar. The floor rises up to meet me.

What the actual hell?

I twist my torso at the last second and my butt connects with the surface. *Ow!*

The breath rushes out of me. My hair swirls around my face. I scramble for purchase, and my knee connects with his leg.

"Watch it." He steps around, stands in front of me.

"You stepped aside?" I splutter. "You let me fall?"

"Hmph."

I tilt my chin back, all the way back, look up the expanse of muscled thigh that stretches the silken material of his suit. *What is he wearing? Could any suit fit a man with such precision?* Hand crafted on Saville Row, no doubt. I glance at the bulge that tents the fabric between his legs. *Oh!* I blink.

Look away, look away. I hold out my arm. He'll help me up at least, won't he?

He glances at my palm, then turns away. *No, he didn't do that, no way.*

A glass of amber liquid appears in front of him. He lifts the tumbler to his sculpted mouth.

His throat moves, strong tendons flexing. He tilts his head back, and the column of his neck moves as he swallows. Dark hair covers his chin—it's a discordant chord in that clean-cut profile, I shiver. He would scrape that rough skin down my core. He'd mark my inner thighs, lick my core, thrust his tongue inside my melting channel and drink from my pussy. *Oh! God.* Goosebumps rise on my skin.

No one has the right to look this beautiful, this achingly gorgeous. Too magnificent for his own good. Anger coils in my chest.

"Arrogant wanker."

"I'll take that under advisement."

"You're a jerk, you know that?"

He presses his lips together. The grooves on either side of his mouth deepen. Jesus, clearly the man has never laughed a single day in his life. Bet that stick up his arse is uncomfortable. I chuckle.

He runs his gaze down my features, my chest, down to my toes, then yawns.

The hell! I will not let him provoke me. Will not. "Like what you see?" I jut out my chin.

"Sorry, you're not my type." He slides a hand into the pocket of those perfectly cut pants, stretching it across that heavy bulge.

Heat curls low in my belly.

Not fair, that he could afford a wardrobe that clearly shouts his status and what amounts to the economy of a small third-world country. A hot feeling stabs in my chest.

He reeks of privilege, of taking his status in life for granted.

While I've had to fight every inch of the way. Hell, I am still battling to hold onto the last of my equilibrium.

"Last chance—" I wiggle my fingers from where I am sprawled out on the floor at his feet, "—to redeem yourself..."

"You have me there." He places the glass on the counter, then bends and holds out his hand. The hint of discolored steel at his wrist catches my attention. Huh?

He wears a cheap-ass watch?

That's got to bring down the net worth of his presence by more than 1000% percent. Weird.

I reach up and he straightens.

I lurch back.

"Oops, I changed my mind." His lips curl.

A hot burning sensation claws at my stomach. I am not a violent person, honestly. But Smirky Pants here, he needs to be taught a lesson.

I swipe out my legs, kicking his out from under him.

Sinclair

My knees give way, and I hurtle toward the ground.

What the—? I twist around, thrust out my arms. My palms hit the floor. The impact jostles up my elbows. I firm my biceps and come to a halt planked above her.

A huffing sound fills my ear.

I turn to find my whippet, Max, panting with his mouth open. I scowl and he flattens his ears.

All of my businesses are dog-friendly. Before you draw conclusions about me being the caring sort or some such shit—it attracts footfall.

Max scrutinizes the girl, then glances at me. *Huh?* He hates women, but not her, apparently.

I straighten and my nose grazes hers.

My arms are on either side of her head. Her chest heaves. The fabric of her dress stretches across her gorgeous breasts. My fingers tingle; my palms ache to cup those tits, squeeze those hard nipples outlined against the—hold on, what is she wearing? A tunic shirt in a sparkly pink... and are those shoulder pads she has on?

I glance up, and a squeak escapes her lips.

Pink hair surrounds her face. *Pink? Who dyes their hair that color past the age of eighteen?*

I stare at her face. *How old is she?* Un-furrowed forehead, dark eyelashes that flutter against pale cheeks. Tiny nose, and that mouth —luscious, tempting. A whiff of her scent, cherries and caramel, assails my senses. My mouth waters. *What the hell?*

She opens her eyes and our eyelashes brush. Her gaze widens. Green, like the leaves of the evergreens, flickers of gold sparkling in their depths. "What?" She glowers. "You're demonstrating the plank position?"

"Actually," I lower my weight onto her, the ridge of my hardness thrusting into the softness between her legs, "I was thinking of something else, altogether."

She gulps and her pupils dilate. *Ah, so she feels it, too?*

I drop my head toward her, closer, closer.

Color floods the creamy expanse of her neck. Her eyelids flutter down. She tilts her chin up.

I push up and off of her.

"That… Sweetheart, is an emphatic 'no thank you' to whatever you are offering."

Her eyelids spring open and pink stains her cheeks. Adorable. Such a range of emotions across those gorgeous features in a few seconds. What else is hidden under that exquisite exterior of hers?

She scrambles up, eyes blazing.

Ah! The little bird is trying to spread her wings? My dick twitches. My groin hardens, *Why does her anger turn me on so, huh?*

She steps forward, thrusts a finger in my chest.

My heart begins to thud.

She peers up from under those hooded eyelashes. "Wake up and taste the wasabi, asshole."

"What does that even mean?"

She makes a sound deep in her throat. My dick twitches. My pulse speeds up.

She pivots, grabs a half-full beer mug sitting on the bar counter.

I growl, "Oh, no, you don't."

She turns, swings it at me. The smell of hops envelops the space.

I stare down at the beer-splattered shirt, the lapels of my camel colored jacket deepening to a dull brown. Anger squeezes my guts.

I fist my fingers at my side, broaden my stance.

She snickers.

I tip my chin up. "You're going to regret that."

The smile fades from her face. "Umm." She places the now empty mug on the bar.

I take a step forward and she skitters back. "It's only clothes." She gulps. "They'll wash."

I glare at her and she swallows, wiggles her fingers in the air. "I should have known that you wouldn't have a sense of humor."

I thrust out my jaw. "That's a ten-thousand-pound suit you destroyed."

She blanches, then straightens her shoulders. "Must have been some hot date you were trying to impress, huh?"

"Actually," I flick some of the offending liquid from my lapels, "it's you I was after."

"Me?" She frowns.

"We need to speak."

She glances toward the bartender who's on the other side of the bar. "I don't know you." She chews on her lower lip, biting off some of the hot pink. How would she look, with that pouty mouth fastened on my cock?

The blood rushes to my groin so quickly that my head spins. My pulse rate ratchets up. Focus, focus on the task you came here for.

"This will take only a few seconds." I take a step forward.

She moves aside.

I frown. "You want to hear this, I promise."

"Go to hell." She pivots and darts forward.

I let her go, a step, another, because... I can? Besides it's fun to create the illusion of freedom first; makes the hunt so much more entertaining, huh?

I swoop forward, loop an arm around her waist, and yank her toward me.

She yelps. "Release me."

Good thing the bar is not yet full. It's too early for the usual officegoers to stop by. And the staff...? Well they are well aware of who cuts their paychecks.

I spin her around and against the bar, then release her. "You will listen to me."

She swallows; she glances left to right.

Not letting you go yet, little Bird. I move into her space, crowd her.

She tips her chin up. "Whatever you're selling, I'm not interested."

I allow my lips to curl. "You don't fool me."

A flush steals up her throat, sears her cheeks. So tiny, so innocent. Such a good little liar. I narrow my gaze. "Every action has its consequences."

"Are you daft?" She blinks.

"This pretense of yours?" I thrust my face into hers, growling, "It's not working."

She blinks, then color suffuses her cheeks. "You're certifiably mad—"

"Getting tired of your insults."

"It's true, everything I said." She scrapes back the hair from her face.

Her fingernails are painted... You guessed it, pink.

"And here's something else. You are a selfish, egotistical jackass."

I smirk. "You're beginning to repeat your insults and I haven't even kissed you yet."

"Don't you dare." She gulps.

I tilt my head. "Is that a challenge?"

"It's a..." she scans the crowded space, then turns to me. Her lips firm, "...a warning. You're delusional, you jackass." She inhales a deep breath before she speaks, "Your ego is bigger than the size of a black hole." She snickers. "Bet it's to compensate for your lack of balls."

A-n-d, that's it. I've had enough of her mouth that threatens to never stop spewing words. How many insults can one tiny woman hurl my way? Answer: too many to count.

"You—"

I lower my chin, touch my lips to hers.

Heat, sweetness, the honey of her essence explodes on my palate. My dick twitches. I tilt my head, deepen the kiss, reaching for that something more... more... of whatever scent she's wearing on her skin, infused with that breath of hers that crowds my senses, rushes down my spine. My groin hardens; my cock lengthens. I thrust my tongue between those infuriating lips.

She makes a sound deep in her throat and my heart begins to pound.

So innocent, yet so crafty. Beautiful and feisty. The kind of complication I don't need in my life.

I prefer the straight and narrow. Gray and black, that's how I choose to define my world. She, with her flashes of color—pink hair and lips that threaten to drive me to the edge of distraction—is exactly what I hate.

Give me a female who has her priorities set in life. To pleasure me, get me off, then walk away before her emotions engage. Yeah. That's what I prefer.

Not this... this bundle of craziness who flings her arms around my shoulders, thrusts her breasts up and into my chest, tips up her chin, opens her mouth, and invites me to take and take.

Does she have no self-preservation? Does she think I am going to fall for her wide-eyed appeal? She has another thing coming.

I tear my mouth away and she protests.

She twines her leg with mine, pushes up her hips, so that melting softness between her thighs cradles my aching hardness.

I glare into her face and she holds my gaze.

Trains her green eyes on me. Her cheeks flush a bright red. Her lips fall open and a moan bleeds into the air. The blood rushes to my dick, which instantly thickens. *Fuck.*

Time to put distance between myself and the situation.

It's how I prefer to manage things. Stay in control, always. Cut out anything that threatens to impinge on my equilibrium. Shut it down or buy them off. Reduce it to a transaction. That I understand.

The power of money, to be able to buy and sell—numbers, logic. That's what's worked for me so far.

"How much?"

Her forehead furrows.

"Whatever it is, I can afford it."

Her jaw slackens. "You think... you—"

"A million?"

"What?"

"Pounds, dollars... You name the currency, and it will be in your account."

Her jaw slackens. "You're offering me money?"

"For your time, and for you to fall in line with my plan."

She reddens. "You think I am for sale?"

"Everyone is."

"Not me."

Here we go again. "Is that a challenge?"

Color fades from her face. "Get away from me."

"Are you shy, is that what this is?" I frown. "You can write your price down on a piece of paper if you prefer." I glance up, notice the bartender watching us. I jerk my chin toward the napkins. He grabs one, then offers it to her.

She glowers at him. "Did you buy him, too?"

"What do you think?"

She glances around. "I think everyone here is ignoring us."

"It's what I'd expect."

"Why is that?"

I wave the tissue in front of her face. "Why do you think?"

"You own the place?"

"As I am going to own you."

She sets her jaw. "Let me leave and you won't regret this."

A chuckle bubbles up. I swallow it away. This is no laughing matter. I never smile during a transaction. Especially not when I am negotiating a new acquisition. And that's all she is. The final piece in the puzzle I am building.

"No one threatens me."

"You're right."

"Huh?"

"I'd rather act on my instinct."

Her lips twist, her gaze narrows. All of my senses scream a warning.

No, she wouldn't, no way—pain slices through my middle and sparks explode behind my eyes.

TO FIND OUT WHAT HAPPENS NEXT READ *SUMMER & SINCLAIR*

STERLING'S FAKE RELATIONSHIP ROMANCE IN THE BILLIONAIRE'S FAKE WIFE BY L. STEELE

READ AN EXCERPT FROM THE UNWANTED WIFE - SKYLAR & NATHAN'S STORY

Skylar

"I can't do this." I lock my fingers together and narrow my gaze at my reflection. I'm in the tiny bathroom adjoining my office at the back of my bakery—my baby, my enterprise into which I've poured my life savings. And now, it's going to shut down. Unless I find the money for the rent next month... And for the utilities to keep the lights on so the sign on the shopfront continues to be lit up in pink and yellow neon... And for the supplies I need to continue baking. *The Fearless Kitten* is more than my dream; it's my whole life. What I've worked toward since I was sixteen and knew I was going to become the most phenomenal baker in the world. And now, I'm going to lose it.

"Sure, you can do it." My brother encourages me from the doorway. "You can do anything you set your mind to."

"That's what I used to think. It's why I started this pastry shop." I was twelve when I discovered I was good at baking. That, combined with my love for desserts, meant I knew what I wanted to do with my life.

Two years ago, I moved to London to work at a well-known patisserie. I began scouting for a location for my place while I saved every single penny I could.

A year ago, I found the perfect place, and my little artisan bakery with coffee shop seating was born. Of course, I work eighteen-hour workdays, which means I have almost no social life. I barely manage a few hours of sleep in my little apartment over the shop. But nothing can dampen my spirits. I'm spending my days churning out cakes and pastries. It's what I've dreamed of for so long. Only issue?

I don't have the money to advertise, and despite having a social media post go viral—which is when a lot of people look at your social media feed—and result in a surge of customers, I'm not making enough to salvage my business.

"Don't give up. You have to believe this can take off." Ben's voice is confident. If only I shared his optimism.

"Oh, trust me, I want to believe. But blind faith in yourself only takes you so far." I wish I could do better at spreading the word about the place and bringing in new customers. I seem to suck at everything outside of baking. It's why my business is on the decline.

"Success is what's beyond the dark night of the soul," my brother, ever the wise one, remarks.

"Is that a saying among you Royal Marines?" I scoff.

"It's—"

The bell over the door at the front of the shop tinkles.

"—your destiny." His lips curve in a smile.

"What?" I blink.

"The bell—it's your future calling."

I roll my eyes. "If you say so."

"Go on, your customer is waiting." My brother walks over and kisses my forehead. "Good luck. Remember, when one door closes, another one opens. Or the one I prefer, she who leaves a trail of glitter is never forgotten."

"Eh?" I stare. "What does that have to do with my situation?"

"Nothing, but it did cheer you up."

I roll my eyes, then can't stop myself from chuckling.

"That's my girl." He pats my shoulder.

Yep, that's my brother. The ever-cheerful, never-surrender person. "You'll see; it will work out." He turns me around and points me in the direction of the doorway leading to the shop. "Go on now."

"Whatever you say, big bro."

I was ten when my father passed, and Ben became the de facto father figure in my life. I'm fifteen years younger than him, an "oops baby," born when my mother was in her early forties. I hero-worshipped Ben, who, in turn, took care of me and never let me feel the loss of my father. And when my mother passed away, he took a leave of absence and came home and stayed with me, until he was assured I was ready to pick myself up and move on. He's the most important person in the world, in my life, in so many ways. And the fact that he fights wars so I can be safe is a source of the utmost pride for me. It's one of the reasons I feel terrible about being on the verge of bankruptcy. I want Ben to be proud of me.

"This is my last chance to get things right. If I can't find a way to pay off my debts, I'll have no choice but to shut down." I hear my words and realize I'm being negative. The exact opposite of my brother. I expect him to tell me off, but there's no answer. I turn to find he's left the shop. Not that I blame him. He has a two-week break before he has to ship out again. I suspect he's gone to meet his current squeeze. Ben never lacks female companionship.

To find out what happens next read The Unwanted Wife by L. Steele

CILLA'S RECIPES

CILLA'S GRILLED HALLOUMI & CUCUMBER MINT SALAD

Ingredients:

- **200g Halloumi cheese**, sliced into ½-inch thick pieces
- **1 cucumber**, diced or thinly sliced
- **2 medium tomatoes**, diced (or use cherry tomatoes, halved)
- **¼ red onion**, thinly sliced (optional, for a bite)
- **A handful of fresh mint leaves**, roughly chopped
- **2 tbsp olive oil** (plus extra for frying)
- **1 tbsp lemon juice** (or more, to taste)
- **Salt & pepper**, to taste
- **Optional: A sprinkle of sumac or chili flakes** for a hint of spice

Instructions:

1. **Prep the Halloumi:**

2. Pat the Halloumi slices dry with a paper towel (important —reduces splatter when frying).
3. **Fry the Halloumi:**
4. Heat a non-stick pan over medium-high heat. Add a drizzle of olive oil.
5. Place the Halloumi slices in the pan and cook for 1–2 minutes per side, until golden and lightly crispy.
6. Remove from heat and set aside.
7. **Assemble the salad:**
8. In a large bowl, combine cucumber, tomato, red onion (if using), and mint.
9. **Dress it:**
10. Drizzle with olive oil and lemon juice. Season with salt and pepper. Toss gently to combine.
11. **Top with Halloumi:**
12. Arrange the warm Halloumi slices on top of the salad. Finish with an extra squeeze of lemon or a pinch of chili flakes if you like a kick.

Serving suggestion:
Best served immediately while the Halloumi is still warm and crisp. Great on its own, or with warm pita or flatbread on the side.

FOR YOUR TODDLER
BANANA OATMEAL MINI PANCAKES

Ingredients:
- 1 ripebanana
- 1egg
- 1/4 cup quick oats (or finely ground old-fashionedoats)
- 1/4 teaspoon cinnamon (optional)
- A tiny splash of milk (ifneeded)

Instructions:
1 Mash the banana really well with a fork in abowl.
2 Add the egg and oats to the mashed banana. Stir until fully

combined. (The batter should be thick but pourable — add a splash of milk if too thick.)

3 Heat a non-stick pan over medium-lowheat.

4 Spoon small amounts (about 1–2 tablespoons) onto the pan to form mini pancakes.

5 Cook for about 2 minutes on each side, until golden and cooked through.

6 Let them cool slightly, thenserve!

Optional toppings:

- A little smear of natural peanutbutter
- A few softberries
- A drizzle of plainyogurt

CHEESY VEGGIE MINI MUFFINS

Ingredients:

- 1 cup finely grated carrot (about 1 mediumcarrot)
- 1/2 cup finely chopped spinach (or any softgreens)
- 1/2 cup shredded cheddarcheese
- 1 cup all-purpose flour (or whole wheatflour)
- 1 teaspoon bakingpowder
- 1/4 teaspoon garlic powder (optional, forflavor)
- 1/2 cupmilk
- 1egg
- 2 tablespoons olive oil or meltedbutter

Instructions:

1 Preheat oven to 350°F (175°C). Grease a mini muffin pan or line with paper liners.

2 In a large bowl, mix the flour, baking powder, and garlic powder.

3 In another bowl, whisk the milk, egg, and oiltogether.

4 Add the wet ingredients to the dry and stir just untilcombined.

5 Fold in the grated carrot, spinach, andcheese.

6 Spoon the batter into the mini muffin cups, filling about 3/4 full.

7 Bake for 15–18 minutes, or until golden and a toothpick comes out clean.

8 Cool beforeserving.

Optional add-ins:

- Finely chopped cookedbroccoli
- A sprinkle of mild herbs likebasil

MARRIAGE OF CONVENIENCE BILLIONAIRE ROMANCE FROM L. STEELE

The Billionaire's Fake Wife - Sinclair and Summer's story that started this universe... with a plot twist you won't see coming!

The Billionaire's Secret - Victoria and Saint's story. Saint is maybe the most alphahole of them all!

Marrying the Billionaire Single Dad - Damian and Julia's story, watch out for the plot twist!

The Proposal - Liam and Isla's story. What's a wedding planner to do when you tell the bride not to go through with the wedding and the groom demands you take her place and give him a heir? And yes plot twist!

CHRISTMAS ROMANCE BOOKS BY L. STEELE FOR YOU

Want to find out how Dr. Weston Kincaid and Amelie met? Read The Billionaire's Christmas Bride

Want even more Christmas Romance books? *Read A very Mafia Christmas, Christian and Aurora's story*

Read a marriage of convenience billionaire Christmas romance, Hunter and Zara's story - *The Christmas One Night Stand*

READING ORDER

Download your exclusive L. Steele reading order bingo card. *SCAN THIS QR CODE TO GET IT*

How to scan a QR code?
1. Open the camera app on your phone or tablet.
2. Point the camera at the QR code.
3. Tap the banner that appears on your phone or tablet.
4. Follow the instructions on the screen to finish signing in.

ABOUT THE AUTHOR

Hello, I'm L. Steele.

I write romance stories with strong powerful men who meet their match in sassy, curvy, spitfire women.

I love to push myself with each book on both the spice and the angst so I can deliver well rounded, multidimensional characters.

I enjoy trading trivia with my husband, watching lots and lots of movies, and walking nature trails. I live in London.

Made in the USA
Columbia, SC
09 May 2025

57740398R00235